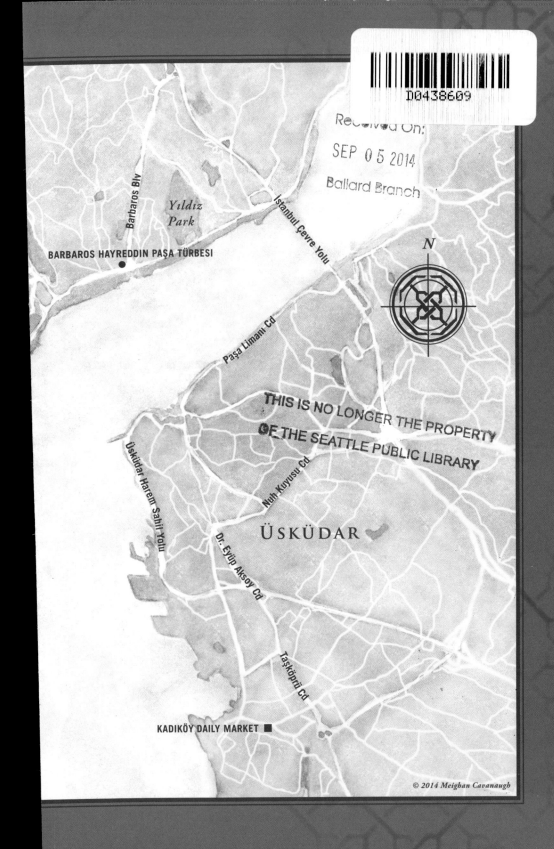

Barbaros Blv

Yıldız Park

BARBAROS HAYREDDIN PAŞA TÜRBESİ

İstanbul Çevre Yolu

N

Paşa Limanı Cd

Üsküdar Harem Sahil Yolu

Nuh Kuyusu Cd

ÜSKÜDAR

Dr. Eyüp Aksoy Cd

Taşköprü Cd

KADIKÖY DAILY MARKET ■

© 2014 Meighan Cavanaugh

THE RED ROOM

THE RED ROOM

RIDLEY PEARSON

G. P. Putnam's Sons | New York

G. P. PUTNAM'S SONS
Publishers Since 1838
Published by the Penguin Group
Penguin Group (USA) LLC
375 Hudson Street
New York, New York 10014

USA · Canada · UK · Ireland · Australia
New Zealand · India · South Africa · China

penguin.com
A Penguin Random House Company

Library of Congress Cataloging-in-Publication Data

Pearson, Ridley.
The Red Room / Ridley Pearson.
p.   cm.
ISBN 978-0-399-16374-6
1. Istanbul (Turkey)—Fiction.   2. Suspense fiction.   I. Title.
PS3566.E234R43   2014   2013051019
813'.54—dc23

Printed in the United States of America
1   3   5   7   9   10   8   6   4   2

BOOK DESIGN BY MEIGHAN CAVANAUGH

. . . as always, for

Storey, Paige and Marcelle

ACKNOWLEDGMENTS

To get a story from brain to shelf takes more than a village, it takes a patient army. For *Red Room* the list of soldiers includes: editors Christine Pepe and Genevieve Gagne-Hawes; assistants Nancy Zastrow and Jennifer Wood; copy editors Laurel and David Walters; literary agents Amy Berkower and Dan Conaway of Writers House; film agent Matthew Snyder and CAA; publisher Ivan Held, G. P. Putnam's Sons.

THE RED ROOM

1

Two men await a delivery van. Nameless men. Professionals. Proficient at blending in. The man with the camera—call him Alpha. The man who stands in the camera's frame is Beta.

A white FedEx minivan appears in the camera's field of view. It serves as the starting gun. Alpha eases the Nikon onto his chest. Turning away from the Şişli Merkez Mosque, he is jostled by Istanbul tourists posing for the perfect picture. It's nearing the end of the day. Slanting sunshine slices through the smog, playing across the mosque's stone dome and adjacent minaret. Hell of a photo.

Beta, looking so much like Alpha they might be mistaken for twins—each in a navy blue knit cap, black leather jacket, blue jeans—sees the camera lower and moves toward the curb. He cradles a canvas messenger bag beneath his right arm.

The van double-parks in front of a pharmacy, its emergency flashers pulsing.

Alpha walks incrementally faster, entering the pharmacy only seconds behind the FedEx deliveryman. His job is to provide cover. Beta opens the van's panel door and slips inside. After five days of surveillance, they know the delivery kid, always in a hurry, never locks the van in this part of town.

THE PHARMACY SMELLS CHEMICAL. Alpha reaches the FedEx kid and, as if trying to slip past, allows himself to be tripped. He brings down most of the contents of a shelf as he falls. Turns and pulls the deliveryman along with him.

There is shouting as employees hurry to help. Boxes of medicine are spread across the floor, causing the employees to tiptoe as they approach. The delivery package has slid out of reach of both men.

The lens hangs broken from the camera's body.

"Idiot! You clumsy bastard!" Alpha speaks English with an Eastern European accent. More training. The deliveryman is young, red-faced and unsure. He spouts apologies in Turkish.

BETA SEARCHES the contents of the first of six plastic bins arranged on the van's open shelves, his fingers flipping through the packages like a collector in a vinyl-record store. He knows exactly what he's looking for: he has its clone in his messenger bag.

Bin two. Bin three. An internal timer runs. The op calls for an abort at thirty. He's at twenty-seven when his fingers stop at the air bill listing:

FLORENCE NIGHTINGALE HOSPITAL
ABIDE-I HÜRRIYET CADDESI
ISTANBUL, TURKEY

Seven packages. More slowly now. The third shows the sender as a Swiss address. He makes the swap, his for theirs.

Forty-three seconds and counting . . .

No reaction. No adrenaline or concern or anxiety. The lapsed time is merely a statistic to be noted. It's filed and processed. He stuffs the switched package into the messenger bag and comes out of the van with his back to the sidewalk. He walks the curb like a balance beam. No one has shouted at him. No one has approached. He slips out his phone and sends the text. The signal.

ALPHA'S PHONE dings at his hip.

"My fault, my fault!" Alpha says. He helps the cautious deliveryman to his feet, making sure to keep the man faced away from the windows. In tourist Turkish, he manages something close to *"Üzgünüm."* Sorry.

He inspects his broken camera, trying to force the lens back into place. He and the deliveryman exchange agonized looks. Alpha extends his hand, a peace offering. The deliveryman is delighted by his change of heart. They shake.

Alpha says in English, "All for some toothpaste." A shared moment of tense humor.

Leaving the pharmacy, Alpha reads the text. It's a smiley emoticon. Success.

He makes a phone call. Hears a click. No voice. He keys in a five-number string followed by three pound signs. Hears a second tone.

"It's done," he says, speaking Hebrew.

2

NINE DAYS LATER

A veil of fog obscures the steep steel-and-glass-clad marvels that rise out of Hong Kong harbor. From the twenty-second-floor offices of Rutherford Risk in the Chamberlain Tower, John Knox thinks the trolleys and cars look like toys. On the glass, pinpricks of mist collect and join, growing into drops and skidding down the glass in a race, obscuring the view. It's not raining, but will be within the hour.

Knox steals a look at his own reflection, while behind his image another appears: an imposing figure of a man, older by a few years, unable to disguise a brutal intensity that impressed Knox when the two first met in Kuwait, another Knox ago. David Dulwich still walks with a limp, although his gait has vastly improved since the car accident in Shanghai two-plus years ago. The men embrace.

"This way," Dulwich says.

Knox notes the lack of small talk, wonders if the brief phone call that detoured him to Hong Kong was as much of the personal stuff as he and Sarge were going to bother with.

The starkly contemporary offices of Rutherford Risk reflect the tastes of company president Brian Primer, whose warm side only surfaces when a client is present. Knox knows Primer as a calculating son of a bitch who concerns himself with margins and profitability, often at the expense of his assets—like Knox. He treats his clients almost reverently and stops short of tolerating loss of life on either side of the ledger.

Down the corridor, the maple office doors, marked only by a number, rise to ten feet and are a full meter across, ensuring that any visitor, no matter how large, feels physically insignificant.

Primer, a proponent of Frank Wisner's "mighty Wurlitzer," required his architect and interior decorator to work with a team of psychologists. Wisner, the first director of the CIA, created front organizations and planted media stooges in order to "play any propaganda tune needed." Primer can work a meeting.

To Knox's surprise, he's led not to Primer's office but to the secure elevator. It drops thirty stories so fast he feels like he's floating. He's ridden it only once before.

Hong Kong high-rises are anchored deeply into the mountains. Lessons learned from mudslides a century earlier have prompted the creation of structures able to withstand both the ground giving way and the pummeling of typhoon winds and rain. Twenty meters below grade, storm shelters and storage rooms are carved into the hillside. It's here, outside a door marked PRIVATE, that Dulwich removes anything containing metal—coins, wristwatch, Bluetooth device, smartphone, belt. He places the items in a cubby, turns the lock and asks Knox to do the same. Knox does so and pockets the plastic key.

Dulwich swipes his ID card and admits Knox to a small vestibule, where they must wait for the door to close before a second can be opened. A body scanner hums. A green light indicates that they are clear.

"The Red Room," Knox says. "So cloak and dagger."

Still, Dulwich is silent. The barrier is seven inches of steel and insulating concrete weighing three hundred pounds, yet it moves fluidly, clicks shut and locks electronically. The Red Room is a twenty-square-foot bunker with pale green walls and a strip of exposed overhead lights. The furniture is clear, ensuring that nothing can be hidden inside it. Knox has heard of it, but took it to be company myth.

"I've never had the pleasure," he says.

Dulwich checks his watch. "We don't have long." He produces an A4 manila envelope. Knox can't believe he didn't see it, marvels at how quickly one can lose one's edge. He's been back to import/export for a matter of months; the operation in Amsterdam is still fresh in his memory but apparently not in his skill set.

Dulwich slides the envelope across the table like it's radioactive.

"Your schedule, not mine," Knox says. He finds the Red Room claustrophobic. He can handle small spaces; a top-secret facility, impenetrable to all eavesdropping technologies, causes undue pressure.

Dulwich taps the envelope.

David Dulwich is usually not the melodramatic type. It's one reason Knox doesn't mind doing the occasional piece of work for him. The rest of his time, John Knox is a trader, traveling the world for rare goods, in business with his younger brother, Tommy. Dropping into a James Bond movie is a little much.

"Sarge?"

"They're of you. The pictures. You love looking at yourself, Knox. So go ahead."

"Moi?" Knox fails to entertain his host. "Why?"

"Why what?"

"I have plenty of pictures of myself, all of them stunning."

An uncomfortable smirk crawls across Dulwich's lips. "Not like these you don't."

Knox suppresses the urge to take the bait. He wants more from Dulwich, who knows that Knox is a reluctant freelancer. His brother, Tommy, isn't in the best shape—the experts call him cerebrally and physically impaired, autistic, mentally challenged. He is, in fact, highly functional with medication and care. Knox can't risk leaving him alone on this earth—but he's attracted to the work Dulwich offers for more than just the money. He has a savior complex that probably bleeds over from caring for his damaged sibling.

Still, he's in no hurry to screw things up by rising to the wrong fly. Dulwich will eventually play the money card. Knox has been robbed, embezzled from by his company's bookkeeper. Things are tight. Have been for some time.

But Dulwich doesn't start there.

"I don't go in for drama," Dulwich says.

"An understatement."

"This is an in-and-out—a week tops—that can do a lot of good."

"Good, like Amsterdam?" Dulwich understands which buttons to push.

"No, not like Amsterdam. Not even close. Frog and the scorpion. Open the envelope."

Knox doesn't understand the reference but doesn't want to appear ignorant. He wants to open the envelope—oh, how he wants to; but there's commitment that accompanies the act, and he can't bring himself to do it without knowing more.

"Political?" Knox wishes he had hidden the astonishment in his voice. Like all private contractors, Rutherford Risk's bread and butter comes from U.S. government jobs: guarding convoys of supplies, providing security details, moving funds, interrupting the Internet, burning drug crops. It's the occasional insurgency Knox wants no part of.

"Open the envelope."

"Wrong guy."

"Turns out you're the only guy, or we wouldn't be locked in the Red Room."

"Maybe you should unlock the door."

"Maybe you should open the envelope. There are good guys and bad guys on every team, Knox. Even good teams have their share of bad apples. But I wouldn't put you on the bad team. Not ever. Now, goddamn it, look—"

Dulwich takes the envelope back, opens it and slams down a handful of 8x10s. Shot with a high-powered telephoto at a good distance.

Knox can't pretend it's not his profile. It takes him several long seconds to digest the look of the café and the apparent location: Bethany, Jordan. That gives him the other man in the photo, a man with Jordanian and Circassian blood, Akram Okle.

"I was never told flat out," Knox says, defending himself, "that the piece was black market. Every antiquity has passed through too many hands to count. Sometimes that includes mine. I'm offered a piece; I know a buyer. More like a matchmaker. I can see how that might be politically embarrassing, but I don't work for you, Sarge. I'm not your employee. I'm a contractor. I—"

"You are so off base you're running around the outfield." Dulwich flips through the stack of photographs. Three show Knox and Okle engaged in what Knox thinks must be their most recent deal; more troubling are the final two photos, which go back eighteen months earlier. There's no way Knox has been followed for eighteen

months; he keeps track of such things. So it's Okle who's being surveilled.

"Okay, I give up. The frog and the scorpion?"

Dulwich arches his eyebrows as if Knox should know this one.
"Frog and a scorpion meet on the riverbank. Scorpion asks for a lift
to the other side. Frog says, 'Why would I do that, you'll sting me.'
Scorpion says he won't and they sign a treaty. The frog carries him
on his back. Halfway across, the scorpion stings the frog. As they're
both going under, the frog says, 'Why would you do this? We're
both going to die!' Scorpion says, 'It's my nature . . .'"

"Akram's a good client," Knox says. "I see certain pieces, I think
of him first. He only buys the rarest of the rare. There aren't many
people who can afford such things. You go where the market is."

"He's a middleman."

"None of my business."

"It is now."

3

Rutherford Risk pays out six figures to employees at various Internet security companies, on top of the seven figures budgeted for their own hackers who roam cyberspace probing for firewall vulnerabilities. When a back door is discovered in an existing operating system, Rutherford receives an alert before Microsoft or Adobe or Sun or Apple can identify the issue, a day or two before they can offer a patch.

During that window—hours, or minutes sometimes—people like Grace Chu, a private contractor based in Hong Kong and specializing in forensic accounting, are able to slip through the back door undetected.

Thanks to other sources on the inside of those companies, Grace Chu is also told when to get out.

Most of her days are spent poring over spreadsheets or money wire transactions, establishing trails and hard evidence for the client, most typically Rutherford Risk. Today she works like a day trader, jumping in and out of the market, seizing opportunity, playing margins. She's attempting to establish and trace an individual's net worth. It's a nerve-racking exercise not meant for the faint of heart. A moment's hesitation and the SEC or FBI will have her location. Get out too quickly and she loses her only chance at access.

Today she's inside the server of a Jordanian bank; tonight or tomorrow, if the current back door holds, an Iranian investment firm. She's curious about the op. Yesterday, Dulwich instructed her to data-mine this man's financials. Dulwich wants her travel plans left open. He sounded uncertain. It's new territory—Dulwich at sea, running her personally. Success will mean promotion; she can taste it. To prove herself as a field operative capable of on-the-fly intelligence gathering and analysis will put her in a class by herself. She knows of no one at Rutherford Risk with this particular hybrid skill set.

She works wirelessly using a "hopper"—a cellular Wi-Fi device that jumps among three carriers randomly, the same technology that makes her jailbroken iPhone impossible to eavesdrop on. It costs her some speed, but she has grown accustomed to the pauses.

She's working from the downtown campus cafeteria of the University of Hong Kong, meaning her IP address is shared by a few hundred at a time, making a quick trace difficult, if not impossible. She's stolen a user ID and password off a nearby, far too casual user.

The bank's firewall is impenetrable. The last effective cyber raid was in 2004. This back door they've been given is far more benign— it's for the bank's local area network, which includes all web searches, most e-mail traffic, video conferencing data as well as the security server.

Grace monitors the cafeteria's visitors, studying the face and body language of each new arrival. It's lunchtime and therefore busy, which is both a blessing and a curse, but she chose the time slot to help support her cover. Her fine features—she's been described as "haunting"—win the attention of males over twenty, many of whom underestimate her age, which is well north of that. She keeps her laptop screen angled slightly down; it wears a layer of plastic film that limits side views, but there's a sweet spot she found from just above head height that concerns her.

She types a long string of commands. A year ago, she was fairly new to this cyber play, made anxious by it. Now she eats it up. Over the months, she's grown addicted to these short bursts of information theft, much the way she imagines runners treasure their endorphins.

Working with remarkable speed, she moves through the root directory hierarchy, navigating to the security servers. In her mind's eye, it's like going down ladders and through tunnels, into anterooms and on to other tunnels and more ladders. Throughout the process, she raises her eyes, tracking newcomers, accounting for those already in place. Her memory is superior. Her mind has been trained to be nearly photographic. She has identified the two men back by the soda fountain, the woman by the trash can, another woman eating alone. Any of these could be a threat. There's a male student who looks like he's hoping to see up her skirt. She'd like to flip him her middle finger but keeps it on the keys.

One thing she's learned about security servers: the systems are organized to accommodate and account for the intelligence level of those meant to operate them. Not every security guard is a Bill Gates in waiting. The video stream is labeled KAYMARA. Camera.

In seconds she's opening a dozen video feeds, like surfing a traffic cam site. She closes them as quickly as they open. She's not interested in the teller windows or the safe or the safe-deposit boxes. Not interested in the elevator interiors, the back hallway or the six exterior cameras.

All the while, a stopwatch app runs in the upper corner of her screen. She's been online 2:07 minutes and counting. Even using a

THE RED ROOM

back door, she may be sniffed and identified for having an IP address outside the known database of approved users. She should be safe staying within five-minute usage intervals.

At 4:22, she clocks off.

The second hack, she heads directly to the camera list.

Her third breach hits gold: the camera is mounted behind four desks, with a view of the teller windows' left side. One of the desks is occupied. Her fingers fly across the keys as she builds a macro that logs in, clicks through to the proper security camera, takes a video screen shot and logs out at the four-minute mark. The macro will loop until she shuts it down.

She hits Enter, angles the screen lower and is caught off guard by the young skirt-chaser's approach.

Terminate or continue? These are the decisions that define her: when to run, when to admit temporary defeat, when to trust her instincts. Right now couldn't be better—the hack is clean, the macro running flawlessly. She has the op teed up perfectly. She just needs the other two desks filled following lunchtime breaks.

This guy's a problem. He asks in Cantonese if the seat is taken. It's a dialect she has nailed but an accent she finds tricky even after two years living in the city. Her rebuff of him is polite but firm; her right pinky finger hovers over the F12 key while her left index finger covers the FN. These two keystrokes combined will log off the laptop and send it into a double-encrypted sleep mode that would require seventy-two hours on a Cray computer to have a hope of gaining access.

Appearances mean nothing. The boy's approach is taken as a high-level threat. If he lifts a finger, she'll break it like a twig, and his arm along with it. Apologies to cock-motivated boys like him are cheaper than excuses to Dulwich.

He offers a smile he's practiced too many times in his dormitory mirror.

"Listen to me, cousin," she says, losing her accent slightly to her temper. "I don't appreciate boys . . ." she lingers on the word, savoring it, "looking up my skirt, or trying to. If you haven't seen one before I'm not interested in you, and if you have, then you know it's a woman's secret treasure and she doesn't wear it like a Shanghai billboard. If I wanted to share pictures of it, I'd post them on the corkboard over there by the register, *neh*? Back up and leave me alone or I'll put my heel so deep in your crotch you'll have shoe leather for a tongue."

His sallow skin tone drains to the color of talcum powder.

The fact that he sits there, standing his ground, is cause for worry: he's a cocky bastard.

She detests the thought of logging off when everything is going so well. She can't bring herself to do it without further provocation. But her instinctive reaction is impatience and she's trained to guard against it. Good things come to those who wait. She'll have another shot at this data, she reminds herself.

So why can't she bring herself to log off? It's him and his obstinacy; she's taken it as a gender challenge and she's not about to cave.

She's angled the screen too low to see what's happening at the bank. The boy's flirting will provide good cover, but the distraction has cost her: she's lost track of who's entering or exiting the cafeteria. Her best chance now is to keep this boy engaged for the sake of anyone who might be watching. The longer she has him with her, the longer her computer continues recording the bank's video camera.

"A woman's secret treasure, or her secret pleasure?" he says now, and draws the opposing chair back with his shoe, making space to sit.

"Pleasure cannot be kept secret," she returns, suddenly enjoying the wordplay, "whereas treasure can."

Keeping her prior threat in mind, he estimates the length of her extended leg and moves the chair far enough back to accommodate. He sits.

"Origin EON seventeen-S," he says.

She wishes she could stop the blush that floods her face. John Knox has told her it's a tell that could get her killed.

The boy has been lusting after her boutique laptop, not her crotch. She's made a fool of herself, and he's so smitten with her electronics that he's played along.

He rattles off specs and she counters with the upgrades she's opted for. Lunge. Parry. His eyes go wide—and then wider. His upper lip is sweating.

Has she misjudged his age? Is he too old to be a student? Teacher's aide? Grad student? Or is he a risk-taking thief who dresses well and chats up girls on college campuses, snatches their laptops and disappears before they can rise from their chairs? The Origin is worth over four thousand USD. Mainland gamers would pay that or more.

If he manages to steal the unlocked laptop, she and Rutherford Risk would suffer. She plays the odds, pressing the two keys and protecting the data. She's angry over being forced to do so, is tempted to knock the guy across the room.

Quoting a proverb, "'Man's schemes are inferior to those made by heaven,'" Grace casually closes the Origin. It's heavy, but she one-hands it into the Trager Tru-Ballistic case.

"I was admiring it. And you. That's all, cousin."

"Next time you might consider antiperspirant on your upper lip, cousin."

He holds up both palms in an act of surrender. Behind his eyes, he hungers to test her threats. That look convinces her he intended to steal the laptop. She has to wonder if he was hired.

She slings the case over her head so the strap, which will hold up to any box cutter or razor, crosses her chest, separating her breasts.

"I think I'm in love," he whispers as she passes.

4

The air in the Red Room is piped in through slit vents in the ceiling. The temperature is perfect. The humidity, perfect. The company, less than perfect.

Dulwich is not himself; he's lost sleep, some color, and his throat is raspy, suggesting he's stressed.

"Are we going to rewind," Knox asks, "or am I supposed to keep up?"

"What do you think?" Dulwich scratches at the burn scar below his collarbone. The line of pink runs down into his shirt. The phantom itch is one of the man's tells. He's editing himself on the fly.

"Akram Okle owns a pair of Indian restaurants, both called Saffron. One in Bethany. The other in Amman. He's done well. Not well enough to afford his last purchase, but the man knows his art and would have no problem forming a partnership to make a buy. He's a family man, no connection to organized crime. Well educated. A pleasure to do business with. You've got the wrong guy."

"His mother is gravely ill," Dulwich says. "As we speak, he's traveling to Istanbul to join some, or all, of his six siblings. Three brothers, three sisters. He's not in partnership. He's a middleman for his brother, Mashe." He pronounces it "Masha." "That's who bought your piece."

"Okay." Knox does not appreciate Dulwich knowing what he knows. He circles back to the photos taken of Akram from a year and a half ago. Police. Interpol. A cultural ministry trying to stem the flow of precious art.

Dulwich's focus can be laserlike. "After I saw these photos, when I realized you deal in more than nose flutes, it seemed so unlike you. So I go back through your college records to find out you were an art history major."

"Minor. My major was sorority girls."

"Save it for someone who laughs," Dulwich says. "Why'd I never hear about this? Too soft for the tough John Knox?"

"I don't tell everything on the first date."

"So you're an art dealer now?"

"Finger cymbals are folk art."

"How long?"

"A while. Here and there, now and then. Better margins when I can find the right piece. It's a pretty tight-knit club, gray market art. I have a long climb ahead of me, but yes, I enjoy it. Sue me."

"You're about to skip a few rungs," Dulwich says. "Move to the front of the line. No more papier-mâché face masks for John Knox. What's the gray market equivalent of Christie's or Sotheby's?"

Knox doesn't answer. His heart is pumping. Dulwich has a disturbing way of knowing how to play him. Knox would love to get away from hill tribe trinkets and into the art world, gray market or not. But Dulwich can't make such promises.

"YOU ARE to offer Akram the bust of Harmodius."

"Harmodius and Aristogeiton." Knox doesn't need Google.

"Apparently so."

Knox can tell Sarge is out of his element. "Athenians who paved the way for democracy. Bronzes were made of the heroes, the first art in human history to be commissioned out of public funds, adding to the gravitas of the pieces."

"Listen to you," Dulwich says.

"The statues disappeared, likely seized in wartime. Copies were commissioned. This is still four hundred years before Christ. A piece—just a piece!—of one of those copies surfaced in the 1980s and sold for millions."

"You will be offering the head and left shoulder from the original Harmodius," Dulwich says.

"That's impossible. No one will believe that. Not even me. The originals were lost two thousand years ago. Come on."

"It's been tested. Assayed. Whatever. It can be tested again. It's the real deal, Knox. And yes, you will have it. I'm told the estimated value is well north of ten million."

"Well north," Knox says.

"You'll be asking five hundred thousand."

"And why would I do that? Why would anyone do that?" But he knows the answer. It's been stolen. It's a piece for one's bedroom, not one that can be seen by others. There are too many questions that need answering. Given the current climate of cross-cultural theft, trying to deal it to a museum would result in jail time.

"If you're trying to court me, you're going about it all wrong. What the hell are you and Primer up to?" Knox has a nose for

Dulwich bullshit. The closest they've been to the truth was the bit about good and bad players on the same team. That line's been running through Knox's head since Sarge said it.

"You deliver the Harmodius. Grace will make sure the money flows in the right directions. You'll make a name for yourself in certain circles."

A name? Knox thinks. He'll be legend, and Dulwich is fully aware of this. He's offering Knox a career change, a gold pass into the inner circles of the art world, gray market or not. *The fucking Harmodius?*

"Grace," Knox says. He works occasionally with Grace Chu on Dulwich jobs. She's a rising star within the ranks of outsourced Rutherford operatives like him. They have a platonic chemistry that Knox welcomes. She's insanely smart, wildly ambitious and enough of a risk taker to keep up with him.

"You're after Mashe Okle's money stream?"

"It's NTK." Need To Know. "You make the offer. You make sure he bites. You and Grace deliver the Harmodius. An in-and-out. Like I said."

"What's the catch?"

"You need to sell directly to Mashe. I need you two in the room with Mashe for five minutes."

"Play the lure? For what, a hit? No thanks." Knox stands. The acrylic chairs are painfully uncomfortable.

"No hit."

"Bullshit. I lead you to him and some sniper takes him out that day or three days later. What's the difference? You think if I never find out, it lessens my role? That's bullshit. Who is he?"

"No sniper."

"Who is he?"

"NTK."

"Fuck that. Good guys and bad guys on the same team, you said. So is he a bad guy on a good team or a good guy on a bad team?"

"I wasn't talking about him."

"The client? You were talking about the client?"

"NTK. I don't need to know. You don't need to know. Leave it at that. I . . . we've been promised no killing. For you: it's fifty thousand on acceptance. How much are Tommy's new meds? Once you two get the five minutes, a hun more. For a week, tops, including travel."

"I won't bait a guy for a bullet. He'd have to be a real monster. I would need proof. Who's the client?" Knox resents Sarge for bringing up his brother's medical situation. They know each other too well, he thinks, not for the first time.

But Sarge is right. There's a compound currently in testing for Fragile X and the treatment of social withdrawal. The results are promising, but Tommy's well above the test's age limit of twenty-one. Getting him prescribed the drug will be tricky and expensive—and even if Knox succeeds, costs are estimated at ten thousand dollars a month.

"I'm telling you, I wouldn't ask you to do this if—" He searches. "Listen, there's no bullet. Not from us, not from our client. Could he take one? Of course. But not from us."

"Who's us?"

Dulwich purses his lips. Knox changes tactics.

"What's the right way for the money to flow? What are you after?"

Dulwich retains his expression.

Knox processes the use of the Red Room, the limited information he's being offered, the eighteen months of photo surveillance. It feels like the work of Interpol's Stolen Works of Art group or a domestic organization like Scotland Yard. He doesn't like it.

"Art theft? That kind of politics? I need guaranteed amnesty," Knox says.

"The client has no say over that. It's beyond borders. Grace is your best bet. Trust Grace. She says run, you run."

Dulwich has revealed more than he intended, a costly and unusual mistake. The client is either nongovernmental or a covert governmental group unable to interfere. Knox can't put it together. He doesn't like hearing that he's to take direction from Grace; she's become Dulwich's star pupil. Knox has always been more the gum chewer in the back row. Grace's importance to Dulwich is on the rise; his own status, he's not so sure about. And it's so out of character for Dulwich to slip up that Knox has to wonder if it's an intentional ruse. Why would Dulwich game his own assets?

Because this is bigger than stink.

"The Brits' stolen-art database is fifty thousand pieces," Knox says. "Yet their total annual budget to investigate stolen art is less than four hundred grand. Italy loses thirty thousand pieces a year. Russia, seven. Stolen art is the most lucrative market out there. And the most underfunded on the investigative side. I like nice things, I deal in nice things, but I've never knowingly participated in the sale of stolen art. I need protection. I don't think I'd like Turkish jail."

"It's not in my interests to see you in jail."

"Well, that's a huge relief."

"Scheduling is critical. Clock is ticking. Lean on Grace. If she does her homework, and we both know that's not an 'if,' we'll know whether or not it's safe for you two to take that meet."

"The clock is always ticking."

Dulwich shrugs.

How much does Grace know? How much will she be willing to share? She can be a real Girl Scout. How much can Knox deduce by understanding what Grace is up to? The stop Knox had planned in

Shanghai is worth a fifth of just the down payment Sarge and Primer are offering.

Knox flashes back to the pile of money Tommy lost to the embezzling bookkeeper, money intended for Tommy's care. Recovering that money is a work in progress, one that currently involves the voluntary help of Dulwich and Grace. In the interim, Knox is trying to cover in-home health care that costs the same as buying a new car every month. Adding drug therapy will kill the goose.

Dulwich's expertise is manipulation, but in affairs of business only. His personal life is a minefield littered with craters behind him and tall weeds ahead. This job offer feels different, as if he's dragging Knox into that field with him.

Knox tries for the jugular. "What makes this personal for you?"

Dulwich doesn't so much as blink. "He's important to the client."

"The brother."

"Correct." He repeats, "I'll backfill as much as possible, whenever possible, assuming the client okay's it. It'll go through Grace. You and I can't connect. Period."

"I'll be watched." Knox looks down at the photographs. Feels a chill. Maybe he's been under surveillance for some time.

"We play the odds."

"What makes a buyer of art special?" Knox asks, thinking aloud. "The dollar value of the art is what's significant. Right?"

Dulwich doesn't want him going there. He says so with his eyes.

"Let's say I'm a black ops agency trying to buy some RPGs or a few million rounds of ammo. I'm trying to back the Syrian rebels or some other Arab Spring do-gooders. My seller is unwilling to take currency of any kind. Currency can be traced. He can't allow himself to be found out."

Dulwich doesn't stop him, but Knox can tell he'd like to.

"So the cash buys a piece of art. It's a value market—a relatively small amount of cash buys a very valuable trade. The art is exchanged for the weapons. Untraceable. The guy who sells the weapons hangs the art in his dacha; the other guy reloads. Everyone's happy." Knox looks for the fallacies. It holds up. "Mashe's facilitating war, insurrections, bloodshed."

He's a monster.

Dulwich can't help himself: a small shrug says close enough.

"So the client—your client—is someone on the other side of the potential bloodshed. He doesn't want the weapons sold. He's looking to limit or shut down his enemy's arsenal."

"I need a go, no-go from you, John. You know how this shit works."

"But the Red Room."

"Don't read too much into that."

"Seriously?" Knox looks around the bunker. "The client can't be seen using private contractors like Rutherford. He doesn't trust his own people—good guys, bad guys. You said so yourself. I find that interesting."

"Don't find it anything. Just give me the go, no-go."

"Stop pressuring me, Sarge. You need me. I'm the one in the photos. How long did it take your client to figure out who I was? To connect you and me? That can't have been easy. Shit. Months? A year? Are these our guys? Homeland Security? The FBI? You can imagine why that would make me just a little nervous."

Dulwich fails to react.

"Don't make like if I pass on this you're going to move down the list. There is no list. It's one name. One guy. Me."

"Lucky you."

"Flip the payments. The hundred now. Fifty if I get the five minutes with him."

"Deal."

Knox shakes his head, disgusted with himself. That came far too easily. He could have gotten more. "I need an agent," he says.

Dulwich smirks.

"I'm no expert on Istanbul. There's a brass worker I do some business with in Merkez. The Grand Bazaar is overpriced. Can I parachute in? Sure. But don't ask for anything ninja."

"Understood."

"If Akram is playing middleman for his brother, I don't see how I ask to meet the guy without raising flags."

"You leave that to Chu," he says, referring to Grace. "She can make that happen. I'm serious about it being an in-and-out for you. Show up. Watch movies in your hotel room. Chu does what she does. You do what you do. She will bring Mashe to you. You set up the deal with Akram. Take the meet. You and Grace hop a plane home."

"How do I get a piece like that in-country? If I'm busted at Customs and spend twenty years in a Turkish prison, I'm going to come out very mad."

"I'm counting on you."

"I won't take a hand-off. Not in a place like Istanbul. Couriers are bought and sold more than the artwork they transport. We need to get it in there ourselves. No middlemen."

"I'm working on it." Dulwich pauses. "In all likelihood, it'll be a hand-off in Amman. After that, it's up to you. You'll think of something."

"If you don't mind my saying so: this doesn't feel like you," Knox says.

"And if I do mind?"

"You're up against a tight schedule. I get that. This guy's only on the ground a short time." Knox feels the ice cracking beneath his feet and he hasn't even accepted the job yet. "Since when do we take on a client with bad guys on his team? You're usually telling me not to ad-lib. You hate that about me. Now you're telling me I'll think of something."

"This is actionable."

"Getting that piece of art from Amman to Istanbul is actionable. You're not the one making the trip. I'm the one making that mistake."

"Glad to hear it."

"Fuck you."

"I'll take that as a yes."

5

B y the time Grace reestablishes herself in a Starbucks on Queen's Road, the sidewalks are quieting down from the lunch rush. She finds a corner table.

The second of the two four-minute recordings made while she fended off her young thief shows a bank officer returning to work. Taking her seat at one of the unoccupied desks, the woman quickly logs on to the bank's computer network. The beauty of high-def recordings and retina displays makes itself clear in the ease with which Grace is able to zoom in on the woman's hands and observe the keystrokes in stop-motion.

She dares not attempt to use this woman's ID and password while the woman is logged on, so Grace reconnects with the live security camera repeatedly. Forty minutes later, the bank officer logs off and leaves her desk. Grace pounces.

SHE MEETS DULWICH on the upper level of an eastbound double-decker tram twenty minutes later and details the encounter with the man in the cafeteria.

"Mashe Okle, our POI," she says—person of interest—"is indeed paying the medical bills for one Delbar Melemet—female, seventy-three—in care at Istanbul's Florence Nightingale Hospital. Mashe Okle's income is bifurcated. His deposits from state-generated Iranian paychecks put him at the mid-to-high end for research academicians. Additional phantom income, the result of pension funds that don't appear to come with any restrictions, bumps that to six figures in U.S. dollars. He appears to have no mortgage, no housing costs. Utilities, even a wireless bill, all these are a no-show."

Dulwich's head pivots back to front, watching the passengers come and go. Experience tells her that even when Dulwich appears distracted, as now, he's listening closely.

Beside him Grace also admires the well-heeled mix of Europeans and Asians crowding the sidewalk, reveling in the cleanliness of the streets and the elegance of the architecture. Nonetheless, despite its reputation as the "London of Asia," Hong Kong carries a whiff of malfeasance beneath its white-collar façade—*probably,* Grace thinks, *due to its pirate heritage.* She waits until the tram is moving again, no new passengers having sat down within hearing distance.

"There was a cash withdrawal from the account on the day following the woman's hospitalization. Fifty million rials. That computes to the cost of a round-trip, first-class ticket, Tehran to Istanbul, with enough left over for living expenses for several days."

"Good work."

"An hour later, a first-class ticket is purchased with cash at an Emirates branch office in downtown Tehran under the name of Mashe Melemet."

"Spell it." Dulwich scribbles onto a busy piece of notepaper.

"Mashe Melemet, aka Mashe Okle, departs Monday," she continues, glowing now like the star pupil in the first row. "With a two-hour layover in Dubai."

"I may be able to pull a passport photo for the Melemet ID." He tries to cover his excitement. She interprets, deciding he doesn't have a photo of their mark; realizes she's given him something he and, by inference, their client, need.

"Book yourself a flight arriving in Istanbul just ahead of his," Dulwich says. "Arrange a driver and surveil Okle. Nothing stupid. You can pick him up again at the hospital, so you don't need to stick to him."

"Yes, sir." Questions hang in the air. Grace wasn't aware this would involve field ops. She's thrilled. She'd love to get out of the office for good. Is she to work directly with Dulwich—no John Knox? She would view this as a promotion of sorts. She's about to ask the obvious question when he subverts her.

"You're Knox's accountant, same as Shanghai," he says. "Use your EU creds where necessary. They'll hold up. But in terms of the mark, you're there in the room to protect Knox from any kind of sting. You and I will need to know the players. You may not hear from me, but I want to hear from you."

His mention of Knox is bittersweet. "Understood. If I may?"

"Go ahead."

"Who protects John Knox from himself?"

Dulwich smiles, which doesn't suit his face. Two of his front teeth are chipped.

"If the POI's cover is broken," Dulwich says, "it will be bad for him and everyone around him."

"Do we extract at that point?"

"You'd have to get in line. A long line, I expect."

"Behind whom?"

Dulwich smirks. "You and Knox make quite the pair. The point is . . . your takeaway is this: we need to know as much as we can about all the players. That's how we protect the POI. It's fluid. White water."

He's telling her that the events in Istanbul are moving danger-ously fast. The mark, along with her and Knox, are all at risk. The information hit her as a welcome jolt. For the last few years, she has lived for such rushes.

"Look: you two are only there to make Knox's deal. Anything and everything you do, Chu, has to make sense when viewed through that lens. Copy? You are Knox's accountant, working to keep him clean in the deal. Nothing more. There's no backstop. I don't exist."

She wants badly to ask about the deal. But Dulwich made it clear when he briefed her in the Red Room that this is a Need To Know op. She has never operated under such restrictions. She doesn't know if Knox has or not, but she can guess he will not respond well to them.

In contrast, Grace can and does follow orders. She's all about team play. A dozen questions crowd her thoughts. She says nothing.

6

Amman, Jordan, is the color of bleached sand. The buildings, the roads, the clothing. The palm trees that attempt to interrupt the sameness of the bigger avenues look like candles on a sand-colored birthday cake.

Knox wears a sand-colored suit with a white shirt and no tie. Loafers without socks. His hair is moussed back. He wears wraparound Ray-Bans. A gold chain bracelet adorns his right wrist. None of this costume feels natural to him.

People who can take photos of a person over an eighteen-month period are people to steer clear of. Their employers are often identified by acronyms. If they can aim a camera, they can aim a rifle. And if they're keeping an eye on Akram, on Saffron, his restaurant—and there's no reason to think they are not—Knox will never know. The casual pedestrian won't spot them; they won't be holed up in a utility van across the street.

They will see him. He will not see them.

The loose disguise is an attempt to separate himself from his former self, to prevent an instant connect-the-dots moment on the part of the surveillance team. The computers may make the face recognition for them later, but for now he's just another patron of an Indian restaurant. That the surveillance team may have an asset or audio/video on the inside must be considered. But Knox embraces such moments. He's as comfortable in his skin as he ever gets.

He fingers the twenty-dinar note in his pocket. On it, written in Arabic, is Akram's name followed by Knox's phone number.

Knox has memorized a line of Arabic. He practices it in a head chaotic with thought.

He orders *palak paneer, dahi gosht* and a beer from a subdued young woman with amazing skin and eyes like black olives.

He finds it impossible to immediately spot the plant, if he or she exists. Is troubled by the feeling of being watched, photographed, accounted for; he'd rather be the one doing the surveillance.

Dulwich had not confirmed or denied Mashe Okle's connection to the weapons trade. Knox's subsequent Internet searches returned only a holistic physician in Oceanside, New York. A Middle Eastern Mashe Okle does not exist. Knox is attempting to spend five minutes in a room with a nonentity, which has him wondering if Mashe is in fact real, or if Akram is the proxy for some other dark lord whom Dulwich cannot or will not divulge.

There's a reason people on this side of the profession are called spooks. Knox prefers things clean and tidy. He already regrets taking this job. Spooks operate in Spookdom with their own rules, their own stakes. They are flag-wavers who can make toxic decisions because they're weighing the good of an entire nation against an individual deed. They're comfortable justifying anything.

Knox doesn't want to be locked on that playground. But he gladly indulges in the adrenaline rush of sitting in an Indian restaurant, dressed as somebody else, waiting to make contact with a man he knows is likely out of the country. It's Spooky behavior, and he enjoys it—it's this stab of hypocrisy that troubles him. Waffling between a sense of displacement and yet enjoying the party . . . it doesn't sit well.

The meal is excellent. As Dulwich said, and Knox planned for, Akram is nowhere to be seen; he's in Istanbul at his mother's hospital bedside. The stop in Amman is what's known as a back door. For Knox to arrive in Istanbul without suspicion, he must arrange for Akram to invite him, to allow the man to think their meeting is his idea, not Knox's.

Knox gives himself time to finish the beer. Orders another. He's a man in no hurry.

He asks after the toilet, despite the sign, despite being aware of the floor plan. He's directed to the back.

He approaches the counter where the waitstaff drop off dishes. His hand finds the bill in his pocket. As he reaches the dish drop, he peers inside at a gaunt, forty-something male wearing a head wrap and a heavily stained apron.

"Do this for me, it is yours," he tells the man, handing him a day's wages.

The dishwasher takes the note, mutters something. Knox translates only: "is mine."

Knox lingers long enough to make sure the man sees the writing on the note. The dishwasher's expression turns more severe as his eyes bore into Knox.

"Go," the man says sharply in English.

The twenty-dinar note disappears beneath the apron.

As Knox urinates into a porcelain hole in the floor, he wonders about the severity of the dishwasher's expression. Was it the result of his attempting to reach the owner? Was it that Knox is a Westerner trying to reach the owner? Will the clandestine nature of his effort cause him to be followed as he leaves?

He hopes so. The beer is tingling his head. He's sorely missed this part of the game.

THE SANDSTORM ARRIVES AT DUSK. Knox witnesses the diminished light from his second-story room at the Canyon Boutique Hotel. The sky darkens dramatically in little time. Parting the privacy curtains, he's presented with a golden shimmer in the air, like a wand has been waved over the city, covering it in pixie dust. It is too beautiful to turn away, yet the color is foreboding. At first Knox mistakes it for toxic smog, an inversion or other weather phenomenon having nothing to do with the desert discharging a hairball.

But over the next five minutes, the sky changes from gold to bronze, from bronze to copper. Strong wind whips rooftop Jordanian flags. Fine, powdery grit infiltrates the louvered window frame, enticing Knox to test the iron lever. Finding it not quite sealed, he lowers it fully into a locked position.

The grit continues to invade.

In the reflection off the glass, the door's security peephole blinks, going dark. Someone is out there. Knox is already moving toward the door, thinking that without the sandstorm, without being drawn to the window, without the contrast between the dark sky and the well-lit space, he wouldn't have seen the flicker suggesting someone is there, in the hallway. Knox doesn't consider himself a fatalist, more an agnostic with inclinations that allow for a force or presence behind creation. Yet he acknowledges internally that he's the beneficiary of a string of events—that he's been offered an opportunity.

He doesn't question Dulwich's ability to place a handgun in his hotel room safe. The man has his end of the bargain to uphold, whether it's documents, background cover stories or small arms. Knox keys in the four-digit combination. Inside is a Jordanian-made

9mm Viper in a SERPA CQC holster. Along with a hundred rounds of ammo is a CRKT folding tactical knife and a pick gun capable of picking 98 percent of all locks, dead bolts and nondigital car locks. Two prescription bottles containing antibiotics and pain medicine. Nine hundred dinars in small bills left in a brown A4 envelope.

Knox pockets the knife and cups the Viper, kneels as he trains the barrel into the wood of the door so he can shoot through it if required.

The glass peephole is now unblocked, but Knox is not about to put an eye to it, not about to announce himself or take a round in the head. Knox cannot be made small, but he can be made less big and lower. The door's interior lever automatically unlocks the dead bolt. Crouching now, he yanks open the door.

The man on the other side is looking for someone at head height, lending Knox a split-second advantage. Knox comes to his feet spreading the man's arms wide. He spins his visitor so the man's throat slides into the crook of his own left elbow, grabs the right arm, wrenching it behind the man's back with the barrel of the gun aimed into the base of the man's skull. One twitch and they'll be scraping gray matter off the ceiling.

He drags the choked man into his room and kicks the door shut. Total time in the hallway: four seconds. His victim has yet to register what's happened. The man tries to speak, but can't in the choke-hold.

After thirty seconds without blood to his brain, the man slumps to the floor. Knox has already ID'ed him by holding him up to the room's mirror: it's the dishwasher from Saffron.

He ties the man's ankles together with a terry-cloth robe belt. Secures his wrists with the laces from the man's running shoes. Gags him with a washcloth. Slips the Viper into the small of his back—no need to advertise. Unfolds the knife, using its tip to coax open the man's thin wallet and clamshell cell phone. He memorizes the last four numbers called. He'll need to write them down in the next few minutes; his memory isn't what it once was.

The dishwasher regains consciousness with a kind of terror in his eyes that serves a purpose for Knox: the man is not used to this kind of treatment. He's new at this. An amateur.

Things just keep getting better and better.

Knox can taste the sandstorm; feel the grit between his teeth. A look out the window confirms a premature nightfall; the city's in the heart of a violent dust cloud. The condition can last for days. It can ground aircraft, stop taxis and buses from running. Be a real pain in the ass.

Knox speaks kindergartner Arabic, hoping his message gets through.

"You were sent?" Knox says. He moves his own head first in a nod, then shaking to indicate "no." He repeats his question.

The man nods.

Knox has found no weapons on the man.

"To hurt me," he states.

The man panics.

"To watch me."

Another violent shake of the head.

"To warn me."

Again.

"To tell me."

The man nods.

Knox plucks the towel from the man's mouth. The dishwasher speaks far too fast. Knox picks out: "Akram," "speak," but loses the rest. He allows the man time to calm down.

"Again," Knox says.

This time he gets: "Akram speak you."

Knox toys with the man's phone with the knife.

"I call?"

The dishwasher shakes his head.

"Not here."

"Where?"

"Machine café." It takes Knox a moment to process "machine" as "computer."

He glances back at the window, moving like the skin of a timpani drum as it's buffeted by the wind.

"Shit," Knox says.

7

Arriving at Atatürk International, Istanbul's primary airport, Grace is both tired and hungry. She doesn't want to do the math to determine how tired, but doesn't require calculations to know how hungry. She has an hour and seven minutes before Mashe Okle, traveling as Mashe Melemet, is scheduled to land. She sits down with a salad at Greenfields, carrying a soy mocha from Starbucks. She calls her driver, tells him to wait. Kills forty-five minutes eating slowly while catching up on iPhone e-mails.

Grace does not do well with free time. Her brain gets ahead of itself and starts tripping over discarded thoughts like a lost hiker stumbling over fallen limbs in the forest. Even at a meal, as tired as she is, she can't help herself.

She embedded code in the Emirates Airline's server to alert her to any outside IP addresses searching the manifest for flight numbers 975 and 123. She built a trap to catch others like herself as a security measure, something Emirates should have done in the first place. Having received no such alerts, she has every reason to believe she's alone in having identified the Melemet alias and flight schedule. But her mind won't let it be.

Ten minutes.

Immigration desks are the fly strips of terrorism pest control. Face recognition software has improved exponentially in the past five years, to the point at which X-ray imaging in an airport's full-body scanner can utilize an individual's skull features to overcome attempts at disguise like glasses and wigs. If the man Grace is set to follow has tripped a list in Tehran or the UAE or is identified passing through Immigration here in Turkey, airport security will follow him. Turkish agents might arrest him. Where does that leave Dulwich's plan? Why weren't contingencies made?

A Knox rule she's absorbed: you can't win the game if you don't know all the players.

Dulwich has either been told Okle is not in the international database of persons of interest, or Dulwich's mystery client is none other than the Turkish government or one of its agencies—meaning the man can enter the country without being stopped. Atatürk Airport offers Grace an opportunity to identify such players if they exist. She notices a series of mirrored windows angled down toward the busy concourse from the mezzanine level. Despite her fatigue, she smiles at the advantage she has just discovered.

She assumes Dulwich will follow Okle once he's out of the terminal, but it's nothing but an educated guess. She begins plotting.

An agent or investigator wanting to follow Okle/Melemet out of the terminal would be far wiser to do so from a chair in a security office than with boots on the floor. Every square inch of the airport is monitored. Once the mark reaches Immigration Control and leaves, through a succession of cameras one would be able to follow him to a taxi, bus, passenger vehicle, rental or parked car.

One agent in the security room, another in a car parked somewhere along the airport exit route. The mark has no way of identifying his surveillance team.

But she does.

She's filled with a sudden burst of energy, defying her fatigue. Her mathematical mind is well suited to strategic planning; she's capable of linear thinking, of laying down stepping-stones on the fly, rarely having to backtrack and correct a step.

Abandoning the salad, she pulls her roll-aboard into the concourse and rides an escalator to the mezzanine and its pair of higher-end restaurants, administration offices and the secured entrance leading into the mirrored window area. She phones her car service, is patched through and informs the dispatcher she will be at the curb in twenty minutes—ten for the plane to land; ten, or more, for Okle to get through Customs and Immigration.

She kneels by a trash can and makes a point of unzipping her bag and rearranging some clothing. She needs the cover.

In the process, she places her iPhone slightly behind the trash can, lens pointing out, difficult if not impossible to see. The beauty of the device is that it allows still or video photography to be shot without having to unlock the phone. Its contents are Cloud-based; if the phone is confiscated, she will be able to access those via another identical phone in a matter of hours. Apple sells well in both Dubai and Istanbul. For now, it's recording live video. She repacks, zips up the bag and leaves, returning to the concourse via the escalator.

Six minutes.

She repositions herself with a view of International Arrivals. A crowd of weary drivers and enthusiastic relatives has formed on her side of a restraining tape, a gauntlet past which she can't see. Despite the heels, she's forced to a stretch as she tries to balance against a spinning rack of tourist pamphlets. As arrivals reach the open end of the roped-off gauntlet, people rush to meet them, further obscuring her view.

She overhears a woman ask an arriving passenger in English the flight's origin. Delhi.

One minute.

The crowd ebbs and flows, sorting itself out. There's a lull. She has a chance to secure a place at the tape, but decides against it. Mashe Okle must not see her; she is supporting Knox and may meet the man face-to-face. Her interest is less in Okle than in who's watching him. That, along with his entourage, if any.

She's also monitoring the elevators and escalators for people like her—those who keep their distance and yet imply an interest in new arrivals.

She sends Dulwich a secure text:

mark on point

He made it clear she won't hear from him over the course of the op, but that only serves to excite her: he's trusting her, solo. Until she and Knox confab, she's independent.

He expects her to fail at following Okle single-handed. Told her she can pick him up again at the hospital. But she has other ideas.

Dulwich's penchant for secretiveness has a chilling effect on Grace. His methods, his need-to-know exclusivity, protects the chain of knowledge, secures the intelligence. Her first field op for Dulwich, in Shanghai, she felt expendable. Recently, she's been led to believe she's not simply secure with her outsource work for Rutherford Risk, but is a highly valued asset/provider. Brian Primer has invested in her cyber intelligence training. He must see big things ahead for her.

Knox knows Dulwich better than she, rarely believes everything Dulwich tells him. She often finds herself defending Dulwich only to wonder why later. She blames her ingrained sense of loyalty to her employer, her Chinese-ness, an inescapable connection to her heritage that she often wears like an albatross.

Time is suddenly impossible to measure. The minute hand of her watch won't advance. It isn't the adrenaline-induced special effect of time slowing, a phenomenon that can be mesmerizing and addicting. Instead it's her anticipation and expectation, which feed her impatience. She wants the curtain to rise.

As so often happens in surveillance, when the logjam finally breaks with the arrival of Mashe past security and into the terminal, Grace finds herself in a perfect storm. She counts two other men traveling with him, possibly bodyguards; they aren't making it obvious, but they aren't hiding, either. They follow a step behind, emotionless and alert.

She sees a Middle Eastern male, wearing blue jeans and a leather jacket, walking down the moving escalator. The rubber rail guides his hand, his eyes on the arriving passengers. It's his practiced scan of his surroundings that cues her: in a second or two he's taken in the surroundings, including egress. He's spotted a uniformed airport security team with a K9, as well as an undercover woman that Grace had missed.

He's wearing iPhone earbuds, the undercover equivalent of the flesh-colored curly "pigtails" bodyguards wear emerging from their shirt collars. His lips move. Could be a phone call, but Grace knows better—he's with a team. Private security? Police? Domestic intelligence? Foreign? Friendlies?

She calls Dulwich to pass along the intel of the extra set of eyes. He doesn't answer the call, pissing her off. She assumes he must be nearby. Providing information like this should help solidify her stature as an effective field operative. There are a limited number of such opportunities on any op. The cream rises to the top because it separates; she must separate herself from the nose-to-the-ground types who can't think for themselves.

For now, she sends Dulwich a text, "company," and leaves it at that. She avoids the man from the escalator. She'll determine his role later. As he reaches the bottom floor, she locates and rides an elevator up one flight. She retrieves her phone, grateful it's still there, and enters two passwords in order to unlock it and view the video. Back on the lower concourse, she replays the video a total of three times: she watches a man emerge from the secure area of the mirrored windows. He comes straight for the camera. Videoed from floor level, the perspective lends drama to his approach. When he's three meters away, she pauses on a clean image of his face. It's the same Middle Eastern man—the agent, the cop—who came down the escalator. A man who has been monitoring Melemet from inside airport security. Such access suggests Turkish law enforcement or an agent.

Like her, this man—*and his team?* she wonders—are surveilling Melemet.

Dulwich is going to love her.

She calls her driver for a second time.

"I'm coming out now," she says. "Please be ready."

8

Knox wears a damp strip of torn hotel towel over his nose and mouth, sunglasses, the spaces against his face stuffed with wet toilet paper. The dishwasher introduces himself as Shamir. He wears a sweat-stained kerchief around his neck. The sidewalks are cleared of all but the stupidest, a category into which Knox puts himself, given the conditions. He now knows what a pork cutlet or tilapia filet feels like when it's dredged through a bag of cornmeal.

Knox is sandblasted from all sides. Cars choke and die, windshield wipers swat at the dust like horsetails, car horns honk at double-parked vehicles blocking traffic. The leaves of the roadside plane trees rattle like the inside of a rainstick. Knox coughs. Shamir spits as he attempts in vain to screen his eyes.

Hunched forward, they stumble up the sidewalk, battling a directionless wind, caught in vortexes that suck all the oxygen out of the air. Knox chops at a wall of swirling sand, hoping to part the curtain.

Instead, it envelops him in an airless cocoon with a dust so fine it seeps through even the wet fabric to be ground between his teeth.

It tickles his nostrils; stains his taste buds with a foul mixture of street grime, desert sand and the dung heap of humanity crushed into a fine powder and snorted. He tastes tobacco, rubber and motor oil, all behind a tinge of latex he doesn't want to think about.

Shamir points across the street. They cut through a line of motionless traffic. Nothing is moving but the air and the street signs, many of which are losing their coats of paint as if in slow-motion animation.

They take shelter against a wall. The wind quiets. Coils of sand swirl at their feet. Plant life clings to crevices, whistling as if crying to hold on.

The sudden peace is shocking. He and Shamir hesitate before charging back into the stinging roar. Knox clears his sunglasses, pockets of trapped sand cascading down his cheeks.

"Not good," Shamir says.

Knox understands him perfectly.

"Bad," Knox says.

By now Knox is wondering about his choice. He might have fought harder to hold his ground at the hotel. The truth is: he loves this shit. The more difficult an op, the more he has to celebrate. But he worries he's come off as soft to Shamir, that the man will report back to Akram how easily Knox was convinced to battle the elements for a meeting or a phone call. Due to the language barrier, Knox is still not convinced which it is to be.

It isn't weather for standing around, and the man's movement catches Knox's eyes. He's off to Knox's right somewhere, sometimes visible, sometimes not. Knox's first glimpse of him was from across the street as he and Shamir left the hotel. At the time, he stood out as an anomaly. Who hangs around outside in such conditions? Survival dictates taking shelter.

Initially, Knox assumed the man was awaiting a ride. But now, the same man is huddled against the sting of the sand, facing away from Knox and into the skin-shredding torrent. But Knox feels the eyes in the back of the man's head. He considers the value of the Harmodius. Is there a group of art thieves after the treasure, too?

Knox signals Shamir back into the sandblaster. They push ahead for a block, Knox not looking back.

As they round a corner, Shamir again extends a finger, this time pointing to a swinging shingle sign at the bottom of which, below the Arabic, says in English: INTERNET! WI-FI!

Knox waves the man on ahead. Shamir hesitates, encouraging Knox forward. Knox speaks some of the few Arabic words he can command: "Go! Wait."

Shamir doesn't like it, but he trudges ahead anyway, entering the café.

The man following Knox is made careless by the storm. He's blind, head down and craned forward in a determined stride. A thick wave of airborne grit envelops the street. The man is a step off his game. Knox hits him from behind. He's good: he manages to drag Knox down with him. It isn't instinct. It's training that allows a move like that. It's like trying to fight on ice. Knox fails to land an effective blow; he is slow to dodge a fist that catches his shoulder. They wrestle and roll. Knox's glasses are dislodged; he can't see a thing. Feels like he took a spoonful of salt in both eyes.

He wipes the grit from his eyes while clenching a fist. Deflects a blow and lands a sharp jab to his opponent's kidney, buckling him. The guy lands an elbow to Knox's head; damn near dislocates Knox's jaw.

Knox's spine is a Twizzler. The whining of the wind covers his howl as numbness fills his fingers and toes; he can't feel anything past his elbows and knees. Tries to block the next blow, but can't lift his arms. Deadweight.

He goes over backward, opening himself to a world of hurt. Prepares himself abstractly for a boot toe to the temple. Thinks of Tommy. Feels the fool.

Nothing happens.

Squinting, he rolls over painfully.

Nothing but the smoky, coarse air—sand and dust traveling horizontally at thirty miles per hour. Ancient rock walls surround him. His world is gray and hard. Pain arrives to his limbs like venom.

The man appears as a specter, fleeing from him, quickly absorbed by the sandstorm.

Running away.

But why?

THE CAFÉ, crowded with refugees from the storm, has the feel of a downtown Detroit bar during a power outage. The air might be cleaner outside, given the interior gray haze of tobacco smoke. Knox finds the bittersweet coffee aroma intoxicating, the loud conversation soothing. It's a mixture of young and old, women and men, and probably the biggest crowd the café has ever seen.

It's clearly not what Shamir expected. He prepays for time; they wait uncomfortably for a computer to come available. Shamir buys Knox an espresso.

"Who were these men?" Shamir asks in surprisingly decent English.

"I thought you were going to tell me," Knox says, trying to play naive. Knox doesn't have the looks for naive. Shamir isn't buying it.

Hell, neither is Knox. Why did the man retreat when he clearly had the advantage? Who does that? Which of them had he followed: Shamir or Knox? All questions that need answering.

"You were followed," Knox says, trying to put this at Shamir's feet and keep suspicion off himself. "From the restaurant? Why?"

"It was you that is attacked."

Knox was hoping the man might have missed that part. "Because I'm a Westerner? Robbery?"

"In this storm?" He doesn't say what they both know: the man was dressed as a Westerner.

Knox takes note of what Shamir chooses not to say. It's as important as what they do discuss.

They both realize they're lying to each other and stop talking. Knox finds the café's atmosphere entertaining; he keeps an eye on the entrance. So far, so good.

When their time comes, Knox is guided to the bar stool by Shamir, who pulls a pair of tangled earbuds from his pocket and plugs them into an older model Mac laptop crudely secured to the wall counter. The name on the Skype account is not Shamir's, but of a woman named Victoria Momani. Knox wants badly to "slip" and open her contact information, which will come up if he can click on her name. Clearly Akram has no suspicions: he instructed Shamir to set Knox up on this account for the call, assuming Knox to be the import/export businessman Akram knows. Knox feels ugly about his true intentions.

"Mr. John?" Akram's voice sounds thin through the earbuds. Knox can't say for sure that it's Akram he's speaking with.

"Akram."

"Shamir tells me you wish to speak to me."

Knox can hear he's confused about Knox's involving Shamir. "The waitress said she knew nothing about how I might reach you. This is time sensitive."

"Please tell me."

"I am sorry, my friend. This connection is not so good . . . I must confirm . . . Let me ask you this, please. In Irbid, you and I once spent a nice hour in the shadow of a mosque as we talked. What is the museum near that mosque?"

There is an outside chance that an agent might be able to answer this, but it would take his team several minutes to collect the information. The timing by the man who says he's Akram is the tell-all. Knox can't believe he has to go to this kind of extreme; he wonders what must be running through Akram's head, given Knox taking this kind of precaution.

"You exaggerate, my friend. The mosque was several blocks south of the museum. It was adjacent to a school."

Knox collects his thoughts. "Listen carefully, my friend. I have a head for puzzles. A woman who tips the scale—think earth-shaking—restored this man's arm."

The line hisses intermittently. "Once again, please."

Knox begins with having a head for puzzles, and continues to the end.

Another long silence intervenes, broken by Akram's surprised voice. "This is not possible. Out of your wheelhouse."

Knox is amused by Akram's use of current vernacular. He reminds himself that this guy is smarter than he lets on. The piece is indeed well out of anyone's wheelhouse. It's so buried in myth as to seem fantastic. Knox has done eight or nine small middleman deals in the past two years. Three have been to Akram. None has been for over two hundred thousand dollars.

"I kind of fell into it." *Keep it light,* he tells himself.

"A nice hole to fall into, if only it were true. I am afraid you have been conned."

Akram's distrust plays into Knox's hand: Akram can now understand Knox's use of Shamir and the secretiveness.

The Skype connection sparkles.

"You have a number in mind for this fantasy," Akram says.

"Mid-sixes, U.S. dollars," Knox says.

Akram coughs as he laughs. "Perhaps another time would have suited us both better."

Knox's heart sinks. He mustn't beg. "As you wish."

"You have other clients, I assume."

"With patience, one can turn water into wine. Not to worry."

"My problem, you see, Mr. John, is that I am not to return to my beloved Jordan for an undetermined amount of time. An illness in my family."

"*As-salaamu 'alaykum.*" Knox waits, hoping he hasn't mispronounced it. *Peace be upon you.*

"If you were to have plans to visit Istanbul anytime soon . . ."

"Plans can change," Knox says.

Shamir turns toward a ruckus in the far corner. Knox quickly opens the contact information for Victoria Momani, copies it. Closes it. Five seconds, tops.

"How shall I contact you?" Knox asks.

"My friend Shamir will take care of it."

"Very well. Until then." Knox ends the call. Opens the word processor. Pastes in Victoria Momani's contact information. Hits Print. Ten seconds.

Shamir is turning back toward him as the print menu still hovers on the screen. Knox loses his balance intentionally, slips off the chair and shoves Shamir aside.

The print menu is off the screen by the time they both recover.

Knox apologizes. Says he has to take a piss. He'll meet Shamir up front.

Shamir tells him he's not going anywhere in this weather. Knox pays the man another twenty. "You may be hearing from me again."

"It is my pleasure." They are best friends.

On his way to the back, Knox places a coin down surreptitiously on the bar and manages to say, "Paper," not knowing the word for "print." He doesn't wait for change, doesn't want Shamir seeing this.

Knox snags the sheet from one of two beat-up printers on his way to the washroom. He folds and tucks the sheet into his pocket.

He doesn't yet see a use for Victoria Momani. But the night is young.

9

—————

Y ou speak English, Besim?" Grace asks of her driver behind the wheel of a Mercedes. Her eyes never leave Melemet, his two bodyguards and the man following them. She has some Turkish, though her Arabic is stronger. She'd rather not show her cards to a driver; such men are known to talk.

One of the bodyguards takes the front seat of the Audi. A moment later he signals. Melemet is in, followed by the trailing guard. Traffic is intense. No one is going anywhere just yet.

The agent crosses to an island, waits and is met by a Land Rover. It stays at the curb, much to the disdain of a policeman who is waving it away.

"Some," her driver responds. Balding, and with a short-cropped beard, he wears a black suit that brings out a caramel tone in his dark skin. She has yet to see his full face.

"Have you ever followed another vehicle?"

"Jealous wife. Jealous husband." The beard puckers. He is smiling.

"I am—was—mistress to this man." She points to the Audi. "We are going to follow him. He is not alone. He owes people money.

Much money. You understand?" She points left to the Land Rover. "You see?"

"I understand."

"I would rather not be noticed."

"Not easy to follow during nighttime."

She passes a good deal of cash into the front seat. He won't want to touch her. She drops it.

"Let us make it as easy as possible," she says, avoiding the use of confusing contractions. "Our problem is: the ones following are very good. They will be watching for people like us. They do not wish to share."

"This, not easy, ma'am."

No, she thinks.

"I tell you," he says, pulling out now, five vehicles behind the Audi, already on the job, "I know this car company." He motions with his head. "My brothel's nephew"—she doesn't correct his mistake—"the brothel to his wife's sister, he is, how do you say, radio man, this company."

"Dispatcher." Grace appreciates his sense of extended family, the intermarrying of cousins, the generations of business relationships between families the size of clans. Tribes. Not so very different from her native China.

"Precisely. Drivers, we together."

"I am sure."

"I call my brothel?" he asks. "He call nephew?"

"How much?" She doesn't mind paying but doesn't want to come up short when the time comes.

"I am your driver throughout stay in Istanbul. No need for these monies, ma'am."

She presses. "I may need an ATM."

Another smile. More a lascivious grin.

"I make call," he says.

HER DRIVER makes three calls. She picks up more of the conversations than she thought she might. Pats herself on the back.

"Is okay," he says, backing off the pedal a bit. "Destination, Florence Nightingale Hospital. Forty kilometers."

Given Dulwich's briefing about the sick mother, Grace has assumed the hospital would be an early stop. The location doesn't help her. She works to keep the irritation from her voice. "After that? His final destination?"

He catches her eye in the rearview mirror, his mental gears clearly grinding. She's following a man, her supposed former lover, who just landed and is heading straight to a hospital; her tone suggests she knows all this and yet somehow knows the hospital is not his final stop.

"His mother is ill, Besim," Grace explains in a more intimate and caring tone, trying to stay a step ahead of her savvy driver. "Of course the hospital must come first. If I am to speak to him, it must follow."

"I have address," he says. "You desire I should drive you this place?"

"Yes. Please. Tell me, Besim, can we arrive at the hospital ahead of him?"

"It is doubtful—possible, but doubtful. Very fast driver, as you see."

The Audi has sped out of sight since Besim's initial backing off.

"I would like that," she says. "No matter, I must arrive to his final destination ahead of him. I must be waiting."

His dark eyes slide into the mirror and out again.

"He has wronged me," she explains.

Besim keeps his thoughts to himself, but he's an open book: she needs a good backhand to the face. A little tune-up. Eye-tunes.

"The money he gambled was mine. The money he lost. The money these other men want." The invented story comes with surprising ease. She's not a natural born storyteller; she's a number cruncher.

The true story reads differently: she has left her first and one true love behind in China, both disallowed by their families from pursuing the relationship. She was eager to do so; he refused, held tightly by the family reins. Besim doesn't need to hear this. For him she is translating the language of the heart to the language of money. *Stories are so interchangeable,* she thinks, wondering why lives are not.

"He has taken my heart," she says honestly. "I want my money back."

Besim's chipped teeth sparkle white. He wants to say something about her being Chinese, to sting her for entering a relationship with an Arab. She knows that look and resents it. Objectified. Reduced to what's between her shoulders and legs. So easy to choke or garrote a man from the backseat. Her emotions swing with every lane change of the car. Besim knows his stuff; they are stitching their way through the congested traffic.

She doesn't want to follow, would rather leapfrog.

"His final destination, please. You will drop me there, then wait with my bags at my apartment. It is okay?"

"Yes, ma'am."

Her decision made, she sits back. Her thought process is linear, mathematical. If A equals B and B equals C, then . . . Were the agents waiting for Melemet, aka Mashe Okle, as they appear to have been? The "why" isn't important to the equation, but the "how" definitely is. They must have been aware of his cover identity prior to his booking the ticket. If a known arms dealer, why not arrest him on the spot? Okle is in Istanbul to be at the bedside of his dying mother. Why put off his arrest? No matter how she manipulates the variables, the equation won't yield a result. It's an unsolvable proof. Unacceptable.

What is Dulwich not telling her, and why? This is the parenthetical product she's lacking, the value that is throwing off the result.

When her phone vibrates and a sixty-four-character string of symbols and alphanumeric characters appears in the Messaging balloon, she knows it's the password she's been waiting for, the one she needs to raid Okle's investment portfolio. She stares at the phone as if it belongs to someone else. The message doesn't come from Rutherford's Data Sciences division, but from Dulwich himself, the most digitally challenged man she knows. It's a small inconsistency, but she's trained to identify such variables.

She drums her fingers on her knee. *What is Dulwich up to?*

Outside the vehicle, the sparkle of the Istanbul lights emerges.

"You like?" Besim asks. He's caught her look of awe in the mirror.

"It's beautiful," she says, admiring the twinkling hills, the dozens of mosque spires, and the sparkling vessels on the Bosphorus Strait. She doesn't want to get her driver talking. She needs time to think.

The illuminated minarets of the mosques look like chalky fingers pointing to heaven.

Besim nods thoughtfully. "You will like this place."

Grace is not so sure.

10

The storm has turned the streets of Amman into a beach parking lot. The grit beneath Knox's shoes gives him shivers; it's like biting into a dry Popsicle. The air quality sucks, but at least he doesn't feel as if he's standing in front of the nozzle of a sandblaster anymore. It's tolerable, and people return cautiously to the sidewalks and streets, their faces protectively covered. Some cars are moving. Many hoods are open, the driver leaning in to deal with a clogged air filter. There is little sense of irritation; such storms are an accepted occurrence here. Knox marvels at the universal adaptability of humans.

A text from Dulwich: Shepard Fairey's Obama Hope poster and an address. A parenthetical: eight P.M. It's coming up on seven. Knox knows not to put this off. A possible rendezvous, though the Obama reference eludes him. Dulwich's cryptic messages can be frustrating. Knox returns to his thought about spooks, wondering what Dulwich and Primer have gotten him into. Rutherford Risk rarely discriminates against its clients. Knox is allowed that luxury. He picks and chooses, though Dulwich has his number, quite literally. Anything in six figures and Knox can't seem to keep his fingers off it.

The corporation is in the business of problem-solving those problems that can't be solved by conventional means. Over half their business is international kidnapping resolution. Knox can't yet figure the client on this job, but assumes it's a government wanting to block an arms sale, one that lacks a security division as capable as Rutherford Risk. Many countries fall into this category, leaving Knox to marvel at the power of Primer's corporation and the leniency it is afforded. He is a small part of that, and often wonders if it's a blessing or a curse. He understands this: the further down the food chain, the more expendable the individual. Working with Grace has taught him as much. In Amsterdam, it became clear that Brian Primer and Dulwich would protect Grace over him, making Knox feel like the team veteran about to be replaced by the rookie. As he does more jobs for Dulwich, does he become more of an asset, or a liability? Again: what the hell has he gotten himself into?

He flags down a share taxi, a white Volkswagen minibus. The driver sits on a backing of wood rollerballs. Talismans dangle from the rearview mirror. Knox crams in with eight others, the smell of body odor overpowering. He feels like Gulliver next to the two women on his bench. Eyes stare at him from headscarves arranged to limit his view. The passengers have gone quiet. The ride through the recovering city is treacherous; the driver does his best to control the skidding. They detour several times because of breakdowns blocking the road. Knox's command of the Jordanian dialect is too pathetic to attempt conversation. He sits uncomfortably, banging his head on the ceiling with every bump. Someone lights a cigarette. No one complains. Knox is close to losing his temper by the time the van pulls over. The driver has to point at him to let Knox know they're at his stop.

Merchants have come downstairs from their second-story apartments to sweep the sidewalk in front of shuttered stores. Women in *abaya*s worn from the shoulders and colorful headscarves move silently and efficiently while men gather in small clusters, smoking. Knox dodges cardboard boxes, discarded appliances and a pair of worn shoes as he passes some unhappy shop clerks who were caught by the storm, unable to salvage their wares ahead of time. Discouragement weighs down their bent backs and slows their movement. The struggle of daily life hangs in the air as thickly as the residual dust left behind by the storm.

Knox's iPhone mapping app reveals that the van dropped him at the wrong intersection. Maybe they got sick of him. Maybe they're all laughing at dumping the American. He walks a winding kilometer uphill to reach Ali Ben Abi Taleb. Walks east and locates the address Dulwich sent.

The art gallery is called "brilliant." All lowercase English. No name offered in Arabic. In the window to the left stands a sandstone egret; to the right, a collage of newsprint, pieces of lingerie and tufts of human hair, all covered in a thick layer of clear-coat. Knox double-checks the address.

He knows what he's doing here: Dulwich has figured out how to pass him the Harmodius. No need for a courier. No black-market transaction. David Dulwich can be a real pain in the ass. As Sarge hinted, getting the bust from here to Istanbul is going to fall on Knox.

He pushes inside. An antique bell chimes. The sandstorm has been good for business—a dozen or more people are milling about. Three bottles of white wine are open on a side table, two empty. Plastic cups. Knox pours himself one. A young woman, nearly six feet tall, greets him. Australian. Nice calves. Fierce eyes. She welcomes him. They small-talk. Knox searches the wall for the Obama poster.

"I've had a recent interest in Shepard Fairey." He laughs at himself. "I'm behind the times."

"Not at all! He's an interesting artist. Began as a skateboarder. Did you know that?"

"A digital Warhol," Knox says, doing his best. "Though that's taking it a little far." He indicates a great distance with his large, scarred hands.

"They say you can tell a great deal about a person by his hands," she murmurs.

"The most difficult part of the body to paint or sculpt," Knox says.

"You have impeccable timing." It sounds loaded. Hers are not eyes he could face when waking.

"How so?"

"We had a bust come in just today—very much like Fairey."

"Not interested in sculpture." He wants to make her sell him. Can't seem eager.

"You should at least take a look."

"I don't think so. Wall art's my interest."

He allows her to steer him deeper into the gallery. It's like a UN conference in here: Indian, Asian, African and Caucasian. The scent of incense intensifies.

He spots it atop a white pedestal. An oversized bust of Obama made from a hideous rainbow swirl of what appears to be bowling-ball plastic. The chins of the other gallery patrons lift; the eyes gaze up at the acoustic tile. Knox is forced to cover his smirk with his hand, as if considering the piece.

"Not exactly what I was looking for."

"One of a kind," she says.

"With good reason."

"As close to Fairey as you'll find in Amman." She adds, "Which is why my owner chose to represent it."

He shakes his head. He wants to be begged.

"Art is so personal, is it not? I cannot begin to suggest taste. But strictly as an investment—and I typically discourage clients from thinking this way—these political pieces, especially those tied to Fairey's influence, are certain to gain in value. Politics is a fleeting business. As you know."

It's selling for six hundred U.S. dollars. Its plastic conceals a piece worth millions.

"Given my tastes, if I bought art as an investment I'd be a poor man."

"I think you underrate yourself."

If not for those eyes, he could play along. A body like hers can tumble. It would be a pleasant way to pass a lonely evening in Amman.

"I'll think on it," he says, wanting to sink the hook. He thanks her and studies a gaudy airbrush of a white horse in the desert. It reminds him of romance-novel cover art. Slim pickings in Amman. The rest is not much better.

He's careful to get a look at everyone in the gallery. Dulwich didn't put the ugly plastic over the Harmodius; he didn't pack and deliver and convince the dealer to display it. There are too many intermediaries, no matter how trustworthy. The bust feels more like chum, and Knox does not want to feed too quickly.

To his surprise, of those who notice Knox, none seem particularly interested. If he's being monitored, he's once again reminded that it's by people so good at their jobs.

Dulwich has handed him a way to take possession of the Harmodius, but moving it into Turkey remains the challenge. Dulwich has his reasons for passing it to Knox here: if the Harmodius "coincidentally" shows up in Istanbul the week the Okle brothers are there, the op could appear forced. If there's a paper trail, no matter how obscure, that shows Knox shipping it from Amman to Turkey, the attempted sale to Akram Okle will seem all the more authentic. But accomplishing the task, given the earlier encounter and the questions it raises, makes things more complicated.

Knox spends a good deal of his time in front of some horrible art, thinking it through. Studying a nude who's offering herself to a man's head on an ape's body, it dawns on him: Victoria Momani, whose contact information he got from his Skype with Akram. With the proper manipulation, she can be used to ship the Harmodius from Jordan to Istanbul with Knox's name nowhere on it. The pieces stitch together better than they do on the fabric art by the window.

He approaches the woman docent.

"The wine must be getting to my head," he says. "In a moment of weakness, I'll buy it. But sadly, I can't leave it behind on show. You won't want me to, anyway, because by the sober light of day I know I'm going to regret this purchase. So it's your call. If I buy it, I'm taking it with me, which I'm already beginning to think is a bad idea."

"I think it will live better on its own."

"It's iconic. An archetype. For that, and that alone, I will find a place for it."

"It's heavy."

"Since it appears to be a melted-down bowling ball, I assumed as much."

He gets a rise out of her, though her eyes are prohibited from showing mirth. It's the depth of the sockets and the smallness of the eyes themselves; she'd do better with Lady Gaga–sized sunglasses. He suggests she call a taxi, owning up to the fact that the storm congestion may delay it.

"More time to get to know each other," she says cunningly, even hopefully.

Knox knows better. He hates to disappoint.

DESPITE THE FACT that the bust is packed and crated, by morning light Knox feels like his X-ray vision can penetrate the box to reveal the hideous rainbow Obama bust. If he'd had the gallery ship it to Istanbul, he'd have left a means to tie him to a missing historical artifact. He can't use a brick-and-mortar express shipping counter for fear of security cameras; he needs to ship it anonymously from a residential address. It could be picked up out front, leaving no face attached to the air bill. But for that, he needs a valid residential address.

In Amman, Jordan.

Victoria Momani answers his call speaking Arabic.

Knox speaks English. "Victoria? It's John Knox, a friend of Akram's."

His introduction is met with silence.

"He suggested I . . . that we . . . that I should call you for a drink if I was ever in Amman."

"I see." Understandably skeptical of a stranger's call.

"I'm in import/export. I've sold Akram some artwork."

"John. Yes," she says, making no effort to disguise her relief.

"Coffee? A drink? Do you have a spot?"

She names a teahouse and address, suggests lunch. One P.M.

"I will try for one. I may be a few minutes late. See you there." He hangs up.

He calls FedEx and supplies Victoria Momani's address and a pickup time of one-thirty P.M. He can't count on her being perfectly on time. He asks the hotel concierge to help with the air bill so his handwriting can't be traced. Lugs the crate into the taxi at twelve-forty-five; arrives at her apartment building at the top of the hour. The teahouse is a twenty-minute walk, a five-minute cab. He waits outside for five minutes and, seeing no woman leave the building, decides she's a walker. He takes a chance, his system charged with the elixir of adrenaline.

He carries the boxed bust up two flights of stairs rather than risk being seen in the elevator. It's like lugging a small car in his arms. He puts it down outside apartment 222 with the air bill on top. He hurries down the stairs, leaving an unguarded fortune in the hallway. Arrives back to the waiting taxi and is off.

He's only minutes late to the Turtle Green Teahouse.

Jordanian women don't need the cosmetics they use. Knox finds most of the over-forty faces severe. Like the Italians, it's the skin of the younger women he finds attractive.

The only woman willing to meet his eyes is sitting alone. Victoria Momani does not cover her hair. Her shoulders are square, her posture perfect. There's no indication of smile lines.

They shake hands. Knox sits across from her and asks for recommendations, then requests she order for the two of them. He wants her to feel in control, to lessen any defenses she may have in place. His primary concern is to keep her here long enough to ensure the package is picked up with her name on the air bill. If he can stretch this to forty minutes, he's in the clear. FedEx is reliable.

Knox orders an espresso for himself. She asks for hot tea.

"Here on business?" she asks. Her English is tinged with a delightful lilt that makes it poetic.

"What else? I'm a slave to it, I'm afraid."

"Trade."

He shrugs. "Too kind a word. You might say I'm an arbitrageur. Move a piece of art or craftwork from one country to another where it's more valued, or where the currency conversion is favorable. Sell it; convert. Purchase. Resale. It's less supply and demand than catching the idiosyncrasies of artistic taste."

"You take advantage of people."

He mugs.

"And me? Do you plan to take advantage of me?"

He might think she's flirting, but her tone is accusatory bordering on angry.

"I beg your pardon." He has already taken advantage of her. He wishes he could feel remorse over it, but does not.

"Why do you lie to me?"

"Excuse me?"

"Akram would never recommend a drink with me. This is your mistake. So you are testing me, yes? A Westerner, no less. Bravo! An interesting twist, to be sure. But I still know nothing. You are wasting your time."

To the contrary, Knox thinks, suddenly interested in how Akram might be testing her.

"You may have me mistaken for—" he says.

"I think not, Mr. Knox, if that is in fact your name."

"Why meet me if you consider me such a liar?"

"To tell you, as I have told all of you before, to back off. What goes on between a man and a woman, it stays between the man and the woman."

"Rarely," Knox says. The word he hears is "before."

"In this case, then."

He's caught between wanting to distance himself from whoever she thinks he is and playing the role in order to work the conflict for "incidental findings," the unintended information she may yet divulge. Judging by her tone, she and Akram were once an item. *Were*—past tense. Akram or his people have tested her since the collapse of the relationship. She believes these people have now gone to the trouble of hiring a Westerner to do their bidding. Boxes inside boxes—he's intrigued.

Their drinks arrive. He adds sugar to the espresso, but it's unnecessary: the bean makes for a smooth and slippery liquor in his throat.

"You like it," she says.

"I do, very much."

"You will please pass my message along."

"I would if I could. Sadly, you mistake me."

"I think not."

"Your prerogative." He pauses. "You recognized my name when I called. Akram has spoken of me."

"You people . . . people like you . . . you can know any of that far too easily. Did you listen to us at the end? Did you enjoy it?" She can't look at him, only the reflection in her teacup.

People like you, Knox hears the echo in his ears. People who eavesdrop. She's talking about surveillance. She fears she's been listened in on. Better with every bite. He says, "You mistake me for someone else. No one is keeping you here."

Her eyes flash darkly.

They share olives, hummus and falafel. Knox could eat all afternoon, the coffee boring a bottomless pit in his stomach. Shredded onions deep-fried in garbanzo flour. The dishes keep coming. The act of sharing food lowers the wall between them; the connection is primitive but palpable. He orders a beer.

"So it was a bad breakup," he says.

She shakes her head as if to tell him he knows this already.

"I've only met him a couple of times, but I like Akram." He thinks he may be getting through to her, judging by a softening of her dark eyes. But she doesn't take the bait.

"Leave me alone, please. You tell them: leave me alone."

"I don't know who they are."

"If this is the truth, then there is no harm done, and I apologize for any inconvenience. But I know you are lying, Mr. Knox, and I wish to make the point that I must be left alone."

"Point taken." He capitulates for no other reason than laziness and the meal's imminent end. He signals for the check, pulling receipts, his hotel key card and his thin wallet from his front pocket. He doesn't want her to see the name on any of the cards. He removes some bills and stuffs everything back.

"These men. Police? Government? Criminals?"

She eyes him warily. Spitefully. Shakes her head in defeat. *You people won't stop,* her eyes shout. "Is there so much difference?" she asks.

11

Mashe Melemet and his two bodyguards take an additional two hours before arriving at the residential address that Besim, Grace's driver, uncovered. It was likely time spent at the hospital, given that one of his guards is carrying takeaway food; dinner was an afterthought.

Grace has failed to spot anyone else interested in the apartment building, though she assumes that Dulwich could be watching. She expected to see the men from the airport, including the agent who descended the escalator, but she has not.

They interest her, and they will certainly interest Dulwich. The more information she can put together on them, the more thorough her work into who's tailing Mashe Okle is, the more she'll impress Dulwich. She has the men pegged as police, immigration officers or possibly Turkey's National Intelligence Organization. Getting it right will earn her bonus points.

Is the takeaway dinner the result of a long day of travel or Mashe Okle's—aka Mashe Melemet's—avoidance of public places? If he's afraid of restaurants, of being seen in public, it explains why Dulwich needed a plan—needed her—to put herself and Knox in a room with him.

To that end, she has to black-hat an investment server before she sleeps. Staying with Melemet is a guilty pleasure from which she finds it difficult to pull away. She left Besim and the black Mercedes four blocks back, going on foot, a scarf pulled tight over her head to hide her Asian features. She enjoyed walking the busy Turkish neighborhood for the past two hours. An operative. She continues walking past as the mark arrives. Takes no interest in him at all.

Comes around the block to the north—for the third or fourth time—and spots two men, one wearing the Euro-ubiquitous black leather jacket. Her suspect in the airport wore a jacket just like it. She's unable to get close enough to see them clearly. They smoke cigarettes while talking, like a million other men in Istanbul.

Their location is significant. From where they stand, they have a view of Okle's apartment building. *His safe house?* she wonders. A family residence? A rental? Are they protecting him, or pursuing him?

At this moment, she can't be sure of anything.

12

Sipping from an eight-dollar minibar beer for which Dulwich will eventually pay, Knox finds going through e-mails tedious. He can't keep his mind off the men following him in Amman, or Victoria Momani's implication that the fallout between her and Akram was related to a team surveilling Mashe. Is there a connection?

He can't believe it, but he misses having Grace Chu around. Her mathematical mind has ways of cutting through the clutter. More than anything, he trusts her. He tries to never lose sight of the economic leash connecting Dulwich to Brian Primer.

Knox has decided the requirement of spending five minutes with Mashe has something do with tracking. He assumes there must be a device within either the plastic outer mold or the Harmodius Obama covers; a tagging device but, according to Dulwich, not for assassination. Maybe Grace could make sense of it. He can't. He pushes right to the edge of drawing a conclusion, only to be knocked back by a screwball piece of evidence: Dulwich's promise of no assassination; the attacker in Amman retreating at the moment of superiority; Akram's level of secrecy.

Knox doesn't feel safe. But he doesn't jump at the sound of knocking. He shuts the laptop and eyeballs the peephole to the hall.

"One second, please," he says.

He keys open the safe and leaves it ajar. He can have the gun in hand in a second, or less.

He opens the room door, his foot blocking it from the inside. She appears to be alone. He admits her and locks the door, security bar and dead bolt.

"I'm sorry," he says, taking her by the forearm. "I'm going to need to search you and your purse."

Victoria Momani's eyes blink slowly, giving her consent. Knox is gentle but thorough, sparing no contact—up between the legs, under and around her breasts from behind. He dumps her purse on the carpet and inspects the contents as he returns them one by one. He pulls the battery from her cell phone and drops them both into the bag.

"Which agency do you work for?" he asks, still working her belongings. "You had me going with all the complaints. I bought that fair and square. A wonderfully executed diversion. Well done."

"You cannot be so ignorant."

"Who but a police officer or agent could find my hotel room in a city this size? And you did not follow me."

"What kind of import/exporter can track who's following him?"

He hands her back her purse, motions her to a chair. "The one thing you learn in my business is this: a simple robbery is rarely simple. At any given time, I might be carrying a coin or a stamp, a letter, a photograph worth a small fortune. One learns to protect his assets."

"Okay."

"You answered a question with a question," he says. "So you're trained at this."

"No. I am a woman." She points to the table. Knox does not want her messing with his laptop. "You pulled out your key card when you paid the bill."

Knox sees his key card on the table next to the laptop. The card's paper slipcase carries the hotel logo. He can't believe he made such a freshman mistake.

"A friend's sister works on the hotel's event staff. Amman is not such a big place. You . . . you stand out. It wasn't hard. I was given five rooms to try. This was my third."

"That's a lot of effort to go to for a drink." He's bent at the minibar.

"White wine," she says.

He pours it into a water glass. "So?"

"Your arrogance is insulting."

"Is it?"

"Your ignorance as well."

"Is that so?"

"Then you knew it's my gallery? Brilliant?"

Bile stings his throat. He works to mask his confusion with a wry smile. His mind grinds. When the shit flies in your face, you'd better be wearing goggles. He's rarely forced to deal with bad luck; is something of an amateur at it.

"I am called by my gallery manager. Told we flipped—I believe you call it—a piece. Buy and sell same day. She describes a Westerner who buys piece. Same man meets me for a drink not so long after. I have neighbors, Mr. Knox, neighbors who saw a big man, a Westerner, enter my apartment building with a heavy crate or box, and leave empty-handed."

He's assembling his explanation as she continues.

"Shortly thereafter, same box picked up by delivery service. Object is heavy, but what? A bomb? Explosives? Ammunition? Something sent to Akram, perhaps? With my name and return address on it, his ex-girlfriend, someone to take blame."

"Too much television."

"I beg your pardon?" Irate.

"Far too dramatic, Victoria. Have you heard of value-added tax? Not nearly as sexy as bombs or ammunition, but I'm not an arms dealer. I'm in import/export. I just exported a pretty ugly piece of artwork I may find a market for outside of Amman. But if I pay the VAT and fail to recover it, I'm out what slim margin I might have to turn a profit. It shouldn't take you too long to determine who might be interested in this artwork, eh? How else would I have gotten your contact information?"

She's visibly upset, and to his surprise, it's not directed at him. Again, he's a fraction late in realizing what's at play.

"You actually thought I was sending a mail bomb? Me?"

She holds a finger to her lips, silencing him. She points to her hairband. The one place he failed to check. It could easily contain a microphone or GPS chip.

Driven by her anger with Akram and Moshe Okle, her mistrust of Knox has resulted in a call to the police. Judging by her pallor— she's an eerie green—she regrets that now.

Knox grabs the laptop, stuffs it into his messenger bag along with its power cord. His Scottevest jacket's many pockets contain everything he values. The gun carries his prints. Can't have that. He retrieves the safe's contents and stuffs them away in the jacket, vowing to be rid of the gun—possession of a handgun will land him in Jordanian prison. Only shotguns and rifles are allowed, and they are hell to obtain legally. He appreciated being able to defend his castle, but out on the streets, he'll need to rely on his wits. An art dealer doesn't carry. He never gives the few clothes and toiletries he leaves behind a second thought.

He picks his hotel rooms carefully. Never takes a room above the third floor for a reason. He's out on the private balcony in seconds.

To her credit, Victoria Momani is up there, shouting as if Knox is with her. She's comparing him to a parasite, attempting to keep the police engaged and at bay.

Knox dangles from his balcony, swings and drops to the balcony below. He climbs over and hangs, facing too far a drop to the sidewalk. His only hope to save his legs is to aim for one of the rattan tables on the sidewalk terrace. He pushes off the wall and drops, knees bent to absorb the hit. Crashes dead center, rolls, clutching the bag. A few bruises. A stiff ankle. A crushed table. He hobbles off, staying close to the wall, working the rigid joint back to life.

The rapid footfalls behind him push him faster as he turns the corner. Police or worse. They think him a bomber or an arms dealer. Lovely. The narrow streets twist and turn. If he weren't being chased, it would be an interesting neighborhood to wander. But whoever's back there knows them better than he.

Testing the fitness of his pursuers, Knox turns to head uphill. Faces a dead end. Squeezes between two buildings ornately covered in ironwork. He vaults a low fence and finds himself in another narrow winding street.

The hill is terraced with major streets, cul-de-sacs and tighter lanes jammed between them. Knox moves in bursts of speed, gaining ground quickly but preserving endurance. He arrives at another thoroughfare and crosses through heavy traffic. Manages to do so without drawing the peal of a car horn. On the opposite side he reenters the puzzle of steep streets cluttered with parked vehicles. Zippered into the pockets of the Scottevest are the tools necessary to jack a car, but he fears the traffic. It's faster on foot.

He smells spicy meat and fried bread and his mouth goes wet with saliva. Hears Jay Z and Justin Timberlake cursing through an open window. Could be Brooklyn.

He pops out onto Khaled Ben Al Waleed and is crossing the wider avenue when a minivan skids to a stop on the skim of wind-blown sand. The side door slides open.

"In here!" The driver is leaning well out of his seat. Knox can't place the accent. It's definitely not Jordanian. The driver rolls a balaclava down over his face.

Knox pauses. He's not getting into the van.

"Now! Or you're with GID." General Intelligence Department. The accent is vaguely Eastern European. Possibly forced. Croatia? Bosnia?

Knox's efforts have done nothing to slow whoever's coming up the hill; he knows only too well the training required.

"Shit," he mumbles as he climbs reluctantly into the tiny van. "Go!" he says.

The van lingers.

"Go!"

Knox reaches to slide the door shut. A hand grabs hold from the other side—Knox assumes it belongs to the man following him, a man also wearing a balaclava. He shoves Knox out of his way as he boards. The van takes off. They don't cuff him. Don't speak.

"What the fuck?" Knox says. There are no weapons showing. He can take the man in the balaclava if he has to.

The flashing blue lights of police vehicles coil slowly up the hill. The van is well out ahead and currently in the clear; the police are searching for a man on foot. Knox puts it together: the one following him radioed how and where to intercept Knox. The why of it lingers. Dulwich is the easiest answer: Knox is being driven to Dulwich.

He wants to connect these two to the man who followed him to the Internet café, but it's too big a leap. The easy answer is never the right one. The Iranian agencies recruit men and women who look like Israelis; the Israelis recruit Palestinians. There's no *Who's Who* of black-ops agents. These guys could be on Dulwich's payroll for all Knox knows.

"Someone going to say something?" Knox says.

The van obeys the modest speed limit as it climbs through a series of turns and then descends, slowing at an intersection.

Knox grabs for the handle, slides open the door and rolls out. He's on his feet and running.

He hears, "Have it your way, asshole." The vehicle pulls away.

He assumes the second guy followed him out. Knox has forced their hand: they're going to kill him.

Or try to.

He glances back to measure his lead.

No one.

Have it your way, asshole! What kind of an accent was that?

He's alone, suddenly wrapped in a swirling dust-dog of wind and sand.

"What the fuck?" he shouts, spinning in a full circle to see who, if anyone, he missed. The night air holds only a red glow, remnants of the sandstorm. The haze crystalizes the millions of lights. White diamonds in a ruby haze. He bends over and grabs his knees, his heart racing out of control.

13

Grace has arranged herself an apartment rented by the week in a building suited for Westerners. The idiosyncrasy—that in a Middle Eastern nation she might be considered Western—is not lost on her. She and Besim made three stops: grocery store, pharmacy and liquor shop. She has everything from feminine products and mascara to Greek yogurt and vodka.

The apartment is furnished and well appointed, with a kitchenette, nice linens, Wi-Fi and a flat-screen television with full satellite. It keeps her out of a hotel, allowing a lower profile.

Already at work attempting to hack Mashe Okle's investment accounts, she maintains an open videoconference with Xin in Rutherford Risk's Data Sciences division, which operates 24/7/365. Her VPN connection has been pinged around the world, aliased and encrypted. Slipping into an investment server undetected is impossible, so once again she must cloak herself. The going is tedious. Data Services is advising her as to the exact time to make the hack. She waits, her finger hovering above the Return key.

Her phone rings, the caller ID on her screen. She mutes the video and takes the call.

"Ma'am." She doesn't like being addressed this way but didn't have the heart to tell her driver. By arrangement, he remains parked outside, on call through midnight.

"You have man friend maybe watching building?"

"Explain, please, Besim."

"Man park twice. First time, west of building. Get out. Walk around building. Move car to see east side."

"How alert of you, Besim," she says.

"This is man you follow, perhaps?"

"Perhaps." She thanks him for his attention. Asks him to let her know if anything changes.

Ending the cell call, she takes the videoconference off Mute. "Xin?"

"Wei." Yes. Thousands of miles away on an island in the South China Sea, Xin sounds as if he's next to her.

"You have my coordinates?"

"Within one meter."

"How long for you to account for every cell phone turned on within one hundred . . . no, let's say, fifty . . . meters of me?"

"How many carriers?"

"Enough to cover in the ninetieth percentile of coverage."

"Soonest? Fifteen minutes. Longest? An hour."

"Put someone on it, will you please?"

"Copy."

A symbol indicates he's muted his line. She does the same, taking note of the time. The minutes drag out. After five minutes, she's reconnected as Xin gives her a countdown to the hack.

She's in. She celebrates the success by pouring herself warm vodka. Wishes she'd given it time to cool. Now, data-mining a major investment firm, she envisions herself as a salmon or sperm swimming upstream, seeking out a specific destination. It's a journey. She knows she must be patient. As in a video game, there are dragons and demons lurking, traps set, awaiting a misstep on her part. Having extracted Mashe Okle's password from the bank server, she uses it here, hoping he's a man of convenience, and gains entrance to his investment portfolio.

She laughs at the irony of the Iranian's savings being heavily invested in the U.S. stock market. She's feeling the vodka.

He's a wealthy man, but it's not the kind of money she might have expected. The stocks and mutual funds favor scientific companies. She is annoyed by the worming thought that this doesn't pass the sniff test for an arms dealer. Did Dulwich ever confirm that, or was it her assumption? She's eager to speak with Knox; he knows Dulwich better. At the very least, he'll have a keener sense of what's at play. Knox is not one to take on in a game of cards.

She clicks through to the portfolio's history, increases the time sample and prints to a PDF file. On point, she flies through menus so quickly another's eye would be unable to keep up. Multiple files are saved and archived in a matter of seconds for later analysis. This is not a time for window-shopping. She prides herself on the speed and agility with which she extracts every morsel of relevant data. When she logs out of Mashe's account, she's at forty-seven seconds. She closes the firm's web page at forty-nine, giving her a total of under a minute. She celebrates by throwing her arms in the air, an Olympian sprinter at the tape.

"Three hundred seventy-one." It's Xin from the video window in the corner of her screen.

"Within fifty meters?"

"Affirmative."

"Of those, how many have called or been called by known law enforcement, domestic or foreign, in the past ten days?"

"Published, or known to us?"

"Known to us," she says.

"Back at you." His line mutes. Xin loves this stuff as much as she does.

She pours herself another drink, this one on the rocks. Warns herself to take it easy. She likes vodka a little too much. Has no remorse about drinking alone. She's always alone. Even in a mixed group she feels isolated, believing her mind more facile than most, her personal history more complicated. The truth is, most people bore her.

"No joy," says Xin.

The trouble with vodka: it skews her sense of time. Ten minutes have passed. She's been surfing Mashe Okle's investment files offline. The vodka level is halfway down the ice.

"Calls and texts placed outside Turkey in past ten days," she states.

"Hang on. That shouldn't take but a moment."

She finds the British accent on her fellow Chinese appealing. It's either Xin or the vodka warming her.

"Fifteen."

"Better," she says. "We can work with that. You'll need a phantom caller ID. Untraceable. Australia. UAE. Israel. UK. Washington. Maybe a rotation."

"Copy."

"I want you to ring each of the fifteen numbers in thirty-second intervals. Wrong number, but sell it. Maybe a child's voice asking for mother."

"Copy."

"Let me know when you're ready. I'm here." She mutes the video window. Considers another three fingers of vodka. Convinces herself it doesn't negatively affect her thought process—if anything, it enhances it. Knows damn well it's a lie. Pours more anyway.

Yum.

She calls Besim. "Can you see him?"

"Yes, ma'am."

"He can see you?"

"Not probably. My seat low whole time. Resting. Who knows?"

"I'm going to keep you on the phone. You need to tell me if he answers his phone. The moment he answers his phone. You un . . . derstand?" She slurs. Thinks nothing of it. Checks the glass. Half of what she poured is gone. She obviously shorted herself. Wouldn't mind topping it off.

"Yes, ma'am."

"Good. Stay on the line please."

Feeling incredibly good, she closes her eyes, celebrating the vodka's ability to cleanse her fatigue, settle her racing mind and warm her limbs. What's not to love? Opens her eyes again when Xin speaks.

"You napping on me?"

"Ready?"

"Will call all fifteen, thirty seconds apart."

"Correct."

"Here we go." Her head clears; she is instantly sober despite her efforts otherwise. This is not the first time this has happened; where the alcohol haze goes, she has no idea, but it's undetectable. She has the cell phone to her ear. She watches Xin. He's gotten a young woman in her early twenties to make the calls. The woman's face glistens with a sheen of nervousness. Grace wants to caution her to do it right, but knows it would only add to the woman's anxiety. She has to trust Xin. She chuckles to herself—his name, a common one, means "trust."

"Something amusing?" Xin asks.

"You had to be there," she says. She drains the remaining vodka. Trust is not found in her personal lexicon. She knows its absence is the source of much of her inner struggle.

The calls go out. The young woman does an excellent voice, sounding about thirteen and troubled. Three calls. Five. Grace keeps eyeing the vodka bottle, knowing she's over her efficacious limit but wanting more.

"He's on phone," Besim says in her left ear.

"Joy!" Grace says to Xin, whose typically quiet face registers a thrill. "That's the one we want."

"Got it."

"Off phone."

She mutes the video. "Thank you, Besim. That's all for the night. But please, don't leave for at least another thirty minutes. I will tell you when."

"As you wish."

She will turn off the apartment light before allowing Besim to drive off. She wants as little connection to the wrong number as possible.

Back with Xin, she says, "I need all calls, text messages and web access to and from that number over the past ten days to two weeks."

"It will take a few hours. Likely a lot of data. I will post here. You can access it once I post. I will let you know."

"Give me the GPS data as well."

"Copy." Xin ends the video call.

Grace is left with nothing on her computer screen but her wallpaper photo of a dog and cat curled together at the foot of a wingback chair. They're not hers. She has no pets. No wingback chairs.

She isn't who she pretends to be. She isn't who she is.

As bad as that makes her feel, she feels damn good.

14

"N*ee-hao.*" Knox speaks over the phone's earbud wire to re-tain his peripheral vision. His feet are tired, his belly empty; he's back down the hill in Jabal, the nearest thing Amman has to a historic district. With each conquering army, one civilization has replaced the next, going back millennia. While the Jabal neighborhood is arguably also the most modern, these con-temporary edifices are built cheek-to-jowl alongside ancient ruins. It's a human stew of body odor, food scents and fossil fuel. Liveli-hoods are made on the streets, other lives are lost on the streets, and still others repair the streets.

Now they are teeming in the evening hour.

"*Nee-hao,*" Grace answers.

"Can you change a FedEx delivery address for me?" He speaks Shanghainese, a specific dialect of Mandarin. Of all the words, only "FedEx" is in English. It stands out like a black sheep.

"Are you sender or recipient?"

"Recipient."

"Must be sender." Grace's tone is deliberate, professional.

"Electronically? Can you hack it?"

"I could check with Data Services, see if we have that capability. I would guess it would come down to timing."

"Immediately."

"No. I would think not."

He hesitates. Victoria turned him in to the police, who will have located the shipment using her address as the point of origin. He's counting on FedEx being so fast that the Harmodius is already in the air, or perhaps landed in Istanbul. The trick is to move it while the Jordanians debate how much to share with the Turks, and if they come to terms, the Turks set up surveillance to trap the recipient— Knox. Given the bureaucratic tangle likely to ensue, he can't see either side anticipating the delivery location changing; it's his one chance to steal the piece back before they seize it. And him.

Grace informs him that the sender can change the delivery address for a small fee.

"Can you impersonate the sender?"

"I am no expert on this. I would imagine there are safeguards. The sender must call from the phone number listed on the air bill. Something like this."

"Shit." Knox put Victoria Momani's number on the air bill.

No names. No small talk. No locations. He and Grace haven't spoken in several months. He likes hearing her voice. It's an unexpected reaction.

He ends the call, knowing no offense will be taken.

FROM A SECOND-STORY stairwell window across the street, Knox keeps watch on the cars—mostly European subcompacts—and pedestrians outside the apartment building across the street. It's a residential area with no cafés or coffeehouses or galleries to hide in. It's going on one A.M., yet swarms of youth and pairs of both men and women fill the sidewalks. Oddly, there are few couples over thirty seen together; the Jordanians in this neighborhood separate by gender when out for the evening.

Knox takes note of every twitch of every tree leaf. Nothing escapes his eye. He spots no solo surveillance, though the complexities of spotting team surveillance that combines mobile and pedestrian remains. He gives himself an extra twenty minutes to make damn sure. The success of the op depends on the next hour. If the Obama bust is studied in depth by Jordanian authorities, if it should end up confiscated, Dulwich's plan is compromised.

He wraps a white scarf bought from a street vendor in an open-air market around his head to fashion a turban. Angles his chin low as he descends the stairs and crosses the street. Enters the apartment building and climbs to the second floor.

Knocks. Waits. Knocks again.

Victoria Momani opens the door. She wears a large scarf like a robe. "Go away," she says. "I was asleep."

"It can't wait."

"You have been hurt."

Knox hasn't gotten to a mirror. The scuffle in the van, he assumes. "It's been a busy evening."

She checks the hall before she admits him. Once the door is shut: "Are you out of your mind?"

"Regularly."

"I could be watched."

He shakes his head.

"Who are you?" She waits. "I knew you people would not stop."

"Stop what, Victoria? I told you: you got me wrong the first time. I am as I represented," he says, still weighing his options. "Why else would you have let me in? You believe me. That's important to me. To us both." *If only Grace were here,* he thinks. She could make this smoother. "But let's stay here for a moment: who do you think I am? What have these people done?"

She appraises him. Shakes her head.

"'You people,'" he repeats to her. "Organized crime?"

She is incensed by the suggestion.

"Police? Special police?" he asks.

His ignorance is winning her over. Her second evaluation of him is more forgiving.

"Are you police?"

She coughs up laughter. Doesn't know what to do with him.

"Innocent bystander," he says. Her eyes go glassy, contradicting her outward confidence. He's a dentist with a pick.

"I need a favor," he says.

"Because we are such old friends."

"What caused the split with Akram?"

Impressively, she manages to keep her obvious emotion from her voice. "It is not yours to consider."

"His brother," Knox says. "Mashe."

It is as if all the air is let out of her. As she contracts, she finds a chair to sit upon while she coils inward. "I knew it."

"I am neither what nor who you think. I am, in fact, as I told you, a merchant. But I am helping others, as I know you would, were you able." He stares her down; he's reached her.

"You think me so gullible?"

"I think you've been hurt. Lied to, more than likely."

"And you are the great purveyor of truth."

Her command of English suggests he should avoid talking down to her. He regroups.

"I fashion the truth as needed," he says. "I lie about another's beauty, my own politics, my vices. But not about this." Having little to no idea of what he speaks, he says, "Mashe Okle is trouble. He can be stopped. I am offering you that chance. The crate contains a piece of legitimate art. I promise you that. But, believe it or not, it's important to my effort. I do not work for any government or police. I am a merchant enlisted by others—neither government nor police, nor any kind of criminal effort—to help expose the man for what he is. By now the Jordanians have alerted the Turks to monitor my package when and where it is delivered in Istanbul."

"I do not believe you. It is a bomb. Something like this. I will not hurt Akram or have him involved in hurting Mashe, no matter what I think of the man. I will not be part of this."

"It is not any kind of weapon or device, nor can it be used to make a weapon or a device. It is as I said." He considers her. "Very well."

He makes for the door, a gamble that causes each stride to seem artificially long and slow. Has he judged her incorrectly? Since when?

"Wait!"

He works to hide the smirk. Successful, he turns.

"A phone call is all. One phone call," he says.

15

tanding in Şişli Square, Grace can understand why a person would return to this place multiple times. Worn like a cocked cap, morning sunlight the color of candle flame catches the top of the minaret. There are more pigeons than people, more cars than pigeons. The mosque's three gray-roofed domes rise above the rectangular entrance wall, trees lurching up from within an unseen courtyard. It's all in the middle of a bustling neighborhood awaking for the day.

She's arrived early, having sneaked out of the apartment and snagged a cab, leaving Besim to sip his morning tea out front for the sake of anyone watching.

There is an answer here, some reason the man following her has repeatedly visited the square. She watches for it, expects it. Awaits its jumping out at her. This added depth of knowledge is exactly what Dulwich will treasure: not just the fact that she's being surveilled, but by whom and possibly why.

Dulwich has failed to answer calls she's made from one of several anonymous pay-as-you-call SIM chips she carries. He had warned her that she and Knox would be on their own. Nonetheless she holds out hope she'll hear from him. She has provided him this place and time. She waits, and then spins once, slowly, holding her head scarf in place.

It reminds her of a Parisian avenue but with Turkish spices in the air and overseen by a towering minaret. Şişli was countryside in the late nineteenth century, transformed into a residential neighborhood at the end of the Ottoman Empire in the early years of the Turkish Republic, when French culture was au courant—wide avenues edged with wrought-iron balconies. It was an area of trade, soon taken over by Greek and Balkan immigrants. There isn't a parking space to be had. The streets and even the newer buildings seem poised to be pushed over by the crush of pedestrians.

On her iPhone, she once again reads the data pertinent to Şişli Square. The man she and Besim identified as watching her the night before, the man from the airport, visited this place four times in three days. His phone's GPS data reveals that he's been in Istanbul but six days. Other than a discount hotel across town, this is the only place he has frequented.

Why? Beauty alone cannot account for it. Given that each visit was between four and five o'clock, it's possible he performed afternoon prayers at this mosque, but it's unlikely given the absence of any other repeated visit in the city. Grace decides to return at that hour if possible.

Her phone vibrates; the caller is listed as "Hopper 1." Dulwich. The "hopper" designation assures her that the line is secure; Grace checks around her to ensure the area is as well. That's when she sees him, sitting on a bench in the shade closer to the mosque, his back to the avenue.

"So?" Dulwich says.

"My apartment is being watched."

"Then you were careless."

"The GPS data from this man's phone reveals a pay-as-you-go SIM chip initiated six days ago," Grace says.

"You have tracked his phone?"

She thrills at the sound of his voice: shock and awe. "He has since visited this place where I sit four times in the past three days." Grace waits. "Hello?"

"I'm listening."

"A policeman, perhaps agent, is most likely to use a pay-as-you-go SIM chip like this. Same way we do. Let us assume, therefore, that this man arrived in-country six days ago. He buys the pay-as-you-go and sets up his phone. From what country he comes, we don't know. You received my text, yes? This man had access to the airport's security room. He tagged the mark upon landing. Access to Turkish security. I later identify a similarly dressed man watching the mark's residence. Could be same agent. He was paired."

"And is that the same—"

"Unlikely, no. The mobile unit surveilling my apartment was a solo. Who are all these people, sir? It is a crowded field." Grace takes in her present surroundings of pigeons, pedestrians with white iPhone wires hanging from their ears and a sea of colorful scarves.

"I wouldn't worry," Dulwich says. "What you're seeing is likely protection. The mark is an important man."

It's her turn to be unintentionally quiet. Wouldn't worry? Since when? She collects more data from Dulwich's body language than the conversation. His posture has tightened with her every revelation.

Grace says, "So why would a man protecting the mark spend extended time on a bench in front of a mosque three out of the six days he has been in-country?"

"He's religious? Do we care?" Dulwich doesn't have to try to sound offensive.

Red flag. A rule of the game is to know more about your adversary than he knows about you. "I am not comfortable with such surprises. Such unknowns."

"You understand the op?"

He's insulting her. She regrets bringing him in without more information. He doesn't want to be offered half a meal. She accepts the mistake as a learning moment. It's all or nothing; he doesn't appreciate being teased.

"Understood," she says.

"Well, then . . ." Dulwich stands and puts his phone away, offers his back and is swallowed by the tumult a few seconds later.

16

W hat the hell?" Knox sits by himself in a waiting lounge in Queen Alia International Airport. A white wire runs to his left ear; his right remains unplugged so he can over-hear the activity in the terminal. He keeps his hand over his mouth to prevent lip reading. He makes the seat look small, like an adult in a preschool parent-teacher conference.

"That would depend," Dulwich says.

The line is secure. But Knox is in public, so he will dance around specifics.

"If we'd wanted help, we'd have asked for it."

"Elaborate."

"I was followed. Lost a step. Right when the guy could have cold-cocked me, he walks. What's with that?"

Dulwich tells Knox more than he intends with his silence. This is new information; the man was not his.

"We may lose the . . . trophy," Knox says.

"You had better not."

"My lady friend is helping with that."

"Your lady friend and I had a chat earlier."

"Bully for you. I'm beginning to think we could use a couple boys from the old team."

"Not going to happen."

"Because?"

"It's an in-and-out. Don't overcomplicate it."

"You said I'd be lying in bed with my feet up watching pay-per-view. That isn't happening."

"So complain to HR."

"You said you and I wouldn't have contact—that you don't exist."

Dulwich teases him by leaving only silence on the line.

"Friendlies? Is that why he walked?"

"Don't overcomplicate it," Dulwich repeats.

"It's doing that by itself. Six months ago, Obama convinces Netanyahu to apologize to the Turkish prime minister for Israeli commandos killing ten Turkish protesters attempting to cross the Gaza blockade. Relations between Israel and Turkey immediately thaw; embassies are reopened. Now, wouldn't you know, Rutherford Risk has an op in Turkey—complete with a priceless piece of art being given away for nothing and spooks that appear out of dust storms and then vanish. I couldn't make this stuff up if I tried."

"You're hallucinating. These are small speed bumps. They happen—especially early on. It'll sort itself out. Don't go all double-oh-seven on me."

"If I'm being shadowed by a bunch of spooks, I could use a heads-up."

"So here's your heads-up: it's not a can-do, it's a must-do. That's why the paycheck is so big. Ask fewer questions, keep your fists in your pockets, and it'll sort itself out."

"He followed me through a sandstorm."

"I read about that. Sounded nasty."

"Who does that? Who goes out in a sandstorm?"

"You, apparently."

"Now you're just being rude."

"Yeah, funny how that feels on the receiving end."

Knox ends the call unceremoniously. His blood pressure lessens. He trusts Sarge with his life, yet he wouldn't trust him to walk his dog if he had one. Knows he would never be wholly lied to by the man, but isn't sure he ever gets the truth.

This operation has started poorly. He'd like to blame it all on the sandstorm. Takes it as an omen. Knox thinks of Tommy back in Michigan, and there's a nagging ache in his chest telling him to abort. He worries he's working for the department of defense, Rutherford Risk's biggest client. Dulwich's emphasis on importance has Knox convinced a government is behind the op.

But there are so many governments, and Rutherford Risk isn't particular. Government work gets people killed. That's why it's contracted out. Knox has wandered off-trail in search of an extravagant paycheck, knowing all along there's no philanthropy in his line of work. He's being overpaid for a reason. Five minutes in the room with the mark, Dulwich said. He made it sound so small, but five minutes can be an eternity.

Knox's flight is called. He has eyes in the back of his head as he boards.

EVERY STUDENT of history should start with a school trip to Istanbul, Knox thinks. It's the Kevin Bacon of history—everything's connected. Throw a rock; dig a hole and try to miss. Turkey's significance over three thousand years of Western civilization cannot be overstated. Knox is no academic, but his import business and knowledge of art history have given him a crash course in Western and Eastern civilization, an unintended consequence he appreciates, even cultivates.

Spends far more time in museums now than he did a few years ago. Beds down with books he'd be embarrassed to be caught reading.

The Demirtas neighborhood of the Eminönü district is a tight tangle of short streets that compress in width the closer one gets to the Golden Horn inlet. Smog-stained Roman columns adorn corner buildings adjacent to the remnants of ancient city walls, all of it surrounded by tasteless two-story apartment buildings that make Knox think of the highway views driving by Detroit. Istanbul has been conquered and occupied by the Crusaders, Ottoman sultans, Romans and the original founders, the Greeks. Built on seven hills, the Golden Horn and the Sea of Marmara, it was made into a fortress of palaces, golden domes, parks and towers. It has been sacked, nearly emptied of its population and rebuilt numerous times. In the middle of the seventeenth century, it was the largest city on earth.

It is currently the home to every ethnicity, culture, religion and sect, a kaleidoscope of the human species. Every scent. Every color of glass, clothing and skin can be found. Every culinary treat. The city's Grand Bazaar, an endless warren of booths and shops, is all this diversity boiled down to commercialism. Knox walks the unbearably crowded bazaar first, just to remind himself of where he is and whose company he keeps. Overpowered by sweat, cinnamon, ginger and cardamom, incense, blue jeans and hammered brass lanterns, Knox roams the concourses in a herd of tourists and locals alike, content and comforted by how some things, some places, never change. Squint your eyes, and it could be 200 B.C.

He keeps the Tigers cap pulled low as he settles himself onto a stone step across town. Doesn't want his height and physique drawing undue attention. He wears his important belongings on his person, thanks to the Scottevest. Needs a stop at a department store for a change of clothing.

He continues his surveillance of the Yurtiçi Kargo storefront. Satisfied he's spotting nothing out of the ordinary at the shipping center, but wary nonetheless, he crosses the street, lengthening his strides to reduce his height. He was with Victoria Momani when she called FedEx and requested an alternate delivery. He trusts that between the hand-off to Turkish authorities by the Jordanians— if such a hand-off ever took place, which is unlikely given the reluctant, sluggish nature of overly possessive international security divisions—any live monitoring of the bust's movements is unlikely. More credible is that its air bill destination might have been shared or be under surveillance. He can't imagine Victoria's redirect to this branch office being picked up on. Bureaucracy has its blessings.

Inside, he presents false ID in the name of one of three covers he carries, John Chambers. The delivery is efficient, no tell apparent from the woman behind the counter. The bulk and weight of the crate creates problems, or would for most. Knox carries it like a hatbox in one hand, stunning the woman, who struggled to move it from cart to scale.

An instant later, he's out in the street, eyes alert for those alert to him. It's a strange and disconcerting element of this work; he imagines it being akin to the weight of celebrity. Knox is rarely indifferent to his surroundings, is perpetually preoccupied with survival. It's a condition shared with animals in the wild—fight or flight, the underlying awareness that every moment is kill or be killed. Some will claim they can feel it, that they possess a prescience that can alert them to surveillance. Knox is not so lucky; he needs some sign. And although he has trained his senses well beyond those of the "average man," spotting group surveillance continues to elude him. His only hope is to identify one of many and expand from there.

This is the task he puts himself to as he climbs into a taxi. His eyes roam, searching for faces he saw during his curbside vigil. He makes comments about how beautiful the city is to satisfy his driver's curiosity. Knox makes an excuse of forgetting something, directing the driver to circle a block to return to the pickup—an attempt to spot mobile surveillance. Feigns discovery of the missing item on his person and redirects the cab once again. It's a familiar routine, but far from comfortable. He's crawling out of his skin within minutes.

He checks into the Alzer Hotel as himself. Is a returning guest and, as such, is treated like royalty. He declines an upgrade in order to remain on the first floor, one above street level. He looks down on the hotel's café seating, has a view across an open plaza and a mosque beyond. Its spires and walls suggest an exotic fortress, a world secreted from prying eyes like his. Such treasures await the unsuspecting visitor on nearly every corner: a Roman bath, a Greek column and a mosque.

He keeps the Obama bust in its crate in the bottom of the armoire, displacing a pair of courtesy terry-cloth slippers and a shoeshine kit. Thinks back to Dulwich's description of the op and wonders if things will settle down now.

They need no introduction when he makes the call, as the caller ID on her end has identified him as Hopper 7.

"We need to get together and go over the books," she says. Her use of their cover, Grace as his bookkeeper, tells him she's speaking somewhere she doesn't believe is secure. He finds it easy to slip into his role.

"Indeed. Work up a budget for me, please, with an eye toward the improving climate."

"My pleasure."

There's something about the way she says it that takes his mind off the job at hand. "Why don't you pick the location, as I've just arrived?"

"I am somewhat . . . preoccupied," she says, choosing the word carefully, "with other clients. I could fit you in around drinks."

She's suggesting she's being watched or followed. Knox mulls this over, compares it to his own situation in Amman. He should have pushed Sarge for more details about his "chat" with Grace; sometimes his wisecracking banter is a detriment, though he's loath to admit it.

"Name it."

She picks a Starbucks near the Firuz Aga Mosque in the old city. Knox knows the adjoining park well: its handcarts selling fresh melon and bananas, the vegetation an unexpected mix of tropical and temperate. The choice of Starbucks disappoints him but is so in character he should have thought of it first. The time is set for three-thirty.

He gets a shower and a much needed nap. Buys two sets of clothes, head-to-toe, and puts them into the hotel express wash. Where once there was adrenaline and urgency, there is routine, a condition he cautions himself against.

GRACE'S FACE REMAINS PASSIVE, but her eyes light up at his entrance. They kiss cheeks and he sits across a small table from her. Before anyone else has a chance to enter the coffee shop, she reviews her arrival to the airport and the tail she collected, speaking quietly and fast.

"If I had to guess, I'd say Dulwich is a lying sack of shit," Knox says.

Grace bites back a smile, chastising him with her expressive eyes, and opens her laptop to actual spreadsheets of Knox's import business. They sit closer and she traces lines on the screen with a blue fingernail.

"You do not think this," she says.

"No. I think he's into something big—we're into something big—that has political ramifications, and is likely another attempt to improve something that will never be fixed. He knows I'm a sucker for lost causes. He uses that. And even knowing that, I fall into it, so it's on me."

"This common interest in Mashe Melemet is shared by others," she says.

"Who?"

"The mother is Melemet. Hospital records," Grace says. "Oldest son, Mashe. Younger son, Akram. The spying is on Mashe."

"You've had company," he says.

She nods.

"Me, too. You ID them?"

She shakes her head.

"Me, neither." He never stops checking out the other occupants. Has them memorized by face and clothing. "So tell me about him— the brother."

"He is quite well off. Income is paid through Iran's Ministry of Industry and Mines." Grace answers before he asks. "Regulation of industry, including mining. Promotion of export of mining products, including engineering and technology."

"A cover for military research?"

"Possibly, though his investments suggest an academic. Sciences. Pharmas. Aviation. Space exploration. He could indeed be a researcher. And get this: all listings are on the NASDAQ and the NYSE."

He smirks.

"I thought you would like that."

"So, a scientific academic in Iran," Knox says, leaving it in the air between them.

"He liquidated investments ahead of your previous sales to Akram."

"He's my collector."

"Indeed."

"And Brian Primer wants us both in a room with him for five minutes, but he swears it's not a hit."

He sees surprise.

"What?" he asks.

"The request is from David, *neh*, not Mr. Primer?"

Ever the realist, Knox thinks.

"My immediate role is to ensure the meet between you and Mashe."

"You do that how?"

Her eyes say, *please.* Her voice says, "You like things clean."

"Cleaner than this. We don't know who we're working for. We don't know who we're working against."

"I . . . in the airport. It's government, or someone who can buy his way into the Turkish equivalent of your TSA."

"Well, that certainly clarifies things."

"Have you made the call?" she asks.

"Tomorrow. I don't want to appear overeager."

"You are flirting. No wonder Mr. Dulwich selected you for this job."

He almost finds it in himself to smile at her.

Checking her watch, she says, "Would you help me with something?"

"Shopping for a new watch, I hope." She wears a Michael Kors aviator, platinum ringed, hinge-snap clasp. Its masculinity has no place on her delicate wrist.

She leads the way outside. Within minutes, they've joined the hordes of tourists that are forced to divide themselves between wonders-of-the-world mosques and exquisite Roman ruins. Soon they break away into Gülhane Park, inside which the city disappears.

"Have you been in?" Knox asks Grace, pointing out the Istanbul Archaeology Museum.

"Never."

"You must."

She checks her masculine watch again. "Not today."

"Are we meeting someone?"

"I am not sure."

They continue toward Topkapi Palace. "It once housed four thousand people. Was a miniature city for the sultan. Included a hospital, bakeries, nearly independent of the outside world. And now, tourists."

"Like the Forbidden City," she says. She turns them around. Knox can't keep from surveying their surroundings.

"Anything?" she asks.

"No. But if they're government . . ."

"I was able to track one. Xin was, actually. Data Services."

"One what?"

"A man following me."

"Track, as in . . . ?"

"I have his texts for the past several days. His locations. GPS fixes."

"And you were going to tell me, when?"

"I just did."

"Jesus."

"He revisited Şişli Square four times in three days. Always between four and five." She pauses. "Sent what could be a coded text at the end of his last visit."

He now understands her double-checking the time.

"There will be taxis at the museum," she says.

"And crowds."

"Just so."

"It's good to see you again," he says.

She hooks her arm in his and they walk. It's an uncommonly familiar gesture for someone as distant as she. It feels awkward until she speaks.

"In case we missed someone out there."

"Yeah," he says. "Of course."

She holds him closer, or does he imagine it? In profile, she appears to be smiling. Or not. He feels off balance. First Dulwich, now Grace Chu. The leaves rustle overhead, sounding dry in the fall breeze. A boat horn haunts the sky. A Turkish kid skateboards past them wearing a Who T-shirt and Air Jordans.

Knox ditches the anxiety. He feels right at home.

THEY SIT together in Şişli Square as afternoon prayers are called. Grace is enchanted by the nasally, electronic summons pealing from the minarets.

"Do you feel it? It is as if the city takes a breath," she says.

"If they take too deep a breath, they'll gag." Car exhaust chokes the city when the breezes off the Bosphorus pause for even minutes. The smog residue crusts the older buildings in a black smudge and, on bad days, causes one's nose and eyes to run—the scourge of the third world.

They both wear sunglasses; Grace, a head scarf. She explains what the GPS data has told her about the man seen watching her apartment.

"The mosque makes the most sense," Knox says. "Afternoon prayers. He didn't have to be attending. He could be surveilling someone."

"By your own admission, there are any number of agencies who would want the mark. Yes? More important to me is not the who, but the why. This man entered the country six days ago. This we can assume. Four different times he spends at least an hour on this bench. Why? How does that relate to us? To say it does not is absurd," she says, cutting off his objection. "A shipment? A middleman? Our safety relies upon—"

"—knowledge of the exigent circumstances. You take this stuff too literally. Chinese violinists are technically the most accomplished in the world, you know, but they lack soul. You need to loosen up." He's thinking: *The frog and the scorpion. This is the Middle East. Anybody could be interested in Mashe Okle. Get in line.*

"You need to consider what you say before you say it."

"You realize we're recording all this?" he says.

They laugh together. He never would have imagined such a moment a year ago.

"What I said," Grace says, "my mother used to say to me. You would be surprised. I was once more like you than you imagine."

"Are you implying I never matured?"

"You are impossible."

"But consistent."

Knox's phone is still recording when a low-battery alert chimes. They end their recordings at thirty-two minutes.

"I'll call Akram tomorrow morning and ask for the down payment. Get things going."

"To be wired. The funds must be wired into the account."

"Impossible. These things are always cash."

"The data will enable me to hack his bank account and determine the source of the deposits."

"Sarge didn't explain any of this to me."

"It is how we win the face-to-face." Grace is unsure how much to share. If David Dulwich did not include Knox, there must be a reason, the most obvious of which is that should one of them be captured, he or she must not have the full picture. That leads her to wonder why the possibility they might be surveilled and captured was never mentioned.

"He's compartmentalized us," Knox says. "That can't be good."

"I was thinking same thing." Grace hears herself drop the article as dictated in her native Mandarin. Knows it signals her anxiety. Sees Knox react to the red flag. They know each other too well; it's a worrisome thought. The op in Amsterdam brought them closer. Not only are they more aware of each other's idiosyncrasies, but also a shared hour in a brothel stripped them of the secrets typically kept between co-workers. They have information only lovers possess, and yet they are far from lovers.

"It's got to be cash. He'll smell it a mile away."

Grace ruminates. "Yes. I understand."

"You don't have to look so glum."

"It is a complication."

"Maybe if it was explained to me, it wouldn't be."

Grace makes a point of weighing her response. A year ago, she would have stuck to David Dulwich's instructions without question. Now, she wonders at the forces responsible for testing her this way.

After a moment or two of silence, she speaks quietly. She is afraid he will tease her. Sometimes this cuts her to her core. "'When the wind of change blows, some build walls while others build wind-mills.'"

She sees Knox winding up to lash out, but he swallows it away. Perhaps they are both different from a year ago, she thinks. Condensing the plan she and Dulwich worked out, she offers it to Knox in its most simplistic form.

"Isn't there some way around the wiring of the cash?" Knox asks.

Knox's sense of what she does amuses her at such times.

He says, "It's a boatload of money."

"Understood."

"Maybe not if you're an arms dealer, but—"

"He is not an arms dealer." She blurts this out. "Or if he is, he is not so very good at it." She explains the relatively small investment portfolio as well as her inability to follow the deposits. "The point is, the deposits are made directly from other bank accounts. If this was questionable income . . . I deal with questionable income. It is what I do for the company. This is not. You see?"

"It's only one account," Knox says.

"Yes. Are you going to tell me how to do my job?"

He's about to. He stops himself.

She wants to reward him. "I apologize."

"No. You're right. You have me nailed."

Maybe he's jet-lagged. This isn't the Knox she knows.

He says, "How certain are you?"

"I should not have said anything. I was mistaken to do so. An opinion is all."

"Are you going to make me beg?"

"David did not confirm the man's occupation to me. Did he to you?"

"What a snake."

"He allowed us our assumptions," Grace says. "Fair play."

"He must have loved that we both jumped to the same conclusion."

"He choreographed this. Yes?"

"I suppose he did." Knox drops his head into his large hands in concentration. "How can Mashe possibly afford the Harmodius if he's not in arms dealing?"

"Investors. A consortium. The money will be kept in a phantom account or will be held as cash in a safe-deposit box or home safe. It is possible it cannot be wired. If cash, it would be safer to carry it in. Physically transported."

"But Mashe is already here," Knox says.

"A friend or family member. A mule he trusts implicitly."

"His wife."

"Or mistress, or cousin. It can be done," she says. "But to convert such amounts of currency? At black market rates? It is very onerous. Funds wired from a ghost account would convert at bank rates, the most favorable possible."

"Mashe would wire the funds here," Knox speculates, trying to follow, "from a fake account. Akram would collect it as cash from various banks, bundle it and deliver to me. Leaving us where?"

"Leaving you stuck with too much cash to legally get out of the country. You say your previous dealings have been cash?"

"Yeah. But we're talking small amounts."

"This time it must be different. Can you take a meeting with Akram?"

"Of course."

"We will need a pickpocket," she says. "Must be a thousand around the Hagia Sophia."

"You going to put out a sandwich board offering employment?" he says.

She looks surprised. "Yes! I suppose it should be something like that."

He wonders: is she mocking him, or is she being sweetly naive? Has she already formed a plan, or is she leaving it up to him? He grins privately as Grace allows a smirk beneath her oversized sunglasses. There is cunning in her expression, a high-spiritedness and a convincing smugness that suggests she is already three steps ahead of him.

17

In order to harpoon his pickpocket, Knox performs a gag he learned off a middle schooler named Cameron Wood on a school trip to New York City. Warned by their chaperone of thieves in Times Square, Cameron and his buddies bought a street vendor wallet and put a note in it reading, "You are being electronically tracked by the NYPD." Cameron then volunteered to be the one to carry the decoy wallet in his back pocket, keeping his real one in the front. When the class returned to the hotel from a walk around Times Square, Cameron realized the wallet was gone; he never felt a thing. He and his pals got a good laugh at what the pickpocket's face must have looked like when he read their note.

Knox's three notes, written in Turkish by the hotel receptionist, read, "I will pay five times this. Look for the tall American by the ticket window."

He, too, carries a dummy wallet showing slightly from his back pocket. But unlike young Cameron, Knox knows exactly when each of the three wallets is stolen. Each carries a handwritten note and the equivalent of ten USD in Turkish liras.

He waits thirty minutes by the mosque's ticket window. The

apprehensive boy is twelve years old with oversized eyes and a choir-boy complexion. He keeps himself at arm's length in case Knox turns out to be trouble.

Knox is trouble, but not in any way the boy will ever know.

KNOX AND AKRAM OKLE meet two blocks from the DoubleTree on Mithat Paşa Caddesi, a narrow street that could be Paris or Brussels except for the occasional Red Crescent on a sign. Art galleries intermingle with boutique hotels. Nothing over three stories. Freshly painted neoclassical alongside colonial. The men are in blue jeans, long-sleeved shirts and sweaters. Running shoes. Not a woman in sight. Knox is spitting distance from the Grand Bazaar, the Beyazit Tower and the Calligraphy Museum. In any five-block area of the European side of Istanbul, there is more history than in all of Athens. He thinks they should put a glass dome over the entire city and preserve it as it is. The Syrians or Georgians or Kurds are bound to destroy it in a forgettable conflict and the world will lose a treasure, as it has lost Lebanon. He absorbs what he can with what little of him is not preoccupied surveying his immediate sur-roundings. He plays far too much defense; he's eager to get himself on the other side of the ball.

Someone is grilling lamb nearby. There's the scent of cardamom in the air, carried on a charcoal breeze. Knox is ready for lunch; to his delight, the source of the aromas is their meeting spot. He passes through a beaded curtain, keeps his eye on a pair of low ceiling fans and asks Akram to switch sides of the table with him as they shake hands, providing Knox a view of the entrance. It is an uncomfort-able moment that neither man draws attention to.

They talk briefly about the time of year and the approach of cooler days. Knox expresses concern over the illness in the man's family. Akram orders for them, telling Knox of a dish this restaurant does better than any other in the city. Knox settles in for a long lunch. Akram likes his food.

There are tourists scattered throughout, none fitting the descriptions provided by Grace, but Knox has every person sized up and he's located the exit by the two restrooms, as well as the entrance to the kitchen. He drinks coffee that should be considered an alternative fuel, tolerates the cigarette smoke. Realizes a dentist could make more money in this city than a bond trader. He's high on adrenaline and the approach of negotiation, feels it in his loins like he's about to try to flirt an underwear model into leaving a party with him.

"So, this thing we talked about," he says.

"Yes."

"Should I consider you interested?"

Akram lowers his eyes in consent. Knox finds the man's face to be a confusion of contradictions. Bronze facial skin covered by a salt-and-pepper balbo beard that adds ten years to what is likely his early thirties. Nearly shaved head to lessen the impression of a receding hairline. Heavy, expressive eyebrows shield wide-set eyes that could be black glass, yet his gaze reveals that he's multitasking. He's an IRS agent who knows everyone cheats on his or her taxes, a priest awaiting the first stone. He'd run a fillet knife through you if you crossed him, but he'll attend your son's bar mitzvah no matter how far he has to travel. He wears a cracked brown leather jacket that might have trouble zipping shut when it reaches his chest. The tight fitting black T-shirt supports this assessment. He wears no jewelry. The face of his rubber sports watch is scratched, its black band cracked.

"It's many times greater than that of any of our prior transactions."

Knox withholds comment.

"First, let me say, my friend, that I mean no insult to your integrity." He allows that to fester in Knox. "I must question how it is an item that has eluded the top archaeologists and researchers for several centuries, suddenly appears in the hands of a . . ." He's searching for a word other than "amateur."

Knox saves him. "Even a good copy is worth serious consideration. We both know that. And this is not a good copy."

"The original Harmodius? This is not possible."

"And yet we are here."

"So it is."

"I expect you will want authentication. I will agree to the specialist of your choosing, but I am to accompany the piece at every step, and I will determine the location. Your man has three days."

Akram purses his lips. "Absurd. Three months, perhaps. Analysis of mineral composition, weathering layers, historical comparison. This takes time."

"I have paperwork with me. An independent, well-respected expert. You can call him directly and he will confirm the contents of the paperwork. As to the funds, half will be placed into escrow. At that time I will permit verification to begin. Time is of the essence."

"Someone has done a good job of selling you, my friend. I do not know whether to feel sorry for you or happy for them."

"I mean no insult to your integrity," Knox says deliberately, "but I will need a credit check, or asset verification. The sum is large and not easily raised."

"I cannot think of a museum that would not do business with you, whatever terms you demand."

"Do you read the news? The art world has become too accountable. What has happened to everyone?"

"Globalization," Akram says. "We were far better off when isolated in our own countries. We wanted blue jeans. We ended up with the EU. If only we had known."

"You are able to raise the funds?" Knox asks.

"For a good copy, certainly. For the original? How long do we play this charade?"

The food arrives. Knox inhales deeply.

"I told you," Akram said. "The chef is an artist."

The presence of food lessens the tension. Akram shares a story about one of his six daughters, who is training as a gymnast back in Irbid, Jordan. She has started to grow taller, maturing early, and it's a family crisis.

"You are wondering how I can afford such artwork," Akram says, as the third course, the lamb Knox smelled out on the street, arrives.

"Not my business. Only that you're able."

"Let us assume it is a copy, to your great surprise."

"Very well."

"It would be wise for us to have two prices in mind. Yes?"

"As to that, the down payment will be held in escrow. If you pass, your money will be returned."

"So confident! Please pardon me, my friend. But are you so naive?"

Knox shrugs. This is some of the best lamb he's ever tasted.

"It's the marinade," Akram says.

"Secret recipe?"

"More precious than your Harmodius, believe me."

"I do not," Knox says. "Five hundred thousand, U.S."

Akram Okle offers his first tell: he pinches his nose to clear it. Knox had taken note of the tic earlier, but now he establishes its significance.

"I offer it to you first out of respect. You have only a matter of days to fund the escrow. I will then deliver the piece for analysis at a place and time of my choosing. It will be very last minute, I am afraid." There are only a few labs in Istanbul capable of authentication. Arranging an ambush at multiple locations will present a challenge for Akram. Knox must cover every base.

"I would request the same."

"As I said, I have test results," Knox says. He unzips two of the nineteen pockets in the Scottevest to locate the paperwork Dulwich supplied. Passes it across the table, keeping his hand atop it. He wants the symbolism of the exchange to register.

Knox says, "I will accept half as a down payment. It must be received at least twenty-four hours before your people assay it."

"Twenty-five percent."

"Fifty percent. No less."

"As you wish," Akram says. He studies Knox carefully as he slides the paperwork his way. He shows tremendous strength in not looking at it. He won't trust the contents, but it will set him drooling. It will help his people know what to verify in the short time Knox will give them at the lab. "Can you handle this, John? A deal like this? This size?"

"Our earlier deals . . . I was testing you," Knox lies. "I thought you ready for this. If I am wrong . . ."

Akram pinches the bridge of his nose again and inhales. "It is impossible, the Harmodius. You must understand."

"Half now," Knox says. "The other half wired to the account of my choosing upon delivery." He goes back to the lamb. Delicious.

18

B ack on the same bench in front of the Şişli mosque, Grace speaks softly.

"Detroit is up in the World Series. Congratulations."

"Verlander is a god," says Knox.

"He cannot pitch every game. I will put ten dollars on the opponent in tonight's game three."

"You, gamble?"

"Consider my heritage. You think mahjong is a game of fun?"

"What do we know of our boy's movement?"

"His chip went unused the morning after we spotted him surveilling. He's obviously careful."

"Or well informed."

Grace respects Knox's ability in the field, is trying to learn from him. This work, the work she is doing right now, is dream work. Out from behind the desk, yet still able to use her accounting skills, sitting on a plaza bench in Istanbul riding an adrenaline high. She senses how close she is to being given a solo assignment. Sees down the road a boutique security firm, her picking and choosing ops that satisfy more than the bottom line—like the work she and Knox did in Amsterdam.

She worries that Knox won't forgive her once he realizes how she has used him. She has evolved from tolerance, through acceptance, to appreciation of her sometime collaborator. Knox is like a piece of contemporary art: meaningless at first glance, but in time comes to speak to you.

"Sarge has withheld information from us," Knox says.

"Possibly." Grace feels a rush. "SOP. NTK."

"Protecting the client?"

"And the mark," she says. "This is how he explained it to me. Yes. Perhaps not only the client and mark. You were rescued by that van, or so you said."

"But then what we're saying is that this is something so heinous a government can't be associated with the outcome. That's the reality break for me. Sarge promised there would be no targeting of Mashe."

"Sensitive, perhaps not heinous," says Grace.

"Their own spooks handle sensitive. This has to be more than that."

"David prefers we perform the operation as assigned."

Knox ignores her. "It could be someone connected to Mashe. I could buy that—using Mashe to lure out a bigger fish. That would allow Sarge to promise me nothing's going to happen to Mashe. I didn't expand the playing field. My bad."

"I could suggest we stay with the operation," Grace says.

"Says the woman doing all the digging around. What's gotten into you, anyway?" When she fails to answer, he asks, "Is there actually any hope that these videos will mean anything?"

Knox gets restless easily. His legs bounce. His feet start tapping.

"There is, of course, something of significance here. Four separate visits by the person we now think of as an agent of the client." She speaks encouragingly. "A few more minutes, please."

"Yeah, yeah."

"If you sit still, the image will be clearer."

"Point taken."

The two ride out the remaining seven minutes. In that time, fifty or more people stream in and out of the mosque entrance. Several hundred cars flow past. It is a remarkable sight. Europeans, Americans, Africans, Japanese tourist groups, Arabs.

"Maybe your guy just likes people-watching." Knox is in a snarky mood. She can't blame him; he's not a stakeout type. More the brass knuckle variety.

"Your opinion of Akram?" She tries to read his face.

"My opinion doesn't matter. Sarge puts him as the messenger. He and his brother know that even an ancient copy of the Harmodius is invaluable. Many times what I'm asking, and I have a problem with a client willing to sacrifice millions—many millions—just so we can spend five minutes with Mashe Okle. Translation: whatever it is we're supposed to accomplish would either cost the client those same millions, or the desired outcome is so impossible for them to accomplish on their own that it's worth those millions. You see?"

Knox has a way of clarifying things. Grace is overly sensitive about her lack of this ability. She equates Knox's faculty with the much-heralded American ability to create and innovate; her own tendency is toward rote technical skills. She thinks of Knox's Chinese violinist example and flushes. Here, he has turned a double negative into a positive. It's not the high price of the art; it's the amount being given up by establishing a lower price that tells them something about the seller.

"You are more clever than you give yourself credit for," she says softly.

"Do you hear me disagreeing?"

"You are also arrogant and rude."

"And I wear it proudly."

She reminds herself never to compliment him. "You can be such an ass."

She expects another of his snide comebacks. Is surprised to see that she has stung him.

"I put out a feeler for a meeting with Sarge. I got back postponement."

"He is here in Istanbul," she says. "I feel it."

"You know what? I hope not. I actually hope not."

"Hope leads to disappointment; action to success."

"Another proverb?"

She doesn't answer. "What do we do about it? About David?"

"We consider the people that pulled me into the van and the people who followed you as allies, at least of Sarge. Probably working for the client. We assume we are pawns, and you know how I feel about that. We need to come up with a way to do the op without their involvement, client or not. I don't trust them."

"Maybe this helps us determine who and why," she says, indicating the two phones shooting video.

"I'd rather shoot a guy in the leg than shoot video," Knox says. "Puts a person in a sharing mood real quick."

"There is a surprise."

"Akram?"

"I have what I need." Grace looks toward the mosque. "Xin and Dr. Kamat will help me to breach the bank firewalls. I have every confidence the plan will go forward as designed."

"You never lack for confidence," Knox says.

"You exaggerate, as usual."

"Don't give me that false modesty . . . that Chinese thing you do, going all humble and demure? It's undignified."

"On the contrary, it is quite dignified, which is why you do not recognize or understand it."

"I won't dignify that with a comment. Look, we wait a day for Mashe and Akram to settle out the funds. You need to be ready by then. Thirty-six hours, max. Then we're on a plane home."

"I may need more time. David's plan is more . . . evolved. I am to challenge the sourcing of the funds, demand an explanation. This provides you—us—with the meet. The five minutes."

"Doesn't mean I like it," he grumbles. "So, we'll make our move once the deposit and sourcing are confirmed. 'Action breeds success.'"

"Given that my work cannot commence until the deposit of the funds," Grace says, "we are presented with ample opportunity to shoot more video tomorrow. We then download it to Xin for analysis. We meet here again tomorrow, sixteen hundred."

"You're putting too much on this," Knox says.

"It is tangible. Actionable intelligence." It will impress David. "We must know why this agent spent time here. Perhaps to meet his control. *Neh?* How pleasing would it be to identify not only this agent but also his control?"

"You've grown your hair longer," he says. "And changed perfumes. This is tangible."

She swallows her surprise, is able to contain her reaction.

"Enough! It is past five," she says. "We are done here."

19

Maybe it's the three beers or the bone-aching numbness of isolation, of time spent in his hotel. It may be the lively patter from the terrace below, the internal echo of the earlier call to prayer still reverberating through his body—whatever it is, Knox's sense is that he's missing out. His dedication to fixing Tommy up with private care for life rules out all else. Undermines him. He's either chasing a deal on rattan chairs in Indonesia or pursuing black marketers in Amsterdam. He lives in airport lounges, discount hotels and the backs of cabs. When he gets a break like this—a four-star hotel in a picturesque location, gorgeous women planting their oversized lips on oversized wine goblets that chime when their nails ring against the glass—and he's confined to his room, whether by dictum or common sense, he curses the likes of Dulwich and Primer—even Tommy and Grace—all those figures who in some way control him.

It's the beer, he decides. Sometimes it fills him with elevated joy. At other times, despair. He guessed wrong tonight.

His big moment of the night comes when he wheels room service into the hall and heads to the hotel business center, an unpretentious glorified closet containing three Dell computers and an HP printer. He transmits the videos he and Grace have taken to Hong Kong as requested. But bored—again he blames the beer—he also uploads them onto YouTube without sound. Posts them as tourist videos. Calls one up on the computer to his left, the second on the computer in front of him. Uses Rewind and Play to closely synchronize the two so they play at roughly the same minute of the day. Requests a fourth beer from room service, letting them know his location. Turns off one of the monitors as the beer is delivered.

With the opening of the door, he hears more activity from the lobby and the pulse of a Killers song. He pays for the beer. Lights up the dark monitor.

He studies the two videos side by side in ten-second clips. Chuckles to himself when he identifies the same pigeon. He can envision a children's picture book, *The Pigeon Is the Spy*. Checking his mirth, he slows his consumption of the cold beer.

Person by person, nearly frame by frame, he compares faces, profiles, shoes, backpacks, head wraps and scarves. Smokers and non-smokers. Right down to the make of cameras being used by the tourists. He keeps notes on a hotel pad using a hotel pen. The sight of the pigeon has him tracking dogs.

A hotel guest enters and prints a boarding pass on the third machine. Nothing is said between the two. But Knox knows the guy's name and frequent flyer number, the flight he's on and the fact that he's not checking bags.

It's the only interruption over a two-hour period. Knox shrinks the open windows when he takes a break to the washroom, returns to work refreshed. The cause of boredom isn't sitting around; it's lack of purpose. Energized by the puzzle of trying to spot similarities on the two screens, time passes quickly. The roughly one hour of video takes three hours to get through.

"Forest for the trees" becomes a mantra for him when he catches himself going screen blind. Rewinding.

When he spots the boy, he's eager to call Grace and loop her in. But he knows the trap of such knee-jerk reactions; it's better to finish the job and deliver a full list. Nearing midnight, he has all but settled on making the call. He's reached the end of the two videos. Both are paused on their respective screens. Catching himself studying a woman's backside, he runs a hand over his face: it's bedtime.

Frozen alongside the woman is a white Mercedes G-Wagen in traffic and he's reminded fondly of a buying spree in Morocco where he suffered two flat tires and was stung by *Buthus occitanus*, a scorpion that caused a painful lump on his calf the size of a navel orange, an injury that nearly itched him to insanity.

"Oh, shit." Knox says it out loud, acutely aware of his own nervous perspiration. "Fucking idiot!" A little too loudly. Doesn't want to set off alarm bells for a sedated night desk clerk. Doesn't like talking to himself. Hits buttons to return the two videos to their respective starts. Does his best to resynch them, but is less concerned with it this time through.

It's all making sense now. Maybe the beer fog is lifting. Maybe it's the stab of common sense, an ah-ha moment when the crystallization of thought coincides with reason. Maybe he's overly tired and making less sense than he thinks. But at the moment, he's Einstein. He's being played by Russell Crowe or Vince Vaughn or Sullivan Stapleton. Tense music.

He deletes the two YouTube videos. Erases the history in both browsers and closes them. He returns to his room, moving with an invigorated stride. He can't wait to call Grace.

"Are you kidding me?" He can hear Grace moving.

"It's early."

"In Delhi, maybe."

"As if you were asleep."

She doesn't have a comeback.

"There's a kid in the video. School uniform. I caught the backpack. Black and white. Unusual. Most of 'em are black or another solid color. This thing looks like a panda."

"We are off the scent?" she asks, her voice more vibrant. "Not about Mashe or Akram, but one of their children? Or the child is to be used as leverage."

"It has to be factored in."

"Listen to you!"

He can hear the mirth in her voice. He's used a math reference. She will take credit for it. Grace wants to change him. He wants to tell her others have tried, but he enjoys the pursuit too much to stop her now.

"You've been drinking," he says. It slips out. It's what his brain was thinking but not what he wanted to say.

An unnerving silence settles between them. He's seen her hit the vodka before. Not often, but hard. Her reaction throws up the guilt flag.

"I've had four beers." He tries to make light of it, to include her in the club. It isn't working.

"Factored into what?"

"There's more."

"We were going to send the videos to Xin. What happened to that?"

"I did as you told me," he said. That isn't a sentence he's used often in his life. Doesn't sound like him. He looks around for anyone else, another speaker, but he's all alone.

"Traffic," he says. "We were focused on people. Faces. Shoes. Repeat visitors. We have the kid—the student, the panda—and maybe he's worth something, but . . . listen, I don't expect this to make sense, it's more of intuition . . . and thinking it is one thing, saying it, another, but we're in the business of speculation, right? Damned if we do, damned if we don't. I watched the videos side by side, just now, trying to focus on nothing but the traffic—the cars, the trucks, motorcycles. Both lanes, okay? Forest for the trees," he says, wondering if she'll understand the reference. "And maybe there was . . . I mean there could have been . . . something I missed. Easily. But I tried to separate out the same vehicles, the same colors by antennas or how dirty they were, wheels, dings, stickers—anything to distinguish them. Okay? And sure, way too many Fiats, Opels and Renaults to know if I accounted for them all. It's something your team back at the office can do better, or do again. But the one thing I did see, the one thing there was no mistaking, was a FedEx truck. White FedEx van in the near lane. North to south. If my timing's right, and it may not be, it was maybe five minutes later the second day. But here's the thing: in both videos, its blinker is on. Driver's hitting the brake lights."

"Pulling over," Grace says.

"Could be."

He hears the blood in his head like a tsunami. It's too late at night. He's had too many beers. It was stupid to call her. He should have slept on it. You maintain your position of strength by keeping your trap shut until you know what the fuck you're talking about. He knows this. Boy Who Cries Wolf, otherwise.

"You are brilliant," she says softly and as intimately as if pillow talk. It arouses him. His groin is pulsing. Warming. Hardening. He wants to switch it off. Feels somewhat sick to his stomach over it. Grace? Since when?

"The text," she says. "Hang on."

He listens. Another rarity. She's up and moving. He can see her in his mind's eye. Remembers what she looks like from that hour in the Amsterdam brothel. His friend in his pants is straining the seam of his jeans. No wonder they put rivets on the pockets.

"The fourth time," she says—breathlessly, which doesn't help matters. "The last time the man was at this GPS fix he sent a fifteen-string number by text."

He doesn't know whether to stroke his friend or ignore him. Checks that the shade is down. Works his belt loose.

"You there?" she says. He can hear her nails clicking on plastic keys.

"I'm here," he says.

"You sound out of breath."

"I get off on this stuff."

"Right. If I am boring you, I can call back."

"No!"

More tapping. More images of Amsterdam. More confusion. What the hell?

"Oh . . . my . . . God. . . ."

She shouldn't have said it. Not that way. His throat tightens. Eyes close.

"FedEx international shipments? The numbers? Fifteen digits."

Say something more.

"This is it!"

Good girl.

"This is exactly what we wanted."

So right.

"That's it! That's the connection. John? . . . John?"

Eventually, he speaks. "I do what I can."

"It may be nothing, but it adds up."

"Certainly does."

"Hong Kong can—No! What am I saying? Hold on."

It's way past that. He's headed for the sink, the phone pinched to his shoulder. Six, seven minutes pass.

"Florence Nightingale," she says. "The tracking number that was texted."

"Brushing my teeth. Speak up."

"Florence Nightingale Hospital. Şişli. Same district. It is on Abide-i Hürriyet Caddesi."

"Say that three times fast."

She misses the reference. Is about to ask him to explain.

"Date?" he says.

"Shipped overnight. Delivered the last day his GPS tagged him at this location."

"Origin?"

"Switzerland. The company is BioLectrics."

He towels off. Puts the call on speakerphone while he Googles the company. Can hear her doing the same. It's a race for him. Everything is a competition.

"Bizarre," he says.

"Strange," she replies.

"Medical electronics? Why would these bozos care about the delivery record for a package containing medical electronics?"

"It is too broad, too large a company. BioLectrics makes everything." She reads, "Vascular intervention. Cardiac rhythmic management. Stents. Pumps. They run clinical trials. We need the invoice to know why this delivery is important. A product number. Product description."

"Is this making any sense to you?" he asks.

"No."

"I got it wrong with the FedEx van?"

"No."

"It's got to be one or the other."

"We need more data. Do we copy David?"

There it is: the question he knew she'd ask. He wants to call her a goody-goody. Teacher's pet. Knows he resents her rising importance in the company, an ascendance he's witnessed over the past two years. If there's a sacrificial lamb on Primer's altar, it's him. She's immune.

"And look like we can't figure this out ourselves?" He knows he's appealing to her profound fear of appearing weak; he's learned to trigger her paranoia as much as compliment her strengths, to feed her the information she needs—filtered, if necessary—to move her off of an idea and into his corner. If he had resisted her outright, she would have gotten her back up and been intractable.

He's learning, or so he convinces himself.

20

Grace chides Knox for his impatience but only because she is no stranger to its irritating and unrelenting hold. It is an unusually warm fall day; golden sunlight floods the vast sea of red terra-cotta roof tiles, spills through the impossibly narrow streets, the ancient buildings so closely packed that, from a distance, they appear as a warped red mass rising slowly to the north, a packed line interrupted by pale chimneys, satellite dishes, minarets, domes and laundry lines.

On the apartment building's rooftop, Grace occupies a patio chaise lounge. Her laptop is open as an iced tea glass sweats on the side table. Grace wears a collapsible hat; her mother has instilled in her a belief that her skin must never be exposed to the sun. She re-checks the ghost escrow account established by a Cayman lawyer's office. No deposit has been made. She's beginning to wonder if Akram Okle and his brother really intend to make a move for the Harmodius. If not, she and Knox will pack up and go home. For every two or three successful ops, there's a failure. She has yet to be attached to one, dreads the day, but knows it will come.

She sloshes some of the iced tea onto the terrace's rough gray tile as a thought paralyzes her brain like a seizure. Returns the glass to the side table with her right hand; her left is already working the computer.

Her vision dances between the expansive view, attempting to isolate a single large structure she knows is out there, and her computer's screen, where Google maps is now open and determining her current location. Her right hand seeks out her iPhone, enters its passcode and texts a message to Knox.

missed overlap

Blames her racing heart on the tea. The map directs her eyes. She gets her bearings. Throws her legs off the chaise, moving to include the area 160 degrees from north.

?

Knox is perplexed by her text.

meet across from FNH—20 mins

He texts:

copy

Grace changes into her only pair of running shoes, not as white as she hoped, a form-fitting Nike T she wears to work out, and a pair of black yoga pants. On each op, she carries five sets of fake glasses. Selects a geeky but stylish pair. Ties a brown scarf over her head, imitating the Muslim women—far more for coverage than looks.

Has the op planned, but continues to hone it as Besim drives her across town. They pass handcarts carrying fruit, clothing and spices. Stall-sized shops manned by a merchant crouched on his haunches. The men smoke cigarettes while women toil. Boys play soccer in the streets.

Besim leaves her three blocks from her rendezvous. She must not attract attention, hopes the scarf hides her well.

On her walk, she passes a three-story white colonial on two acres behind twelve-foot rock walls. She wonders about its history, its former residents, but her mind makes no attempts to supply a story. Grace yearns for imagination. She questions what she and Knox are doing so far from home. She finds Istanbul's continual reminders of history and the passage of time daunting. Its confused cultural identity dispirits her. She longs for the simplicity of China.

She wonders if this is contributing to her sense of vertigo. The concrete beneath her feet is undulating.

Grace locates a uniform supply store and purchases a slightly oversized nurse's uniform. Pulling the dress on over her clothes in the dressing room, she now wears the uniform out onto the street. She carries two different colored head scarfs stuffed into her purse— tricks of the trade. Hide and seek.

Knox is enthroned at a café table, his legs stretched straight out, impossibly long as he semireclines. He's well through a double espresso. Looks half asleep. Detroit Tigers baseball cap low over his eyes. That same windbreaker he always wears, with its many interior zippers concealing his worldly possessions.

For a split second she wonders once again what the world looks and feels like from inside the head of John Knox. Dismisses it quickly; there are times she doubts he has a single thought in his head. She has no idea what that would feel like.

He kicks back a chair for her.

"Now you're messing with my fantasies, Nurse Jackie," he says, admiring her garb.

On the facing street, seven-story office buildings trade places with apartments, the street-level retail space occupied by designer boutiques, camera shops, shoe stores and cellular carriers. It could as easily be a street in Moscow or Paris as Istanbul, the road divided, the island planted with scrawny immature trees. The city can go from fascinating to boring in a block.

Knox catches the attention of a twenty-something waitress with wide eyes. It's clear she's been awaiting his signal. She delivers a black tea with sugar substitute and milk on the side.

Grace doesn't know whether to thank him or be annoyed with herself for being so predictable—an attribute to which she attaches negative connotations.

"So," he says, studying the nurse's uniform in a John Knox way that makes her incredibly self-conscious. "I can pretty much guess the first part of whatever's going on." He contemplates the hospital across the street. "But I seem to be missing something."

She mixes the tea like a lab scientist. Sips. Adds a speck more sweetener. Examines her lipstick residue on the cup's white china.

"The mother," Grace says. She, too, looks across the street.

"Oh, shit. How stupid can we get?"

"It was late."

"We're idiots." Knox attempts to process the FedEx shipment, to suss out how it connects to Akram Okle's sick mother, who occupies a bed across the street. "What the hell?"

"I know, right?" Grace hears herself sound American. She attributes it to the two years in grad school in Southern California. Wonders if Knox notices. These expressions bubble up occasionally, catching her by surprise. She thinks of herself as entirely Chinese; not a view shared by her father, who considers her a traitor to tradition.

A young boy skateboards past. Grace instinctively squeezes her purse between her thighs.

"Why would they care about the mother?" Knox's face is not meant for confusion. He looks boyish and lacking in confidence.

"One wonders."

"Come on. What the hell do you hope to accomplish dressed like that?"

Knox is threatened by her fieldwork. She takes this as a compliment, but knows she still has much to learn. She wonders if a person can learn to ignore the ordered, logical, straight-line thinking that defines her. Envies the ability of his mind to spark and jump as it does.

"Before you go in there, we need to work this backward," Knox says, his voice soft now. Sexy. "First, we have to consider whether or not the client is simply ensuring that whatever medical device the mother needs is on schedule. Perhaps he is literally tracking it, making sure no one messes with it en route. In that case, Mashe's in league with our client and our client is simply looking out for his mother. Right?"

It's like listening to chamber music, a melody going to an unexpected place.

"Or, the opposite, of course," he says. "This agent interrupts the delivery of a medical device. Steals it in order to determine the true extent of her illness. Knowledge is power. Perhaps they want leverage over Mashe? Then there's substituting one device for another. It's more difficult and tricky, but possible." He ruminates. She isn't about to interrupt. Two years ago it might have been different, but they've both learned the footsteps of this dance. "Oh . . . God." Her system charges with adrenaline as she meets his intense gaze. He's looking through her. *Into* her. "Long shot," he announces, warning her. "The medical device is part of a dead drop. The device being shipped contains a data chip intended for Mashe. No Internet, no chance of interception. All you need is an insider at the device manufacturer who solders an extra memory chip into the device, and you've shipped information across borders. Which begs the question: who is Mashe Okle, or Mashe Melemet, or whatever name he's traveling under this week? An Iranian arms dealer? Your financial investigation says no. An art dealer? A rich businessman? Maybe an agent, an Iranian agent? And what are the Iranians up to these days that they might be seeking classified information?"

Grace has the urge to reach across the cigarette-scarred table and take his rough face in her hands and plant a kiss on his lips. But Knox would take that as her handing him her hotel keycard. All she can do is let a ripple of excitement surge through her, sit back and sip the tea.

"You're the computer tech," he says. "Find him."

"You think I have not tried? Mashe Okle's past has been expunged."

Knox says sarcastically, "Try harder. His university records. Scour the West for immigration records, trips abroad."

Why is he able to conceive of a strategy she's missed? She has asked Dulwich for Okle's immigration records, but looking at that request through Knox's suspicious eyes, she wonders if Dulwich has been honest with her, if there really is no significant travel out of country as Dulwich earlier reported.

"There are more than two hundred universities in Iran," Grace says. "Do you know how long it would take to hack each of the admission servers? Years. Do you think you can throw a switch and hack a national immigration database? You think the terrorists wouldn't love to control such information? It is impossible, John. Firewalls as thick as the Great Wall."

"He's an agent," Knox says.

"No. He is an unknown."

"The device is a package. The mother, an unknowing courier."

"The first step," Grace says, "is for me to get in there and see her chart. To determine the extent of her illness. The office is working on this, too, but I can speed it up. Determine what device might have been shipped. Slip a piggyback onto the hospital's network as I did in Amsterdam."

Knox drags his hand down his face in frustration. "We're off-mission," he says. "Way off."

She imagines Dulwich's appreciation for her delivery of the information—her insight into Mashe's true role and her discovery of the agent working behind the scenes. She doesn't want to seem too eager, conceals her excitement from Knox. "You are right. We should perhaps go back to our respective rooms. Await contact from Akram. Proceed as intended."

"Says the woman in the nurse's uniform."

Grace hangs her head demurely. Caught. These acts of contrition seem to be in her DNA, passed down a hundred generations. There is no place for such reactions in her professional life; she wishes she could rid herself of them. She strains to lift her head, but her neck muscles resist. Rigor mortis.

"We need Sarge to come clean."

"David has been consistent, John. He has emphasized Need To Know protocol and demanded we protect the wishes of the client. You are correct, we are off-mission." Knox reacts best to reverse psychology.

"Drastically."

"We should return to our lodgings. Regroup."

"Of course we should," Knox says.

"If you go in the hospital, you are impossible to miss," Grace says. "Whereas I am far more invisible."

"You sell yourself short."

She wonders if she was fishing for the compliment. Worries she was.

"How do you expect to find her room? It's a big hospital."

"Taken care of," she says. Answers his inquisitive look. "I was forced to pull her account financials to get the lead on Mashe. Her room number is four-three-one."

"Four-thirty-one," he says correcting her. "You can be so Chinese."

"Just imagine."

"I'll flag a taxi," Knox says. "I'll find an alternative exit— something other than the front lobby—and text you my location. You will call me now, leave the line open. I want to hear everything you're up to."

"Agreed," she says. It's standard operating procedure, at least for the two of them.

"Nothing absurd," he cautions. "You may meet some of these people later."

"Understood."

"An in-and-out." A look overcomes him.

"What?"

"That's what Sarge called it. Made it sound so—"

"Simple."

"Yes."

"That is his job," Grace reminds him.

————

GRACE SLIPS into the nurse's role as effortlessly as she donned the uniform. She crosses the hospital lobby head bent, shoulders slumped and the head scarf worn down her forehead as a brim to screen her face. She rides the elevator aware of the likelihood of security cameras.

She walks out onto the fourth floor wanting to impart a sense of familiarity with the floor plan when in fact it's foreign to her. Many of the men in the waiting area wear the ubiquitous black leather jacket and she wonders if any of Mashe Okle's bodyguards are among them. She angles her head away.

She marvels at how small the op's boundaries have become. They are shrink-wrapped by a need for secrecy, by the clandestine nature of the work. Everyone wants the same thing while no one knows exactly what they want.

Three hallways extend like spokes off the hub of a semicircular nurse's desk that roils with activity. It's like an airline check-in counter twenty minutes before the flight. Doctors, nurses and orderlies swarm together with a clear delineation of power visible in who concedes to whom for countertop space.

Spotting an incorrect room number, she pivots in a course change and bumps into a doctor. Recovering, she moves toward the Melemet mother's room. She didn't need the tea; she's riding an unhappy marriage of caffeine and adrenaline. Visitors crowd the rooms into which she peers. Some emit laughter. Some stifle sniffles or tears. Grace processes it in her gut rather than her head, suddenly weighed down by loss and shattered hopes. She harbors a fear of illness. Is worried that someday one of these beds will hold her mother or father; recognizes that her mother would welcome her company, but would her father allow her in? Worries she has waited too long to repair the damage between her and her father—heritage, genera-tional tradition, familial honor. She allowed the love of a boy—a mere boy!—to separate them. Her father has not reached out to her since; but neither has she.

She must focus. The trick—the skill in such situations—is invis-ibility, to move among others in such an obnoxiously mundane manner as to not exist. The scarf and glasses create a decent enough disguise. What she must prevent is anyone addressing her or paying her any attention. She will, with any luck, meet Akram Okle in the near future.

Grace counts on a degree of racial prejudice as well as the white dress to help her blend in. Having already determined that the pa-tient charts are stored at the foot of the bed, not in wall racks in the hallways, she knows she must infiltrate. She clears her throat; if re-quired to speak, she will affect a moderately high, annoying voice with a Chinese accent, much like her mother's. She can adopt the identity without thought, so accustomed was she to mocking her mother when with her brother.

Barely checking her stride, she enters room 431. Seeing only the far bed occupied, she walks steadily toward the chart that waits for her like a raised finger.

Beyond the partially pulled curtain sits a man; he's facing away from her and toward the older woman in the bed. Occupying a stool on the window side is a man in his sixties with a thick white mus-tache and thin white hair.

Grace's throat is dry as she slips the clipboard from the clear plas-tic pocket.

She has already asked Xin and the Hong Kong office to work backward from the woman's hospital charges to determine her likely illness. It's ongoing. Grace's mission here is to look for scheduled surgery prep or the mention of a medical device that could be one of the many BioLectrics products. She scans the first page. Nothing. She senses all eyes on her as she flips to the second. Scans this. Nothing. The third.

"Everything is good?" In Turkish.

Grace is confident in her execution of a limited vocabulary. "Yes," comes easily. "Routine," follows, also spoken well. She keeps her eyes low out of deference and respect, lowers her head, takes four steps and encounters a leather jacket.

"Excuse me," she says, head still down.

"You are?" English, with a thickly Arabic accent.

"In a hurry, if you do not mind?"

The younger man behind the curtain, Akram or Mashe, she assumes, laughs.

"Easy!" this man says, instructing the one in front of Grace. "Let them do their work."

"This one is new to us," the bodyguard says.

The sitting man is standing now. He rakes back the privacy curtain angrily. "You have interviewed the entire hospital staff, I suppose?" Persian. Iranian. His irritation with his guards intrigues her; she compartmentalizes it for later analysis. This one, she is sure, is Mashe. "Let them do their jobs! The sooner my mother is well, the better for all of us. Do you hear me?"

The jacket steps aside. Grace has yet to look higher than the guard's belt.

"I am sorry, nurse," Mashe says.

Grace nods and passes into the corridor. She hears rapid footsteps approaching from behind.

An orderly runs past.

Grace bites back a smile. She eyes the chaotic nurse's station, checks down the hall and spots one of Mashe's guards. He is watching her, compounding his earlier distrust.

The guard sidles toward the nurse's station. He's calm and intro-spective, exceptionally smooth and practiced at appearing that way. In a few short steps he tells her more about Mashe Okle's impor-tance than she knew even following all her research.

Grace must not overreact. She and this man are testing one an-other. The crush of bodies is claustrophobic, preventing her from a quick escape. She eyes the elevators. The stairs are her second op-tion. Men like him are deceptively fast in spite of their size. She'd rather not test him.

Grace doesn't want a close quarters confrontation. She's capable of self-defense, is as well trained as he. But the man has eighty pounds on her and a longer reach. It will be possible to postpone the dam-age, but only that. Instead, her best bet is to get out front and then keep it a race, all the while not allowing him to realize what's going on. It's time for smoke and mirrors.

The best way to accomplish this reality break is to instill doubt, to reaffirm her cover. Rather than separate herself from the nurse's station, she turns and briefly joins three nurses studying paperwork. The guard can't force his way into the nurse's station. Instead, he comes around the front, eyes boring into Grace's back.

Grace manages to block the background noise like noise-canceling headphones. She hears the guard ask someone if he could please speak "with her." She feels the heat run up her spine. He explains he's unfamiliar "with her" and that he wishes to discuss why she was just examining the chart in 431.

As this mostly one-way conversation carries on behind her, Grace quietly introduces herself to the two nurses as an employee of the Ministry of Health, an introduction that runs shivers up their spines. Her Turkish is passable, but since the ministry might easily employ doctors and scientists from around the globe, Grace is not overly concerned. She allows them to hear that she's checking standards and practices and that the annoying man at the counter behind them is about to unintentionally expose her, which will defeat her purpose here and might reflect poorly on the hospital.

She leaves it at that. No direct request, no suggestion as to how they conduct themselves.

When the woman at the counter tries to gain Grace's attention, the older of the two nurses turns and chides her. They are not to be disturbed. If a patient's guest needs something, they should apply to the attending nurse.

Grace keeps her attention on the paperwork.

A minute later, she overhears the receptionist asking the man to move on, pointing out the posted signs requesting that guests occupy either the waiting area or a patient's room, but leave the corridors clear. Grace wishes she'd had the time and foresight to print bogus business cards—so useful at a time like this. The bodyguard has chosen the small waiting area, more of an alcove with airport seats, enabling him to keep an eye on the elevators and stairs.

Grace studies the metal engraved fire diagram mounted in the nurse's station. There's an exit at the end of each of the three corridors. Physical therapy takes place in the east corridor; she spots several patients walking slowly, holding on to the rolling stands carrying their IVs. It's the busier of the two corridors available to her.

She leaves the station without so much as a glance toward the waiting area. She has at least a thirty-foot lead. She must pull this off without arousing suspicion, without compromising the op.

It's a magic trick she has planned. She notes the location of a mobile laundry bin well down the corridor. She can use the knot of the slow-moving patients and their nurses to her advantage. Assumes but does not confirm that the guard is following her.

She can imagine that from his vantage point, he will briefly lose sight of her among the addled parade of staggering patients when she enters a patient's room. He will slow, maintaining a position that provides him with a line of sight to the doorway. But his view will be obscured for at least several long seconds.

He will try to see around the patients walking the corridor blocking his view.

When and if he dares to enter the hospital room, he will find its privacy curtains pulled back, exposing occupied beds. There will be no attendant in sight. No nurse. Nothing to suggest the woman he was following. She has vaporized.

He may try several more rooms. Eventually he will return to the nurse's station.

"The woman? Brown head scarf? Short?"

The nurse stares at him as if he's daft. "No idea."

"The woman you were talking to."

"Who are you?" she asks. "Why do you ask this?" The nurse knows that the Ministry of Health can make a world of problems if it so chooses.

He will not think to look into the laundry bin parked in the hallway, would have to dig to see a white nurse's uniform and brown head scarf buried two layers down. Has only a vague recollection of a woman slipping into the stairway. Was she wearing yoga pants and an Under Armour top? He gives it no weight whatsoever, his full attention on finding the missing nurse who paid an unexpected visit to 431, who glimpsed the man there he's sworn to protect.

Grace's descent of the stairs is controlled but hurried. She moves quietly and stays close to the wall; she will not be seen nor heard by someone peering down into the narrow slit separating railings. She moves landing to landing like a wraith. Arrives at the street level and walks out into the cool air.

A taxi waits, a dark figure looming in the backseat.

Knox throws open the door. She climbs in. Knox says, "Go!" in Turkish. The cab rolls.

"Well?" Knox says.

Grace looks straight ahead as she shakes her head.

"Nothing?"

She repeats the gesture.

"No procedure scheduled?"

She looks into his gray-green eyes, chameleon eyes, sometimes blue, sometimes nearly brown. Lets him know that she's as puzzled as he.

"Then why? Why the package?"

She has no answer that will satisfy. She can run them in circles, but imagines he's already there with her, coming back around in an endless loop that will begin to ring like feedback in his ears. No easy explanation. No concise meaning or rationale for a probable agent tracking the movement of a shipment of medical supplies, but too many coincidences to discount.

Knox is taking them in the direction of his hotel. The cab leaves the busy streets for back alleys. The Chinese know how to keep their cities clean and free of litter. The Turks could learn a thing or two from them, Grace thinks.

"The package could be something pertaining to an earlier procedure," she suggests. "The pieces must fit. They are not random."

"Sarge knows," he says accusingly. Emphatically.

"We are expected to operate blind."

"Because he knew we might have questions," he says. "Questions he doesn't want to answer. So the real question is: why doesn't he want to answer them?"

The cab pulls over. They stand on the sidewalk across from the Alzer Hotel.

"The client sent the package," Knox speculates. "There's a courier in the hospital who's supposed to get something from the package to Mashe. It can all happen inside the mother's hospital room—a controlled environment."

"Protected by bodyguards," she said. "They were afraid maybe I was planting a listening device, a camera. Just now. At the hospital."

"But if this is about an exchange, then why the Harmodius and my five minutes with Mashe? What's the point?"

"Electronics hidden in the sculpture?"

"No. They'll X-ray it as part of the authentication. It has to be clean. Even so, what could be gained? Why do they need those five minutes?"

"I agree. I do not see the purpose of our involvement."

"You need to contact Sarge."

Her neck makes a pop, she spins her head so quickly.

"Use Xin to track him. I won't contact him electronically. I understand how that could compromise us all. But in person? In the right setting? That's different. If he fires us, he fires us. We need answers."

"It is a mistake, John. We need first to know who Mashe is. My trail, the electronic trail, is nonexistent. But the brother . . ."

"Will never tell me anything," Knox says. "And to ask . . ."

"There must be someone who knows this man!"

In his mind's eye, Knox sees a woman opening a door for him. Sees her plaintive expression as she realizes she has betrayed him to the Jordanian police.

"Maybe there is," he says.

21

When Knox picks up the voice mail, he extends the iPhone to arm's length, studying it as if it's from another planet. He's so nonplussed he doesn't hear the message clearly the first time, only the woman's voice; he has to start it again. Takes it off speakerphone and puts it to his ear. The SIM chip in the device is the phone number he uses for op contacts. He routinely checks it for text and voice messages.

He considers himself calm and rational, avoids emotional response and drama as much as possible when on the job. But he knows he can't keep his heart out of his decisions or his head out of his motives. He doesn't take kindly to coincidence; he's programmed toward paranoia when it rears its head.

Years ago, inside a hotel room in a distant province of China, he complained to his roommate that hotel housekeeping had failed to leave complimentary bottles of filtered water; less than three minutes later, there was a knock, and the water was delivered. Coincidence? Only if the word is spelled "eavesdropping."

But how could anyone have eavesdropped on his thoughts? He didn't actually tell Grace that gallery owner Victoria Momani might be able to shed light on Mashe Okle. Yet it is her voice speaking cryptically from his phone.

"Orhan's minis. Before fourteen."

She is in Istanbul. His stomach turns.

This is an in-and-out, a week tops.

Knox didn't give her his number, but her phone trapped his original incoming call. This shows him she is facile and a quick study. But what does she want?

He's overreacting; he was going to have to contact her anyway; she has done him the favor.

But he thinks back to the water bottles in the hotel regardless.

Shit!

The cryptic message can be taken one of two ways: she doesn't want others to quickly or easily know the location of their meet; or she wants Knox to take her precautions as an indication that this is between the two of them when she's actually leading him into a trap. As she's betrayed him once already, she doesn't have history on her side.

Quickly he switches SIM chips, starts walking while searching the midday traffic for an available taxi. He never uses the op SIM chip anywhere near his lodging in case callers intend to trace his location through a GPS fix. He's up near Vatan Lisesi, a high school well away from the Alzer Hotel, when he dials.

Grace answers on the second ring.

He says, " 'Orhan's minis.' Mean anything to you?" He only has twenty minutes to make the rendezvous. He's counting on Grace.

"Orhan Pamuk," she says. The name resonates with Knox, but he can't place it so he stays quiet.

Knox has it. "The writer."

"The Nobel laureate. Correct." She sounds as if she is barely tolerating him. "Dr. Pamuk has said his novel *My Name Is Red* was inspired by Islamic miniatures."

"Orhan's minis," Knox says. "Where do I find them?"

"Stand by," she says. He hears her nails spiriting along a plastic keyboard. "Turkish and Islamic Arts Museum. Down by—"

"The Topkapi."

"Terzihane Square, more accurately."

"I know the museum."

"What do I need to know?" she asks.

A dozen wisecracks fill his head. He says instead, "Making progress. Might have Xin track this number for the next two hours."

"John?"

"Just as insurance."

He ends the call before Grace becomes all motherly.

ENTERING THE PALACE GROUNDS, Knox proceeds through immaculate landscaping over grouted stone, gets the impression of a cloister or an Oxford garden. With the sounds of the city reduced to a distant hum, he hears a bird sing brightly and marvels at the age of the massive tree that leans in an ungainly fashion against the sign directing him to the museum entrance. A four-foot-tall pottery urn rests against ground cover. The interior courtyard housing the museum has the feel of a monastery. A confluence of architectural devices and methods causes Knox to think Turkish Tudor.

Once inside, the museum is warm colors, tapestries and dioramas. Dark wood posts support the ceilings. The smell of lanolin is in the air. He passes ancient brass bells, stone sundials and Asian armor.

"The Turks must have had superior eyesight to do such intricate work," Knox says, speaking over the shoulder of Victoria Momani. If she's a spy, she's not a very good one; she's more interested in the displays than Knox's arrival.

And he answers himself: perhaps a very clever one.

He has taken his time. He questions if the man with the newspaper tucked under his arm, a man currently studying a tin incense burner, is in fact listening to the recorded guided tour. Has the audio player been replaced with a two-way radio? Maybe Victoria isn't paying attention to him because the others surrounding him are.

Having located two security camera bubbles, he keeps a post between himself and one camera while using Victoria to partially block the other.

"The first writings of magnifying lenses date back to a play by Aristophanes. Four hundred years before Christ," she says, continuing to study the details of a hanging rug.

One cool woman, he thinks. It's as if they'd rehearsed the meeting.

"On vacation?" he asks. "You should have told me ahead of time."

She moves to the next hanging rug, Knox following like an obedient dog. He knows of only one alternative exit, and it's not close by.

"I meet you in courtyard, ten minutes. I am not finished with gallery."

He suppresses a flash of anger; it's not easy, given his fatigue. Wants to wring Dulwich's neck for not being more up-front with him and Grace.

Outside, he doesn't know if he has the right courtyard. Finds the building as beautiful as the artifacts it contains. It's a Muslim Frick on steroids, possibly the most architecturally stunning museum he's ever been inside.

He sits outside at a two-person table in the shadow of plane trees. She approaches with a model's gait, a confident swagger that puts him back on his heels. A yellow head scarf frames her face; her brown cardigan hangs open over a yellow and green floral top, flared white linen pants. She wears the scarf for fashion, not out of religious obligation; many Muslim women are Westernized here. Gold and silver bangles rattle. A beaded metal necklace bounces against her chest.

Once she reaches him, she hesitates. Knox stands and draws back the chair; she sits. She places a gray leather clutch in her lap. Waits for him to take his seat across from her.

"I have not seen man move as you did when we last met."

"I was a gymnast in college."

"Yes?"

"No," he says. "I majored in Budweiser."

Her condescending expression says: *If you are trying for charming, it is not working.* She doesn't speak.

His eyes reply: *When I try for charming, you'll be the first to know.*

She frowns.

"I'm tired," he says, apologizing. "Sleeping with one eye open has that effect on me."

"Afraid? You? I think not."

"Cautious. I'm not a fan of surprises. Though I make exceptions for a phone call from a beautiful woman."

"So quick with flattery," Victoria Momani says.

"I'm hoping this is a social call."

"After your escape," she says, "I was detained by authorities."

"I don't doubt it." He looks around. "And now? Are you working with them?"

"I was questioned by Ministry of Culture," she says. Her dark eyes catch the sky and go pewter. She looks alien. "I believed your VAT explanation," she adds. "Stupid of me. When Ministry of Culture is involved I think to myself, What is Obama hiding? Why would ministry make such involvement?"

"What did you tell them?"

"I am an art dealer." Victoria considers him. "You? You are government agent? Working for Mashe? Who else? You are selling to Akram. Yes? This puts him at great risk. All for the older brother. Of this, I have little doubt. Mashe gets whatever he wants. Always. He runs Akram around like his slave. I will take twenty percent of whatever deal you are making, or I report you to Turkish and Jordanian authorities. At very least, they interrupt your sale and detain you. Make business difficult for you."

"You think?"

"Perhaps ministry discover you hide stolen art—I am guessing an antiquity—and they put you in jail for long time. I come out hero. Paid reward."

His chest tightens like stepping into bitterly cold air. "Extortion?"

"It would be mistake to doubt me," she says.

"Seven-point-five percent," Knox says. "Even this will make you rich."

"Twenty."

"Seven-point-five."

"Fifteen."

"Ten is final," he says. "And I get everything you know or have ever heard about Mashe Okle."

"You are government agent," Victoria claims.

"I am not. We've done this before, you and I. Make the call. Turn me in. They'll never find the piece. You'll have ten percent of nothing. And I'll walk."

"Why Mashe?"

"Because he's the buyer, according to you. Possibly for the other pieces I've sold to Akram as well."

"Definitely. Mashe is collector. Mashe will go to great lengths to acquire. It is maybe disease for him. Like drugs to addicted."

"I make a point of knowing my buyers better than they know themselves. Keeps me out of trouble."

"This, I understand," Victoria says.

"The full download on Mashe. You know 'download'?"

"Yes!" She's insulted. He reminds himself: don't talk down to her.

"And ten percent." Knox adds, "Rich. Very rich."

She eyes him cautiously. He knows how the rugs inside must have felt. "I will be present at appraisal."

"Not going to happen." He adds, "Understand?'"

"Akram will trust appraisal one hundred percent more with me in room."

"I am not involving you."

"In this way I know true value of sale and ensure I am not cheated."

"What will Akram think of that?" he says testily.

"I just explain. You will propose me as person in middle. Akram remains in love with me. You will see."

I don't doubt it, Knox thinks. "Middleman," he quips.

She nods faintly. "That, or Turkish cultural ministry. You make choice."

Reaching inside his jacket and searching among the many zippers, he pulls out a small journal. Raises it. Shows her the pen he intends to write with.

"I won't agree until I see how much detail you can provide."

"The start? The first time I meet Akram?"

"Why not? I'm a good listener," Knox says.

The story she tells plays out as a tale of promise and expectation. Victoria and Akram—Knox starts thinking of them as Victoria and Albert—met at one of her gallery openings during a Saturday-night gallery walk in the former embassy district, now the artsy, chic neighborhood of Jabal al-Weibdeh.

She knows his restaurant, has eaten there and is impressed by his humility, his knowledge of art. He's ruggedly handsome yet soft-spoken. She spends more time than usual with him, while she knows she should be spreading herself around the crowded gallery. He buys two pieces, both from her back room, regional artists he collects, pieces she would have liked to own.

He charms her without outwardly trying. Avoids flirting. They talk history and architecture and film. Tells her to call ahead if she's planning on coming to his restaurant—especially if she's coming alone.

She sees it as an irresistible offer, puts an anxious week between the gallery walk and the dinner. He has held a window table for her. It's set for two. The meal lasts three hours. He gives her a ride home on the back of his vintage American motorcycle and never once fishes for an invitation upstairs.

For their next date, he flies her to Istanbul, where he owns another restaurant. They gallery-hop, feast and spend the night in a two-bedroom hotel suite. Victoria blushes. Skips ahead.

Akram travels a good deal between Irbid, Amman, Istanbul and Ankara, where, at the time, he was starting a fourth restaurant. The courtship is romantic, undemanding, the best months of her life. She imagines giving him a family and knows he, too, is thinking about it.

On a trip to Istanbul, Victoria is introduced to his vacationing older brother and family elder, Mashe.

"Akram was different around Mashe. Weak. No spine." Her voice tightens. "Mashe . . . how would you say? . . . He *asserts* himself. We fight over something unimportant. Imagine how I feel when Akram takes brother's side."

"A fight?"

"As territorial as dog is Mashe. I needed hair dryer. This is all!"

"He got angry over a hair dryer? You've lost me," Knox says.

It pains her to talk about it. "I went into his room, you see? This is where hair dryer was to be found. On bed is ring. Stupid plastic ring. I look at this ring. It is blue. Has different family name. I ask him about this ring with different name. He makes explosion. Yes?"

"What kind of blue ring? Turquoise? A gem stone?"

"I tell you! Plastic ring! Worthless. Ugly. Very big," she says, spinning several of her own rings on her fingers.

"His name was engraved?" Knox's interest is heightened.

"Labeled. Like hospital bracelet. Not decorative ring. Functional. Not his name. Different last name. No big thing. Correct? Just on bed with keys. Wallet."

"A blue plastic ring."

"Are you listening?"

"I am," Knox says. "It was big. It had a name on it. He was upset you had seen it."

"Upset? He did not mention the ring, but he grabbed it up like a gambler with the die. Pocketed it. Exploded, shouting about how a man's room is private, about how I had no permission to intrude upon his privacy. It is cultural." Her expression changes to astonishment. "I am telling you these things, but I do not know your name. Is it Knox or Chambers?"

"Chambers" was the name he used on the FedEx package. He assumes she has discussed him with Akram, that the use of two names won't surprise her given the fact that he was trying to smuggle out art. They've reached a tipping point. The ring, the argument with Mashe—it holds significance. His skin prickled with sweat tells him so. Close.

"Knox." The truth is easier to defend.

"In our culture, John Knox, even Jordanian women . . ." She doesn't complete the thought.

He needs to move her away from the ring's importance. Doesn't want her connecting the dots the way he has. "It caused a rift. Between you and Akram."

She assays him. Her eyes grow nervous. "I will be watching you, and I will turn you over to the ministry without a second thought. Do you understand?"

"Mashe is the collector. I need to know it all." He pauses. He's gone too far. Decides on a more direct approach. "The last name on the ring, for instance. Something . . . it would allow me . . . I could run a credit check against that name. My accountant is here in Istanbul." He tries to seed his operational cover; hopes Victoria might pass this tidbit about Grace along. "She will run the credit check, do background. You don't sell this particular work without a firewall in place. You understand?"

"Perfectly."

"You don't approve."

"I am art dealer, Mr. Knox. You are art smuggler. The enemy."

"The competition."

"Same things," she says. "A divorce, perhaps. Adoption following a remarriage? It was never explained to me. Akram would not discuss it."

Knox tries not to hide his confusion.

"Okle is the mother's family name," she says.

"Both brothers took their mother's maiden name? Doesn't sound like a remarriage to me."

"The name on the ring. Mashe—"

"Melemet," Knox says. The ring, "labeled like a hospital bracelet," holds significance. Is Mashe Melemet a medical doctor on some kind of mission? Based in Iran? His brain spins, seeking out the most outrageous possibilities. An MD whose patient list includes Mahmoud Ahmadinejad?

Knox recalls Grace mentioning that Mashe's investments were heavily weighted toward scientific companies. He sees Mashe Okle in a new light.

"How could you know this? How could you possibly know this?"

Knox chides himself for always needing to prove he's a step ahead. His mind races, looking for an out.

"A man named Melemet was the owner of the Jordanian restaurant prior to Akram. Records show he sold it for a third of its value. I never understood that transaction—but now I see: it was Akram selling it to himself after he changed his name. Simply updating the new name on the property would have left too easy a trail to follow."

"Who are you, Mr. Knox?"

"John."

She nods demurely.

"One cannot be too careful," he says.

"Nor too thin, nor too rich."

He appreciates the attempt. Grace is humor-challenged, pragmatic and grounded in fact. The few attempts she makes at jokes register with Knox as lame clichés. As with so many people, she's at her funniest when it comes unintentionally. Why he's thinking about her is beyond him.

"You and Akram. Were serious?"

"Was I sleeping with him?"

Together they stop and appreciate a trio of intricately inlaid tables. The style is too busy for Knox's taste, but there's no dismissing the artistry. Why, he wonders, is such detail only seen in coastal Mediterranean cultures? Turkey. Morocco. Libya.

She says, "As if it is any of your business."

"As if."

"You wish to make it your business. Our business." She establishes eye contact. All knowing. Serene. "It makes things messy."

He's thinking bedsheets. She is not.

"Ten percent. I am expecting six figures U.S."

He coughs. "Low fives if we're lucky."

"I call the ministry now? I believe they will be interested in what Mr. Obama is hiding."

"I think we can hold off on that."

"You would not like Turkish prison, Mr. Knox."

He remembers saying the same thing to Dulwich. What happened to a week of pay-per-view movies in the hotel and a five-minute meet-and-greet?

22

Grace has to see his face when she tells him. Though she's unsure when competition became an integral part of her relationship with Knox, she nonetheless cannot resist a chance to put a hash mark in her column.

She video-Skypes his phone. When he doesn't answer, she sends a text. Five impatient minutes later, Knox answers her video call. He looks tired.

"We could not have been more wrong," she says, enjoying the look of confusion overtaking his face. It's a handsome face, though she hopes he doesn't know she sees it this way. "Actually," she confesses, "you were close. In some ways, close."

"You're enjoying this way too much," Knox says.

"The brother's blue plastic ring is a Landauer dosimeter ring. Science, yes. However, a specific medical—"

"Hazmat. Dosimeters measure exposure to toxins—"

"And radiation," Grace says, interrupting. "Landauer manufactures radiation dosimeters. In this case, a finger ring that carries your identity, as your lady friend said." She enjoys needling Knox about his promiscuity; though she's plucked the occasional businessman off a bar stool, she's not proud of it. Currently her sex life is dismal to nonexistent. She is far more conservative than Knox, but that doesn't take much. It also means she doesn't see him as competition to her current life plan, which includes great financial gain and—eventually—her own security company. Rutherford Risk has paid too little attention to cyber crime and financial malpractice, two areas on which she would like her investigative company to focus. She cannot compete, nor would she, with Knox in the field. She considers it a symbiosis, mutualism more than parasitism, but if necessary she can see herself learning from him and draining him of his knowledge at his own expense, like a tick.

"A radiologist?"

"Perhaps."

"Ahmadinejad is being treated for cancer?"

"Who said anything about Ahmadinejad?"

"Since when do bodyguards and agents follow a doctor around if—"

She brings a file up on the screen that hides him for a moment, though the video connection remains active in a window beneath.

"Mashe Melemet is a PhD, not an MD. He may design medical radiation equipment, but he does not practice on it." Grace blames Knox for this cat-and-mouse gameplay. Prior to her working with John Knox, Grace was all facts and figures. She bowed at the altar of numbers. Knox has trained her by example to tease with information. She has come to enjoy the game. Immensely.

"What have you done?"

"I placed a call requesting his university transcripts, which were e-mailed to me."

"This is why you are calling. You're calling to crow."

"Mashe Melemet took his doctorate at the Physics Institute's LHEP—the Laboratory for High Energy Physics at Universität

Bern. His early research and published material, highly regarded." She gives him the best smug look she can conjure. "He studied abroad eleven years. Returned to Iran. He teaches for eight months and then goes off the grid."

"Mashe *Okle* surfaces," Knox says, speculating while emphasizing the change in family name. Nuclear physics. *This is the Middle East.*

"I love puzzles." It's true. Grace's attraction to accounting, forensic accounting in particular, is the precision of the numbers always needing to agree. She loves a world where everything balances. Harmony. It's the polar opposite of the family discord that drove her to seek independence.

"Jesus," Knox says.

Grace gloats. She wants so badly to see his face. Is about to minimize the file in order to see the video window when the door to her apartment breaks open behind her.

Two men come at her, closing the distance before she fully swivels in her chair. Sitting is a position of vulnerability. She knows it. They know it. As she flexes to stand, one of them stiff-arms her back into the chair. Grace swings her foot, aiming for the outside of the other's knee, but it's a powerless blow and he barely reacts. Grace could try to fight, but reason gets the better of her.

The men reach for her, clearly expecting resistance. But Grace uses their tactics against them, allowing them to turn her back to the keyboard. One pins her arms as the other struggles to get a cloth bag over her head. This gesture triggers the floodgates of terror: confinement, torture, rape. She screams, bucking and writhing and straining to be free. A hand clamps over the bag, muffling her, hits her hard enough that her lips swell and she tastes blood. This, in turn, causes another instinctive struggle to be free.

Rutherford Risk deals with kidnapping on nearly a daily basis.

Negotiation. Dead drops. The tracking and freeing of hostages accounts for over half of Rutherford Risk's revenue. In this matter, Grace is far too well informed.

She is overpowered—itself a dreadful feeling. Her left hand stretches blindly for the keyboard. It's a three key combination. Her first try misses. She fights to pull her right arm from the man's containing grasp. He's now bear-hugging from the side. She snaps her head decisively, knowing that the crown of the forehead can deliver a head butt with surprising strength and sustainability.

But that's unavailable. Taking the blow just above her ear sends sparks shooting across her vision. Her opponent didn't see it coming, though. He loosens his hold. It's not much, more a reflex relaxation as the nervous system is stunned, but it's enough for a final blind try at the keyboard.

Grace slides the index finger of her left hand across the keys, feeling for the raised bump on the F. Her middle and ring fingers form an isosceles triangle and she pushes down, with no way of determining if she has succeeded.

She hears the lid of the machine smack closed. Her hands are secured with a plastic tie. She's gagged with duct tape; then the hood is lowered a second time. Stuff flies noisily off the desk. She imagines them taking both the laptop and iPhone power cords. In her mind's eye: a face similar to one of the men guarding Mashe Okle. The same man?

Hears something dragging across the floor as she's moved toward the door. Each man has her under an armpit. She makes herself dead weight, letting her bound ankles drag.

They bump her down the fire exit stairs, indifferent to her pain. She's shoved into a car; a minivan based on the sound of its sliding door.

"Her phone?"

"Yes."

"Turn it off. Pull the SIM."

Some noise indicating effort. "Yes."

"Battery from the laptop."

"Done."

The discussion between them is in Persian and surprisingly level-voiced. She retires any thought of overpowering them—it's impossible with her wrists and ankles secured. The poison of fear has overcome her. She attempts to see through it and focus on the story. Story is everything. Story is the key to her survival.

23

Because of his brother Tommy's often unstable and unpredictable condition, Knox uses a phone app to automatically record their video conversations. The same app records Grace's abduction.

The video is jumpy, contributing to its surreal look. The first nail of panic spikes his chest; he works to remove it, strains to emotionally distance himself from Grace, knowing the importance of his response to her recovery.

His voice is deliberately, eerily calm, though his fingers tremble slightly as he dials Rutherford Risk's emergency response number.

A fax tone. He keys in his ID. Three pronounced clicks.

"Case number?" A man's voice.

Knox doesn't recall being given one. "Unknown." He recites his contract ID.

"ID comes back 'on leave.'"

"Leave? I'm on an op, you idiot! My partner's a two-oh-seven! Do your job. I need a track-and-trace ASAP. Give me Digital Services!" Two-oh-seven is the police code used for a kidnapping.

"Stand by."

He connects with Kamat, Xin's boss. Again, Knox uses the police code 207. Kamat's reaction is professional and immediate.

"GPS tracks two blocks south-southeast and goes off-grid."

"That's all?"

"I will prioritize her signal with the lat/longs to be transmitted to you. Text number, please." He sounds like he's asking for a pre-scription.

Knox recites the phone number for the SIM chip currently in his phone. He repeats, "South-southeast?"

"Affirmative."

"CCTV?"

"For Istanbul? They are not web available. Is it possible for us to hack the system? Likely. Probable, even. Six to ten hours."

"You've got operatives in theater here!"

"You're shown as on leave. I see no case number. Admin error, I suppose. But we are currently blind to you and the op."

"Well, how about we change that?"

"Yes. Agreed."

"And I need traffic cams! Now!"

"Copy."

Hearing his own tone of voice, Knox apologizes. No sense in taking this out on Kamat. Sarge or some bean counter has screwed up the paperwork. Murphy's Law.

He puts himself in Grace's shoes.

"Set alerts for traffic incidents or accidents," he tells Kamat. "Alarms. Police, fire and ambulance deployments. Traffic violations. Erratic driving."

"Copy," Kamat says.

"I'm sending over a low-rez vid of the abduction. Request face recognition. Clothing. Voice. Tats. Anything you can give me on these two."

"Understood."

Knox e-mails the video in three parts. Wants to do more. *Now!* The "rapture of capture" that he typically experiences—the palpable excitement brought on by his being hired for an extraction—is absent. Instead, he cares, cares deeply about the outcome, though he knows such emotion is more of a liability than an asset. The mantra that reverberates through his mind is this: *Grace can take care of herself; I know her; her captors have no clue what they've taken on.*

Through the anxiety, a hint of a grin steals across his face. Then a grimace, the sting of impatience. Her abduction implies her flat was under surveillance.

Knox calls Kamat back. "The cell phone Grace had you geo-track. Has that number popped back up on the grid?"

"That was Xin, I believe."

"Yes, sorry."

"I can check the records. One thing to consider is an IMEI trace."

"Give me the shorthand."

"A different way to follow a phone. Hardware versus phone number. IMEI information moves with your billing. In a couple hours—"

"I need this now."

"Affirm."

"One last thing . . ." Knox has been considering how to approach this. He doesn't want to admit that he's out of contact with Dulwich; that could raise a red flag. Given that he's listed as "on leave," it might look to Kamat like Knox has gone rogue.

He continues. "Dulwich doesn't want me contacting him directly on this op. This info is top priority."

"I can contact him. No problem, John. You want to dictate the message? Stand by." A beat. "Go."

"G-C two-oh-seven. J-K Alzer." The police code "207" to inform Dulwich about the kidnapping. "J-K" to indicate Knox is registered at the Alzer under his own name, not an alias.

Knox waits for Kamat to read back his message.

"Perfect," Knox says.

"It's gone."

So is Grace.

KNOX'S PHONE VIBRATES as he's on his way to Grace's apartment. It's a text with three lat/long coordinates and times; Knox transfers them to the phone's mapping app. The coordinates are eight, four and two hours old. Kamat has managed to lift a phone's IMEI from a cell carrier's logs. It's for the man who kept vigil outside Grace's apartment, the man who sat on a bench at the Şişli Mosque. A patient man. The eight-hour and two-hour locations are within a block of one another—at their center, the apartment housing Mashe Okle/Melemet whose address Grace provided to Knox.

Knox rides the Metro to Kabataş and the funicular up the steep hill to Taksim. Out on the streets again he enjoys the view across the Bosphorus, which is busy with white-wake ferries and boat traffic, to the city's Asian side. Knox is unable to appreciate the beauty; instead, his head is crowded with plans. He shuffles imaginary tiles, trying to form an outline of the steps to come, the steps that will give him the greatest chance of success in his attempts to recover Grace.

Timing is everything. If she's not already dead, he has twelve to twenty-four hours. After that, it will take a ransom to return her, a ransom he can't imagine receiving from Rutherford Risk. It's irrelevant, though: Grace was not taken for money, but for information. They'll either dump her or kill her once they have whatever they're after, and Knox is not willing to play those odds.

He returns to the Metro and rides to Şişli, the modernity of the train system juxtaposing everything else about the former Constantinople. It surfaces in front of the Sony Center and the enormous shopping mall. He takes a taxi to within a block of the lat/long locations, then pulls the Tigers cap low and stops to use the glass storefronts as dull mirrors, assimilating, memorizing. He's in combat mode, as if a switch has been thrown, everyone's a suspect, an enemy. No friendlies. His isolation armors him. He thrives, relishing the overwhelming data he must analyze, process and file. The woman with the two children is not dismissed, nor the squatting old man with the turban and a cigarette stitched to his lower lip. An aproned shopkeeper leans against his wooden stand of ripe red fruit, surveying the street no differently from Knox. There's a baby stroller pushed by an attractive woman in her twenties who hides her waistline beneath a maternity blouse.

No one gets a free pass. He studies shoes, knowing they can often reveal impostors. Looks for bulges suggesting radios or weapons. For lips moving without the appearance of Bluetooth or earbud wires.

With a half block to go, Knox's pulse elevates as his body works to keep up with his mind. His senses heighten to a point at which every sight, sound and smell is analyzed in nanoseconds. Possible threats enter his mental hotbox, a quarterback's read of a sudden change in defense by the opposing team.

It's four cigarette butts lying on the asphalt outside the driver's door that alerts him to a man behind the wheel of a Fiat parked at the curb. The driver's seat is cleverly laid back to take advantage of the frame between front and back window, and to position his head with a clear view of the apartment building now directly in front of Knox.

Across the next intersection, Knox lifts his phone as if checking a text but uses its camera to snap a photo over his right shoulder that includes the parked car. At the next intersection, now twenty meters past Mashe Melemet's apartment, Knox crosses to the west. Out of sight of the car, he enlarges the photo until he can see the last five digits of the license plate. Progress. Texts the partial plate and the vehicle model to Kamat. Circles around the block, a plan of action defining itself. Feels sure he's the victim of a conspiracy, one that's primarily the result of Dulwich's autonomy.

Rounding the final corner, Knox catches a wink of light in a passenger-side rearview mirror. The location of the car is consistent with what he's observed. Whether it's the driver or a second man in the passenger seat, it suggests the occupant of the car could be watching for him. This, in turn, indicates sophistication, a level of training that doesn't match with a basic bodyguard or police. It kicks his opponent up a level to operative or agent, and reminds him of the surveillance conducted outside the Şişli Mosque and the tracked FedEx package.

What the hell has Dulwich gotten him into?

If these are operatives defending Mashe Okle, then the closer Knox draws, the more trouble will ensue. If he's to play out his role as Knox the art dealer, he can't be recognized as Knox the provocateur. The duality won't work.

On the other hand, if Mashe's people grabbed Grace, then this person or persons, also connected to Mashe, can likely provide information. Currently, Grace's recovery is all that matters. Her abduction possesses him. It's personal. It's wrong. More important: it's urgent.

Timing is everything.

He lowers the brim of the cap to disguise his face. Closer now, he sees it's just the driver. The wink of the mirror must have resulted from its adjustment on the driver's side. It moves again. Knox slips through two parked cars, coming up on the car's left.

The agent will not anticipate Knox's pick gun. Nor will he be prepared for Knox's approach point. He may shoot Knox, but not if Knox is fast.

And Knox can be very fast.

The car's trunk lock yields to the ingenuity of the pick gun—springs tripping tumbler keys at the squeeze of a trigger. Knox turns the device and the trunk pops open. His eyes go wide at the sight of the armory—Tavor assault rifle with nightscope, MP5 shotgun, stun grenades.

The Tavor confuses: Israeli-made, it could as easily signal a Mossad agent as someone pretending to be Mossad. This flashes through Knox's mind as he rears back and kicks down the car's backseat. He dives through, pulls like a swimmer and comes up behind the driver. Knox's invasion has caught him by surprise.

Knox grabs the driver's unclasped seat belt and pulls it tightly against the driver's chest, pinning him to the seatback. Knox one-hands the seat belt and pats with his left hand, pinning the man's hand as they both encounter the concealed handgun against the man's hip and ribs. Knox briefly eases, giving the man a false sense of victory. Then Knox steals the gun from under the leather coat, drops the seat belt with his left hand and leans around to lock his forearm across the man's throat. He grabs the man's wrist and applies the chokehold. The driver bucks off his seat so hard he smashes his groin into the steering wheel. Knox feels him momentarily go limp.

"Where is she?" Knox asks in Arabic. From his time in Kuwait, his accent is good enough to mask his country of origin. "The Chinese woman. Where . . . is . . . she?"

The driver tries to shake his head. Knox releases long enough for a single gulp of air. "Do not know!"

The man's move is swift and decisive. The driver has freed the seat adjustment with one foot while driving the seat back with the other. He crushes Knox's knees, pins Knox into the broken back-seat, and drives his right elbow into the gap between the seats, catching Knox on the cheek. The driver rips the rearview mirror from its support and swings awkwardly for Knox's head.

Knox counters the blow with his forearm. His right hand goes numb, his arm wooden. The driver propels the back of the seat into Knox's lap, pinning him further, and comes over in a reverse somersault, a move that has to be practiced. Knox doesn't often find himself in over his head. He battles an unfamiliar surge of panic, pushes back the lactic acid that threatens to stiffen his joints. Pulls his right knee free. Feels something nearly lift his kneecap off the joint.

The driver, inverted and leveraging his strength by pushing against the ceiling, wedges his weight into Knox's chest. The effect is like a scissors lock—Knox cannot breathe.

Knox scrabbles to find the man's ear and pulls hard, like he's trying to undo a stuck zipper. A scream, and blood.

Through it all, Knox hears the click of metal. Recognizes it immediately. Struggles to shift right, reaches down and yanks the cigarette lighter from where his knee has punched it. Plants it into the driver's palm as the man chops at him. Knox pulls it back and makes contact with his adversary's neck.

The screaming is deafening.

Knox punches the man in the temple, dumps him off, pops open the car door and rolls outside. He's up and gone, running down the street as fast as his legs will carry him. The man's words, *Do not know,* reverberate in his head.

Knox takes them as genuine.

24

G race pieces together the events of the past few minutes. She's blinded by the hood over her head, so must reconstruct what has happened without the benefit of sight.

Upon being stuffed into the vehicle—a minivan, again—they took away her phone. The man closest to her was instructed by the driver, in heavily accented English, though the accent was not immediately revealing—to remove the SIM chip. The van took two immediate rights and a left, increased speed, and has remained on this street since.

The driver swore—in Persian—complaining bitterly about his watch. This was followed by the rattle of a wristwatch's metal band, then the sound of an object—the wristwatch?—hitting the floor.

Interrupted, the man closest to Grace, who is now her interrogator, repeats himself—also in struggling English.

"You are to tell me who is this that employs you."

Her wrists are bound by a plastic tie—in front of her body. A mistake on their part.

Grace's mother is overbearing, highly manipulative, not merely fast-talking but verbally dominating. Throughout her teen years,

Grace deployed imitation to challenge her mother. As fast as her mother could dish it out, Grace could reciprocate. She and her brother would take turns mimicking their mother and playing her foil. Now, in response to her interrogator, Grace spews a stream of Mandarin from a verbal fire hose, drenching the man with a continuous high-pitched rage of indignity and offense. She levels a half-dozen curses on the man and his lineage while insulting the size of his sex organ and comparing his testicles to kidney beans.

Once past the curses, still speaking Mandarin, Grace explains that she is but a humble accountant in service to a Westerner and that both are in Istanbul on business and that it is by no means any business of the men in this van.

Not that her captor understands a word. The idea isn't to be understood; it's to take control of those trying to control you. To get away with as much as allowed. To test the boundaries and buy time and look for a quick way out. She has her best chance of escape while in transit. Once locked down in a fixed location, her chances of survival sink quickly.

Grace is further benefited by the van's mechanical problems. Apparently the two men chose a lemon for an abduction vehicle; even as she continues her Mandarin assault, she hears the driver complaining. The engine misfires amid the storm of her cursing. The two men argue about what a poor job the driver is doing, taking the heat off Grace, who continues to protest her innocence defiantly.

"Fucking yellowtail," her interrogator complains. "Cannot shut her up."

"Fix it!" the driver says. "She spoke English when requesting the transcript. Get it out of her!"

Grace translates this from Persian while her tongue lashes out in Mandarin and her brain hears a translation in English. Mention of "the transcript" runs cold through her as she determines the nature of the house call. Points connect with vectors, arrows weave through her thoughts: these men are tied to her call to the university; the university connects her to the records of graduate Nawriz aka "Mashe" Melemet, who holds multiple degrees associating him with advance studies in particle physics.

They will beat the English out of her, she thinks. Rape her, gladly. Share her with every man.

She begins to fall down a tightening spiral of defeat. Too much knowledge can be dangerous. She has lived such outcomes through their clients, but always at a healthy distance.

Grace clutches at the unrealistic: the van will quit; they will be forced to move her on foot. But where? Is there a destination planned, or is it to be an interrogation and dump? Get what they can, as quickly as they can. Kill her. Move on.

"This fucking piece of shit!" the driver says, pounding the wheel.

"English!" her interrogator roars, attempting to create a wedge in her tirade.

"I am humble accountant," Grace says suddenly in Mandarin-accented English, still breathless, "serving Westerner making sale of art. Due diligence. Background. Credit checks. No understand what you want."

She buys herself time as he processes her statement.

"Simple background check," she continues. "Do so dozen times. Banks. Investment. Education. What you want? What I do wrong? Simple phone call. No more. You have no reason treat me like this."

"Working for who?"

"This my client!" Incensed.

"Who is this client?"

"I wish all things foul on you and your children. Your children's children. This none of your business. This confidential."

There's a foul smell of fuel; the engine's choking continues.

Maybe she's going to get her wish after all. Maybe divine justice is real. Maybe all the incense-burning her mother does means something. A twenty-foot golden Buddha with fruit piled at its chipped feet swims across her mind.

"What the fuck!" The driver keeps cursing—in English now. She wonders about a culture that apparently can't come up with its own expletives.

Flung off the floor by a sharp turn, Grace is thrown back against the side door. Had her hands been bound behind her, this would have been her moment; she might have found the recessed door handle and bought herself freedom. Instead, she smacks her head. Her head sack catches and, as she bounces back onto her bottom, a few threads snag and fray at the bridge of her nose. The van shudders to a stop, coughs and dies.

Grace is thrown back, a forearm to her throat. The door comes open and she's dragged out, held by her collar. She can see dark, looming shapes through the snag. It's a parking garage.

She's led up concrete stairs to a landing, and then on to a higher floor.

Her internal processor slowed by the blow to her throat and the adrenaline compromising her system, only now does she identify the square object mounted to the concrete block wall a level below. A fire alarm.

She's forced to climb higher. At level two, another fire alarm in the same location on the wall.

Hands bound in front of her.

She knew that would cost them.

25

The plaza across the street from the Alzer Hotel is an oasis of flagstone, immature trees and park benches, reminding Knox of a museum's café courtyard, one where the coffee is overpriced and the quiche tastes store-bought. Well-dressed tourists and locals crisscross the space, their attention on the drama of the mosque to the east or the hum from the Parisian café tables in front of the Alzer to the west.

A man sits unmoving amid the plaza's activity, his shoulders as wide as a gate, his face as ordinary and uninteresting as that of any school's gym teacher.

David Dulwich might be a piece of urban art—*Man on a Park Bench*, sculpted from concrete. But his collar riffles in the breeze and he squints against the street dust and litter. Focused on the entrance to the Alzer, and now Knox, who has exited the building and is looking in his direction, Dulwich sits unmoving and stoic. Let the mountain come to Mohammed.

"You bastard!" Knox stands, hands shoved deeply into his jean pockets, looking nine feet tall.

"You want me to walk away, I will."

"Go ahead and try."

For a moment, as Dulwich shifts on the bench, it appears he might challenge Knox. But all he's doing is making enough room for Knox to sit.

Knox remains standing. "Takes a two-oh-seven to hear from you."

"I've had contact with Chu prior to this. You know that."

"They've got her. And you're sitting over here singing a chorus of 'Feed the Birds' like you haven't got a care in the world." Knox takes a step closer, a drunk begging for a bar fight.

Dulwich sits up taller, though he clearly doesn't mean to give Knox the power in the conversation. "It's what we do," Dulwich says. "We're good at this."

"For our clients. We do this for our clients. Not our own people. Not like this."

"Clete Danner," Dulwich says, reminding Knox of the Shanghai op and why Knox took it in the first place.

"Fuck off."

"You can't contact our company directly."

"I did, didn't I? Apparently I'm on leave. You said 'an in-and-out.' Wait around in a hotel room. What happened to that?"

"Grace is the company contact, not you. We can't risk losing your cover. Grace can be replaced. You're too important."

"She's indisposed, so I texted you."

"And I handled it. We're on it. What part of the assignment did you not understand?"

"They've abducted her!"

"Keep your voice down. Sit." Dulwich indicates the space next to him. "Tone it down. Or I'm gone."

"You say you're 'on it.' How? What's the plan?"

Impassive.

"What are you doing for her?" Knox closes the distance, putting his face an inch from Dulwich's. "What the hell am I into? The Red Room? 'On leave'? Some spook watching Grace, who's monitoring FedEx shipments of medical devices?"

Dulwich is so well trained he has few tells, but Knox picks up a change of pulse in the flesh near the burn scar. "Digital Services has your video," Dulwich says calmly. "They're monitoring Istanbul police radio traffic and CCTV available cameras as you suggested— quick thinking on your part, for what it's worth. If we're lucky, we pick up some scraps. I'm here for your debrief."

Knox hands over his phone, cued to the video. Dulwich produces earbuds. Knox doesn't need to hear. He remembers nearly every word.

He cringes as he tries to read Grace's lips.

"He studied abroad eleven years. Returned to Iran. Taught for eight months and then goes off the grid."

"Mashe Okle surfaces."

"I love puzzles."

Her abduction feels faster this time. Knox wonders how time can condense and expand as it does in these moments.

"You know one of those guys," Knox says, astonished, studying Dulwich in profile. "Who is he?"

"There's a methodology, a science to it. You know that, Knox."

"There's not going to be a ransom."

"No." Dulwich's first concession. One that Knox does not want. "What is she doing talking to you about the POI's education? Where the fuck does it say she takes a flyer to dig into this guy?"

"It's Grace, Sarge. You assigned her his finances—"

"But his education? You know who these people are?"

"That's rhetorical, I trust."

"Christ almighty! She hacked an Iranian university? What kind of response did she expect?"

"Not this. I guaran-fuckin'-tee you that. This thing is nine layers deeper than you let on. Surveillance on Grace. Hostiles chasing me and the Obama. Package intercepts. Sick people who maybe aren't. Well people who may be sick."

"What the hell are you talking about?"

"You're not here. You don't want to know."

"Let me be the judge of that."

"I don't think so. It's Grace's intel. You recover Grace, she'll download you." Knox hopes that if Dulwich didn't have enough motivation to throw everything at this extraction before, the fire's lit now.

Dulwich stabs the bench. His fingers look like big pieces of broken sticks, most, but not all, with full fingernails. "This thing . . ." He shakes his head. Bears down on Knox with intensely angry eyes. A conversation passes between them, a dust devil dropping pieces of friendship, frustration, fear. "You are to sell the Harmodius. You and Grace spend five minutes in the room with the mark. You get the fuck out and go home to Tommy. What was not clear about that?"

Knox knows better than to answer. He has Dulwich right where he wants him: in need.

"What is this about the mark's health?" Dulwich asks.

"You'll need to ask her."

Dulwich stabs the phone too hard. Knox takes it back and pockets it. "Motherfucker." He tries to reassure himself. "She's a big girl."

"She's tiny."

"Inside, asshole. Brass onions, that girl. Clanging brass onions."

"And we both know that's what'll get her killed. No way she's going to talk," Knox says.

"Not right away."

"Iranians. You're saying they're Iranians who responded that fast to someone cracking a university site? Give me a break."

"They responded that fast to cracking Mashe Okle."

"His name's Nawriz Melemet. He's a nuclear physicist." Knox would have gotten the same effect by delivering a blow to the man's solar plexus. Sarge has gone slightly pale. He looks up to take in the pedestrians, the drivers, the dozens of men and women across the street at tables.

"You two fucked up. You fucked up good."

"You encouraged Grace to dig."

"Not with a backhoe."

"Kick Xin in the butt," Knox says. "Get me some reliable intel. We're not waiting on this. We're not handling this the way we tell our clients it should be handled."

"Agreed." Dulwich shoots him an unreadable look. "It's only bigger—nine layers deep, you say—because you two dug the hole."

"Present time."

"Primer will disavow. There's no protocol for something like this."

"Bullshit! It's an extraction."

"I don't mean it like that."

"There are two of us. We're going to get her back. Right now."

The two men exchange several years of personal history in a single look.

"Damn right," Dulwich says.

Dulwich seldom admits to Knox being right about anything. The win comes at a time Knox can't appreciate it.

"We . . . owe . . . her," Knox says.

"I know. I know." Dulwich nods.

Says nothing more.

26

There are few advantages to being small. Grace has rarely had the opportunity to celebrate her feet, breasts or hands. If she so much as looks at food, she gains weight. In the department stores, they point her toward the children's floor—there's no fashion for the diminutive. One of the few advantages is expectation: size is mistakenly equated with strength. Her two captors each have six inches and fifty pounds on her. What they don't know is: it's not enough.

As if to illustrate the point, as the three approach the steel door on the second-floor landing, Grace drives her right elbow into the groin of one man, then uses her bound hands as a ramrod, a piston propelled into the unsuspecting chin of her second captor. She chops the glass on the fire alarm, cutting herself. Hooks her fingers around the lever and pulls so hard she loses her balance and falls flat onto her back as the alarm sounds.

To her surprise, her second captor is already on the floor. A glass jaw. Her single blow rendered him unconscious.

She rolls hard into the shins of the first man, who won't urinate without pain for a week. He falls forward onto his knees like he's in the midst of afternoon prayers. She attempts a last-minute penalty kick—just her and the keeper—splitting his thighs from behind and striking him so hard he vomits before falling fully forward.

Her phone is all that can save her. Her laptop would be nice, but it's too much to carry. Hands bound in front of her, she awkwardly searches the downed man, recovering her iPhone from his jacket pocket. No chip, rendering the phone useless.

She wants so much more: personal ID from both men; weapons; a look at any tattoos; clothing tags; currency. The fire alarm is a sharp peal of possibility; she has bought herself precious seconds.

Her wrists are bound, her hands bleeding. It's not as if she can blend in. Temptation points her down—toward the street. Fresh air. Freedom. It's what any hostage would do.

Instead, she climbs. One floor. Two.

A voice from below: one of the captors calling it in.

Damn wrists.

She tops out on the fifth floor. Nowhere to go.

What now?

27

D ulwich limps away from the bench. His bad knee has apparently given up along with the rest of him. His bulk looks cartoonish in comparison to the Turks on the plaza. A stovepipe arm lifts what looks like a toy phone. Then, slowly, the man's shoulders pivot as he turns.

Knox knows the call has to do with Grace. He rises from the bench and closes the distance, moving with extended strides. His pounding heart drums in his ears.

"What?" Knox says.

Dulwich's expression is patronizing. He says, "Got it," and shuts down the call.

"Her," Knox says.

"You told Kamat to watch the grid for fire alarms?" Perplexed. Annoyed. "You going to run all over town chasing mattress fires?"

"Talk to me."

"It's a confirmed safe house. On a list we got from the Pakis before things went to shit with them."

"Iran," Knox says. Gets no pushback from Dulwich. "How long ago?"

"Came in just now."

"It's her."

"Could be. Trouble is, we don't know."

"Address?"

"You can't make a one-man raid on a known Iranian safe house."

"Two-man. Address?"

"There are so many reasons why this is a no-go. I don't have time to list them all. We can ask the local police to roll a fire truck to the scene. Nothing wrong with that. They can do a room-by-room for us. The Turks are friendlies. We can—"

"I'm on that truck."

"Not possible."

"We'll see what Primer thinks."

"Thin ice, my friend. You have no idea how deep and dark a hole you're digging."

"We're digging. This is Grace. I'll tell you what: you get on the truck. You give me the address in case they're tardy or lazy."

"If she tripped that alarm, they beat her senseless and/or moved her. By now she's a dozen blocks away and moving fast."

Knox steps forward. "If she pulled that alarm, then her hands are either free or in front of her. I've seen her in the field. You, too, in Amsterdam. You gotta pity those bastards. Now give me the fucking address."

Dulwich spins his phone to reveal the message from Kamat. Knox types the address into his map app, careful of each number and letter. As precious as pearls.

"I'm going to need you as backup," Knox says.

28

Thinking is not an option. Grace reacts because she's been trained to react by the PLA's intelligence force. There's a communal laundry wire strung between this building and the next, barely ten feet away, open windows on both sides. A vinyl basket tied to the wire holds clothespins. Handicapped by her bound wrists, Grace dumps the clothespins inside, unties the basket with her teeth and places it over the woven wire, holding the basket by its opposing handles. The basket collapses under her weight but serves as protective strap to guide her across the wire. She tests it against her weight, throws her ankles up onto the wire, contracting her knees to pull her along. She does not look down, but can't ignore the basket's vinyl is being slowly sawed into by the wire. She says a few prayers, grateful it's ten feet across, not twenty, and speeds up her efforts. The basket about to break, Grace switches to her bare hands for the last few feet. The wire cuts through the flesh of her fingers.

Once she reaches the far building, it takes her three precarious tries to get her feet through the opposing window, and she's losing strength by the time she manages.

An older woman in a hijab sees Grace's bloody fingers and wrists and silently withdraws back into her apartment, shutting her door.

Grace hurries downstairs, before realizing she should have asked the woman to cut the ties.

No one follows. She would like to attribute her continuing freedom to her evasive skills, but Grace knows better. It's not as if she incapacitated both her captors, so where are they? She pushes into a busy bodega, self-conscious at the stares caused by her lack of a head scarf, her bound wrists and the sweat cascading down her face.

A pair of scissors is chained to the counter alongside a beat-up calculator.

"Please," she says, extending her wrists to a man in a soiled turban.

The clerk looks at her wrists and then meets eyes with Grace.

"My husband," Grace says, appealing to a matronly woman behind her. "My husband. He beats me. Please!" She raises her voice. "He did this to me. He's coming for me."

"It is God's will," the clerk says. His eyes are dark brown, dead.

"Step aside!"

The woman who comes to Grace's aid is college-aged and dressed unconventionally in a zippered jacket and blue jeans. She wears a head scarf, but fashionably. All eyes are on her as she shoves past the solemn matrons in line.

The clerk places his hairy hand over the shears, pinning them to the counter.

"It is inhumane," the young woman says. "Only a coward must bind his wife's hands like a prisoner."

The sound of approaching sirens carry down the street outside, giving everyone pause.

The young woman doubts herself. "What have you done?"

Grace pleads, "Please! There isn't much time!" The sirens form a chorus. "Whose side will they take?"

The young woman isn't going to touch the man's hand. She snags a butane lighter from a basket and lights its blue flame. She looks down at the curls of black hair on the back of the man's hand.

Minding the flame, he takes his hand off the scissors, but the young woman and Grace are of like mind. Grace has angled her wrists and the girl is melting the plastic tie that binds them. It catches fire, emitting dark black smoke, and then pops as Grace applies outward pressure.

The matrons jump away as the burning plastic whistles to the floor.

Grace utters a Muslim blessing to the girl, who returns it.

"There is a door through the back." The girl speaks English, her all-knowing look holding Grace. "Do not worry." Again, English. "I say nothing."

Grace rushes toward the rear of the shop.

The streets are narrow and as thick with people as the air, which hangs heavy with the smell of spiced food and human sweat. Smog cloaks the tops of the low buildings like morning fog over a river. She hears coughing and the scratch of grit beneath shoes, the roar of car engines, children's voices and a barking confined dog. Despite its uncanny similarity to Shanghai's claustrophobic neighborhoods, it is foreign to her. She is a stranger here, in looks, height, dress. She has no money. Her phone is worthless. She has no idea where she is in relation to the Bosphorus or any other city landmarks. Senses she is a target, that they are coming after her.

She swipes a head scarf from a woman's shopping bag as she passes; pulls it on and cinches it beneath her chin. Wishes for a pair of dark glasses. Needs some sense of bearings. More minarets than chimneys in Dickensian London. More people than a parade route. The buildings are too crowded, the street too winding for her to get a glimpse of the landscape. And all the while, there is the inescapable tension of the Pamplona bulls coming up behind her.

Head down. Long strides. She uses car mirrors to check the street. Cuts in front of taller vehicles, using them as screens. Looks for a bicycle, anything to move her faster. A part of her cannot believe anyone could find her given the crush, but she knows better. Rutherford Risk is in business because of the suffocating hold kidnappers maintain on hostages—even escaped hostages. Informal networks of payoffs. Corrupt cops. Gangs. The underground world is five times the size of the legitimate one. It runs on a currency of favor and fear, is a place where debts are final and betrayal is met with punishment that extends across generations.

Her phone vibrates in her pocket, stunning her. She fishes it out. The carrier is written in Arabic. Glancing back all the while in search of anyone following, she stops several people, asking in Turkish: "Please!" and holding out her phone. Finally, a woman stops.

"My phone," Grace says, speaking Turkish. "What does this mean?"

The woman tries English. "This says, problem. How you say, problem? Difficulty?"

"Emergency!"

"Just so. Emergency. Yes. Like hospital."

"I can dial an emergency number?"

"Yes, I believe so."

"What do I dial for police?"

"This number is the one, the five, the five."

"One, five, five. Thank you."

"May I help, please?"

Grace fights back a surge of emotion. Her eyes glass over. The Turks are such warm people.

"You have. Thank you so much. Indebted."

She spots a man a half block back, recognizes him as one of her captors.

Her newfound girlfriend picks up on the sudden fear coursing through Grace. Looks back and forth between the two with troubled eyes. "This man make trouble you?"

Perhaps she has seen the red, raw rings on Grace's wrists or the dried sweat and smeared makeup. But no. It's Grace's feet: she is shoeless, wearing only ankle socks.

Even with its chip pulled, the phone can dial emergency calls.

"One-five-five. Thank you!" Grace speaks even as she runs from the man approaching.

29

"G o around," Knox instructs the cabbie in crude Turkish.

The cabbie's posted ID reveals a Muslim name to go with his Egyptian face. The vehicle skirts a small fire engine and two police cars pulled to the curb, negotiates the crowd of curious onlookers. Knox strains to look up from within the cab. It's a nondescript apartment building, a perfect safe house.

He's traveled by ferry to the Asian side of the city. Now the cab. Knox has no idea what he's looking for, only knows that he'll recognize it when he sees it. Tops on his list is the clothing seen in the Skype video—a distinctive light brown leather jacket on one of the two men; a more ubiquitous dark windbreaker worn by the other. Turks, Greeks, Spaniards, Italians—the stadiums of any *futbol* match are filled with a hundred thousand clones of the men he seeks.

To his left, a group of young boys flees down the sidewalk—following someone in a hurry? Somewhere nearby, sirens; hopefully Dulwich with the cavalry.

"This address?" The cabdriver points to the meter. He has tired of Knox's impatience, wants to be free of him.

Knox isn't much of a gambler. Feels himself coming apart. Raid the building or follow the boys? Pictures Grace, her hands free enough to trip a fire alarm. Her captors playing her for the female computer hacker she is. A nerd. They wouldn't expect her punch. No one would ever expect a woman as complex as she.

The sky in front of them is brighter than rain clouds behind. Knox knows the psychological reaction of someone frightened, someone fearing for her life, would be to move in the direction of the light.

The direction the boys were running.

"Drive on," Knox says. "I will tell you the way."

The driver huffs.

Grace needs a sanctuary, he thinks, somewhere to lose herself in a crowd. A mosque is too male-dominated. A restaurant is too static, and therefore risky. The neighborhood around the safe house is up-scale: sidewalks of hand-laid pavers, trees in abundance, a mixture of contemporary and ancient architecture. The sidewalks remain a Benetton ad: Western, Indian, Arab, African. Not a Chinese in sight.

"A market? A street market?" Knox says.

"The Grand Bazaar, mister, is most famous—"

"This side of the strait! The south side!" Knox's abrupt tone is off-putting to the driver. The man looks away from the rearview mirror, pretending his cab is empty.

Knox drops some liras into the front seat. "A food or spice market. Clothing? Household goods? A street market near here."

"Kadiköy is not familiar," the driver says.

"Call someone! Find out!" Knox says. "Turn here." He points right. Directs the cab left at the next intersection. He's all raw instinct—a water witcher. The purpose of training is to make you unpredictable, and Grace is well trained. She's likely stuck on foot if she's not dead in the safe house. He shudders. "Call someone now!" he shouts. "Public market!"

Cursing beneath his breath, the cabdriver reaches for his phone.

Knox attempts to further untangle the knot of Grace's abduction. Mashe Okle, a nuclear engineer. The record of his higher education obscured but not redacted. Grace's captors will want her to explain her interest in the man. To kill her would be to invite others to follow the same path. If she has escaped—as Knox is assuming—the Iranians will be trying to recapture her.

"Street market today," the cabbie says, ending the call. "Many apologies. I forget the day it is."

"Near here?"

"Up the hill. Quite near."

"Up the hill?" Grace has played contrarian, assuming that, like Knox, her pursuers will head downhill.

"I take you there?" The man wants Knox out of his cab. Smells trouble.

"You take me there," Knox confirms. He wants Grace in the backseat with him. And he wants any one of the personnel pursuing her, too. Wants to confirm them as Iranians, wants to tune up someone to rid himself of the adrenaline poisoning him. Experiences a pang of guilt: he should have protected her from this ever happening.

Knox's phone vibrates. "Yeah?"

"Police emergency line." It's Dulwich. "Woman speaking English says kidnappers are after her. Said she's near a bull."

"Bull!" Knox says to the driver. "Cow. Steer."

"Yes. I tell you already. This is Kadiköy market."

"Got it," Knox says to Dulwich, ending the call. His mind is stuck back on Dulwich having access to voice traffic on Istanbul's police emergency line. Can that be explained by Kamat's or Xin's involvement? Does it suggest outside resources available to Dulwich?

Knox drops more liras onto the passenger seat. "Fast!"

30

Traffic is Grace's enemy. Stopped with dozens of other pedestrians, she awaits a light change at a three-way intersection of wide avenues. The island in the center of the interchange is the destination, but the longer the light drags out, the more it feels to her as if she'll never make it.

Adrenaline has given way to fatigue; her blood feels poisoned. The people are well dressed; Gap and Abercrombie anchor the intersection on opposite sides of the square. She clutches her phone, her lifeline. The emergency operator's English was atrocious. Grace's Turkish failed her. Grace told her she could see a bull, a sculpture of a bull. The woman operator told her to go there and wait. Help is on its way. At least that was what Grace thinks she said.

The man rudely pushing his way toward her clearly has other plans.

Grace tries to summon her strength, but while the physical power feels within her reach, her emotions are taxed. She is empty, unable to find a spark to light her will. She knows the terms to describe the psychological disconnect of hostages, has read the case studies;

she saw these things firsthand on the Shanghai op. Her abduction was less than an hour long. How could it have affected her so?

And yet, she wants to sit down on the curb and tuck into a ball and hope no one sees her. She's broken free and escaped; she's beaten the odds. But this man aims to crush any hope she has of victory. She doesn't think she can survive a second abduction. A part of her is tempted to run into the speeding traffic and take her chances, stocking feet and all.

The changing of the traffic light robs her of this option. It results in a footrace; the fresh legs of her pursuer against her own elephantine limbs. The police expect her at the rendezvous. It's impossibly far.

And then a hallucination. Of all the faces she might have invented as her savior—her longtime lover, Lu Jian; her cadet training officer; her father—it is John Knox she envisions coming toward her through the undulating mass of pedestrians. It must be a hallucination because he doesn't see her; he looks beyond her, his face caught in a stony expression. She angles in his direction, trying to catch his eye, struggling with vertigo amid the riot of people spinning around her.

"The taxi's waiting across the intersection," Knox says.

It sounds like Knox, but the man walks past without so much as a glance in her direction. Grace spins, trying to get a look back, but is turned again by a collision with a stranger. Finds herself facing the giant bull, realizes she's only yards from the curb. The statue is a massive bronze beast in the exact center of the island. Curious tourists surround it.

Feeding her fantasy, she glances across to the far side of the intersection: a waiting taxi. Coincidence? The mind of the hostage is susceptible to all kinds of impressions; she supposes she must have spotted the taxi before inventing a Knox who instructed her to go there.

The crush of pedestrians disperses at the curb. Taxi or not, she'll never make it. She knows better than to look back, to let her adversary know she's on to him. It would only hasten his attack. But she forsakes her training and glances over her shoulder.

Gone.

She only looks for a split-second, but it should have been enough. Now she looks left and right, expecting him to come at her from another angle.

Car horns sound well back. The knot of pedestrians ahead begins to move; the traffic light is in her favor. She steps off the curb, the asphalt warm on the soles of her feet.

31

Wrists crossed and held low in front, protecting the sternum. Chin averted to the side, in case his opponent's head snaps forward, a rare but painful unintended consequence. A quick step to his left like a defensive tackle in a stunt. Knox plants the block perfectly, lifting the small but sturdy man fully off his feet and laying him back onto the street. His head hits concrete with an audible thud.

Knox drops his right knee into the man's crotch. There's no mistaking the parts caught between his patella and the asphalt. A good percentage of his two hundred and twenty-seven pounds are balanced on that knee.

It's not the wallet that interests him—leatherbound fiction. Nor the 9mm handgun in a belt holster, which Knox removes, ejecting the magazine with one hand and skidding the weapon deeply under a truck that has stopped to allow the pedestrians to cross. The flurry of car horns doesn't bother him; in truth, his focus is so intense, he barely hears anything but the blood whining in his ears.

It's the man's phone he wants, his data. Ones and zeros that connect this man to another, and he to she, and she to it. It's the "it" he wants. Needs. The "it" may put this all into perspective, something Dulwich is clearly loath to do. If the data suggest Iranians, so be it. But if Israelis or another faction, it moves the five minutes with Mashe Okle/Nawriz Melemet into far more dangerous territory— the arenas of international politics and national security, a zone in which friends and allies are no more than conveniences. Though he doesn't want to, Knox must consider the possibility that Dulwich and/or Primer have entered into this op naively, that he and Grace are now in too far to abort but may have been set up, intentionally or not, as scapegoats.

The inside zippered pocket. Knox has the phone practically before the man's facial skin stops dancing from the contact with the pavement. He's off him and moving. Elapsed time, seven seconds. Knox continues in the direction, away from Grace, alert for others like this one, who now lies unconscious in a thinning intersection.

He passes a yogurt shop, a jeans store, a window with more discount electronics than anything in Times Square. Crosses at the next intersection, reducing his height by bending his knees and taking longer strides. Same old tricks. Same old circus.

As he nears the far curb, the taxi jerks to a stop. Knox rounds the vehicle and climbs into the back, throwing his arm around her without saying a word. It's Dulwich driving the cab.

Grace clings to Knox like a child.

32

"Who is this?" Victoria Momani comes out of the chair at the small desk in Knox's hotel room. Her eyes narrow; her shoulders square, lifting her chest and reminding Knox of a tropical bird announcing its claim on territory.

"My accountant," he answers as if on cue. "She's been through hell. Give us a minute, a long one."

Clearly, Victoria considers her options. She and Grace meet eyes, and Victoria nods, more to Grace than to Knox. "I am downstairs." She collects her purse and cell phone, taking her time. Finally, she leaves.

"You make things so complicated," Grace says weakly as Knox leads her by the arm into the bathroom and starts the shower, supporting her all the while.

"Sometimes, they make themselves," Knox says. He unbuttons her shirt and helps her out of it. Unbuttons her pants and unzips them.

"That's enough, John." She forces a grin. Her eyes are sad and tired and he thinks he could kiss her. "Thank you," she says.

"It's not as if—"

"I need no reminder."

Knox has seen her naked. Another time. Another op. Little remains about these two that would surprise the other. It's as unique a relationship with a woman as Knox has ever had; platonic, yet deeply intimate.

"Call me," he says.

She nods and again he wants to kiss her, to express how pleased he is to have her back.

The shower runs for twenty minutes. Finally, Knox taps on the bathroom door; when there's no answer, he opens it to find the room a thick cloud of steam. Grace is sitting in a tight ball, arms around her shins in the corner of the shower, the water beating down on her. He opens the shower, takes her hand and leads her from the stall. Wraps her in a towel, the steam swirling magically around her, crosses it in front of her and hugs her. She hesitates, then accepts the embrace, locking her tiny hands around his strong forearms and holding to him, her grip painfully tight.

"It was nothing," she says finally. The water is still running, the steam enveloping them. "I do not know why I should feel like this."

Knox closes the embrace, their bodies pressed together, his front to her back. She sags her head against his biceps, her wet hair soaking through to his skin. He feels himself growing aroused and releases her out of embarrassment. He shuts off the water and slips past her. She reaches out for him, her fingers catching his shoulder. He pauses. It's her way of thanking him.

GRACE EMERGES in one of Knox's long-sleeved T-shirts and a pair of his boxer shorts rolled at the waist. Her black hair is neatly combed.

The room is small. He's in the desk chair. She tucks her legs beneath her and lies back against the headboard in a riot of pillows.

"What the hell?"

She so rarely curses, Knox has to look over to make sure it's her.

"You tell me."

"They knew that I'd called the university and breached their fire-walls. They tried to sound like Eastern Europeans speaking English, did a decent job of it, but they swore in Persian."

"Makes sense. The safe house is Iranian. Phone numbers from the cell I recovered in the street? All Iranian country code."

"You made contact with David." She can fill in the blanks; he appreciates this about her.

Knox doesn't have the heart to punish her for drilling so deeply into Nawriz Melemet, to inform her that Dulwich's star pupil has gone too far for once. She's in as fragile a state as he's seen her.

"He's being a bigger bastard than usual," he says, "but played good backup to your rescue; I'll give him that. Honestly, I think this one is getting the better of him. He doesn't seem like himself." He could easily mention Dulwich's discontent with her efforts; he has teed up his own ball. Elects otherwise.

"All they got from me was that I am your accountant. That I was hired to conduct a background check. Had my escape failed . . . We would be facing a more difficult situation." Her eyes wander to the door, and he knows what she's thinking.

"Her name's Victoria Momani. I used her as a cutout in the shipment of the Harmodius. She . . . It didn't work out exactly as I planned. She shows up here wanting a cut. Has me in a bind. She's involved herself—not the way you think; there's none of that—in a way that I can't undo. We can't have her compromising the deal. So, for now she squats. You know the expression?"

She nods.

"Basically, we're stuck with her."

"The client may want her killed."

"Which makes it all the more tricky. That's not going to happen."

"What is Mr. Dulwich's opinion?"

Knox says nothing.

"You withheld this information?"

"Need to know," Knox says, mocking Dulwich.

Grace shakes her head, mulling it over. "This is a mistake."

"You'll stay here with me," he says. "I'll put her in another room."

"She is in this room? With you?"

"She won't let me out of her sight. Doesn't trust me."

"I cannot return to my apartment, but I do not need to stay here, John."

"You do, and you will. I have the Harmodius in a second room down the hall. I need to move it. If she finds out where . . . She'd as soon steal it as take a cut." He considers his options. "It can't be here. At some point, my room will be searched. I'll think of something."

"I have inconvenienced you."

"You have." He wins a faint smile from her. But she looks scared. "It'll be over soon."

"No worries," she says.

It's an expression he uses with her; her using it on him gestures to a larger conversation. He tries to find an appropriate retort, but he's at a loss.

"You are a good man, John Knox."

"Don't let that get around."

She closes her eyes, looking as if she will sleep.

KNOWING VICTORIA'S greed to be the most immediate threat, Knox pays a bellman to move the crated Harmodius to the bell stand storage. A priceless relic, or a hell of a good copy, now sits in an intermittently locked closet on the lobby level, along with the roll-aboards of guests waiting for rooms to open up.

The conversation with Victoria takes place outside on the sidewalk terrace beneath a string of colorful lights surrounded by dancing bugs. It's a cosmopolitan crowd drinking exotic martinis. The women are beautiful, the men competitive, the cigar smoke annoying. Victoria holds her own, her posture erect, her lips moist, her eyes alluringly tired. Made peevish by Grace's intrusion, she taps out a distress code on the sweating cocktail glass with her index finger.

"If you are making lies, you will regret it," she says.

"That's not happening. She is necessary to the deal. Akram may have been compromised."

"I would know this."

"May be working for the ministry, setting a trap for businessmen such as myself. My partner excels at following money trails. She will ensure the financing is legitimate. I will not walk into a sale where the cash has been supplied by police or the ministry."

"The cash comes from Mashe. Possibly small consortium of men like Mashe—art lovers not willing to let piece like this escape. It is not entrapment."

"And for all I know, you're part of the ruse. Convenient that you showed up here just before the sale, isn't it?" Knox enjoys twisting the story back on her, watching her squirm as she sees her actions from another point of view. They both know it's not true, but he pushes her back on her heels, right where he needs her.

"I swear!"

"And so would any woman sent into a sting operation to convince the middleman the deal is safe. You don't think I know the price I'll pay if caught? You don't think every move I make is motivated by the consequences of failure? You are a variable I hadn't planned for, and I plan for everything."

"Do you threaten me?"

"I caution you: the consequences are not mine to bear alone. My reach is longer than you may think. No jail, no morgue will prevent this from coming back on you. You betray me, and neither prayer nor pistol will protect you."

He's gotten through. Victoria's eyes alight with fear, the blue and red bulbs above her head setting off a kaleidoscope of concern. She uses the gin and tonic to busy herself.

Knox thinks his dark rum and tonic has never tasted quite so perfect. He appreciates meeting a challenge head-on, facing a powerful threat. His life with Tommy can't supply this. He feels on edge, one foot on either side of a self-imposed line.

He would welcome being free of chess sets and tribal reproductions in exchange for gray-market Kandinskys and Bernards. The commissions on such sales would fast-track Tommy's safety net and grant Knox an independence he hasn't felt in five years. He cautions himself to not allow his hunger to get ahead of thoughtful precaution.

"She did not look well," Victoria says from an intended position of authority.

"She's not. And if I find out you had anything to do with it, you'll think she looked good." It's the booze speaking, but the thing is, he likes it. This is a John Knox he enjoys playing, is comfortable playing. Alcohol could be his downfall.

Victoria tries to contain her surprise.

"You are extorting me," he says. "Don't think I don't know it. For all your beauty and charm, I'm reminded that poisonous snakes are often the most alluring."

"You think my bite so venomous?"

For two nights, this woman has slept beside him in the same bed. They have lived like a married couple, sharing a bathroom. He has fantasized about her bite. It has been one of the oddest forty-eight hours Knox has spent with any woman, especially one as beguiling as Victoria. Also like an old married couple, they have not touched, have not shared so much as a glimpse of nudity.

But now there is an offer on the table.

Knox brushes it away along with the corpses of brown bugs that have orbited the hot bulbs for the last time. They silently float to the sidewalk, snowflakes of wasted lives.

He takes her in her new room, starting by pinning her to the wall, her long legs wrapped around him and hooked at the ankles. They laugh as he fights to tear loose her thong and it stretches to an absurd size. It's around her knees as he drops his jeans and together they direct him to the treasure. Then her eyes roll back and she says something in a language he can't translate but understands. When her eyes come back to him, they say, *You're kidding me,* and a smile seen only on women creeps across her lips. She laughs, groans and coughs, and drops her hand to join in her deliverance. It's frantic and awkward, hard core and hard driving. Her eyes are open again and far away.

Knox feeds off that, thrills to it, loves the feel of her bottom in his hands and the spasms of muscles flexing and rippling as she exhales in a rush and shiver that connects to him and sends him over the top. He turns her and lowers her to the bed, her insides contracting and sparking, her throat cries guttural, her chin thrown back.

Later, she is leaning against him, and he against the headboard, both of them half undressed, her underwear now around a single ankle. They are dozing, not saying much. Occasionally she giggles and then holds his arms tightly around her.

He doesn't tell her that it rarely feels like this. Doesn't share that it's hard to share. There's usually some reserve held in the tank for the sake of self-preservation and self-respect. But she demanded all of him and she got it and he can't say that there are no more tricks or secrets held back within him.

He wants to say that it happens so rarely he can count the times on one hand. That it has as much, if not more, to do with the mystery about her, the situation they are in, the hold she has over him, as it does the intangibles of physical perfection and connection. To her credit, she doesn't press for another throw. Perhaps she's as surprised as he. How incredible if that were the case, if a man and woman could not only scale and reach their own peaks, but summit the same mountain.

Also to her credit, she hasn't spoken. They are basking in an afterglow so intense that a single word would spoil it.

Another thirty minutes. He kisses her on the top of her head, and leaves her slumbering but not quite completely out, on the pillow. Pulls up his jeans, covers her and moves toward the door.

As the latch is about to click shut, he hears a faint "thank you." In English.

THE CALL from Akram comes as Knox is walking down the hall back to his room and Grace. He checks the time. Jesus.

"Yeah?" Knox says, answering.

"Where Itfaiye Caddesi crosses the aqueduct. How long?"

"Ten minutes."

"Fifteen." The call ends.

It takes Knox five minutes. A single streetlamp pours yellow light onto brown stones sixteen hundred years old, piled sixty feet high in double-stacked arches. The bottom arch leads through to a tree-lined pedestrian way.

The Turks are not superstitious or afraid of the dark, but Muslims are devout and wary of displeasing Allah. New Yorkers, certainly a man from Detroit, would think twice about loitering along the aqueduct's nearly thousand meters of randomly darkened arches at this time of night. The Itfaiye intersection, while busy with street vendors by day, lacks the lighted and noisy cafés and bars that abound near its Atatürk Boulevard crossing. Itfaiye Caddesi looks more like a pedestrian tunnel. Knox peers inside cautiously. The aqueduct is ten meters wide at its base. He sees no one.

While he appreciates the activity, even in the midst of it Knox can't stop his mind from grinding. He's not an analyst but an operative. He's here because he was a truck driver in another life and he saved Sarge's life. He's been put in a position of doubting everyone and everything. His only touchstone is Grace, and she's been through a psychological wringer from which it's not easy to immediately recover. The setting feels like the Berlin Wall in a Cold War film; he's a spy who doesn't know which side he's on. He took precautions to make sure he wasn't followed from the hotel, but his efforts feel in vain as he itches under the invasive sense that he's being watched. His skin crawls. He's sweating despite the cool night air. He convinces himself he can smell the Bosphorus—a muddy, turgid tang swirling up in faint gusts along the aqueduct's ancient route.

A figure of a man in silhouette appears beneath a cone of streetlamp light on the south side of the Valens Aqueduct. A dramatic image, it triggers a series of defensive reactions. Knox establishes two modes of egress, though neither provides much cover. In fact, the rendezvous exposes both men unnecessarily. It's a poor choice.

The constant hum of city noise is shrouded by a whine in Knox's ears. It's the sound of increased blood pressure and hyperawareness.

Knox practices the Native American art of rolling his feet as he walks, eliminating all sound of his advance. Keeping his legs slightly spread and his arms from contacting his torso as they swing, he moves silently through the darkened arch, pausing at the far side and allowing his peripheral vision to account for anomalies, any possible threats lurking to either side. Seeing none, he continues toward what appears to be a black cardboard cutout of a man.

As Knox nears, the man moves closer to the streetlamp's post and sits on a metal bench that faces the promenade. The posture puts him in profile. It's Akram. He wears wire-rim glasses tonight, moving him away from a well-dressed tough toward academic.

Knox doesn't like the choice of the bench, which exposes his back. He retreats to the ancient wall and leans against it. A minute passes. Two. Akram stands and walks slowly toward Knox. He joins Knox, the two of them looking down the long promenade, before a word passes between them.

"The provenance is impressive," Akram says in an overtly doubtful tone that suggests he believes the Harmodius paperwork has been forged.

"It is indeed," Knox says, playing it as if he missed the man's implication.

"You will explain please Victoria's participation."

Knox works to keep surprise off his face. "There were complications in Amman. You would have heard this from your man, Shamir. Yes? It wasn't me who used Victoria's Skype account to try to cloak our conversation. You and Shamir brought her into this and apparently I'm stuck with her and her demand of a commission." John Knox the occasional gray market art dealer would play up the unfairness of the payout and little more. "Which brings us to the deposits due in the escrow account."

"We have lost our joy, my friend, you and I. And while it is true I trust Victoria's judgment and expertise when it comes to the world of art, this is not for her."

"Feel free to tell her that. Seems as if you two know each other well enough."

"I will accept her participation," Akram says, backing down quickly, not wanting to tackle the woman any more than Knox, "but I must make clear she is in no way associated with me in this transaction. Any commission is between the two of you." Back to business; he doesn't want Victoria costing his brother.

Knox spots movement in the reflection off the man's eyeglasses. He lowers his voice to a whisper. "You've been followed." He feels Akram stiffen.

"Impossible." Equally soft.

"Move your head slowly to your right as I shake you." Knox bumps Akram against the wall, then pins him at a slight angle. Knox uses the man's glasses as his eyes.

"There's a second," Knox says. "A shadow showing from an arch. The other is in this side of the building to your left." He bangs him again. "Straight up! Are they yours?"

"Do not be ridiculous."

"Your brother's?"

Akram snaps his head up to face Knox.

"Did you or your brother arrange the kidnapping of my accountant?"

The resulting silence is slowly replaced by a loud whine in his right ear. It's a sensation Knox has experienced only rarely since his truck-driving days; they ended abruptly when a vehicular IED took out a stretch of his convoy and nearly killed Dulwich four years ago. Knox was rendered partially deaf for two months following. He lived with the intermittent whine for the next six months. Its return frightens him; it's loud enough to make him deaf in that ear, is occasionally accompanied by sharp pain, and leaves him off balance and sound-blind. He has to turn in the man's direction to clearly hear Akram.

"I know nothing of this kidnapping," Akram says.

"Your brother's doing, then. Same as these two."

"We are done."

Before Akram can take a step, Knox has him by the arm.

"We are not done, my friend." Knox holds the man against the stone wall. Akram does not fight back, but looks paralyzed, a man unaccustomed to physical violence; it speaks volumes to Knox. Akram is more of a fish out of water than Knox. "I have gone to great trouble in order to offer you this piece. You walk away and you will have much explaining to do."

Akram leans back and looks up at the night sky. "The deposit has been made. You only must check."

"I will," Knox says. He wishes Grace were awake to handle this for him. He's not great with the iPhone, but he manages to access the correct site. Akram inputs the account number and a password. The screen shows 250,000 USD. The figure swims in Knox's head, distracting him. It's not an amount either man can walk away from, and they both know it.

"I don't know who your brother is, and I don't care. But I don't appreciate people kidnapping and interrogating my accountant." He hopes to confirm what Grace purposely allowed during her inter-rogation in the back of the van. It has become an unsolvable 3-D puzzle for Knox. One he can't seem to get through and from which he sees no way out. "I don't appreciate your allowing people to fol-low you—"

"But I swear—"

"Yeah, yeah. Enough of that, my friend. Clean up the way you do business or the Harmodius is gone."

"That is surely why these men exist, is it not?" Akram sounds legitimately convinced. "So that you do not cut and run—I believe that is the expression."

"We all have much to lose," Knox says. "Advise your brother that any finalization of the deal must now involve him. And no babysitters. The next phase is verification."

"Dr. Adjani," Akram says. "Victoria is able to arrange this. These two have met."

"We'll see about that," Knox says. "Following verification I will expect the remainder of funds to be transferred within six hours."

Akram sucks air through his teeth but does not counter.

"Upon full deposit, you, your brother, me and my accountant will meet at a mutually agreed-upon location."

"It will never get past verification."

"If you believed that, we would not be here. Yet, here we are." Knox manages to keep an eye on the shadow caused by a man in hiding in the next arch. Unless Akram is wearing a wire, the two cannot possibly hear the conversation, yet have made no move despite Knox's roughing up Akram. It makes no sense, but Knox is not going to push his good fortune. He speaks quickly, "So let's talk transfer of the remaining funds."

"As to the funds, the primary investor," Akram says, as if he's pretending the person is not his blood relation, "never moves without security. Impossible."

"You have wasted my time. I will not forget this." Knox heads for the archway.

"Twenty-four hours," Akram calls out, stopping him. "I must have this name of your financial analyst. I will have him checked out."

"It's a her. Grace Chu. Chinese national. Residence, Hong Kong."

"If I cannot confirm her—"

"You can, and you will." Knox crosses through the darkness of the arched tunnel to Itfaiye. He moves fast, taking the first of the routes he planned. The alley between two cafés is narrow enough to touch the walls by reaching out to both sides. He runs, pauses, reaches the end where a courtyard frames a trio of apartment houses. Cuts sharply to his left. Back to the wall. Pauses.

The whining in his right ear has reached a fever pitch. Why now?

The footfalls of a person running cough from the mouth of the alley. It's how Knox would have done it: one on Akram; one on the meet, Knox. It's the reason for him having positioned himself where he stands. He doesn't want a confrontation, just the knowledge of what he's up against. He remains in shadow as much as possible as he moves away from the alley and across the cobblestone courtyard. There's a street entrance that's too logical a choice; Knox doesn't take it. Instead, he crouches alongside a foul-smelling plastic trash bin wedged between it and moss-covered stone steps that rise to a red door. It's not looking good. In the realm of fight or flight, Knox never gives the options much thought. He's wired a certain way. *So sue me.*

The man pursuing him is no longer running; he's standing still. He's onto Knox's ruse.

The problem for Knox is that the guy knows his stuff. As did the Iranians who snatched Grace. As did the agent in the sandstorm in Amman. Knox can understand the Iranians keeping a short leash on Mashe's brother. Taken together, the radiation-sensing ring Victoria discovered and Mashe's PhD in nuclear physics explain why Mashe comes so well protected. Grace's Iranian abductors wanted to determine who was attempting a background check on their nuclear expert. The Israelis have secretly assassinated a handful of such assets; in response, the Iranians are guarding Mashe "Okle" Melemet closely.

Yes, Knox can paste this much together. But who would be tailing Akram?

Mashe's Iranian guards make the most sense: shadow the brother to ensure he stays in line. Follow the people he meets in dark ruins late at night to determine what Akram—the vulnerable brother—is up to.

The bin crushes in from Knox's left, surprising him and disrupting his swarm of thoughts. The force of the impact drives Knox into the stone of the building's foundation. He brings his arm up as a shield. The bin slams into him a second time; then it's kicked aside and a knife tip is placed just behind and beneath Knox's left ear, in soft tissue where a gentle push will drive the blade into his brain and kill him instantly. Silently. It's a brutally fast and agile move, one Knox did not see coming.

Knox cooperates, led by the pressure of the knife tip. He rolls onto his face, but not before catching a glimpse of stitches and a butterfly bandage on the man's ear. It's a wound Knox recalls inflicting.

His right arm wrenched high and painfully up his back, Knox is making out with trash scum and soggy cigarette butts. He's frisked hurriedly, everything coming out of the jacket's obvious pockets like confetti. But with its many zippered compartments, the Scottevest is tricky even for the owner-operator. This guy finds only four.

The blade draws blood on Knox's neck. Knox's senses heighten. He picks up a trace of cedar over the foul trash, a smell like that of his family's linen closet. But it's sweeter, slightly medicinal. Worse: he knows that smell. It's stored somewhere within him.

His wallet is liberated from his front pants pocket courtesy of an extremely quick draw of a straight razor. The leather slaps to the ground as the wallet is then discarded. Hurried footfalls echo through the courtyard. It has been made to look like a mugging—it is anything but.

Knox counts to five before moving.

Sits. Stands. Checks the neck: a nick. The thigh is worse—the straight razor got a piece of him. Grabs his wallet. Not a single piece of paper inside. His credit cards are gone, but it's not a big deal. He has two more in the room. His driver's license and insurance card are in the muck. No paper. Knox moves, maintains pressure on the thigh. Walks without a limp. He's well practiced.

The few blocks to the Alzer is not the problem. It's the woman behind the registration desk he doesn't want to deal with. His left thigh will face her. He buys a Turkish newspaper from a street vendor hoping the hotel receptionist won't take note of the language. Uses it as a compress and to hide the wound. Tries to keep her eyes off the bloodied hand holding the newspaper in place by saying, "Beautiful evening!" as he passes.

She looks up smiling, but her expression decays as she takes him in.

He understands her response better once he's inside the small elevator with its smoky mirrors and a framed advertisement for the Alzer's all-included breakfast. The left side of his face is smeared with disgusting, shit-brown slime. A cigarette butt is adhered to the sludge. In his eagerness to hide the gash in his thigh, he neglected to clean up his leaking, bloody neck.

Before triggering a floor number, he pauses to electronically open the elevator car doors.

She's behind the front desk, still staring in his direction, just as he suspected.

"I was mugged. You understand? My money."

"The police! A doctor!"

"Will only make it a very long night for me. These things happen."

"Not to our guests!" She's distraught.

"To this guest, yes. But we both know the police can do nothing. A statistic. You understand statistic?"

She nods. "Of course."

A guest enters through the main entrance. Knox backs away to keep from showing himself. Hits his floor number and the car is his. He rides it interminably. Doesn't want to bother Grace. May need some stitches, but can make do with Super Glue. He carries a small tube in the Scottevest. Hopes he got through to the receptionist.

Thirty minutes later, a complimentary cheese and fruit plate and a bottle of red wine are delivered to his room. The knock awakens Grace.

She switches on the bedside light, catching sight of Knox in his underwear waiting for the Super Glue to fully dry in his wound. Shakes her head at him like a disapproving mother, apparently not the least bit surprised to see a five-inch slice in his thigh.

"I'll get it," she says.

Knox is the one to get it, once she places the tray on the corner of the bed and addresses him. Oddly, of the two of them, she looks worse for wear, the shadows from the only lamp uncomplimentary, the fatigue weighing on her puffy eyes and downturned lips. It's psychological versus physical, and the results are no contest. She's had the confidence scared out of her; it sits, spilled limply at her feet like the stuffing from a plush bear. He's lost a little blood and no resolve.

"You could have woken me," she says. "That will scar."

"A souvenir," Knox says.

"If I had applied the glue while you pinched it shut . . ."

"Bad timing. But I appreciate the offer."

"I am not as fragile as you think." Grace's expression belies her words. "Leave the girl sleeping? We are partners."

"Aren't you going to ask?"

"It was not random violence. I know this much."

"Yet, it was meant to look that way. I was mugged for my cash. He left my cell."

"You, mugged?"

"I miscalculated."

"I do not believe it. How many?"

"One."

She scoffs.

"With a very sharp knife and the element of surprise." He tries to make light of it, but the truth is difficult to face. One. He got taken out by one man. Knox is well aware of the professional athletes and military men who lose a step and stay on or in the field too long. Can he be one of them? His stomach turns. In the web of disgust with himself he doesn't feel his wounds.

"Please. You do take me for a child." She's pulling out of her haze, resurfacing. It's nice to see her.

She sits down on the bed and bites a slice of cheese. Chews thoughtfully.

"Who was he?" she asks.

"One of two men watching Akram. The one who was sitting on the bench awaiting the FedEx." He explains the earlier struggle and Knox tearing the man's ear half off.

Her eyes battle to focus on him through the swelling. This news brings matters into her realm. Knox's mention of the name and, by extension, a meet jolts her.

"He searched me. Took all the paper out of my pockets. Grabbed my cash as cover." He waits a beat and adds, "An Israeli."

She gasps, chokes on her piece of cheese. "You cannot possibly—"

"Took me a few minutes to place his deodorant. Smells like

cedar. There was this guy in Kuwait. A member of our team. Same stinking stuff. Something Rosenbloum—the brand, I mean. A designer's name. Red top in a spray can. I borrowed it a couple times. Distinctive. Besides, he had good teeth."

"You are toying with me."

Knox says, "Israeli."

"He took only paperwork? Receipts?" She's like a dentist, probing.

"Sarge warned me. Listen," he braves the topic he's been avoiding, "he doesn't appreciate our background work."

Her back straightens, brow creases. Incredulity.

"Your background work," he continues. "You apparently misunderstood him. The Need To Know was for both of us. He kind of flipped out." He feels badly for her, can see the hurt he's causing. But he thinks he can reverse the effects. "If it's any consolation, I don't think he knew half of what I did. He seemed surprised, informed, but cautiously appreciative. It's like he knew we might be under surveillance, but not from whom. The Iranians grabbing you troubled him, but it was the mention of the Israelis that scored points."

"He was angry?" Girlish.

"More surprised."

She takes a moment. "Not your phone. This mugger. He did not take your phone." She wants to stick to the business at hand. Expressing emotion does not come easily to Grace. In this way, they aren't so different. But the news of Dulwich's discontent has shattered her and her lofty ambition she tries so hard to keep hidden.

Knox plays along, but feels the pit of his stomach. "He's followed Akram, not me. I promise you. He took me on only after the meet. I assume the other guy stayed with Akram. My guy searched me, wanting it to look like a mugging."

"But left your phone," she says.

"That's explainable. Phones can be tracked."

"You could be wrong about him being Israeli," she says.

"I could, but I'm not. The Israelis are watching Mashe. That includes keeping track of his younger brother and any late-night contacts said brother makes. Mashe works for Iran. The pieces fit: he's going to be terminated, whether Sarge knows it or not." He speaks what he's only dared think: that Dulwich has screwed up mightily.

"Speculation."

"It's what the Israelis do to Iranian nuclear scientists, Grace. They stake out restaurants in Amman; they follow the brother; they terminate the Einstein."

"You let him get close. You took this risk to study him." She is definite and irate.

"It happened fast. It wasn't exactly like that, though I appreciate your concern." He's practiced at silencing her: imply an emotional component, and the professional in her shuts it down. The unspoken truth is that their relationship is important to her. Its crumbling walls must terrify her. Such walls can seldom be rebuilt.

He says. "The deposit's in escrow."

"You are changing the subject." She eyes the wine bottle.

"I can have vodka sent up."

"Coffee," she says, but only after an internal battle. "What do we tell David about the Israelis, John? What does it mean to you? Go? No-go?"

"Leaving my ID behind was a mistake," Knox says.

"Time plays into such things," she says, trying to figure out his mugger. "He drops them. It is dark."

"You're missing the point of view. This guy saw me meet Akram. He empties my pockets and keeps every last piece of paper, but leaves my license. An accident? The Israelis? Come on."

Grace says, "They believe the brother, Akram, to be a courier or cutout. They think he passes you something. They want to know what."

"It's hard to see it as anything else. But leaving my phone while taking every scrap of paper? That's its own message."

"Yes. That whatever is being passed is being done physically, not electronically."

"Bingo. You know bingo?" he asks. He irritates her.

"A note given to Akram by Mashe and intended for . . . for whom?"

"Someone watched by governments. Someone you can't reach electronically without it being intercepted and putting everyone in danger. Old-school stuff."

"They believe you are also a courier," she says. "But if so highly sensitive, why not a true cutout? Why not a legitimate dead drop where the cutout picks up a message from one hiding place and delivers it to another? You catch the cutout, and there is no way to connect the message to anyone. If the Israelis are watching Akram, they are not here to kill Mashe, but to find out whatever information Mashe is using Akram to pass."

"Or to identify who's buying the intel." Knox feels his wound, tries not to wince. "This guy risked a lot, searching me the way he did."

"Is he the client? The Israelis hire Rutherford Risk because you have a relationship with Akram. They are watching him. They need to see what Akram is couriering for his brother, so they need your connection to the man. This is why David can attempt to promise no one is to be killed."

"It fits," Knox says.

Grace meets his eyes and inhales sharply. "A note being passed from an Iranian nuclear physicist." She pauses. "I wonder also: intended for whom?"

"Plenty of buyers. Could be plans, going to the North Koreans. A shopping list of embargoed parts. Hell, it could also be medicines needed for the mother," Knox says. "The question is: how much does Akram know?"

It comes out of his mouth bitterly, leaving behind a taste that won't leave his tongue.

33

Knox nears a boiling point five hours later when Dulwich has yet to return his messages.

"It's like one of those fad restaurants where you eat in the dark," he tells Grace bitterly. "We're being served warm dog shit when we ordered the pork sausage."

"Let us hope David was not 'mugged' as you were."

Thanks to nearly uninterrupted work by Grace, Mashe Okle's finances are tied up with a neat little bow. He has some explaining to do about his sources, and this will require Grace to be part of the meeting, as Dulwich intended. Grace feels as proud as a schoolgirl. She's drinking coffee on top of coffee.

"We can present this any time you want," she says. "I am prepared."

"I'm nearly there, too." Knox is dancing with the devil. He claims he has involved this woman, Victoria, because she has contacts in Istanbul that offer him a "remarkable opportunity." Grace detests the idea, but concedes its necessity. Work with the resources you're given. He's been texting Victoria, although she is just down the hall. The entire arrangement feels wrong to Grace.

"You trust them so little," she says.

"The Harmodius is worth millions, Grace. That's a number, something you know intimately. If we hand it over so they can test its authenticity, you and I are the only things keeping them from walking off with it. I'm being the good Samaritan: I'm leading them away from temptation. The problem is, I haven't accounted for the Israelis."

"If that is who they were."

"Oh, ye of little faith. He was wearing Red Top. Trust me: Israeli. It adds an element of the unknown. Poses a big risk to what's already a risk."

"You know I do not mean their nationality, but their role. These men could be private, like us. They could represent the same client as us. More likely, they are art thieves who mugged you hoping to lift a storage receipt or business card that will lead them to the Harmodius. It doesn't take a nuclear scientist to realize you succeeded in smuggling the piece into Turkey. Perhaps they are part of a global team that intercepts stolen art."

"So why are they tracking a particular FedEx shipment?"

"We do not know it is the same people."

"Nawriz Melemet, aka Mashe Okle, has attracted more flies than shit," says Knox.

"If these ancillary people believe you are being used as a courier or cutout, then it follows that someone is set to receive information from Mashe Okle." Grace feels opportunity returning in her favor. She recognizes her condition as related to that of an addicted gambler—the more one loses, the more all-in. With a little more effort, she can deliver the kind of actionable intel Dulwich needs. He will forgive all if she can pull it together. It's loose ends he abhors. There is no choice but to pursue the intel. And Knox proves the perfect sounding board: the more she counters his theories, the more he puts forward, giving her all the more angles to pursue.

She feels awkward manipulating John in this way, playing games within games. But she has hurt herself with Dulwich and needs to make it right. Knox would be the first to do the same.

"At the minimum," she says, "we are dealing with two separate interests: the Iranians and these others—possibly Israelis—who mugged you. The Iranians want to protect the asset, Mashe Okle. The Israeli objective remains uncertain. We must not discount the possibility of a third party: the end recipient of whatever information the Israelis believe you were carrying."

Grace presents the information clinically. Knox is more seat-of-the-pants field op than strategist, but he's often a full step ahead of everyone else. She can feel it now: he hasn't put the mugging behind him. They have not discussed the fact that Akram may indeed have slipped a note onto Knox without Knox's knowledge. That Dulwich may have put Knox in Istanbul with an ulterior motive—a motive like the drop—in mind.

"Mashe is a nuclear physicist—" Knox says.

"What little evidence we have supports this."

"—who works for Iran. A government under severe sanctions."

She inhales sharply. "A shopping list!"

"—can't be sent electronically."

"Too easily intercepted," Grace continues, enjoying the repartee. "The Iranian government assigns one of its scientists, a man who travels to see his ill mother, the role of mule. A dead drop. A double blind. Something to protect your scientist but make sure the list reaches the supplier."

"And if you are the Israelis and you can intercept Mashe's parts list, you have a better idea how far the Iranian nuclear program has progressed. Invaluable."

"It is well beyond the charter of Rutherford Risk," Grace says.

"Aiding a governmental agency? If caught, Mr. Primer would face his company being shut down. No such intercept would be contracted out to the private sector. Besides, the Israelis are better at such intercepts than anyone."

"Which brings us back to Sarge and his client."

"I tell you: Mr. Primer would not accept the job."

"Your argument is also an explanation," Knox says, testing her. Does he dare go there? It's like telling the star pupil the teacher cheated in college. When she pauses, he fills in the gap. "Who says Primer knows anything about it? Have you had contact with him? Any contact at all?"

Grace's eyes go wide, then vacant.

Knox continues. "Sarge told me I couldn't contact Digital Services directly. Had to go through you. Since when?"

She whispers now. "I have been wondering this myself."

"No one will get killed, he told me. Implied we were saving the world."

"However," Grace adds, "the pretext of the sale—the Harmodius—the requirement that we are physically with the mark for no less than five minutes . . . these do not so easily add up if the goal is to intercept a dead drop."

Knox counters. "The art sale is to get me in a room with Mashe. At some point during those five minutes, the shopping list is supposed to be put on me without my knowledge. I walk out of there an unknowing cutout. We would never have considered anything like this if I hadn't been mugged. Israeli agents—Mossad?—were never part of the Iranian plans. Without meaning to, the Israelis have tipped us off. By jumping the gun, they've told us that they have no idea when the exchange is scheduled."

"But, John, David would not . . . How can we even think such a thing?" Grace sounds unconvinced. "Crap," she says. It's as close to cussing as she usually gets. As close to acceptance as well.

"If he's rogue, then by association we're part of it," Knox says, thinking aloud.

"We lack sufficient evidence."

"We have plenty of circumstantial evidence. And consider this: if we run, they follow. This isn't Boy Scouts. You don't get a pass. Neither of us want to say it, but I think Sarge got taken. He rose to the bait and bit and now it's us—you and me—with the hooks in good and tight."

"Just because the column adds up to a particular sum, it does not mean the original values were accurate. One misplaced decimal—"

"I was more of a wood shop guy," Knox confesses. "Gym. Cafeteria. Not exactly AP math."

"What I am saying—" She wears panic awkwardly; it doesn't suit her. Grace Chu is a team player; the idea of being separated from the collective appears to nauseate her.

"I get it," Knox says. It can be cute when his joking goes over her head, but it's frustrating as well. She doesn't want to face what he's suggesting, knows that once it's inside, the rat can't turn around in the maze.

The hotel room has become claustrophobic. Victoria texts him to say that she's made the arrangements for Adjani to assay the Harmodius. Knox stares at the message for a long time, wondering where to put his trust. He's uneasy and twitchy. A response to caffeine or the right impulse? It comes down to whom he trusts more: Akram Okle, or Victoria?

He presents his plan to Grace, trying to read her face.

"The mind cannot be in two places at once," she says, quoting a proverb.

"We need a fourth," Knox says. "Without Sarge—"

"Besim," Grace says, drawing a blank look from Knox. "My driver."

"Who must be wondering where you are."

"He can watch your Victoria for us. He has helped me in this way. David need not know."

"Your driver could be working for Sarge."

She shakes her head. "No. I hired him. David did not want any connective tissue tying him—" She can't finish the sentence.

Knox compliments her on her solution. Her lips purse to contain a smile. She appreciates being appreciated; it is a card he can play when needed, though it slipped out this time of its own accord.

"I will call Besim. You call Akram," she says. "It is not the cry, but the flight of the wild duck that leads the flock to fly and follow."

"We say, 'actions speak louder than words.'"

"And we Chinese say, 'Man who runs in front of car gets tired; man who runs behind car gets exhausted.'"

He thinks she's trying for a joke. Reconsiders. "We need to stay ahead on this," he proposes.

"Just so," Grace says.

Knox holds up his phone as a signal for both of them to make their calls. It feels more like jumping off a cliff than joining a path.

IN THE DARK, the narrow, twisting streets make Knox claustrophobic. The hills of Istanbul have enough dead-end streets to get a man killed.

Knox keeps his phone's map app on. The tiny blue dot representing him inches along, providing some solace. Grace sits beside him in the back of the cab, their shoulders warm where they touch. She's quietly meditative, perhaps rehearsing her role. Hers is a planned and practiced life, organized and prepared. He has no idea what that feels like.

The location and timing of the meet have been dictated by Akram for the second time. The first didn't go so well.

"I felt better near the aqueduct," Knox says after the car engine strains for several minutes to climb, the power steering crying with each turn to the left. "More public, more touristy part of town."

"I understand." It's all Grace says.

Knox takes it as her signal that she has no interest in conversation. The talking is behind them. He suspects she, like him, is leery of a trap; she, like him, understands the op has passed a point where they can abort; she, like him, doesn't appreciate the feeling of being a puppet instead of a player. He can't help himself; his mouth has a mind of its own.

"Nice view," he says, turning around.

She does not look, does not speak.

A patchwork of yellow light filling the apartment windows they pass reminds Knox of a nativity calendar. He thinks of Tommy and feels guilt over his failure to stay in touch while on the job. He sees men smoking inside tight rooms; families gathered; television light pulsing. He's never lived like that in his adult life. He wonders now if he could hack it. Dulwich is responsible for getting him re-addicted to adrenaline after Knox's successful withdrawal following their contract work in Kuwait.

Would Dulwich willingly sacrifice him and Grace for some wish list of maintenance parts, for the chance to gain intelligence about Iranian nuclear capabilities? Would he see the lives of two colleagues, two friends, as a necessary sacrifice in the bigger picture of Middle Eastern stability? Would he convince himself that despite the risks, Knox can and will prevail, that the danger is worth the reward?

"I'm not liking this," Knox says, again breaking the silence.

"Act in the valley so you need not fear those who stand on the hill." She speaks Mandarin, allowing Knox to appreciate the nuance of the proverb.

"Did I miss something, or are we as prepared as can be expected?"

"We shall find out," Grace says with more dread and apprehension than confidence.

"On convoy, when I felt like this, I ordered us to turn around. Or at least stop."

"The choice is yours." She isn't going to stop him. He can smell her fear.

"We're going to be all right."

"Is that for me, or are you thinking with your mouth?"

On the phone, the slow-moving blue dot arrives at the red destination pin.

"Shit," Knox says.

The location is a quaint tea shop, the sweet smells of chai and tobacco burnished into the nut-colored walls. In a city of Greek, Roman and Ottoman influence, it feels strangely and warmly British. Akram waits at the far end in front of a waterfall of beads that obscures a doorway to a private room that holds floor pillows and a large round table. The table is scarred with cigarette burns around its edge and stained interiorly by a thousand overlapping circles left by wet mugs.

Akram is genial and relaxed. His shirt is white linen under a forest green vest of hand-tied knots, paired with black trousers. His mustache is bold, his cheeks covered in five o'clock shadow, his hair cropped. His bloodshot eyes contradict his congenial smile; he's uncomfortable, exhausted and uptight.

"I did not expect two guests," he says, sitting across the large table from them. "Especially one so lovely as you, Miss Grace."

"You honor me," Grace says, demurely.

Akram's eyes inform Knox that Grace's presence is not appreciated.

"You can understand, my friend," Knox begins, "that in a deal with a sum so high as this, all precaution and due diligence must be conducted. I must ensure that there are no surprises."

Akram nods. "So," he says, palms down on the table. "Tea?"

His eyes flick toward the door, no doubt anticipating the fact that Knox has brought the Harmodius with him to be assayed, its authenticity confirmed. He has another think coming.

An aproned man waits on the other side of the beaded doorway. Grace orders green chai; Knox, Assam with milk and sugar. They wait until the server is out of earshot.

"As Mr. Knox's accountant," Grace begins confidently, "you can understand the need to determine the source of funding for a transaction such as this. It was imperative not only that a deposit be placed in escrow, as you have so kindly done, but that the source of the funding also be confirmed. A drop of water does not make a well."

Akram's distrustful eyes dart between Grace and the silent Knox.

"Furthermore," Grace continues, "due to the sensitivity of such an exclusive exchange, both the source and the depth of the well comes under consideration."

"I assure you, the funds are there."

"Yes. And I can only hope you do not take this the wrong way, but again the source of those underlying assets is of keen interest to me and my client. In order to protect my client from possible malfeasance, a sting arranged by law enforcement, you understand."

"I do not appreciate the implication, Miss Grace." Again, his basalt eyes flash at Knox. "Since when—?"

She interrupts calmly. "A piece such as this . . . Authorities would go to great lengths to acquire it. Great lengths, indeed. No man, no country, for that matter, would be able to prevent such an operation. I am not accusing you of anything. I am merely paid to take precautions, so precautions I take."

Akram's nostrils flare. He's ready to get off the pillow and choke her.

"Which is why I took the liberty . . ." Grace reaches into a portfolio and slides a spreadsheet across to Akram.

The proprietor returns with the iron teapots and black iron demitasse cups, placing everything on the table just so, aiming the spouts and handles away. He genuflects and backs off through the beads. Pomp and circumstance. Akram must have tipped well for this room and for his privacy.

Akram's dark complexion and day's growth cannot conceal the color that invades his cheeks. Grace recites from memory the amounts and dates of the cash of which he has taken delivery, the banks that facilitated those deliveries. In some cases, a matching wire transfer to the bank has been highlighted. Akram's withering expression denotes his astonishment that she has obtained such information.

"I will not put my client in harm's way, Mr. Okle. The majority of the escrow's funding is through wire and cash conversions originating in Iran."

"Inaccurate!" Akram's adamancy is matched by the darkening of his complexion. Knox deduces it must have been his job to wash the wire transfers and make the deposits.

Grace calmly slides several pieces of paper across. "You'll notice the various withdrawals, ATM transactions and how the sums match with the resulting deposits and payments."

His eyes track and he goes pale. He's a chameleon reacting to his background. Pale, like the color of paper.

Grace keeps him off balance. "You are aware that the United Nations Office on Drugs and Crime has placed into motion what it calls 'an innovative initiative to support the Islamic Republic of Iran' in protecting its cultural heritage and combating trafficking in cultural property?"

Her steadiness and resolute determination to win the information from Akram is apparent in Grace's steady voice and controlled motions. She is a professional driver so accustomed to high speed that she can take her eye off the track to calm her passenger.

"It is a matter of procedure, nothing more. Mr. Knox has assured me he does not doubt the intention behind the exchange, but alas, I cannot take such luxuries."

Alas. Knox must suppress a grin. Where does she come up with this stuff? Knox strains and pours his tea, adds sugar and milk, and then a bit more sugar. Stirs. An elixir of the gods. But Akram has not touched his. Grace is ahead of both men.

"The Iranian funds originate from the investment accounts of one Mashe Okle, your brother. These accounts received recent deposits. I am unable to verify the origin of all deposits. For this reason, I must speak to Mashe Okle and be provided records of these transactions."

"Impossible. Absurd!"

"It is no problem—your being a proxy. The way of business, of course. But either I meet the buyer and vet his funds, or there is no sale. I will not have my client spending the rest of his days in a Turkish prison. How will I collect my retainer?"

She smirks. *She should copyright that half-grin,* Knox thinks. Trademark it. As subtle as the Mona Lisa.

"What prison? What the fuck?" Akram addresses Knox. "We have done business before."

"Not on this scale, we haven't," Knox replies stonily.

"Out of the question."

"So be it," Knox says, playing the only card left.

"If you should change your mind." Grace passes a business card across the table, steering it with a painted nail.

Akram is nonplussed. For a moment, he hesitates, expecting Knox to raise the price to accommodate the risk involved. When it grows apparent that the two have every intention of leaving—never an easy thing to determine—Akram is up and following.

"What do you expect?" He sounds desperate. "It is unreasonable."

Grace spins. Akram stops short. "It is the very definition of reason, Mr. Okle," she says sotto voce. "Nothing more." Now, so quietly it sounds more like a sigh, "There is no shortage of buyers, I assure you. Each with its own uncertainties and possible consequences. Mr. . . . my client," she says, judging the space around her, "favored you because of your personal history and your industry."

Knox says, "I'm sorry, Akram."

The man's feet are cemented to the wood floor. He has no choice but to interpret this as gamesmanship. A ploy. A day will pass. Two. Knox will be back, for certain.

"Out of the question!" Akram repeats loudly.

Knox tips the proprietor, asks him to call them a cab. He and Grace wait on the sidewalk, not a word spoken between them.

"Nine o'clock," Grace says without looking at Knox. She isn't referring to the time.

"Yes." Knox is impressed she picked up on a man who has been surveilling the meet. A wink from the rooftop of a building up the hill. Grace continues to surprise him.

The taxi arrives, finally. Knox provides a destination he will change in a minute, but his true motive is to compare the face of the driver against that of the face on the driver's ID and to evaluate the ID itself, making sure it does not look as if it's been printed in the past ten minutes. It passes muster. Ali is their driver. Knox and Grace climb in.

Grace has a compact out and is about to touch up her lips when she says, "Damn!" and pulls Knox forward with her as she lurches into a crouch, bending from the waist.

Knox feels heat on the back of his head. It coincides with the *thwap* of what turns out to be a hole in the taxi's rear window. For Knox, it's the bee sting on his skull, the warmth on his neck and the dizziness that wins his attention. The dizziness turns out to be external, not internal. The taxi, aimed downhill, careens off a parked car and ricochets to the opposite side of the street, gaining speed all the while.

It's only as Knox notices the bullet hole through the Plexiglas barrier and another hole in the driver's headrest that the red spray across the dash makes sense. This, because the bridge and right nostril of the driver's nose is lying across the defroster vent. Ali is slumped against the wheel, his body shifting as the car jerks with each new collision. It's a pinball ride. As if gravity isn't enough to contend with, Ali's dead right foot is leaden against the accelerator.

Knox has it in an instant: Grace saved his life by yanking him down with her; a bullet grazed his scalp and took out the driver; the taxi is heading downhill at an ever-increasing pace, checked only by repeated collisions with other cars parked on opposite sides of the narrow street; Grace is white-knuckled, still hunched over. Each time Knox is about to clear his head, the car crashes again. Neither he nor Grace are seat-belted, and the Plexiglas barrier meant to secure the driver from his passengers proves effective. Knox tries to force his hand into the swiveling pass-through intended for payments. No way.

"Shit," he says.

Heads are bleeders. His inch-long gash has soaked his hair and spread rivulets of red down his face and neck. Grace gets a fleeting look at him in the strobe light from the streetlamps, and her training fails her. She screams.

Knox pounds on the barrier. The taxi is tearing down the hill at breakneck speed. Their necks. Their breaks. It flies through an intersection. The front wheels get air and Knox's raw scalp impacts against the ceiling. He swears, loudly.

Grace screams again. She reverses herself, turning so her back is to the floor. She kicks out at the rear window. The safety glass cracks and cubes with each hit but does not yield. Knox tries the same on the Plexiglas barrier, with the same results.

He's braced for one of the collisions to stop the taxi cold and smash them both into the barrier, but it's as if the vehicle's on a track at an amusement park ride. The collisions propel it forward in a rain of metal, which pries loose with a shrieking cry amid the clash of broken glass.

The taxi bumps into a second intersection. A severe collision spins it like a top; they've been hit by another car. Grace is thrown into Knox; the two are pressed into the rear door—which pops open. Knox grabs for the unused seat belt and it plays out from its geared mechanism. He falls out of the car, Grace atop him, caught at last as the belt's speed triggers it to latch. He's a crewman for the America's Cup, hiking out over the leeward hull. The taxi's spinning slows almost gracefully. It skids to the precipice of the continuing hill, teetering there. Seconds before it stops completely, before Knox's blurred vision can make sense of what the hell's happening, the taxi dips over the edge and picks up speed.

Backward.

"Fuck!"

Knox rocks forward, carrying Grace with him, driving them both into the backseat as the vehicle's rear door collides and bends against the frame.

Crying out at a fever pitch, she pulls away from him and returns to kicking at the rear window, this time with twice the power of her initial attempt.

Knox feeds off the adrenaline, his mind clearing quickly. Her efforts are admirable, but it won't do them any good to climb out of what is now the front of the moving vehicle. The taxi crashes left, right, left in quick succession. The hill is steeper on this stretch, and though the front-wheel drive is still active and sending out plumes of burning rubber, and Ali's body has shifted and his weight is off the accelerator, it's not enough to counter gravity—they are once again gaining speed in their descent.

Knox reaches out and pulls mightily against the snapped door. He's making progress when Grace grabs his shoulder: the taxi sideswipes a parked car, a collision that would have pancaked him. It removes the door completely.

Survival is about timing now. Knox's bloodied head is on a swivel. The back window is so destroyed he can't see out of it. He has to judge the taxi's erratic movement from one side of the street to the other.

"You are not!" Grace hollers, seeing his intention in his eyes.

"I am," he says, making his move. He lurches out the open cavity, grabs the driver's door handle, and pulls. The awkward angle allows it to open only inches. He dives back in with Grace as she shouts words he can't make out. The taxi smashes into another parked car, accordioning the driver's door. The jolt destabilizes Knox, but he kicks out and opens the crippled door; taking a two-handed hold on the frame, he swings out and around and feetfirst into the driver's area, kicking Ali's corpse over. The driver is seat-belted, so the face-less body only leans away.

Knox throws himself into Ali's lap, digs down between the dead man's arm and rib cage, and sets the emergency brake. The taxi skids to a stop.

For a moment: silence, intermingled with the mechanical sounds of the car settling and Knox's heavy breathing. For a moment he expects the vehicle to come to life again, like Stephen King's Christine. For a moment, his and Grace's defense mechanisms are held in stasis as they inventory their injuries, seek to determine major from minor, life-threatening from unimportant.

"I'm good," Knox announces, looking like death warmed over.

Grace slaps the barrier and nods, her eyes like those of a scared horse.

Knox backs out and off the driver, having picked up some of the man's blood to add to his own wounds. He's testing his legs and joints as he stands. His wounded thigh hinders him. Grace slides out.

Curious bystanders emerge from the doorways of the four-story apartment buildings on either side of the hill. Knox is less worried about his face being remembered than he is about being surrounded and contained. Crowds form fast in Istanbul. Thick crowds. Deep crowds. He and Grace can ill afford questioning by the police.

He reaches for her hand. Grace places hers in his sticky palm; for a brief moment, she can't take her eyes off the blood. They're in shock, but Knox has been here more often than she and so he navigates his way to the sidewalk and starts them off downhill.

At the first intersection, he turns them right. Several daring males follow, a matter of yards behind. Knox can't find the translation. "What's Turkish for 'back' and 'off'?"

Grace looks up at him, too disoriented to reply.

Knox releases her hand, spins around and shouts a growl at their followers that so surprises Grace her knees give out.

The men turn and run.

Knox supports her by the elbow, dragging her with him. His mind is beginning to return: he needs to clean up before they go much further. The wound will have to wait, but he's losing blood, so at the least, compression is urgent. Grace needs a strong drink and a toilet. Transportation. A new location. Time to think.

Something about the way she looks at him; he knows exactly what she's thinking.

"No," he moans.

She nods. "He's our only chance."

"I don't trust him."

Sirens punctuate the night.

"Very well."

Ever the geek, Grace snaps a screen shot of the phone's map app that shows the blue dot representing their GPS location on the streets of Istanbul. She texts the image along with what could easily be mistaken for a failed attempt at a social media hashtag but is something else altogether, something worked out days ago.

#+#

KNOX ASSUMES there will be an attempt made to confirm the kill. When only poor Ali is found in the vehicle, the shooter will try to complete the assignment. Given the distance the taxi traveled down the hill and depending on whether or not the shooter is on foot, they have anywhere from a few minutes' head start to ten or more. But Grace is in no condition to outrun an executioner, and Knox cannot find a single spot on his body that is not throbbing with pain or bleeding.

The sirens draw closer.

"Damn."

She tells him, "We need to get you cleaned up if we are to have any chance of running under the radar."

Her use of the expression "under the radar" amuses him. It's a non sequitur coming from her mouth. He cracks a smile and winces.

Grace works her phone. "There is a *hamam* three blocks"—she looks in both directions to determine their orientation—"this way." She points to the right. East, away from the wrecked taxi.

"No thanks. No appetite," he says.

"Turkish bath," she tells him. "Neighborhood bath." She adds, "It could have been a solo back there, or there could be a dozen of them after us."

Knox hadn't considered a team effort. He nods. They help each other along, arms locked, both hobbled. Sitting ducks if they stay out on the streets.

The Turkish bath dates back to the fifteenth century, when a lack of running water in homes inspired public works. The numbers of such baths mushroomed in the eighteenth century and then dwindled again; only twenty survive. Some served other functions in the interim, like cheese storage, until the tourist industry discovered them. Grace describes this one well as a neighborhood bath, more a spa for affluent Turks in the hills above downtown. It's one of the few segregated spas, offering a man's and a woman's side, though men attend the women.

"I hit my head," Knox tells the attendant, a surly man who gives him a curious look.

Grace translates, adding that her friend found himself in a romantic tangle with a woman belonging to a powerful man. She's trying to cover in case their pursuers should inquire. The Turks are romantics at heart. She nudges Knox, causing him to wince.

"Tip," she whispers hotly. "Big tip!"

Knox puts out a hundred dollars on top of the seventy for the bath.

"We do not wish any trouble," Grace says.

The man smiles, displaying two gold teeth. "Nor shall you have any," he says in English. "No blood in baths." He points to a sign: NO BODILY FLUIDS is listed as one of twelve bathhouse rules. "You need help, my friend," he tells Knox, pointing to his own head.

"Tape," Knox says.

"Takes more than tape."

"For now," Knox says, testing. "She will help me." He has the Super Glue in the Scottevest.

"Scissors," Grace says. "A razor?" She pushes the hundred dollars closer to the attendant. "We can help you."

The entrance opens into the *camekan* and a number of changing stations. Fountains. They are given *peştemâls*, checkered cloths they are told to wear. Knox keeps the Scottevest with him, which draws the receptionist's attention as the man shows them into the women's restroom, dragging an orange traffic cone to ensure their privacy.

Wearing the *peştemâl* like a toga and carrying her phone, Grace clips, cleans and shaves the area around Knox's scalp wound. Cleans it again using hand sanitizer. The burn makes Knox curse. Cleaning it the second time is a mistake; the partial clot comes free and it's bleeding again, badly. Grace glues it, tapes it and glues it again, but it's a mess by the time it stops bleeding, and there's a 4x2-inch strip of missing hair on the dome of Knox's head. He jokes about needing a comb-over, but she doesn't understand the reference.

Both are troubled by the fifteen minutes that have passed. If it's Turks after them, it won't take long to search the neighborhood. Grace has texted their new GPS icon. Their nerves, on top of their physical exhaustion, leaves them spent. Grace cleans up the small space.

"So?" she says.

"Into the baths," Knox says. "Women's is over there."

"Where we will be naked and defenseless should they find us."

"The steam room is first. The *hararet*. Hard to see in, which gives us the advantage. Be near the door to get the jump on them. Hopefully, it doesn't come to that. We'll each be led into the bath and the warm stone area, where we'll be scrubbed and cleaned before bathing. Tip your man before the rubdown."

"Man?"

"Most places, yes. Now focus. These places have to have exits, so there will be a way out. You hear a shout, that's me. I'll head east, toward the river. We both text him again. With any luck—"

"Agreed. The plan is a good one," Grace says, uncharacteristically complimentary.

Still, Knox can't relax. The steam soaks into his joints and removes some of the pain but his head wound is screaming, and the accompanying headache makes it nearly impossible to think.

He gets through the steam room without incident, though he's naked and a Westerner and this attracts envious attention from the other men. It's been this way since middle school, through the sports locker rooms of high school and dorm showers in college: John Rocks. Knox Johnson. Long John Knox. He's not sure why women don't appreciate being objectified, at least a little; for himself, he loves it. If he attempts to cover himself, it only draws more attention because it requires a two-handed effort, so he carries himself with an upright posture and lets them marvel. What the hell?

His attendant, a potbellied forty-something with so much hair it grows from his shoulders, draws closer and winces audibly at the ripe bruises covering Knox. Knox wishes he knew the word for "gently." But the man gets the point. He scrubs Knox tentatively, like he's bathing his own grandchild.

Thirty minutes have passed since they abandoned the taxi.

Knox's attendant looks up, as do several others surrounding the water, their clients prostrate on the hot stone. They're looking at the receptionist, who quickly crosses the room, moving toward Knox.

"Your woman asks meet her at desk. She waits for you."

Knox thanks him.

Five minutes later, Grace and Knox ride low in the backseat of a sedan driven by Besim. He drives conservatively. He's barely acknowledged them. Finally, he speaks Turkish into the rearview mirror.

"He says you need a hat," Grace translates. "He will stop and buy you one."

Knox thanks the man directly.

Fifteen minutes later, they briefly visit a teeming street market under sagging strings of lightbulbs that remind Knox of shopping for Christmas trees. Besim delivers the hat, falafel, dolmas and two sodas to the backseat.

Knox and Grace eat greedily.

"I need to return to the hotel," Knox says once they're moving again. He dons the trucker's cap Besim bought. It boasts the red flag of the crescent moon and single star with TURKEY stenciled in all caps beneath. It looks stupid on him. "Then to the airport via a taxi arranged by the hotel. We stick to the plan."

"Impossible!" Grace spits small pieces of falafel onto the seat. "Too dangerous. A safe house. Some place Besim knows."

"There's a ritual to act out," Knox says. "I need to leave bread crumbs."

"A blood trail is more like it." She pauses. "It is the woman, is it not?"

"It is not," he says avoiding the contraction in order to mock her. "They must know the transaction is off. No sale. Without playing that card, we lose Akram, trust me."

"Whoever shot at us will be watching the hotel."

"Presumably. Which will give you and Besim something to occupy yourselves."

"You joke?"

"No. I'm serious. We stop and buy you a camera. Besim can find us one. We pass the photos to Hong Kong without getting Sarge involved. Run face recognition on them. It's time we fill in some of the blanks."

"The hit to your head was more serious than I believed," Grace says, scrunching down again to keep her profile out of the rear window.

"The item . . ." Knox says. "It's there as well. Arrangements must be made. I cannot leave the hotel with it. No one coming for it would have tried to kill me. So we know that much."

"The attempt was made because you were mistaken for the cut-out," Grace says. She doesn't miss much. "Insurance. Covering all bases, all possible meetings. Am I correct? They must make certain that if there is a list, it goes no further." When Knox says nothing, she continues. "So it was not the Iranians shooting at you because they wish the information to be passed, the exchange to be made."

"Doubtful, as they would want the list passed on to whoever it's intended for."

"The people who mugged you," she proposes.

"Likely. Or a third party who knows more than we know and wants to start preventing loose ends."

"They'll kill Akram," she speculates.

"I would," says Knox. "Not Mashe—he lays the golden egg. But the brother? Why not?"

"I do not like the way you talk, John."

"Maybe it was the same people who mugged me. By killing me, they force Akram to try again to pass the list. He might be safe for now."

"David would not betray us," she says. Her words hang in the car like a foul smell.

"I'm not going to say I told you so."

"Ha-ha." She adds, "Too many variables."

"For us and for them. Yes. Knowing the way the world works, no one knows shit about anything. That's when people start getting killed." He waits, bracing himself as Besim takes a sharp turn too fast. "The point being, we can only deal with what we know. Move forward while trying to limit casualties."

"So far, we have not done such a good job at that."

"We stick with the plan. If they let me leave, I leave. You, too."

"Just like that?" Grace is appalled.

"I'm open to suggestions." Again, he's mocking her. They don't know enough to do anything more than Dulwich planned for them. If they can't get the five minutes with Mashe, they head home. Sarge controls them even from a distance. Resentment burns through his body; Knox uses the last of the soda to combat the flames.

"Too dangerous," Grace complains. "Besides, I must search the Nightingale hospital. This package? The FedEx that was intercepted? The operation suggested agency involvement."

"It did, didn't it?"

"This now makes more sense. *Neh?* Fit into bigger picture. Need follow up."

"When you get angry, you speak like a Chinese girl learning the language," he says. He's insulted her. Honesty kills.

A minute elapses. Two. Shutting his eyes, Knox hears Grace talking with Besim. They're discussing cameras.

He grins, leans his head back and passes out.

KNOX RETURNS to the Alzer and its busy sidewalk café scene in the shadow of the mosque. Victoria sits at a café table alone, drinking a South African Chardonnay and smoking an American cigarette. She leaves the table and follows Knox as he passes, the silver cigarette smoke rising like an antenna into the festooned umbrella.

Wisely, she boards a separate elevator. Proceeds to her room. This is where he finds her.

"That's a stupid-looking hat," she says, securing the door behind him. No comment about his bruises and lacerations.

"I have a better one."

"Sit down beside me." She pats the edge of the bed.

"Can't stay. I'm heading to the airport, Victoria." He waits for her to collect and contain her emotions. She is remarkably in control, this one.

"It looks as if you are not terribly popular."

"Maybe too popular."

"Police?"

He shakes his head. "I promise you—I promise—that I am not taking the sculpture with me. It remains in safekeeping here in Istanbul. I am in no way attempting to distance myself." His eyes convey what she most wants to hear. He hides that he's using her to let Akram know he's serious about leaving the country. Hates such tricks, but they're his bread and butter. "It must be done. If I don't leave the country, and I'm hoping I won't have to, I'll text you." He pauses. "I'll text you either way, but if I do leave, I'm not returning. Can't."

"And the art?"

And so she shows her true colors.

"Will be retrieved by its owners."

"I thought you were the owner."

"You might call it more a consortium, and me, its front man."

"If you leave Istanbul, I'm out of the deal. How convenient." The bitterness with which she says this makes him worry she'll have him pulled aside at Immigration.

"It has become dangerous." He takes a risk by revealing the lump of gauze beneath his cap.

She emits a sharp, horrified sound at the sight of his patched wound.

"I don't want it spreading," he says. "Best if you trust me. I'll give you your commission if and when I complete the sale."

"Why would you?"

Indeed. He can't afford honesty, can't tell her how he feels without sounding trite and adolescent. Can't afford to have her be the one with a bullet in her skull. "A crime like this crosses borders. Countries, governments, they disagree on a hundred different fronts, but they defend each other's cultural rights. You don't seek asylum for art theft, for gray market resale of a national treasure. There's nowhere to run."

"There is no need to run. Dr. Adjani is available," she says, reminding him of his own plan. "I could tell Akram the schedule must be moved forward. Made more to hurry." Now she's getting the idea.

It's tempting. "No. Too much of a risk. Better I leave."

"Let me explain for you something: Akram is in love. You understand? He never knows when I am not telling the truth." She adds, "No man knows when a woman is being honest." And punctuates her words for Knox's benefit.

"The only chance you have of profiting from this is to trust me. To find a new hotel and take great care in doing so. Wait to hear from me. End of story."

"It is not the end of the story."

They kiss. More is said in the kiss than in all the conversation that has gone before. There is trust, longing, hope. Surprise, as he pulls away, because he doesn't want to. Enchantment.

Victoria wears a mask of indifference. Knox knows better, or hopes he does.

THE ROMAN NUMERAL "II" appears on Knox's phone. He switches to the second of his three SIM chips as he packs the interior pockets of his vest. As the phone registers cell service, a new text appears: a single period followed by "11:00." Sent by Grace, it tells him that a lone wolf is watching the hotel from eleven o'clock, a spot to the left of the hotel's front door.

He is the model of physical efficiency; there's not a wasted motion as he downs three extra-strength Tylenol, double-checks the contents of his windbreaker using gentle squeezes and pulls it on. Uses a toenail clipper to notch two tears in the bedsheet. He knots three six-inch-wide strips, inspects and tests his knots, and then heaves the bed against the exterior wall, ties one end of his improvised fire rope to the frame and tosses the remaining length of it out the window. Lowers himself to a connecting rooftop. Is crossing another roof when he unexpectedly disturbs a pair of lovers who have made a privacy lean-to out of drying beach towels. The woman is topless, her skirt around one ankle; her screaming boyfriend more terrifying than the presumed assassins Knox is fleeing. The young man hollers at Knox in Turkish at the top of his lungs. The damage is done before Knox finds the propped-open doorway leading down. The kid has announced him to the world.

Knox is out on the street and hoping for a cab, listening for his phone to chime, signaling another text message from Grace. He expects to be told his surveillants are on the move.

The cab activity is two streets away, serving the hotel and café guests. As the only Westerner standing alone on the busy sidewalk, Knox might as well be wearing neon.

Grace has gone silent, likely having had to move away from her observation point. He won't be suckered into returning to the hotel.

An explosion to his left. Knox dives and rolls only to realize it's a flowerpot dropped from the rooftop by the young man, who is attempting to avenge his lover's modesty. The blow would have killed him. *Love complicates everything,* he thinks. He's up and moving away from the Alzer when his peripheral vision picks up a man moving in concert and slightly behind across the street. Knox grits his teeth, clenches his fist. He can imagine such a man squeezing off a shot at the back of the taxi. Can see Ali slump forward, lifeless. Feels responsible. Feels like crossing the street to return the favor but knows he's outnumbered, outgunned and likely weaker than his opponent.

This last thought is the most difficult to embrace, but he's been repeatedly wounded and is physically and emotionally exhausted. The more troubling thought is that assassins who take potshots at the backs of taxis and openly pursue you from a sidewalk across the street are not in the business of taking prisoners. Abduction is a team effort. Killing is a solo enterprise. This guy's brass has Knox worried. He doesn't care if Knox sees his face because in his dim view of the task at hand, Knox won't be telling anyone who he was.

The next time Knox steals a sideways glance in his surveillant's direction, his bowels threaten: the man's right arm has ceased its pendulum motion at his side. Only his left swings. He's holding something at his side, something he wants concealed.

Knox is about to be shot at by a marksman who only fractionally missed his target through a back windshield at sixty yards. He's unlikely to miss from across the street.

He turns left at the intersection and crosses the street, running along the wide pedestrian boulevard in front of the majestic Fatih Cami, a white-stone mosque that rises in domes and towers seven stories high alongside an even higher minaret. Tourists are gathered around it, admiring the artistic geometry of the mosque's spotlighted walls. Knox aims in a jagged dance for the queue of taxis, where drivers hawk for customers.

He's gambled correctly: his assassin won't risk killing a tourist. Knox waves a cabdriver into the driver seat as he approaches, shouting one of the few Turkish words he can properly pronounce: "Fast!"

He's in the back of a taxi stitching through traffic like a rabbit through underbrush. Head low, he checks out the back and watches the assassin take the next cab in line.

"Airport." Drops liras onto the passenger seat. "Fast."

The ride is marked by bone-numbing, axle-bending collisions with potholes and poor surfaces. The contest with the trailing cab never reaches the level of NASCAR; his tail maintains a manageable distance, looming back like a hungry wolf waiting for his prey to tire. Knox is beyond tired. He's exhausted. It's everything he can do to fight the movement of the cab, keep it from lulling him to sleep. The dissonant Turkish folk music from the radio doesn't help. Knox asks the driver to silence it. Earns a scowl in the mirror. Feels friendless.

Maybe he has it wrong. Maybe this tail is nothing more than

what he wants: Mashe's Iranian guards following Knox to the airport, realizing he's serious about leaving the country if the meet doesn't go his way. Maybe the device held at his tail's side was nothing more than a cell phone. Maybe his fatigue isn't helping anything.

The order of the taxis holds, keeping Knox in the lead for the remainder of the trip to the airport.

As Knox arrives at the curb, the trailing cab pulls over well behind him and . . . nothing. The rear door does not open. Knox sees no motion on the other driver's part, no attempt to stop the meter. The two cabs sit curbside, twenty meters apart. A few moments later, the space between is filled by other vehicles. Knox no longer has a clean view; he angles to pick up the curbside in his own taxi's passenger mirror. His driver repeats several times, "Please," in English. He motions to Knox's door.

Knox ignores him, watching the side mirror, waiting for the timing to be right. His moment comes when a minivan disgorges a three-generational family whose numbers could challenge the *Guinness World Records* book. Knox uses the cover to make it safely into the terminal. Once inside, he looks back. His taxi is gone. The other sits, unmoving, reminding him he remains the prey. The occupant could be calling in his status or awaiting an order.

More likely, he is painfully aware of the inescapable security cameras covering every square inch of the airport from multiple angles.

THE ABSENTEE Dulwich is on Knox's mind as he waits overnight in the airport terminal. The waiting taxi was shooed away hours ago by a police officer, and Knox has not seen it again.

International airport terminals are among the safest places on earth. The only real threat would come from people posing as police or security officers, and if Knox makes enough noise, others will come to verify his attacker's credentials.

Knox wonders fuzzily why he's still alive. The man trailing him could have had him at any number of red lights. He wonders if his going to an airport didn't save him in more ways than he'd intended. What if whoever shot at him simply wants Knox out of the equation? What if trying to reason him into leaving the country was too risky, beyond the scope of his pursuer's mission? By arriving at the international terminal, Knox has signaled surrender. Perhaps that's enough to buy him a pass.

The Israelis again? Mashe's assassination appears less important to the Israelis than the status of Iran's nuclear program. Five Iranian nuclear scientists have been covertly assassinated in the past seven years, four while inside Iran. Yet Mashe Okle lives.

Dulwich promised no killing. He would not appreciate being made to lie to Knox. Silence is the easier alternative. He has stressed repeatedly that Knox's sole mission is to get into a room with Mashe for five minutes. Knox anticipates the asset being placed onto his person, but how?

Lack of verifiable information is what gets operatives like Knox killed. Ali's death, his murder, sits badly with him. Operatives deserve what they get, not taxi drivers. All this concern and confusion, and yet, in the end Dulwich has given Knox exactly what he loves: the irritable panic of uncertainty and an irretrievable confidence that makes every footfall tentative. He's living the life.

Booking his ground transportation through the hotel desk was an intentional risk. It pays off at six A.M., three hours before his scheduled departure, when an exhausted looking Akram Okle traipses across the nearly empty expanse of marble-tiled air terminal. His face is a contortion of patronizing disappointment, regret and relief as he sits alongside Knox.

"Do not do this," Akram says.

"Such art comes and goes. It will come around again. We both know this. I had a bit of a scuffle after leaving you. For the second time. There was a similar encounter after we met near the aqueduct. A man knows when to leave."

"A scuffle."

"I was shot at." Knox removes his Tigers cap—the Turkish flag hat long since pitched—and spins his head to give the man a good, ugly look.

"Disgusting!"

"Think how I feel," Knox says.

"Who?"

Knox chuckles, stares down the man's profile, shakes his head and looks directly forward.

"We are being filmed," Akram says, bringing up his open hand to cover his whispering mouth. "Possibly eavesdropped upon."

"'It's wonderful, isn't it? I feel safe here."

"John—"

"Obviously, Akram, compared to you I'm a simple man. I can do without the intrigue, without being shot at. Lied to. Without my accountant being kidnapped and my taxi crashing because the driver's been head-shot. I work extremely hard to make sure I avoid doing business with what we in the U.S. call 'organized crime.' The Russians, for instance." Knox tosses it out there, pauses, and picks up a slight nostril flare from Akram, but nothing else. Wonders how much significance to give it? "I came to you for this very reason: I wanted to avoid all this shit. Now, I come to find—"

"I am not who you say, but who you think. I am the man you know me to be." His voice exudes pride.

"It was supposed to be a simple transaction."

"Given these numbers, not so simple, my friend." Akram is noticeably loosening. "But as to that: it can yet be made such. No?"

"No. It's not important. Nothing is worth getting shot. Abducted. Are you kidding?" Knox drums up a frightened voice; works hard to sound appalled. "You want it for free, that's not going to happen. If you kill me, you'll never find it. And don't tell me you weren't trying to kill me." He returns the cap to his head, pulling it on gingerly.

"These are people—" Akram checks himself just as Knox latches on to his words. "You tell your accountant to do what she must. I respect her efforts to protect your interests. But I tell you now: the buyer is my brother, a humble university professor and, because of this, an adviser to . . . interests outside Turkey. The window to make this deal was short to begin with and now it is closing fast. My brother is to be leaving soon."

Akram is no agent; he's disclosed more than his brother would wish. The information exchange—whatever data is being passed along—will happen soon.

"If your accountant must also meet with him," Akram continues, "this can be arranged. But it must be on my brother's terms. It is only to happen after authentication of the Harmodius and, respectfully, the application for information on specific investors by your accounting partner. There is no point in making such a meeting as this should the loose ends remain."

Knox eyes him, feigning disinterest. "It was never supposed to be half this difficult." He adds, "Or risky."

"It was night, was it not?" Akram inquires. "One can only assume this bullet was intended for me."

"Then you have issues you clearly need to work out." Knox believes otherwise: his presence has troubled one of the players and his removal is now seen as a way to simplify the op. "I'm scared, Akram." He lies, savoring the role. "This is well outside my purview. You understand 'purview'?"

Akram nods. "My brother has pulled together several investors, as I have mentioned. This has not been easy given such short notice. These investors cannot be, will not be, revealed to your accountant. I would not wish to upset such people."

"Your reputation is not my concern," Knox says.

"No, of course not."

"I was nearly killed."

"I . . . that is . . . I believe my brother could arrange for protection."

"No, thank you. If we're going to do this, it's going to be today. Authentication. Dr. Adjani. Then we will make the exchange, the four of us. My accountant will ensure that the remainder of the funding is clean. All remaining funds must be deposited into escrow within the next three hours. From there, she will—"

"Today? Impossible! That kind of money—"

"Is either available or not."

"Authentication of the piece will take weeks."

"You will have to be satisfied with what is possible given the limited time."

"Absurd."

"At your request, I have arranged for Dr. Adjani to evaluate the Harmodius. That was scheduled for early afternoon. Now, given the threat level, we will have to wrap the deal by tonight or I leave and take the piece with me."

"Be reasonable, John. The deal is easily within our grasp, but such a sched—"

"I was shot at," Knox says, "following a meeting with you. You will meet my conditions, Akram, or I will be forced to move on. The choice is simple, and it's yours to make. The safest place for me is on the other side of security."

Akram stands. "You will contact me." He walks away, clearly less tired than when he arrived.

34

I wish to speak to your office manager." Grace slides the woman a business card left over from the op that sent her and John to Amsterdam that identifies her as a midlevel United Nations employee. It does the trick.

"Regarding?" The woman's English is impeccable, her choice of nail polish and hair coloring regrettable.

"Your mail room."

The receptionist references her computer terminal. "Our post clerk leader is called Kaplan. You are to find him in S-one, eighteen. Elevators to your right."

Grace repeats the office number, collects her business card, thanks the woman and finds the elevators. She turns to the elevator mirror to check her face. There's a man alongside her—Turkish, mid-thirties. The look he's giving her is either a compliment or a cause for concern, because it's not accidental, even though he plays it otherwise. The elevator car opens, and she steps off.

The mail room manager, Kaplan, is clean-shaven and thin, in his early thirties and going bald. She considers him exceptionally ordinary, though his voice is appealing in a stagecraft way. She gives him a quick look at her business card and then gives him the FedEx tracking number.

"This is a confidential inquiry, sir. If you pass along anything to do with my being here, or the nature of my inquiry, your actions will be considered criminal. This includes your co-workers and senior executives. Do you understand?" Grace came prepared. The accountant in her knows that paperwork intimidates far more than anything said aloud. She presents the man with a nondisclosure form downloaded from the Internet; it has little to do with their situation, but a quick scan of the consequences that stem from dissemination of "anything said or witnessed, or understood to have been said or witnessed" is so severe that the man barely reads a word before signing at the bottom. The click of his ballpoint pen nub retracting is as loud as the snap of a bear trap on his ankle.

To her credit, she could name the date and time, as well as the shipper, BioLectrics, which makes the request all the more convincing.

Kaplan carries out his duties, consulting a computer terminal silently and efficiently. With his eyes on the screen, he confirms receipt of the package on the day Grace has gleaned from FedEx. "Delivered in hospital the following morning."

"To what department, floor, office or doctor?" she asks officiously, allowing a degree of impatience to seep into her voice.

"The Kazan Building. Floor five. Cardiology. Dr. Osman."

"Contents?"

Kaplan looks up, suddenly terrified. "I am sorry, ma'am. I . . . we . . ." He looks befuddled. "Rarely, if ever, are we made aware of a package's contents."

"Yes, of course." Grace considers her options. She feels electric.

High from acting out her role convincingly, and from the man's palpable response to the pressure she applies. Control is its own endorphin.

For dramatic effect, she paces in front of the desk, then turns authoritatively to face Kaplan. "I cannot make this inquiry. Do you see?" She is counting on him being unable to see anything of the sort. "It must come internally if it is to remain anonymous." She pretends she needs a few more seconds to pull her thoughts together. "You will call Dr. Osman's office and explain that there has been confusion about a certain package—this package, you understand? The contents of this package. They will please consult their invoice and confirm the contents of the package and that they received the contents in working condition." She places her hands on the desk and leans toward him. "Do you understand?"

"Yes."

"Exactly as I have said. You are doing your job, Kaplan. There must be nothing in your voice or your attitude to imply differently. Are we clear?"

The poor man is sweating from his forehead and hairline—what's left of it.

"We process such shipments from BioLectrics regularly, ma'am. Every three to four weeks, without fail. Always approximately the same weight and size. Cardiology. They are pacemakers."

A clap of thunder could not have been louder. Grace nearly squeals. Nearly runs around the desk and hugs the man. Chastises herself for her own stupidity.

Maintaining her calm, she asks that he not speculate, and to please confirm the contents of the delivery. Inside, she's bubbling.

The clerk makes a show of collecting himself before placing the call. *We're both acting,* she thinks. Though most of the Turkish escapes her, the man's tone does not. He is annoyed, concerned, perhaps implying that an employee of his has come under suspicion of theft—she can't be sure. He carries out his assigned duty and hangs up the receiver.

"One dozen pacemakers. Exactly as I have said." His confidence borders on cocky. How quickly the attitude of men changes as their testosterone is reestablished. Grace moves to gather her documents and once again swears him to secrecy. She thanks him on her way out and phones Knox from an area outside the hospital's main entrance, where a group of people stand smoking. She cups the phone so she can't be overheard.

"Go ahead," Knox says, answering.

"The package they substituted contains pacemakers."

"How certain—?"

"Confirmed."

"Someone's going to have heart trouble. We need the POI's medical records."

She notes the care he takes not to refer to Mashe by name. "We will never get them," she says. "I go through those firewalls, I bring the lions to our door again."

"The package has to involve him."

"But not directly. The switch was made days before either of us arrived in Istanbul. It is the mother who is hospitalized."

"Shit," he says. "Ali. The taxi. What if all of that has nothing to do with Mashe and the sculpture and everything to do with our spending time on the mosque terrace, shooting videos and chasing down FedEx shipments?"

"And hacking bank accounts and breaching Iranian university firewalls. Yes. I see."

"Sarge said no deaths," Knox blurts out.

"We should work with that."

"How? He's lying!"

"We can assume he knows nothing of this. Without a good deal of work, we would know nothing as well."

"The more we know, the less we know," Knox says irritably.

"Do you wish to abort?"

"Not an option. Victoria can blackball me with the Turkish cultural ministries. I ran from the Jordanian police. We moved the shipment on them. They have plenty of cause to bring me in if she stirs the nest. It could make it tricky for me and Tommy. The import/export. It's important I satisfy her—"

Grace clears her throat.

"If I cut and run without paying her a commission . . . It'll likely follow me." Knox backtracks, reviewing his most recent conversation with Akram at the airport for relevant details. "Look, no matter what, this is over later today. We get our five minutes, and we get out. We can still do this."

"We continue as scheduled," she says. She pronounces it "sheduled," like the Brits. She didn't pick that up in China, but from living in Hong Kong. She hears herself speak and it triggers a picture, a complex self-portrait that jumps from her parents' traditional home to university, to her army service, to graduate school in California. The flashing images leave her with a sudden keen sense of her own mortality. She wonders if she's getting old or if it's only the poison of fear that makes her feel so. "Your Victoria is the connection to Dr. Adjani. She transports the art while you meet with the younger brother. I must remain here, collect pacemaker." She hears herself sounding Chinese, knows it signals her stress level to Knox; hopes he doesn't call her on it. They have agreed on the importance of knowing the role of the devices. No more surprises.

She hears Knox hesitate. Suspects that though he supports her, Knox is about to remind her that Dulwich doesn't want them digging.

She intercepts him. "Do you trust her?"

"Of course not."

"We arrange a driver for her. Besim keeps watch."

Knox goes quiet on the other end of the call. She can sense that he's considering arguing with her, and she takes it as points in her column when he says, "That works." It's spoken with more than a whiff of resentment.

35

For Knox, the op has been reduced to base objectives. Victory will be defined by survival. Working off the idea that some force he can't yet ID wants him out of Istanbul, he buys a one-way ticket for Gebze, Turkey. He uses his company credit card, assuming his transactions may be watched—by Dulwich? the client? the Israelis? He's not sure.

In-country travel does not require him to pass through Immigration, where he fears interference by Victoria or yet another party might lead him to be red-flagged. The plane is still in turnaround as he waits at the gate. He pays an additional seventy-five dollars at the desk for priority boarding. Walks the air bridge behind the first-class passengers, arriving outside the jet's entry while the food service crew is still at work in the galley. The food service truck is parked opposite. Knox steps out of line to tie a shoe that doesn't need tying. Two people pass him. The flight attendant moves down the aisle to help push a bag into an overhead. The food service man stumbles past with a crate of sodas.

Knox moves straight across and into the raised back of the service truck. It's all about the appearance of confidence. He doesn't hurry, doesn't stoop. He waits until he's deep into the truck, where he pushes himself behind a stack of dirty trays. When the worker returns, Knox attracts his attention by making rodent scratches on the wooden floor. Silences him with a blow to the trachea and choke-holds him into unconsciousness. Takes the man's shirt and airport employment ID lanyard. Works the hydraulics to lower the raised truck bed and drives away a few minutes later. Leaving via a secure airport ramp in Turkey amounts to driving up to a security booth and watching the mechanical arm raise fifteen seconds before being close enough to require an exchange. Food service trucks are a regular sight, apparently.

Knox boards the Metro and rides to Beyoğlu. Doesn't spot anyone following. Rides a bus northwest to Tepebaşi and goes on foot the final distance, taking twelve blocks to accomplish what could have been done in eight. His nerves are on edge, an uncommon sensation that causes him to walk faster than usual. Hoping he has lost the tail, he reverses direction and reaches the street Akram named in a text forty minutes earlier.

The latch hums. He's through. He climbs to the first floor, conscious that this is but the first of a two-stage process. Here he must convince Akram the Harmodius is legitimate enough to merit investment; next, he must leverage that authenticity to bring Mashe into a room with him and Grace for five minutes.

The apartment is on the right, likely a flat belonging to a friend of Akram's. Maybe a mistress, Knox thinks, given a few feminine touches. There's a ceramic bulldog sitting on a handmade doily atop a tube television. Furniture, that to Knox's American eye looks like it belongs in a 1960s period film, crowds the small room into which Knox is welcomed.

Akram wears the same cracked brown leather jacket, dark T-shirt and designer jeans. He looks wider and stronger than Knox remembers, more threatening.

"The piece?" Akram says. "Where is the Harmodius, please, John?"

Knox spots the open laptop that Akram was instructed to bring. He sets up a wireless connection over his iPhone, connects to the Internet and places a Skype video call.

"Dr. Adjani," Knox says. "As you approved."

"I do not see him," Akram says irritably, gesturing to their surroundings and the studio apartment that barely accommodates himself and Knox.

"I have taken precautions, given the challenges you and I discussed at the airport." Knox indicates the laptop's screen, which now shows an image of a university lab.

"This will not do."

"It will, or I'm gone."

Adjani, personally selected by Akram, stands alongside the Obama bust in what could double as a high school science lab. Just off screen, at the back of the room, Knox sees Victoria. Is it Knox's imagination or is Akram more interested in her than the professor?

"We are ready at this end," Dr. Adjani says.

"I do not understand," Akram complains. "What is the meaning of this?"

"You and your expert have two hours. Victoria is there, as you can see, protecting your interests. I cannot travel with the Harmodius. Not after that earlier business. Victoria transported it for me. Two hours. Use it well."

Akram appears poised to call it off. Knox is paralyzed with anticipation.

"Let us see what we have, Hassan." Akram sits down in front of the laptop.

Minutes later, Adjani carefully drives a flat, wide blade into Obama's left shoulder. With a black rubber mallet, he applies small, studied taps. His blows are calculated and efficient. He works a rent into the seam and pries; the plastic separates and two pieces calve away, revealing a lump of gauze in one half. Knox watches Akram's face. Impressed. Apprehensive. Overly eager for the gauze to be removed.

Adjani pries the lump from the cast plastic. It's heavy. The man dons surgical gloves and peels away the veil, revealing a bronze head and partial torso broken below the shoulders, which are angled forward. Akram does his best to suppress a gasp, but his eyes pop. Knox has studied Harmodius and Aristogeiton enough to know that if it's a copy, it's a damn good one.

Good enough to be crafted by Kritios and Nesiotes? he wonders. If so, the value is incalculable.

Akram has had the same thought. "The second copy was also lost to the ages."

"Yes."

Akram doesn't say it, but his face shouts, *Could this possibly be real?*

As the bust is fully revealed, it is seen to still contain dirt and gravel, seams of earth packed into its crevices. The piece looks like it was dug up an hour ago and barely cleaned. Knox knows the condition serves a purpose: the dirt and the existing condition can help date the bust, often more than the bust itself.

"I'm telling you, it is possible. Confirmed by my experts." Knox says this and then recalls that his expert is Dulwich, whom he no longer trusts. If Dulwich burned him on the Harmodius, there's no way he'll get the five minutes with Mashe—and no way Victoria will let him off the hook with the authorities.

Knox continues, faking a confidence he doesn't feel. "Adjani should be able to determine the fundamentals. If it's a copy, how old a copy? The chemical lab work is speculative at best."

Knox wears an earbud that Akram hasn't asked about. It's an open phone connection with Besim, who's surveilling the university building where Victoria and Adjani are working. Knox has a chauffeur he's never met guarding several million dollars' worth of sculpture. Grace told Besim that Victoria is her husband's mistress, and that she suspects they have colluded to appraise a piece of art, which they will sell without Grace's knowledge. Knox is a good friend monitoring the situation. Every element of the op is based on a lie.

With the veil removed, Adjani's meticulous methods suggest more than an expert doing his job. He's reverential. The man attempts to start a video camera to record his work, but Knox stops him. Akram speaks Turkish with Adjani. Knox puts a quick stop to that, though ostensibly Victoria is in the room to protect Knox's interests.

The lab work draws out. Soil is scraped from the bust and tested. The piece is subjected to ultrasound. Adjani dons surgeon's glasses and examines the surface of the bronze in a dozen places, picking at it with dentist tools. Nothing is heard but the occasional scratching, Adjani sniffling or Victoria, offscreen, rearranging herself. The silence is painful. Knox breaks it to maintain his sanity.

"The remainder of the funds?"

"It is as we discussed. To be transferred upon delivery should the verification prove out."

Knox enjoys getting what he wants. "My associate must meet him. As discussed."

"I cannot confirm this demand at present."

Knox doesn't belabor the point. He'll let the Harmodius sell itself. It will give him leverage. Adjani is already obsessed with the piece. He rolls up a stool and faces the camera.

An hour has passed. To Knox, it feels like most of the day.

36

D r. Osman's offices are on the hospital's cardiology floor, beyond a waiting area and receptionist desk. Grace might as well try passing through the Topkapi's Sublime Porte during Ottoman times. She's not going to be able to steal the pacemakers. She faces having to accomplish the next best thing: get someone to give them to her.

Her Chinese heritage affords her many benefits in the West, among them the fact that Western men appreciate Asian women. Or the fact that the West secretly considers all Asians academically smarter and less physically able. Grace can use these stereotypes to her advantage. Because it worked so well in the mail room, she presents her UN business card to the receptionist, a matronly Turkish woman with an enormous chest, a double chin and pigmented green contact lenses that make her look like a Martian.

Grace tries English. The woman isn't ignorant, but she's far from fluent. Together they stitch together some Turkish and English, which works in Grace's favor because she doesn't want to present her needs in technical speak.

There has been a shipment from BioLectrics that may have been sourced in China, Grace informs the woman. The parts are possibly counterfeit and unsafe. She needs a sample from the following shipment. She presents the FedEx tracking information.

A nurse is called out, arriving ten minutes later. Grace repeats her story. The woman is younger and unfortunately her English is good.

"The UN's interest?" the nurse inquires.

"Is regulatory," Grace says. "You need not concern yourself. I've traveled a great distance, and have farther to go. Istanbul is not the only location that received a shipment, as you might imagine."

"World Health I could understand."

"You need not concern yourself."

"These are expensive parts."

"Inspection purposes only. The parts will be returned within the week. If they sustain damage in the process of inspection, they will be replaced at no cost to the hospital."

The nurse is acutely suspicious, but there's so much downside for the hospital should the parts prove counterfeit that she relents.

"We . . . the truth is . . . there is no order to our supplies."

"In the case of the pacemakers," Grace says, vamping, "protocol calls for FILO." First-in-last-out. "If you are so disorganized, you can, at the very least, look at the expiration dates on the pacemakers themselves. Correct?"

"I suppose. Yes."

"I would appreciate a single sample from the batch with the latest expiration date. You can first check and copy the invoice for me. I must leave with at least one sample of each of the items shipped."

"It will take a few minutes," the nurse says unpleasantly. She leaves.

Grace checks her watch.

37

Knox was not made for waiting. He moves to the window and parts the blinds an inch to peer out at the street below. Isn't sure what he's looking for. Something different. Something unexpected.

But Istanbul is unexpected—the hustle, the street side conversations, the smells, the mix of Western and Middle Eastern dress. He viewed most of this as an obstacle when he arrived; now it's under his skin and welcome. The mayhem is damn near comforting, a kind of elixir; its absence would be troubling.

He and Akram have been waiting twenty long minutes for some word from Adjani. For any word. Knox reaches for the laptop and mutes their end of the conversation.

"Tell me about Victoria," Knox says.

Akram appraises him. "I think not."

"You haven't taken your eyes off her."

"I do not believe this your business, John Knox."

"She is in possession of my artwork—she, and a man of your choosing."

"Hassan is no thief."

"And yet you are on a first-name basis with him," Knox says.

Akram demurs.

"Not the first time you've needed a piece of art authenticated."

Still nothing.

"She speaks fondly of you. She was hurt. Is hurt." Knox hits the target.

Akram is all flashing eyes, a wicked temper caged. His carotid artery working overtime.

"Perhaps you two can patch things up," Knox says, hoping to give his being alive added value.

"She will have none of it."

"I wouldn't be so sure." Knox sees a crack of hope. "The only way a person hurts is if she cares. And she hurts."

Knox doesn't have to work too hard. Akram wants this to be true.

"They are more a prize than any piece of art, *neh*?" Knox hears himself add the Graceism to the end of his sentence; the gesture sends him tumbling through his own spiral of emotions. Is he talking to Akram or to himself? What drove him to this line of conversation? Just how much trouble is he in? And with whom?

"You would do this for me?" Akram's childish tone reminds Knox a woman can bring a man to his knees. "Do you know my ringtone for her? 'Brown Sugar,' Rolling Stones." He quotes, "'I'm no schoolboy, but I know what I like.'"

Knox arrives at the moment for which he's aimed: the reveal that he, Knox, knows more than expected. He measures his words carefully. "She is afraid of your brother." Pauses. "I have a younger brother. It is not easy for the younger to escape the elder's shadow."

"You know nothing of this matter."

He's testing. "True," Knox says cruelly.

"Family blood is thick," Akram says, rubbing his fingers together.

"Sticky," Knox says, supplying the word for him.

"Exactly this! Sticky."

"Our sense of family evolves."

"She asks too much." Akram's anger is overshadowed by his pain. This is not the first time he's reached this particular crossroads.

Knox shrugs. "Not every deal can be negotiated."

"Why would you do this?" Akram must read some tell on his face; Knox has slipped. "The truth. Eh?"

Knox chuckles. *The truth evolves as well,* he thinks. "The last time we met, as you will recall, I was shot at within minutes." He touches his baseball cap. "There is no reason for me to think this will not happen again."

"You want to be of value to me."

"I am of value to you. What I want is protection as I leave here."

"If I help you live, I get my woman back."

"Something like that."

"You drive a hard bargain, John." It's the first time Akram has smiled in some time.

Dr. Adjani's face distorts as he arrives too close to the laptop's camera. As he does, Knox taps a key to remove the Mute. The lab man's eyes sparkle with excitement as he speaks.

"The soil carried on the bust is consistent with what was once termed the Great Rift Valley, now part of Israel and adjacent to the Jordan Rift Valley. That is, there are high percentages of rock salt and gypsum. Unique to that area. This is in sharp distinction to the red and gray-brown podzolic soils that cover nearly a third of Turkey. The bust is almost certainly Greek. The soil is not. It would not be the first Greek treasure unearthed in the Rift, though the Harmodius was believed lost in Greece, as you must know. The casting, metalwork and craftsmanship are consistent with the era. As to the metallurgy, I took a small sample from inside the cast and subjected it to gas chromatography." Adjani pauses to move his glasses in a nervous tick. "The composition of the bronze is unique to the epoch in question. Extremely difficult to reproduce, I should add. I should also caution that this is not a wholesale endorsement.

"It's suggestive, but such things can be duplicated, no matter how unlikely.

"That said, if duplicated, it is exemplary work, well above anything I have seen outside of authentic pieces."

Akram and Knox watch the screen, awaiting the bad news. None is forthcoming. Adjani fiddles with his glasses again, shakes his head and says, "Extraordinary, gentlemen. Upon cursory inspection this object would appear to be a fragment of a bronze casting forged approximately five hundred B.C. It might easily have been recovered from the Jordan Rift. Soil compaction would suggest it has been buried for, shall we say, several hundred years at minimum. Such soil compaction is extremely difficult, if not impossible, to reproduce. Only months of exhaustive testing will confirm its authenticity. Such testing should begin immediately. It would be . . . criminal"—he leans on the word intentionally—"to not complete such tests regardless of the outcome of the piece's future. This is a work of major importance. I urge you to allow the proper testing—confidential testing, if necessary—to begin at once."

Knox masks his own surprise as Akram stares him down. Both men know Knox is too insignificant a player in the art world to be trusted with such a piece. The only possible explanation is theft, and clearly Akram did not believe Knox up to such a task.

For his part, Knox is wondering where and how Dulwich came up with such a piece and, by extension, how important Mashe Okle must be to the client to sacrifice an antiquity worth millions for the sake of an op. It's an inconceivable price to pay, forcing Knox to question once again if the sale will ever take place. If Mashe is not to make it out of Istanbul alive, that's a play Knox wants no part of. His own life is at stake, too: if the client proves willing to sacrifice a piece as valuable as the Harmodius, what kind of chance does a low-level operative like Knox have?

A single word floats in Knox's consciousness: *Israel*. It is the sun around which all logic spins.

On-screen behind Adjani, Victoria lurks like a beta wolf awaiting the sating of alpha's appetite. Knox's offer of 10 percent must be titillating. More important, she has to realize that to attempt to steal a piece of such extraordinary value would likely get her killed or arrested. The Obama bust was destroyed to reveal the Harmodius; something equally clever and effective will need to be devised and installed in order to smuggle the Harmodius out of Turkey.

He texts Grace a thumbs-up emoticon signaling the verification is good. Understanding the role of the Israelis and the switched pacemaker is more important now than ever. Fearing Dulwich may have been misled by the client, they must attempt to determine the purpose of their proposed five minutes with Mashe.

"My protection," Knox says, reminding him. Akram has yet to admit openly he's under watch by the Iranians.

Akram's eyes grow distant. "You will please to tell her I love her."

38

The text of a thumbs-up spurs Grace on. Time is more critical than ever—if they are to understand how the Israeli intercept of the pacemakers fits into Nawriz Melemet's purchase of the Harmodius, it comes down to the next few hours. Knox works to avoid frightening her; sees her as a neophyte in the field. The great unspoken that lies between them is that the bullet that killed their driver, Ali, was meant for her. Her meddling in Mashe Okle's identity resulted in her abduction. It was nearly immediately followed with an attempt to kill. Although she considers valid Knox's theory of a possible exchange between the heavily sanctioned Iran and one of its trading partners, she can't dismiss her own role. There could have been a trip wire in the FedEx server that sourced the shipment of the pacemakers; a mistake could have been made that alerted others to her probing. Working off the axiom "knowledge is power," Grace is controlled by her training: the more she knows about the Israeli switching of the pacemakers, the more negotiating power she and Knox possess; the more possible it may be for them to talk, instead of fight, their way out of this.

They won't win a fight against Mossad.

The nurse is taking her sweet time, leaving Grace to wonder if she's been set up, if the delay is a stall tactic to allow hospital security time to reach them. The wall clock appears to be part of the conspiracy. Grace makes her move into a hallway that accesses examination rooms. She steels herself, prepares for a rebuke or reprimand. But within a few paces, she's just another patient among many keeping appointments.

As she reaches the nursing station, she identifies the woman she talked to by the woman's wide-eyed response. The tell is the woman's glance to the phone, as if it will save her. That is when Grace knows security has indeed been called.

"I need that device, now!" Grace says sharply. "This is a matter of international security, of the utmost importance." She draws the attention of two other nurses. "Your call to hospital security will only delay the inevitable and put you in a situation with which you will wish you had never involved yourself." Her guess proves accurate. Mention of hospital security devastates the nurse.

"If I am not out of here before they arrive, if I am delayed because of actions you have taken . . . I hesitate to think of the repercussions for you."

"When I spoke to the doctor—"

"Do you think a doctor has any say in the United Nations' efforts to police manufacturing standards? Do you think it is in the best interests of your doctor to install defective devices? I will speak with this doctor now." Grace appreciates the resulting terror that crosses the nurse's face. "That, or you will give me one of the pacemakers from the lot I specified. Your choice."

She allows the woman time to consider her options. "I am happy to await security. You will be less so."

The nurse reaches into her pocket—she had the pacemaker all along. It is sealed in hard plastic against a thick paper backing and rattles like a child's toy as she passes it with a trembling hand.

Grace accepts the package with a sniff. "An exit, other than reception?" She turns in that direction at the moment a tall man in sport coat, dark slacks and black athletic shoes arrives at the end of the short hallway. He carries an intensity that immediately identifies him to Grace.

The nurse's eyes flick, perhaps unintentionally, to her right.

Grace is off in that direction before anything more is said. Turns down a hallway, picking up her pace. Hears voices back at the nurse's station, including a man's. She reaches a T, looks right, then left. Spots a green EXIT sign with an arrow left.

It's a maze. She's running now, painfully aware that the security man can be but a matter of paces behind. By running, she has tipped her hand, a mistake she now regrets. The starting pistol has been fired. This man, double her size and weight, is certain to match or exceed her speed. He has full knowledge of the building. She has only her training, her wits.

Grace punches through the exit and into an echoing stairwell, her hand already fishing lipstick out of her purse. She tosses the lipstick down the stairs straight ahead and then bounds up the flight to her left, two treads at a time; dives onto and across the landing as she hears the door *smack* open behind her. She lies prostrate on the cool concrete. She will lose precious seconds trying to get to her feet if he guesses correctly and follows her up.

But the descending sound of the rolling lipstick carries him down. His shoes clap on the landing as he leaps and turns the corner. Grace nimbly finds her footing and scurries silently up the stairs. A volley of footfalls below stops abruptly as the security man suspends his descent to listen, perhaps to look down the narrow gap between the rails. Seeing nothing, hearing nothing, he prolongs the silence. They are a landing apart, unmoving.

The moment she hears him speak into his radio, calling for backup or video assistance, she moves. She's outnumbered and the technology she so loves is now working against her. She has no choice but to move, as silently and quickly as possible. She's aware now of unseen cameras bearing down on her, of security personnel rallying to intercept her. Of Knox needing her at the university. Even if she's able to talk herself out of the situation—however unlikely—she can't afford the delay.

She's up the stairs as lightly as her feet will carry her. Perhaps not lightly enough. The security man has reversed, ascending as well.

Reaching the fourth floor, Grace takes the door. Faced with another long hallway, she balks. This is the OB/GYN wing, judging by the presence of stirrups on the exam tables. She backs up to the first exam room, closes herself in and climbs onto the table fully clothed. She throws her feet into the stirrups and pulls a linen over her, hiding her face behind a tent formed by her bent knees.

She hears footfalls stop in the corridor. He's measured the empty hallway, perhaps. Believes he should have caught sight of her.

The door is thrown open. A pause. Grace sees the problem now: if he looks into the mirror above the sink, the angle will allow him to see her. She turns her face away.

The door shuts without a word. She exhales.

39

---

kram makes a phone call and less than five minutes later there's a knock on the door of the safe house, and Knox knows the Iranian guards were never far away. He has no qualms about seeking help; for the next few hours he's in league with Akram, Mashe and the Iranians. There's no way to hide it.

He must consider the possibility that Akram has been followed to their meet, and that the Iranians would not have picked up on it if it was the Israelis trailing him.

"This is going to go a little differently," Knox says to one of the two men. "You understand?"

The man grunts his assent. But no love lost.

Knox spots the white van they're walking him toward and his world spins—Grace was abducted in a white van.

He says, "You're going to slide open the side door for me to go inside. You'll close it all up, wait twenty seconds. You understand?"

"One . . . two . . ." An accent so thick Knox has to interpret.

"Correct. To twenty. Then drive off."

The guard furrows his brow, having no idea what Knox has planned.

"Exactly as I've said. You understand?" He nearly adds, "You didn't think I was actually going to get into that van, did you?"

Moments later the guard opens the van's side door. Knox steps in front of the man and drops to the curb like he's been Tasered. He slips between the curb and the undercarriage and is gone from sight by the time the perplexed guard steps into the van. Knox belly-crawls beneath the rear axle and differential then scurries beneath the truck parked closely behind the van.

. . . twenty . . . The van pulls away from the curb and into traffic.

Knox has to keep an eye on his wristwatch because he's lost all sense of time. At ninety seconds he crawls back out and takes to the sidewalk, brushing himself off. He feels clever and proud and wishes Grace had been there to witness it, wondering a moment later where such thoughts come from and what kind of hold he's allowed her to have on him. He's not in the habit of caring about others' opinions, wants to be liked but not at too high an expense. Tries to clear his head, wondering when he last ate.

He keeps the Tigers cap pulled down low. Still, he can't stop himself from remembering Ali's head blowing open as it slumps against the wheel. Knox moves quickly and somewhat erratically, hoping to make himself a difficult target. Wants off the street.

The neighborhood he's in is not on the Star Tour maps. His height and coloring call out for attention.

He tightropes the curb to stay away from street-side doorways. Any one of them could suck him in and swallow him like Jonah into the whale. He keeps alert for new vehicles while measuring the nerves of those within reach of him. Body language and posture can telegraph intent. He pays particular attention to anyone wearing earbuds. Wishes he had backup. Curses Dulwich. Wonders if he should have risked a ride in the white van.

The woman approaching is low to the ground, thin and proves

herself deceptively fast. She's in her twenties, a loop of silver pierced through her eyebrow. Something slips into her hand from up the long sleeve of her flouncy top, like a derringer in an old Western. Knox figures it out only after the rebar is swinging for his shins. She connects there like a polo player. She was aiming for his kneecaps, but Knox leaps instinctively, straight up. Even deflected, the impact stings—cracks—he returns to earth collapsing to the sidewalk.

Loses his vision to the pain—a gooey purple orb swims before him. Sensing a second and perhaps final blow coming, he attacks blindly, working off the sound of her sandals and the adrenaline of threat.

He dislocates her knee with an elbow butt. She buckles and comes down on him like a felled tree. His eyesight returning, he tears the loop from her eyebrow, winning an animal cry. He bucks her off.

An ambulance races up the street.

Ingenious. Creative. Expensive.

He rises onto his knees—nothing can hurt this much—and breaks her ribs with a fist blow; makes peeing blood a part of her future and dislocates her jaw to cut the chatter. Men rush to attack Knox for assaulting a woman.

Knox grabs the rebar and defends his turf as he hobbles into the street. The ambulance pulls up. Knox drives the butt end of the rebar into the grille and through the radiator, releasing a torrent of steaming green water that falls hissing to the street. Hauls the rebar up, cracks the windshield and catches the legs of the imposter emerging from the front passenger seat. Tit for tat. Takes two of the most painful steps of his life and greets a motorcyclist trying to sneak down the side of the stopped traffic; sends the man airborne. Walks stiff-legged like Frankenstein, recovers the fallen motorcycle, its engine still running.

Gives a look to the ambulance driver, who rounds the nearest vehicle. The guy is poised, ready to pull a concealed weapon on him. But to what end? To shoot Knox in the back with a dozen witnesses watching? Possibly?

Knox gives himself the cover of smoke from his back wheel, cussing with each toe shift as he screeches away.

40

The funicular, dangling from its thread of twisted steel, floats down into the Tophane district. Grace feels like a spider off to mend her web. The street address and name of her contact are written on opposing palms—the scribble on her right nearly impossible to read.

Across the dark green waters of the Bosphorus, sliced white by wake and the occasional ship, she sees southern Istanbul on the Asian continent. Below her, a patchwork of rooftops spill toward the water, broken by the green of an occasional park. Its picturesque quality is opposed to her thought. She's cranked and unable to appreciate it. If she knew more clearly the exact location of her destination—an electronics shop Xin has arranged for her—she could likely see it, so clear is the view. But it's lost on her.

Forty-five minutes later, having ferried across the river and ridden the back of a hot taxi through a decidedly more Oriental Istanbul, she resents the lack of anything more from Knox. She has switched SIM chips and texted all three of his numbers.

Nothing. *Asshole!*

The wheels are coming off the op. They have only a matter of a few hours before the proposed meet with Mashe Okle and she has yet to determine what their secreted role is; what purpose the five minutes with the POI is to serve.

She is alone. Knox is alone. Together, they are alone. For a time, her mathematical mind could project a resolution to the op, but now it's more ephemeral; Knox believes them both to be sacrificial lambs, and she has no evidence to dispute this. Dulwich has expected them to do this alone. There is no exit strategy in place.

A strong scent of cloves mingles in the air, tinged with cinnamon. It somehow permeates the taxi's cigarette-stained interior to intoxicate her and remind her of life now past: leisure time in a Hong Kong café with a cup of chai, the *Financial Times*, under a clock with no minute hand. She can envision herself flipping through family photos she recently downloaded to her phone in order to make a birthday collage for her somewhat estranged father, who turns fifty in three weeks. Imagines herself smiling at memories. Laughing internally. Of shopping irresponsibly, of making herself feel pretty and feminine and maybe even available.

But she feels none of these things. Instead, she's bound in servitude, rough and unkempt. She is predatory and hostile, optimistically ambitious enough to believe there may be a way out of this yet. Some heads will likely be broken before it's over: Knox's job. Which heads: her job.

The sidewalks are crowded, the Asian, southern side of the city more dense, more ethnic. Conflicting Middle Eastern melodies pour from shops and loudspeakers; the grating dissonance of half-toned scales that rub together caustically do nothing to prolong the fantasy.

She arrives at a shop with rain-gray windows and peeling forest green paint. It's marked with a rusted sign, the letters faded until they're unreadable. Taped on the inside of the glass is a computer-printed typewritten sheet with an oversized single word: ELECTRONICS.

The shop matches Xin's description. She hadn't fully trusted his information, given that she'd caught Xin in an inebriated state in a Hong Kong bar well past midnight.

Inside the shop, the air hangs heavy with the cloak of serviceability mixed with the sting of sour perspiration, tobacco smoke and a smell she doesn't want to place. The atmosphere speaks of young men and Internet pornography and turns her stomach. She thinks she must be getting old: at university they laughed about places like this; now they merely disgust her. A man-boy is summoned from the back by the electronic chime that died with her entry.

"Xin," she says.

"May I see please?" He speaks with a British accent. Wears an ill-fitting brown vest over a royal blue T-shirt. Stretch jeans. Thick-rimmed black glasses that enlarge dull brown eyes. He's left-handed, according to his tobacco-stained fingers. Diminutive, his flesh has shrunken onto a frame that could and should support more.

She produces the pacemaker.

"You want?" he says.

"Is it operable? Correct voltage? Able to hold a charge?"

"Medical," he says, turning the packaging over. "Cardiac."

"A pacemaker, yes."

He steps back, away from the device. "Such pacemakers are programmed and communicated with via radio waves. I lack any such equipment. I'm afraid—"

"The battery," she says.

"Sealed. Interior." He spins it over, examining it. "Without cutting open, primitive analysis, best offer."

"Please."

"You wait?" He cuts the plastic packaging with a box cutter. She doesn't appreciate that being in his hand.

"How long?" She doesn't like his question. She scribbles out the phone number of her least used SIM chip. Paranoia sickens her stomach. "Text me."

She heads for the door.

"Please. One minute, ma'am!"

She gives him twenty seconds of the minute when his effort to touch the tester's probes onto the leads from the pacemaker turns her once again for the exit. She's crawling out of her skin. He's so obviously nervous he can't connect a probe to a wire. No matter that the wires are tiny, it's a task he must have performed thousands of times. So why fumble?

She's thinking: *Xin, you bastard.*

She turns the dead bolt. Hurries back to the counter with an urgency and energy that causes the technician to step back.

"Charge is complete," the man-boy says, looking up at her. "Battery life—measurement of ampere-hours is calculation of voltage and known load. According to specs," he says, indicating printing on the flip side of the disk, "this runs for years."

"You are certain? A healthy battery?" Grace's own internal battery is overheated and sparking. She expects someone to arrive at any moment, drag her kicking and screaming into the street.

"You make joke? 'Healthy battery'?"

"It is a normal, working device," she states.

"I not know this without opening."

"Opening . . ." she mumbles, allowing the thought to escape her. "Yes. Please."

"It is sealed unit. Replace unit, not battery."

"No way to open it?"

"Correct. Short of destroying it."

"Please."

He studies her curiously. "It will be destroyed if—"

"An extra two hundred liras." Grace digs out the cash as she glances toward the street. "Quickly, please."

The technician takes a hacksaw to the device. The five minutes needed to saw off one end feels much longer to both of them. His face is perspiring. She doesn't think he exerted himself enough to explain this.

"Your loyalty is to Xin," she says.

Removing the internal circuits of the device, he pauses to meet her eyes.

"We both understand that," she continues. "This work, it is a matter of a human life. You understand? Misinformation on your part could cost a human life." She leans in, trying to penetrate the wall he has erected between them. "That will be on you. Not me, not if you misinform me."

He nods, looks at the microcircuitry he's holding. "This will take additional time."

She wonders. "I must know!"

"Understood."

She moves past him into the back of the shop.

He calls after her, "Please, lady. No customer in—"

"To be fair," she says, interrupting, "tell Xin I was not expecting this of him. How long do I have?"

He doesn't answer at first. "I cut open for you. You wait?"

"You will contact me. If you tell Xin or anyone else the condition of that device before you tell me, you could kill a man."

She's out the shop's back exit and into an alleyway barely wider than her shoulders. It's a place that, as a tourist, she would have loved to discover. As a possible target, she finds it claustrophobic.

Her feet seem to move independently of her brain, carrying her past terra-cotta urns meant to collect rainwater, now put to use as the skies have opened in a deluge. She's soaked through by the time she escapes the space.

Gray rain bounces up off the sidewalk in a hypnotic display of fountain magic. Vehicles are pulled over, wipers throwing fans of water. The only people not waiting it out under doorways look like lost pets with their slumped shoulders and pathetic attempts to screen their heads using soggy newsprint. All but the well prepared, who carry their umbrellas so low they look beheaded.

One of these, a tall, wide-shouldered man whose canvas sport jacket she recognizes long before the umbrella angles to shelter her, approaches at a steady gait.

Everything about David Dulwich is steady, Grace thinks, tracking him with her eyes as he draws near. He likely came out of the womb that way.

41

Grace is soaked through, sitting on a raffia-seat chair across from an unreadable, expressionless yet intense David Dulwich. The tobacco haze in the café reminds her of Beijing in winter.

She thinks back to their lunchtime Red Room briefing, their meeting only days ago when she was certain he was condoning her off-the-books digging. She now feels like the schoolgirl about to get an earful. Dulwich's composure indicates a new level of cold, the kind of cold that turns metal from icy to brittle.

Shifting uncomfortably, she thinks about having a hot bath and warm terry-cloth robe, a double vodka and a man. She wants what she can't have: to be away from all this. The earlier excitement has been steadily eroded by exhaustion and starvation. She orders falafel and hummus, hoping food will reinvigorate her. In contrast, Dulwich's engine runs on espresso. He uses this as a pit stop.

"Do you want the download, or would you prefer we—?"

"Please," Dulwich says.

It's not a word she often hears from him. It sticks in his mouth, like a dog with peanut butter.

"The POI, aka Mashe Okle, aka Nawriz Melemet, is a nuclear particle physicist," she says. "The initial funding of the escrow indicates four private investors." She watches Dulwich's pupils flare, dilating briefly. "The sourcing of those investments appears legitimate." She writes names on a napkin from memory and slides it across to him. "I have not had time to trace them out." Dulwich turns it over, will not accept it. "He is being protected by at least two Iranian bodyguards. John and I believe he and Akram are being surveilled by Israelis—unconfirmed." The shutters of his eyes react a second time. Grace feels like a prize student arguing her dissertation. She's impressed him; she finds it impossible to keep from going further. "There could be terminate order on John or me or both of us. Our dealings are complicated by the owner of the gallery in Amman where you placed the Harmodius." She wants this to sting; sees no sign of it. "Regardless of this, the meet appears on track for later today. We will get our five minutes."

Dulwich could be partner to the Harmodius, he's suddenly so still.

"A pacemaker manufactured by the Swiss firm BioLectrics that was headed for Florence Nightingale Hospital, where the Melemet mother is under care, was intercepted and/or substituted by an individual believed to be Israeli, possibly Mossad. I assume you must be aware of this as you were waiting outside the shop Xin directed me to for its analysis." Unreadable. "John and I theorize the pacemaker is part of a dead drop involving the Iranian nuclear program." Still no indication he's even hearing her. She feels anger bubbling up and pushes it back.

"John is clearly compromised. I advocated an abort." She pauses. "Declined."

"See it through," he says, his upper lip holding some of the dark, oily coffee. "There are no surprises—"

"—only opportunities," she says, finishing the Dulwichism. "In this case, more players than *Henry the Sixth, Part Two*."

She can't win a reaction. His stoniness, she will pass on to Knox. Dulwich is not typically without humor, though his jokes are often dark. He has chosen to contact her away from John. Because of the importance of the pacemaker and her curiosity over it, she wonders, or because he doesn't want to face Knox's combustibility?

"John's situation requires continuance," she says.

Dulwich is clearly amused by her inconsistent vocabulary. There's no explaining Grace Chu.

Grace is tempted to insult or challenge him; she's running out of patience. But her pragmatism won't allow it. Dulwich and Rutherford Risk are a stepping-stone to something entrepreneurial for her; it lacks form but is beginning to reveal itself, a shape emerging from behind a sculptor's chisel.

After the falafel and hummus are delivered along with a black tea, Grace asks, "If you could share with us the Israeli op, perhaps we could steer clear." She articulates what Knox would have demanded in far different terms.

Having laid the trap, she eats greedily. She hadn't realized how hungry she was. But it's a bottomless stomach kind of hunger, one that can't be satisfied, that has little to do with food.

"Part of our company name, remember? Risk?"

She considers spilling hot tea into his lap. Packs the last falafel into her mouth. Should have taken it in two bites. Stands.

"Sit down."

Her chewing can't get ahead of her thoughts to allow her to speak. She collects her purse.

"Now!"

Slings it over her shoulder. Finally swallows.

"Do not make a scene," he warns.

"It is not I who makes the scene." Her tension reveals itself too easily. She must work on this.

She leans into him, speaking in a forced whisper. "You have deliberately concealed information vital to our safety. I was kidnapped. John has a pair of fresh wounds. He is being pressured by the gallery owner in a way that could cost him his company. He and I are apparently operating in the dark, unaware of what is or is not fair play. You—purposely, it would seem—avoid communicating with us!"

"Sit . . . down!"

She slumps into her chair as Dulwich looks around. His glance confirms that the waiter and barista are the only ones paying attention, and they are far enough out of earshot.

"I might expect this from Knox," Dulwich says. "Not you."

"John wanted to take it to Mr. Primer."

"No!" The sharpness of his reprimand reminds her of a petulant boy not wanting a teacher to know of his misdeeds. She realizes belatedly that Knox's suspicion and distrust of Dulwich have taken root, something she'd hoped to avoid.

She whispers, "If this op is off the books, you should have told me. Perhaps not John, but most certainly me." Tries for eye contact, but Dulwich won't give it to her.

Primer relies on U.S. government contracts for a large part of the company's business. She has never heard of Rutherford Risk running a black ops group. John claims he was chosen for the op because of the preexisting relationship with Akram, causing her to wonder if the op is on or off the company books.

"You will complete the op. Do not concern yourself with exigent circumstances. The pacemaker is off limits."

She arrives at a critical moment. Cannot believe she says what she does. "I will not condone using John as a scapegoat."

His face is sheened with sweat. The espresso? she wonders.

"Is it so damn difficult?" He spits as he speaks. "You hand over the Harmodius, for Christ's sake. You spend five minutes in the room. It's a fucking delivery, Chu." His eyes roll. "Stop thinking so much and handle the fucking op!"

His voice is so quiet it wouldn't reach the next table, but his words knock her back as if he has shouted.

"This is not right," she says, examining him objectively for the first time. It slips out, but she doesn't regret it. "We are good at this, John, you, me. I think of Amsterdam—it took the three of us to succeed. No difference here. You are the conduit for the intelligence. But where are you? Not to be found. Then you are lurking outside electronics shops like a sexual predator. Keeping your own operatives under surveillance."

Dulwich drags his hand through his hair, purses his lips and exhales. Frustrated. "Jesus, you two. Do this thing. Do not question it, do it."

"They will kill John." She stares him down.

"No one has yet."

"I do not understand you."

"And I do not seek your approval."

The waiter returns, perhaps to referee; perhaps curiosity or a bet with the barista has encouraged him to get close enough to hear. But Dulwich is aware of every movement in the room, as well as those out on the street. Grace tries to learn from him; he knows more than even Knox about such things, and Knox has three times the instincts of anyone else.

Waving the waiter back, Dulwich leans in to Grace. "This isn't a courier for a construction company. It isn't a twelve-year-old girl in a sweatshop." He's referencing previous ops. "You two play games in the sandbox and give no thought to the playground, much less the school that built the playground in the first place. This thing . . .

what we're doing . . . Jesus, I don't owe you this. Carry out the fucking op and stop your whining. No one asked you to play detective. I told you: Need To Know. You misunderstood our last meeting. I would expect this of Knox, not you."

"Do not attempt to manipulate me."

"Be careful he doesn't infect you, Grace. Knox can be a poison."

"John saved your life. Twice. And, perhaps, mine. I can live with such poison."

Dulwich is perspiring.

She says, "Outside the Şişli Mosque you asked if I understood the op. You were appreciative of the intel I had—"

"Appreciative? I was—I am!—pissed off at all your unnecessary digging!"

"Of course," she says, hanging her head like the regretful courtesan, and hating herself for it.

"Here's your problem, Chu: a little information is a dangerous thing. A lot of information is fatal. Stick to the program. Have a little faith."

She can't find the strength to lift her head. The only sound is of the chair sliding back and the rustle of bills.

"Sit down," she says, head still lowered.

"Say whatever it is you have to say."

"Sit . . . down." It's a matter of pride now. Of face.

He sits. She raises her head, exuding a determination she has never shown him.

"We need an exit strategy," she says. "For tonight."

"It can't look like that," he says. "You can't go through this and climb onto a private plane and—"

"Who said anything about a private plane? A strategy. Options. A safe house. This is your side of things. Do what you do. You must." Unconditional.

He doesn't speak; merely silences her with the rush of color to his face. All but his lips, which take on an eerie, bloodless pallor.

"What this is," he speaks slowly and deliberately, "is bigger than stink. How exactly do you think I was able to come up with the Harmodius?"

"We have asked ourselves this same question."

"You two talk too much. Do your fucking jobs. Go home. Someday—" He cuts himself off, a drunk who knows even the bartender cannot hear what he wants to say.

"What? Someday we will hear the truth? Someday you will explain? You are a storyteller, David. It is your job. Promote the op. Coach up your players."

She wins a slight grin, some blood returning to his lips. He appreciates her Americanized metaphors. She believes he will always see her as Chinese first, a woman second, an operative last. She can't forgive him that. He lives the bias she sees on so many faces. Not Knox's, to his credit. She's not sure how Knox sees her, or sometimes if he sees her, but he's not one to label without justification. David is more predictable.

"I can tell you this. I," he corrects himself immediately, "we were hired—contracted," another correction, "by an individual. Not a government. There's a reason for that, a subtext that would be nothing but speculation were I to share it with you. I may have misled you. Maybe I appeared impressed with that early intel you provided. If you'd thought it through, you might have come to the conclusion that it was because I am in the dark on this one. I know less than you do. But I know to keep my nose clean, something you and Knox could use a lesson on. How to stick to the op. You . . . this intel . . . obviously this thing is—"

"Bigger than stink," she says, quoting him.

"Yes."

"Big enough to lose John in the process?"

Dulwich answers with inquisitive eyebrows.

Her stomach tightens: he'll accept whatever losses there are.

"Look, complete the op. Knox understands the risks. He lives for shit like this, and don't let him convince you otherwise." Dulwich pauses. "He's playing you; you're playing him. I'm playing both of you. It's what we do." He repeats somewhat mournfully, "It's what we do."

He hoists the espresso to his lips, but the demitasse is empty and the miscalculation embarrasses him. He doesn't know whether to lift the small cup toward the waiter, calling for another, or return it to the table. It surprises, even troubles Grace, that so small an act can hang so significantly between them.

"I? We? Which is it?"

Here, she thinks, *is the root of the problem,* but the clanging of the demitasse back into the saucer jolts her and she loses her train of thought.

"I'd be extremely careful if I were you."

Grace watches Dulwich go. She doesn't like having her back to the street. She comes around the table and sits down, wanting time to compartmentalize the highlights of the discussion. Still, her wet clothes bother her. The waiter clears the table, a sympathetic look on his face—Dulwich's open hostility has crossed the room.

She is thinking in the third person, hearing the voice of a Chinese army intelligence officer from her long distant past: what do we know now that we did not know before? What needs to be discarded to clear our heads? Of what we have learned, what could be disinformation? Retain only absolute truths. Do not be swayed by subjectivity or opinion. Hold your source in high regard, regardless of appearance or manner.

She filters the conversation accordingly, only bits and pieces making their way through the various layers of screens: the Harmodius; limited resources; NTK; his reaction to the mention of the Israelis; his resistance to Brian Primer's involvement. His confession about the nongovernmental client.

The waiter brings her more tea. She orders a sugary pastry, unable to resist the thought of more food. There was a time when she would have rushed to inform Knox, to involve him in the puzzle. But with experience comes confidence, and with confidence, patience and understanding. Better to present Knox with information he can use than gush out a riot of confusion. Knox has his own filters. She knows better than to edit her information for him.

Grace squints, savoring the pastry. That butter, sugar, salt and flour can combine in so many different ways is a testament to the supremacy of man's evolution; she pities animals their bland diets. Returning from her revelry, she spots a man in profile on the sidewalk, passing the café. Bile leaks up from her esophagus; she recognizes him from the hospital elevator. Mid-thirties. Nondescript. One of Dulwich's? She finds herself hoping so. The alternative is less than promising.

An instant later, she reverses her defensive attitude. This stranger is a bridge to the truth between what she believes and what she knows. More to the point, she feels she is justified to take the offensive. She elects not to run from this man, but to challenge him, take him on. She doesn't ignore her earlier abduction but feeds off her anger over it; does not enter into the task naively but remains alert and hyperaware of her surroundings, convincing herself that they wouldn't have succeeded in taking her the first time if she hadn't been so focused on running firewalls and prying open electronic trapdoors.

With the sidewalk underfoot, sounds and smells swirl around

her; she submits to the tease of nerves and her resolute determination to reverse the injustice.

If the man from the hospital took up a position down the adjacent alley, intent on keeping watch on the front and back of the café, he sorely miscalculated his own confinement. He has no choice but to move away from Grace as she appears at the end of the alley. Slowly at first. Scheming. Perhaps he plans to circle around; perhaps he's lost interest in her.

But not she in him. She closes the gap quickly, clear-minded and fleet of foot. Confrontation and combat require emotionless focus. This man is her prey now, their roles reversed. If he wants to turn and face her, it will be at his own peril.

There's no such resolve. He's on the run—a surveillant assigned to see but not be seen. He's out of luck; she has him in her sights.

Disguised within Grace are power, coordination, training and experience. She brings this combination to bear on the man, who is attempting to pretend she does not exist. Chops his right knee from behind just before he exits the alley.

He didn't come looking for a fight. She drops her purse and its contents spill. His right arm swings in a failed attempt to maintain his balance. Grace grabs the arm as it passes, throws her right shoulder into his armpit and steps forward, thrusts her right elbow into his back, ducks beneath the arm and turns his wrist as she lifts it to connect with his shoulder blades. He drops down to his knees, stunned with pain.

No gun. She takes possession of his phone.

"Who?" She tries Turkish then English. Kicks him between the legs from behind. That wins his attention while dropping him lower. Repeats herself in Chinese, wondering too late if she's revealing too much.

"Besim!" he moans.

She releases his arm. It sags to the pavement as if a prosthetic.

"To watch you. Protect you." Turkish.

Grace steps away and collects her belongings.

"The password to your phone?" She speaks in his language. He recites four numbers; she clears the screen and looks up his most recent calls. Three of the five are to Besim's phone. She double-checks her purse; searches the area for her penlight. Finds it.

"You were at the hospital."

"Yes," he says. He comes to his feet and turns around. He's embarrassed by her superiority, cannot look directly at her. A woman, of all things! "Two others. A woman, a man watching the hospital. Israelis. Saw you."

Grace nearly gasps. "You know this, how?" Condescending disbelief. "It is not possible you could know such a thing."

"As a boy, I fell through the ice on the Bosphorus. Lost my ears, three years. Learned to read mouths. My grandmother is a Jew. This man, this woman? They spoke in the car. Hebrew."

The tightness in her chest remains. Israelis. Watching the hospital or watching her? She asks him, already knowing the answer, but wanting to test his honesty.

"The man followed you inside. The lady left the car. Walked the block on phone. I go opposite side, much luck. Saw you in elevator."

"Unlikely," she said. She checked for tails.

He shrugs, indifferent. "As you wish."

"And they?"

"These two not follow. Lost you, I think."

Grace doesn't know when they transitioned to English but they're speaking it now. Crafty, this one, perhaps explaining why he was Besim's choice.

"But not you," she says. "Besim did this."

"Besim is good man."

"Yes. Yes, he is."

"Istanbul is not so kind to women alone."

"Chinese women."

"Any women. Better with man at side."

"Is that so?"

No response. He looks to be about thirty. Could stand to lose a few pounds. She keys her number into his phone and returns it to him. "The knee––?"

He moves it. Stiff, but working.

"Keep your distance. Should you spot others watching me—"

"Yes." He holds up the phone. "I understand."

"Do not engage with these people." Her words are intentionally forceful. "Promise me that."

"As you wish."

"Besim should have said something." It's as close as she'll get to an apology.

"Besim is man of few words."

She's not sure if something was lost in translation. "A good distance. You mustn't be associated with me."

"I saw what you did not see. I followed you when they did not."

She's thinking of the Chinese proverb: *Jiāo bīng bi bài*. The arrogant army will surely lose. Pride goeth before the fall. "As much as I appreciate it, you do not want to tangle with those following me." She adds, "With anyone following me."

"You are popular woman." He smiles, his teeth gleaming in the dark alley. "I understand Besim's concern."

A minute earlier, she was prepared to dislocate his elbow and shoulder. Again, she marvels at the excitement of fieldwork, the joy she feels, the visceral sense of being alive at this moment. This place.

"My phone," she says. "Others may see it. Text me only the

number of those watching for me and their direction. You understand? Like a compass. You know the compass points in English?"

"Of course."

"Just like that," Grace says. "In relation to me, not you."

"This, I understand."

"Thank you." She leaves him, returning through the deep shadows of the long alley, eager to find Knox.

42

My God!" Grace blurts out as Knox admits her to the toilet stall at the back of the falafel shop. There are two unisex toilets. Knox has been sitting on the closed seat, awaiting her arrival.

Her reaction is in part to his pants being down at his ankles, but primarily to the bloody lacerations and ugly raised lumps on his shins. Hopefully she's not paying attention to the red stab wound on his thigh or the similarly repaired injury to his scalp.

"I wouldn't have called, but it's nearly impossible to walk."

Grace stares at his legs, her face pale. "What—?"

"A woman. Rebar. I was supposed to end up in an ambulance for what I assume was a 'debriefing.' Did you get it?"

She digs into the paper bag she carries and removes a small brown bottle. "This is meant for toothaches, John."

"It'll do the trick, believe me. I usually carry some. I'm out. What about—?"

Grace removes a prescription bottle from her purse. "Vicodin. Take two—"

"How did you—?"

"You do not want to ask." Yet she explains anyway. "Habit-forming drugs require prescription. Antibiotics, antidepressants? These do not. I used my considerable charms—and my UN identification—to obtain eight pills. One day's worth. Not enough to satisfy an addiction."

Knox uncaps the vial, dispenses four and swallows them.

"Size triple X," he says.

He spills some of the toothache ointment over the injuries, wincing at the contact. Grace kneels and patches him up, using cream, gauze and tape from the bag.

"Any one of these wounds is enough to require you to rest, John. We should abort."

Knox studies her pained face. Her position makes them both uncomfortable; she's looking up at him, her eyes level with his waist. He sees something beyond concern flash across her face, but exactly what it is remains out of reach.

"You'd better explain that."

An impatient knock.

"Let us get you out of here first," Grace whispers. "Can you walk?"

Knox flexes his ankles. Shoots of pain race through him like fever chills. He puts his weight on both heels. Winces a second time. "Sure. Why not?"

Grace reaches out to help with his pants, but Knox takes over and Grace stands back as he lifts them gingerly past the wounds and fastens them at the waist. She collects the contents of the bag, including the trash. Leave no evidence of injury behind; give your opponent no sense of advantage.

He hobbles forward two steps.

"It'll be better once the drugs kick in."

"That will not be soon enough. We will wait here. Put food in you. Medication to be taken with food. When is the last time you ate?"

"Look who's talking."

"David just bought me falafel," she says.

Knox wonders if it's the pain or her words that stop his diaphragm. "O . . . kay."

At a table against the wall, Knox sits, long legs elevated on the chair next to Grace; across the table, she takes him through the meeting with Dulwich and her encounter with Besim's agent provocateur. She talks at length with the waitress, who brings two bags of ice. Grace places them atop Knox's wounds.

"You cannot continue, John. Not like this."

He tells her that the testing of the Harmodius, including the soil samples, indicates Israeli soil. Grace nods; relates that this matches with Besim's man lip reading the Hebrew spoken by her hospital pursuers.

The reputation of Mossad is not lost on either of them. Mashe Okle's scientific credentials. The fact that a half-dozen Iranian nuclear scientists have died under suspicious circumstances. Dulwich's assurances that no killing would take place, when all evidence points to the contrary.

Grace walks Knox through what Dulwich told her about a single client, informs him that they are in the midst of a black op multilayered to ensure deniability. She impresses him with Dulwich's apparent surprise at hearing about a possible dead drop, adds that Sarge's emphasis remains on the two of them getting their five minutes with Mashe Okle. "Your condition, John, is the perfect excuse for us to abort," she finishes.

"What about all his flag waving?" This is the part of her story that intrigues Knox—Dulwich's plea to stay with the op. Dedication to the job is one thing, but the way she described it, it sounds more like passion. Knox knows Dulwich to be truly passionate about one thing only: the flag and all it represents.

"Let us accept this: the Harmodius was dug up in Israel. Real or a copy, it hardly matters. It is presumed to be extremely valuable. The client, either acting alone or on behalf of the Israelis, has used it as bait. What if the Israeli agents we have encountered are assigned to ensure its security? Its eventual return?"

Knox likes her explanation, appreciates her ability to be concise. She takes his relaxation the wrong way.

"I am boring?"

"Of course," he says.

She laughs, covering her mouth, an annoying habit of hers he has failed to break.

"It's the drugs kicking in." He feels good. Too good. Recognizes that he's speaking too freely.

"You were supposed to take only two," she reminds him.

"Sarge claimed ignorance regarding a drop," Knox says, attempting to clarify.

"I am reading into this something that may not be accurate," she says, carefully prefacing her words, "but I would say David was not surprised by the suggestion of a dead drop, although it was news to him, if you are able to discern the difference. The trip here serves two purposes, it seems. This makes sense to him, but troubles him, too."

"He's not the only one." Knox lets this information roll around in his head. It's getting gooey in there. The rough corners are smooth now, his body warm. His shins pulse but no longer scream. "You know what this means?"

Grace shakes her head patronizingly. He must be slurring his words.

"Either the Israelis or the Iranians are responsible for the mother's illness."

A ceiling fan creaks. Cars rumble past on the street.

"It's what got him here. Mashe. What created the excuse for him to come."

"A son cannot possibly condone such a thing."

"Maybe he doesn't know. He won't have put it together. And we don't know what he condones or what kind of hold, if any, they have over him. Perhaps the threat is that they finish her. It's impossible to say. If Sarge knows, he isn't telling."

"We either have two unrelated ops," she says softly, "or we misread your mugging."

"I'm listening."

Grace says, "Let us assume the Israelis are assigned to keep track of the Harmodius. They follow you. They account for your every move. They search your hotel room when you are away. The Harmodius is gone. What is next?"

"They search me for a receipt or locker key—evidence of where I've stashed the statue. They make it look like a mugging. Ergo, no dead drop."

"It is a possibility, *neh*?"

It's genius, but he doesn't tell her so. "Then what's with the pacemaker?" Knox would rather be telling than asking, but the shock of the wound combined with the medication is limiting. He'll let Grace take the lead for now.

"It could be nothing more than proactive intelligence. Let us assume the Israelis have connected a Swiss medical supplier with a foreign intelligence organization. Medical devices are being used to convey intelligence. The Israelis cannot take the chance that software vital to the nuclear program might be smuggled to the Iranians inside the electronics of sealed pacemakers—"

"So they interrupt the supply chain and place clean pacemakers in the hospital. They collect the suspicious shipment and deliver it to their lab for analysis." Knox exhales. "Clever bastards."

Grace overreacts instinctively, worried about his pain. "John!"

"I'm good." There are warm marbles rolling around behind his eyes. He could sit here for hours. "Doesn't explain the shot Ali took. You don't try to kill the guy who's hidden what's yours." It's an unintended slap in the face.

"No," she says.

"What are you keeping from me? Sarge told you something."

She does not hesitate. "He said, I quote, it is 'bigger than stink.'"

The expression hits Knox. "He said that? Those exact words?"

"Yes. Why?"

Knox inhales through his nose, feels sick. Knows it's not the drugs. "Well then," he whispers. "Phones off." He digs his out and turns his off and waits for her to do the same. Tries to stand. "They'll have this location by now. We need an alternate exit. And we've got to stay moving."

"John?" Grace allows fear into her voice. She helps him to stand. He's unsteady.

He allows her to help. It surprises them both. He talks to himself. "I'll need to turn mine back on: Akram's going to text me the location for the meet. But for now . . ."

He's rambling. Scared, she repeats his name, imploringly.

Knox steadies himself with hands on both her shoulders. "Bigger than stink. It's a Sarge expression: the end justifies the means, which in our case is us." He meets eyes with her. "We're fucked."

43

The city bus smells of human sweat and greasy food. Grace had to help Knox climb up into it. Now that they're seated, Knox has no intention of ever getting up again.

Neither he nor Grace was willing to risk a taxi. Walking any sort of distance was out of the question. The Alzer Hotel is off limits. They ride the bus to have somewhere to be, like the homeless, and receive their share of stares from the predominantly Turkish passengers. The driver has taken to watching them in his oversized mirror.

"So, we wait," Grace says. As if they've done something else in the past ninety minutes. Knox dozes in and out, grateful for her presence and for the drugs running through his system.

"I've been thinking," he says, coming awake.

She dismisses this as delirium.

"Given the circumstances, the complexities, there's no reason for two of us—"

"You are delirious. Go back to sleep."

"Plans change based on the conditions. These are unusual conditions."

"I know where you are going with this. No chance, John. None. We wait for the text or the call. We do this together."

"As what, martyrs? Why?"

"The plan has not changed. Two of us in the room with him for five minutes. We hand over the Harmodius. We go home."

"I don't like going home. Home is what got me into this." She can see he regrets his words, but his tongue is loose. "Sarge pushes whatever buttons are required to get what he wants. Same as anyone else."

"Tommy?"

"A new medication. Did I tell you?" He looks delirious. She should have let him go back to sleep. But she can't control her curiosity. Wonders if it's an asset or a liability.

"Expensive," she says.

"Insanely so. Yeah. I must have told you."

"You are a good man. A good brother. You must not equate Tommy with—"

"I'm a fraud. I'm the Harmodius. I look like the real thing, test like the real thing, but I'm a copy. An old copy."

"You should sleep."

"Do I do this work out of benevolence? Brotherliness? No. I do this because it takes me away from all of the shit back there. I live for this." He touches his cap and the wound beneath it. "I don't want to die. Far from it. But this shit matters. You know? You realize that, right, Grace? This shit matters."

He's drunk on the medication. Adorable, in an oversized, testosterone-laced kind of way. "She sure as shit better deliver it as promised," he mutters, and appears to doze off.

Besim is tasked with watching Victoria, who controls the Harmodius. Grace is unconcerned. She studies him, feeling honored he would share such things with her, whether the drugs or not. His relationship with his brother is as complex as hers with her father.

She feels close to Knox and knows that it's unhealthy; but so is vodka, and that never stops her.

Twenty minutes pass. She has no idea where they are. It's late afternoon, the sidewalks crowded once more. She catches a glimpse of the Bosphorus and reorients herself.

"We're traveling northeast toward the university," Knox says, his eyes still closed.

She doesn't understand how he does these things, worries it's what separates successful field agents from wannabes like herself. Admires and resents him at the same time.

"It's bus 61-B," he says, as if reading her mind. "Did you think the choice was random?"

She did, in fact, but she's loath to admit it.

"Tepebaşi to Taksim," he quotes. "Gets us close to the river. The meet will take place on the Asian side in an area where Westerners like me can be more easily spotted."

If Knox is the target of a kill order, this is risky territory.

Under Besim's watchful eye, Victoria has returned the Harmodius to the Alzer Hotel's bellman storage. When the remainder of the payment is deposited into escrow, Grace will be with Knox to vet the sourcing—requiring at least five minutes while in his company.

Given the okay, Victoria will meet one of the Iranian guards and pass along the claim tag. The moment the Harmodius is in the guard's possession, she and Knox are nothing but witnesses. Dulwich has made no allowance for an exit strategy, a fact his conversation with Grace did nothing to change. Knox's safety relies on no one being followed to the meet and on no connection existing between Mashe and whoever killed Ali.

"Makes things interesting, doesn't it?"

He's been reading her mind. Again.

"Don't worry so much," he says.

"You can barely walk, certainly not run."

"Never discount the miracles of modern medicine. Believe me, I feel very good right now."

"You are doped."

"Umm." He closes his eyes again.

Grace wants to doubt him, to question him, but entreats herself to listen and learn. Dulwich has a dozen men and three women at his disposal, all contractors for Rutherford Risk. He subcontracts Knox for the intangibles. If she's smart, she can learn from Knox's arrogance. His relentless efforts to set himself apart from the status quo run contrary to her Chinese heritage and training. If she's to become like him, it will require a personality change, a psychic shift that's well out of reach. She sags back into the uncomfortable, slippery plastic bench, discouraged.

44

Knox is not asleep. Despite the meds, his mind is overactive. It's easier to focus without looking at the weathered faces of the old Turkish women riding the bus, the wide-eyed toddlers in strollers, the men reading newspapers as if they plan never to disembark.

He hears the bus wipers engage and realizes it's raining again. A few seconds later, the report on the roof confirms: it's pouring. His legs twinge; the pain presents a real problem, though he's unwilling to admit it. He thinks back to Grace pushing him around in a wheelchair in Shanghai as cover, marvels at how things change. He works through the possible variations of what could go wrong at the meet and how to react. He stores each reaction, a bullet list of responses depending on the situation. Into his assumptions, he must fit his disability.

The pieces do not mesh well. If Dulwich or the client pulls something, if Knox was supposed to escape by his wit and physical prowess, the plan has failed before it even started. He's going to hobble in and hobble out. They will all have to wait for the Harmodius to be in Mashe Okle's custody. If they are to be used as unwitting couriers, the complications will escalate due to his infirmity.

"We have to bring it with us," Knox says, eyes closed.

"Impossible. The funds will never be transferred."

"Sarge wanted us and the prize in the room for five minutes. If it plays out the way I planned, using Victoria, Mashe may not see the piece until he's back in Iran. We'll have done all of this for nothing."

"There is nothing inside it. It was X-rayed. You said so yourself. It is a piece of metal sculpture, that is all."

"We don't want to wait around for its retrieval. That kind of down time is too dangerous. Sarge kept stressing an in-and-out. Why? What if he didn't mean the op as a whole, but just the five-minute meet?"

"He would have told me this when I met with him."

Knox knows Dulwich to be a pragmatic man. He'll defend the op first, the operatives second. Grace filled the man's head with evidence of a possible dead drop. From that moment on, Dulwich was thinking only of preserving his side of the op. "I'd like to think he'd hate to lose us, don't get me wrong. But his flag waving with you was meant to drive home a point: the op's success is bigger than any one of us. Any two of us. What you have to know about Sarge is this: the man's a patriot. First and foremost. His ultimate loyalty is not to you or me or even Brian Primer. He's an agnostic whose higher power is life, liberty and the pursuit of happiness. No one's going to change that. If he perceives that the gain will require loss . . ."

Knox sits up. It's a deluge out there. Looking through the windshield is like trying to see through Saran Wrap. "The one thing we haven't given serious consideration to is the idea that Sarge has gone rogue."

Grace is unblinking.

Knox says, "Use of the Red Room. Mine was at lunch hour. Yours?"

She doesn't answer. Doesn't have to.

"Fewer people in the office during lunch. No one using that room."

"He made it clear that Mr. Primer was not to be involved. Was upset when we made direct contact with Xin."

"When I called, the op wasn't listed. We took that to be a security measure. But maybe it isn't listed anywhere. The Harmodius is tied to Israel. Sarge is in bed with the Israelis. We are now in bed with the Israelis."

"Speculative. And how does any of this help us?"

Knox shuts his eyes again. Listens to the slap of the wipers. A man clears his throat. The air brakes wheeze. Knox checks his watch. Turns on his phone.

In a painful heave, Knox sits bolt upright. "Mashe's going to defect. It's an elaborate plan to allow him to defect! It could never look like it. Never be connected. His own guards would kill him. Sarge never said people wouldn't die; he said that the POI wouldn't be killed. The POI is going to defect to the Israelis through us, a private company. If he does, Western intelligence of the Iranian nuclear program takes a giant leap forward. The program itself loses another scientist."

"But since it is arranged privately," Grace says. She's going along with him, though he can't tell from her face how much she's buying it. "The Iranians do not know to which country he has defected, making it the more difficult to track him down and—"

"So who takes out the guards?"

The bus rumbles. Knox can't make sense of it. So close . . .

"Akram," Grace is gloating. "We will be searched, certainly. But the brother is no threat. He is familiar to them. The last person they will suspect of such a crime."

"That's all well and good but there are pieces that don't fit." Knox can't be sure if he spoke the words or only thought them. He experiences another rush of sensational warmth from the Vicodin. Doesn't see the point of arguing. Of anything. "Akram," he hears himself say.

He's not echoing her conviction but looking at his phone's screen, where an alert shows. He passes the phone to Grace.

"It is an address," she informs him. "We have twenty minutes."

45

A taxi drops them off in front of the Blue Mosque. Several hundred tourists mill about in a way that makes the crowd feel like several thousand. Above their heads, squadrons of pigeons arc through the rain as if it isn't falling.

Knox and Grace take shelter beneath a plane tree but can't avoid getting wet. Grace checks her watch impatiently. Knox's phone chimes a minute later: a license plate number. A dark blue minivan pulls to the curb, where a police officer waves it off. Grace waves at the driver from twenty yards away.

"That the same van that took you?" Knox asks.

"No."

The last thing Grace sees as she climbs inside is Besim's accomplice straddling a pale blue motor scooter back by the gesticulating police officer. As she steps in, a hood is pulled over her head.

"Where is sculpture?" a heavily accented male voice asks in struggling English.

Knox answers, "The woman makes her case with Mashe." He speaks through the darkness of the hood. "When she is satisfied, you will release her and she will text me once safely away. Then, and only then, will you see it."

"No!" Grace objects.

"Shut up!" Knox counters. It's a hybrid plan that meets his requirement of keeping at least one of them safe.

"Unacceptable. No sculpture. No meeting."

Knox supposes this would fill Dulwich to bursting—the enemy begging to be in the same room with the Harmodius.

The man searches and empties the outside pockets of the Scottevest but, feeling more contents, unzips the windbreaker and starts emptying its nineteen compartments. The man starts a dialogue with the driver in Persian, clearly impressed by the garment.

"Where you make jacket?" the man asks.

Knox scoffs. "If you want the sculpture, before you shut off my phone and pull the SIM," he's assuming they are well into making sure no GPS signal allows them to be followed, "you need to text the number ending in six-seven-six and request a curb drop."

There is discussion between this man and at least two others. Knox does the math—three at a minimum, including the driver. Knox is spun around and pushed to the floor as if he's praying backward, into the pew. His bruised shins strike the floor of the van and he goes faint. The op has reached the point Dulwich intended— the five minutes are nearly upon them. He wonders if they'll be his last.

The hood is lifted as the van pulls to the curb. Knox sees gray cloth upholstery and, in the reflection off the seat belt's chrome tongue, flashing pieces of a face and a Makarov PMM trained on the base of his neck.

"You do this!" he's instructed. "I am watching."

His phone has been set up to text Victoria's number, as Knox indicated. The guy probably can't write English. Knox types:

curb drop. supply address. now.

The phone pings, an address being texted back. His captor barks it out to the driver, pulls the hood over Knox and returns him to the seat bench. He stretches the seat belt across Knox and fastens it—a gesture that has nothing to do with safety.

He can hear the guy working. "Where you make jacket?" he repeats.

"You can get 'em online," Knox answers. "Pants. Shirts. FBI uses them."

The man repeats the part about the FBI to the driver. Another exchange. His captor peels the Scottevest off Knox. The work is intimate, providing Knox several lost opportunities to knock the guy into another postal code.

"What is going on?" Grace asks.

"You wouldn't believe me if I told you."

"Shut the fuck! No talk."

Knox hears the windbreaker being passed up to the driver, who shakes it, studying it as he drives.

"Scott-y-vest," Knox says, drawing out the pronunciation.

The man repeats it. It's a language lesson. He gets the hang of it.

"Google T-E-C. It'll be there somewhere near the top."

"I keep."

"No," Knox says.

"John!" Grace interjects. "It's a jacket!"

"It's my jacket."

"No talk!"

Knox says, "You take my jacket, I take your gun."

The man clobbers Knox through the hood, but stuffs the jacket into his gut after the driver says something nasty.

Grace clears her throat as if to say, *Happy now?*

311

Knox coughs to let her know he's thrilled. His hands roam the jacket. They've left him his phone, though it's certainly shut off and currently without its SIM.

"No talk!" the myna bird says.

The guy opens and chews a stick of gum, failing to offer his guests any. Knox's mouth is dry; he feels groggy. Wakes up when he slumps into Grace, who catches his head.

"Off!" Their captor shouts. He's in the front seat, judging by the sound. There has been no attempt to bind their wrists or ankles. Ostensibly, the blindfolds are about protecting the location of Mashe Okle. That, in turn, tells Grace and Knox that Mashe Okle's situation has changed, the turning point likely the attempted assassination in the taxi cab that left Ali dead. Grace and Knox are too shorthanded to know if the elder Okle has visited the mother's hospital room any time since. Doubtful. More likely lying low.

If their theory is right and Mashe Okle is a defecting nuclear scientist, he may have realized that his mother's illness was either faked or forced, as Knox and Grace have. May understand that all the visits in the world aren't going to improve her health. Only crossing the imaginary line, the border between Iran and whatever country he has struck a deal with, can save her now.

Unless they are wrong about his defection. This is the part of the spook world Knox detests, why it never attracted him: too many unknowns. Dulwich made him believe they were doing something good, something that has to be done; Knox can't shake the feeling he has to play this out.

Grace helps Knox to sit up straight; there's an unmistakable tenderness in her touch. It communicates concern, caution, patience, apprehension. They are in the lion's den. Together. Separately. Their single agenda: to watch a clock tick out five minutes in Mashe's company. Both are assuming an announcement or an action on his part will occur before time expires. If not—if he's not defecting—it's anybody's game.

Knox wonders silently if the perceived dead drop was simply misunderstood by one or more foreign agencies. The expectation is the passing of information; in reality, it may be the willing exchange of a human being.

What's beyond doubt is that neither he nor Grace possesses enough reliable intelligence to have any idea what to expect, which makes planning their exit strategy impossible. That, in turn, explains Dulwich's inability to address the subject at the falafel shop. Knox's mind is too dulled to pull all the pieces together.

And lurking at the back of his consciousness is a voice reminding him about the pacemaker battery.

Knox's wrist warms beneath his watch. He ascribes the sensation to the meds until he hears cursing from the front seat and, seconds later, hears something strike the rubber floor mat. A fist knots the fabric of the hood and his shirt.

"What the fuck is this?" the man asks.

"What the fuck is what?" Knox asks, gritting his teeth against the burning of his watch against his skin.

The man bounces Knox off the seat back. "Fuck you!"

"Microwave," the driver says. Apparently the same word in Persian as English. Knox is able to make out most of his explanation. "Listening device. Americans. Microwave. I have heard of this."

"Then shut up!" the passenger barks. Only seconds later, he says softly, "From where? You watch for tail, yes?"

"You are a prick. Of course I watch. It is your job, also."

"How large, this microwave?"

"No idea. Maybe nowhere nearby. Maybe satellite."

Grace toes Knox gently, and he wonders if she's amused that Okle sent Cheech and Chong to fetch them or if it's something more. The

Vicodin has relaxed him to a point at which everything's amusing. They could cut off his hand and he'd thank them. But Grace isn't enjoying herself. She's an accountant in wicked shape, trained as a Chinese spook. She's ambitious, pragmatic, professionally androgynous, socially challenged, mildly alcoholic and lonely. She's not playing footsie to win a chuckle, but to literally nudge him. He must be missing something. If his watch wasn't approaching the heat of a laundry iron, he might be able to think, but in another few seconds they're all going to smell his burning wrist hair.

The van jostles him in the seat. He's attempting to focus enough to rehearse the upcoming meeting. Anticipation is nine-tenths of survival. But Grace's nudge interrupted his preparation, like throwing a trivia question into a conversation. He can't keep his ideas separate.

It doesn't help when the van goes into paint-shaker mode and his thigh wound hits a pain pitch that could shatter glass. Inside the black hood, it's too warm; he sucks for air, claustrophobic. His injured shins pulse. The food isn't sitting right, a mass lodged somewhere around his collarbone and swelling. He tries swallowing away the burning feeling, but his mouth may as well be stuffed with cotton balls.

Grace relives the events inside the van during her abduction: the driver's watch warming to the point he dumped it; the van experiencing engine problems. Engines that run on computers; computer boards running on batteries.

Grace toeing Knox serves its purpose, the connection made. Similar, perhaps identical phenomenon—abduction, vans, overheating wristwatches. Knox isn't thinking clearly and he knows it. Resents it. He would trade the pain for a moment of insight. It's often called "connective tissue": the threads that exist or can be strung between events or persons. It's here for him to see, but he does not. He wishes he could get a look at Grace to know if she's come up with the answer or only the question.

The van slows. His wrist is either beyond pain or the watch is cooling. He and Grace are pushed down as doors bang open and closed. Grace has been made to lie across Knox, while Knox's bagged head is pushed against the van wall. Their captors want to limit any chance that the head sacks will be seen by a random street dweller.

Grace says in a forced whisper, "My phone. Five minutes."

The van is moving again. Knox and Grace are pulled back to sitting positions. He assumes the Harmodius is onboard; Victoria delivered. She had better leave it at that, had better return to her hotel room and await a message. No time for heroes.

Grace's phone. Five minutes. What the fuck?

Goddamned Vicodin.

46

The head sacks come off inside an apartment building. Grace and Knox are ushered upstairs as their captors struggle with the crate holding the Harmodius.

Grace is thinking that if Besim's friend spots surveillance, she'll never know about it. Her phone is off, its SIM pulled. She believes it was returned to her purse, but she isn't about to check. Instead, she's trying to help Knox from behind as he struggles to climb on painful legs. With the ascent of each stair, she considers another bullet point on her list of financial topics to cover with Mashe Okle.

Like Knox, she has a role to play; unlike Knox, she does not ad-lib. She recites her lines, considers her strategies and steadies him by holding him around the waist, impressed by the sense of physical power that comes with the contact—even a wounded John Knox would prove a formidable foe.

The sparsely furnished apartment is a safe house. Not lived in, judging by the lack of personal touches. Drawn drapes lend a sense of claustrophobia to the scant items of furniture: imitation leather couch; a glass-topped stainless-steel coffee table, badly scratched. Several of the floor tiles have been cracked and reglued.

Akram looks nervous. Mashe does not. He's smaller than his brother, wiry but with a big head, his black hair trimmed over the ears but fashionably long on his neck. He wears heavy-rimmed glasses with thick lenses. Gray suit trousers, a collarless pressed white shirt. The matching suit coat hangs over a ladder-back dining chair at a table that may have never seen a meal. He carries an air of aloof overconfidence, no doubt perpetually aware that he is the smartest man in any room.

Knox sits down on an orange-cushioned chair that hisses under his weight. It's positioned facing the coffee table at a right angle to the couch. The chair is too small for him; his knees stick up high. He's chosen it because due to a jog in the wall there's no way anyone can come up from behind him. It's a defensive position. Across the room, Grace takes note of his choice.

Mashe Okle shakes their hands and introduces himself as "Akram's brother." He then approaches his two handlers and stands by, await-ing the unpacking of the Harmodius. It's an ordeal. Grace is won-dering if Knox is thinking what she is: they're halfway to their five-minute deadline already. This is made more evident by Mashe's twisting of his wristwatch.

She believes her phone is directly connected to the overheating wristwatches, though the mechanics make no sense. She has shut off her phone on multiple nights with no odd consequences. How would powering off a device or removing a SIM card create such an effect in the first place? More to the point, her phone has never been out of her possession. Who could have rigged it, and when?

But the empirical evidence contradicts all her arguments.

Three minutes . . .

If he's defecting, why is he continuing to act out the role of art collector?

"Out," Mashe Okle instructs his two security men, one of whom takes in Knox warily. Knox grins for the man, ever the wiseass.

The guards leave the apartment though their conversation carries through the door; they want Knox to know they aren't going anywhere.

Mashe Okle studies the Harmodius with deep reverence. He dons a pair of white cotton gloves and touches the piece sensually. "Akram and I have discussed the results of the preliminary lab work. I must say: it sounds promising."

"There is the matter of the financing," Grace says, firmly embedded in her role.

"If I were part of a cultural police force, Ms. Chu," he says, making it known he's researched her at least to the point of knowing her name, "you two would have been arrested upon entering this apartment."

"Such investigations take months, even years. We both know that." She's wondering if he considers her a midlevel bureaucrat with the United Nations or a freelance accountant in Hong Kong. The man gives off an intimidating presence, especially for a person so small and thin.

"Point taken," he concedes.

"The recent deposits into your investment account require adequate explanation and sourcing, or I am afraid this transaction cannot go forward."

Everyone knows that Mashe holds the cards in terms of the transaction going forward. They are in his safe house, with no idea what part of the city they are in. It's his goons outside, and his brother standing to Knox's left.

The sounding of a ship horn in that instant works against the

Okle brothers. Its proximity and clarity reveal that the apartment is located no more than ten blocks from the Bosphorus. Rain clatters against the windows on the other side of the mauve drapes. The sound is metallic, suggesting a fire escape. Grace assumes Knox has catalogued this and more, though she doesn't appreciate the faraway look in his eyes. That, coupled with his shit-eating grin, is reason for concern.

"Fellow investors," Mashe Okle says.

"I tried to—" Akram says.

His older brother lifts a hand, silencing him.

That demonstration of control liquefies Grace's bowels. She wants out of here. Now. The sound is of rain on metal gutters.

Strength demands strength. It is the rule behind all escalation.

"I will require documentation of the source of those deposits. Canceled checks, copies of wire transfers. And I caution you: I must source the origin of each deposit, the originating accounts."

"I respect such thoroughness."

"I will need a computer and time. Such work is not easy, nor is it without risk."

He purses his lips. "I am under the impression that you, Mr. Knox, require the transaction to take place today. Now. That you have a plane to catch."

"My accountant is quite capable, Mr. Okle. An hour or two is all." Knox looks to Grace for confirmation.

She nods. "It would be a start."

Mashe Okle draws close the ladder-back chair that holds his suit jacket and sits. He speaks more softly. "I am afraid we lack the computer you require. I am also sorry to say neither of you will leave this apartment until the transaction is completed. You see, I have the same concerns as you, Ms. Chu. Mr. Knox is not known to trade in such rare artifacts. Now we are to believe he has come across one of the rarer treasures in the history of Western civilization. A treasure carrying traces of Israeli soil."

He blinks rapidly, revealing a deep-seated fatigue. Grace needs no reminder from Knox that this apparent change in his behavior comes after the five-minute mark, though she lacks an explanation for it.

She's distracted by the recollection of her admittance to the Red Room. She and Dulwich surrendered their phones to shelving outside the secure space. Other than the two abductions, it was the last time she can remember being separated from her iPhone. She knows Knox was briefed in the Red Room as well. Her throat, already dry, is parched.

Their phones were tampered with, perhaps cloned and replaced during their briefings. Dulwich's choice of the Red Room had little or nothing to do with secrecy, and everything to do with separating them from their devices. The degree of the conspiracy expands exponentially—she and Knox have been carefully manipulated from the start. Everything Dulwich has put them through is part of a well-crafted plan. Knox's paranoia is justified.

Mashe Okle has gone pale, perspiration covering his face with a sweaty glaze. The room is hot, and Grace says so. Akram, also sweating, agrees. He disappears behind the drawn drapes and the street sounds intensify as fresh air flows across the space, the wind billowing the curtains. Akram reappears.

"Brother?" he inquires, focusing on the man's sallow skin tone.

"Tired is all."

Has Mashe been anticipating this? Is it part of his plan to defect? He must not seem ill; he must be ill. Is Akram privy to any of it?

Knox stands. He speaks, sounding sleepy. "You're in possession of the lab results. You've seen the piece in person. You will either bring a laptop and some food and coffee or release us and the Harmodius until such time as my associate can complete her due diligence."

Mashe looks like he's had enough. His body language shows weakness. He shakes his head as if disappointed.

"Brother?" Akram's concern comes across as nerves.

"I am fine." To Knox, Mashe says, "I doubt these men have been terribly accommodating, and for this I would like to apologize. I suspect the present arrangements have made you and your colleague uncomfortable. Again, I apologize. While I respect your desire to leave, I believe you will find my security personnel less agreeable." He addresses Grace. "I will request a computer, as you wish. I must caution you: they are likely to decline the request, as any Internet access could, I presume, locate the three of us in ways I doubt I must elaborate upon. Therefore, I will suggest we are in something of a stalemate. I seriously doubt, Ms. Chu, you will be availed of your desire to vet my accounts and, while I understand the desire for such verification, it simply may not be possible given the present circumstances.

"This leaves us with two choices: I can transfer one half of the funds to any account you choose, the balance to remain in escrow, or I can direct these men to make sure the two of you are in no condition to follow me and take the sculpture without compensation."

He allows the silence to settle.

"I am not a thief. I have no desire to make a reputation as one. Nor do I desire to threaten or aggravate the two of you to the point at which you might consider exposing the Harmodius, no matter that once I leave here, no one will ever find it. My brother is a man of honor. I am, as well. However, if you force my hand . . ."

47

Knox is painfully aware that they have passed the five-minute mark. As far as Dulwich is concerned, he and Grace are free to go. Knox has been waiting for a wink and nod to indicate Mashe Okle's plan to defect, but it hasn't come. The only thing he's witnessed is a marked decline in the man's color and his decaying demeanor. It looks as if the air is leaking out of him.

This fits with Knox's earlier theory that the defection might be related to a medical complication. Whatever the intended end game, Knox wants out before anyone accuses him and Grace of causing whatever's about to happen. A Glock in the small of his back would help matters, but he's clean. The op is complete. They have served the required five-minute sentence. It's Dulwich's mess to sort out from here.

Mashe Okle appears to be going south. Grace can see it; Akram, too. The man is unaware of his own condition, making it all the more pitiful and painful to observe.

"As soon as the source of the funds is confirmed, the Harmodius is yours," Knox says, staying stubborn. He can't give in too easily.

Mashe nods solemnly, a benched athlete. "I am sorry, but this is unacceptable."

"Brother?" Akram says.

Mashe's eyes roll to the top of his sockets, his head unmoving. "Give me a minute."

"You do not look well, brother."

Surprisingly, several minutes of sitting quietly return color to his face. His shoulders square, his posture elongates. He's like a flower set out in sunlight. Mashe says with surprising confidence, "One half of funds to remain in escrow until additional testing confirms authenticity."

"The only testing—done by your man—is behind us now." Knox straightens his back, plays his role. He watches Akram for any change in body language.

Knox stands with difficulty and limps toward the bust. There's no need to verbalize the threat. If he were to throw the bust through the window to the pavement below, it would be rendered worthless.

Mashe's skin turns the same awful yellow it was only minutes earlier. Noticing the change, Knox understands the nature of the op in a sickening rush—though he has no idea how Dulwich pulled it off.

"My phone," she had said. *Our phones,* he's thinking.

Grace moves toward Mashe Okle. Simultaneously, Akram moves protectively to his brother's side. No one has spoken. One of the guards in the hall coughs; he's smoking a cigarette. The smell of tobacco smoke seeps into the apartment.

"Let us forget this for now, brother," Akram says. "Let us visit Mother."

He's trying to convince his brother to let him take him to the hospital.

"You had your chance," Knox says brusquely.

"You see?" Grace says to Knox. Her acting is impressive. "The situation so often alters when the money becomes real."

"Salim!" Mashe shouts.

The door opens with alarming speed. Knox grabs hold of the Harmodius, but his legs betray him. Salim has taken a cue from Mashe and runs interference; Knox doesn't make it to the window fast enough. Salim passes and comes at him from the direction of the windows, driving a stumbling Knox back into the room. Knox could smash the heavy bust to the floor, but it would likely only hurt the floor; the thing's as solid as a piece of armament. Still, the threat of it, as Knox struggles to press the Harmodius overhead, brings Mashe to his feet.

Knox's arms tremble. He can't hold it much longer. "All, or nothing!" he says once again. "I . . . don't . . . trust . . . you." Sweating now, he manages to look Akram in the eye. "Apologies, friend. You, I trust."

Mashe acquiesces. "Agreed! Agreed! Now, help him!"

The guard assists Knox in lowering the Harmodius. It's returned to the table where it previously perched.

Knox aches. He sizes up the guard who stands closer; decides he'd go down quickly. It's the man at the open door holding a Makarov PPM that concerns him.

Mashe Okle makes a phone call, holding up a finger to request silence in the room. Knox's pained breathing competes with the sounds from the street. The man talks in clipped Persian. Ending the short call, he works his phone and passes it to Grace.

"Internet connection. Do what you must." Mashe Okle sits back down as if he's just run a marathon.

"I'm with Akram," Knox says casually. "You don't look so hot."

Mashe addresses his brother. "It is nothing. Fatigue is all." He reaches into the side pocket of his suit coat where it hangs on the back of the chair. He withdraws a business card. Extends it toward Knox. Knox avoids glancing at Grace, who is certainly processing the offer as Knox is: the exchange. If Knox accepts the card, he is a cutout. If he does not, he and Grace may lose their value for Mashe Okle and his guards.

Mashe waits for Knox. The moment borders on awkward. Knox accepts it and thanks him.

Mashe says, "If you or your colleague should have any questions or complications when attempting to leave the country, you will please present my card and ask them to call number on back." He pauses. "You will find I am extremely well connected, Mr. Knox. In your game of Monopoly, this is same as 'Get Out of Jail Free' card. City police, MIT, it makes no difference. Do not misplace it."

Grace works the phone she was given. She must go through sourcing the funds to make their story credible and convincing.

Knox flicks the card's edge, and then pockets it. Everything he and Grace have theorized whirs through him, arriving back at the idea of his being used to unwittingly courier intel. The man's business card feels as though it weighs several pounds. He figures he's supposed to encounter trouble along the way, is supposed to offer up the card. In doing so, he, Knox, passes along Iranian intel. A piece of old-school spycraft. As he thought.

"You have your information?" Mashe says to Grace.

She meets eyes with Knox. "Because of time, I chose one of the six accounts at random. It checks out."

She returns the phone to Mashe Okle.

"It is a treasure," Mashe says, his voice filled with gratitude. "I want you to know it will be treated as such, its beauty and historical significance enjoyed by many."

Knox winces a smile. He doesn't give a shit. He resents being used. Assumes he is part of a dead drop, with the emphasis on dead.

If he gets rid of the card, he'll be tortured and torn to pieces to find it; if he keeps it, he's got a target on his back. A target with two bad legs and a busted shoulder and head wounds that need weeks to heal.

Mashe Okle is fading once again. His eyes are shut, his face pallid.

"We're good," Knox says, wanting out, wanting to separate himself from Grace. By accepting the business card, he's been made radioactive.

"Perhaps," Mashe says to his brother in Persian, "a visit to Mother is not such a bad idea." To Knox, he speaks English. "I am sorry to say that you must suffer the indignity of secrecy in leaving here today. My men will accompany you to a location that offers many forms of public transportation. I trust you will forgive me this precaution. It is not to be avoided."

"I would prefer to name the destination myself," Knox says, not wanting to be delivered anywhere on a platter, "once we are in the vehicle."

"As long as it is within reason, it shall be as you wish," Mashe says, surprising Knox with his agreement. He speaks to his men.

"Remember," Mashe says, rising to show them out and pointing to Knox's pocket. "Any kind of trouble. This card is your passport. Use it."

"It is kind of you," Grace says.

"Pleasure is mine." He bows for her and extends his hand to Knox. "I thank you, sir, for this opportunity. You do me and my brother a great honor."

Knox wonders if he means the sale of the Harmodius or the involuntary sacrifice of carrying the business card. If Dulwich's hysteria is to be believed, the fate of the world now rests in his pocket. Knox is caught in the middle.

At the bottom of the stairs, the hoods are readministered. There is a pause, as perhaps the guards allow the sidewalk to clear. Then Knox and Grace are rushed outside through the rain and into the van and driven off.

Ten minutes of abrupt stops and poor driving, and the hoods come off. The door slides open and the two are politely pushed out into the wet as the van drives away.

"Bastards!" Knox hisses. They've been dropped in front of a non-descript building—a sign reveals that it's the city's naval museum. It's miles from the Metro stop he requested.

"Inside," he says. Grace takes him by the elbow and steers him toward the museum's stairs. "Don't!" he says, admonishing her for her nervous glances in every direction.

They are well on their way to being soaked by the time they step inside. Admittance is four Turkish liras. Knox has the cash, but their captors have stuffed his belongings into two of the windbreaker's many pockets, leaving him disorganized. It takes a moment to lo-cate his wallet. In the interim, Grace returns her SIM to the iPhone and the device powers up.

Knox pays. Grace's phone chimes, signaling incoming text mes-sages. Once clear of the receptionist, Grace reports in a whisper, fighting the echoing, oversized room with its stone floor and gray marble wainscoting.

"Besim's man. We were followed from the meet." She slips the phone away.

"Currently?" he asks.

"Two men. Northwest of us." She gets her bearings. "Outside the main entrance."

Knox is moving better even if she doesn't notice it. "Remember the ferry dock. The Huangpu?"

It's rhetorical.

"Not exactly like that, but timing is everything." Knox moves her through the museum with the grace of a dancer. Now, she notices.

"Look at you."

"Amazing what a little motivation can do."

"Will they kill you? Us?" Said so matter-of-factly. So Grace.

"Depends who they are. But why not? Who knows?"

"His health. His failing like that. That was us."

"So noted. Do you know how?" He steers her through a room with paintings.

"My phone. Maybe yours, too. That is only hardware we carry."

"Turned off. Chips pulled. Is that possible?"

She is already a few steps ahead of him. "Dulwich switched them on us. I left mine behind when entering the Red Room. It had to be then."

Knox stops abruptly. They're in a room with five majestic wooden vessels. "Use of the Red Room wasn't about secrecy," he proposes, "but about disconnecting us from our phones?"

She nods vigorously. "Digital Services needed time to clone our data into matching phones already engineered to interfere with Bio-Lectrics pacemakers. Replaced them before we were out of the Red Room."

"Are we just guinea pigs? We field-test a new technology for them? If successful, they use it on some dictator? If we fail, it's not blamed on them!"

She prattles on about how iPhone batteries cannot be removed, how the trigger had to be the phone being switched off and the SIM card removed in combination. She talks about exciting lithium but it's not exciting him the way it is her. "The driver's wristwatch overheated. My captors. Lithium battery! The van malfunctioned, which could have been the failure of computer cards controlling the engine. His pacemaker lost power."

"Then he should have dropped dead."

"Depends if his condition was serious. He grew weak, quickly. Resting restored his health. Remember? He was not faking. No matter, it is not our concern, John. You are our concern. You and that card you now carry."

"I won't play along. I refuse to play along. I told Sarge: no way."

"No longer our concern."

"You think? The plan is to make him weak knowing he'll head to the hospital."

"Where he defects. Not our concern."

"Or they install one of the switched pacemakers into him. This is the Israelis, count on it. This is Iran's nuclear program, Grace. Sarge can't make a promise like that. Once the device is in him, then what? They kill him, like in *Homeland*." He can tell the reference is lost on her. "We'd never hear about it, and if we did, Sarge would claim the guy had a heart attack."

"That is a great deal of speculation, John. Too much."

"Xin's pal never got back to you about the pacemaker's innards, correct? Now there's a surprise."

She had asked for his analysis of the pacemaker's circuitry. "True."

"Listen to me. We cannot afford to have Mashe's blood on our hands, Grace. You think no one will remember him getting faint during our meeting? Seriously? The Muslim culture can be unforgiving. I have family. I . . . we . . . can't endure a fatwa. I can't live that way." He pauses, fixes his eyes blindly on the wooden boats.

"We have to stop him. Get him to another hospital where the pacemakers haven't been switched. We can still make their plans go to shit."

"That will help us, how?" She pauses. "John, let us say what you propose is accurate? Then we have finite time to leave country. The business card is our exit strategy. Mashe said this." Knox remains silent. "I like job. I like work."

Knox shrugs. He leaves her the choice to join him or not. It will be more difficult without her. She has no trouble reading him.

"Text Akram," she says. "Tell him he must switch hospitals."

"Get real. What? I send him a two-page text? He won't believe a word of it."

"This is his problem, not ours."

"No. It's on us. That's the way this'll work. Now. Six months from now. This is on us. Sarge fucked us. Maybe not on purpose, but he fucked us." It's the Vicodin talking. "There's a ferry dock behind the next building to the east. Make sure you're the last to board the ferry, so no one boards after you. We need the definitive word on what's with the switched pacemakers. Then, the same again, you need to be last onto a return ferry to Karaköy. From there, catch the tram to Tophane, Taksim and the Metro to Şişli. Repeat it."

She repeats the instructions, but is shaking her head.

"I need your help," he says. "I can live without it. I won't beg."

"We switch SIMs. Remain in contact," she says.

Knox takes that as a yes. "Tell Besim to meet me here at the museum. Your job is the pacemakers. I will run interference on Mashe Okle."

"I can do this. But I must remind final time: we lack proper intel to make a reliable assessment."

"Israelis and Iranians. That's reliable."

"If we interrupt a defection, the Israelis will not be pleased."

"I'm way too stoned for that," he says.

Her laugh echoes. She rises onto her tiptoes and kisses his cheek. For a moment, neither knows what to do next. "I will go to the ferry," she says.

"Relax," he says. "Deep breath. At all times be yourself. At no time—"

"—be who they expect."

Knox hears something grumble from deep in his throat. He's grateful no words have come out.

48

---

race finds it difficult to reconcile the beauty and tranquility of the Bosphorus with her current assignment. A sense of impending dread and impatience feels misplaced among the churning green waters, the bobbing boat traffic, the stillness of both shores. Men have fished these waters since before Christ. The Crusaders crossed this way, as did the Romans and the Greeks before them. Western civilization's storytelling origins connect to these twin shores, and though thousands of years behind that of her own Chinese culture, she can't help but respect the history.

Indeed, she's left with no choice but to appreciate the few minutes for the respite they offer. A lungful of sweet air, a study of the silver beads of rainwater as they plunge from the awning's edge to the deck and splatter. The murmur of Turkish. A child's self-conscious laugh.

It ends too quickly with her feet working furiously to fight the crowds. She window-shops, using the glass as a mirror in which to search for predators. As she catches sight of her own reflection, she understands herself, believes in her abilities, defines herself through this work in ways her forensic accounting cannot. The fieldwork strikes a balance that suits her, allowing her to exercise two sides of her being. Yin and yang. Her father would be proud, would understand, while her mother would fear for her and counter any justifications Grace might have with concerns for her safety.

But it is exactly that, her safety or the threat thereto, that thrills, that excites, that boils away the tedious hours of searching spreadsheets for inconsistencies and leaves behind a hard layer of purpose.

She boards the return ferry so late that she has to talk the deckhand into reopening the chain that blocks her way. She has yet to spot a tail but knows she will not if Mossad are involved. Knox has made a decent plan, but it can be easily defeated if there's a team surveilling her. She heads toward the electronics shop cautiously, still stinging from her last visit and Dulwich's presence. Xin had obviously betrayed her to the man—something she would have considered impossible. It's an odd and indifferent world, she thinks, when the only person left to trust is John Knox.

By the time she climbs into a taxi in Tepebaşi, she can't sit still. She itches all over. Her throat and mouth are dry. Her feet are sweating and her eyes sting.

She circles the block on foot twice before entering the shop and confronting the young man behind the counter for a second time. She locks the door behind her.

"What did you discover about this pacemaker? Why have I not heard from you?" she asks. Her underlying confidence and intention cause the kid to lean back from the counter separating them. She was the last person he expected.

She leans across the counter. "What was found inside this device?" The chill resulting from Knox's suggestion that Mashe Okle's death, now or later, from his apparent heart condition will result in Knox being a scapegoat, has not left her. Perhaps the pacemaker is to cause a stroke, or permanent disability; for Knox, perhaps for her, the result will be the same.

For her and this kid, it is as if they are picking up an ongoing conversation. But he has no desire to participate. From the looks of him, he'd as soon vaporize than face this fire-breathing woman with her bloodshot eyes and sour expression.

"Programmed with a timer? What makes it different?" She considers other possibilities. Mashe's passing of his business card and his emphasis of its importance suggests it must carry the spycraft, leaving the pacemaker as a weapon against Mashe. "The battery contains compounds that respond to radio waves? Depletes the charge?"

The mention of radio waves wins a tell—the kid's right eyebrow twitches perceptibly.

Adrenaline floods her veins and she vaults the counter, terrifying the young man, who outweighs her, is taller by nearly a foot and has a sizable reach on her. But he cowers as she takes him one-handed by the front of his shirt and, dropping her purse, pushes him out of his chair and against the wall. He raises a hand defensively and she gut-punches up under his ribs.

"Tell me what you told our people about it." She knees him in the groin. She wishes the punishment didn't feel so good, wishes she didn't want to keep going. Three or four more blows, and he'd be on the floor unconscious. The urge is so great she has to battle it to prevent herself from losing the information she's after.

A blink of light on the wall makes her knees go weak. She drops, bringing the man down with her, a response conditioned by training and instinct. The immediate thought is of a rifle scope's lens. But a second look out the shop and across the street tells her it was likely the face of a cell phone. She focuses in on a strongly built man with a phone to his ear.

John was right. She's been followed.

The impossibility of it won't allow consideration. Her brain won't go there. She took every precaution boarding the ferry; circled the block twice. Never an inkling of a surveillant.

How? she wonders.

Her heart is working so fast, pounding so hard that she can't get a word out. She has the boy gagged with her palm, his ear lobe twisted and ready to be torn from his skull in a bloody mess. In a nanosecond, she relives her exchange with Knox, the ferry rides, the tram and funicular.

"Oh, my God!" The man outside didn't follow her here; Dulwich didn't follow her here.

She stares into the eyes of her captive, awaiting confirmation.

Terrified, he looks away.

Grace's immediate thought is to stop John, but first there's the agent watching the shop from across the street and the witness on the floor whose allegiances are well known.

"A GPS chip," she says in Turkish, although she's asking him a question. "You found a GPS chip inside the pacemaker." Dulwich hadn't been told by Xin, he'd followed the GPS signal. The man outside didn't follow her, he's been watching a store indicated by the same signal.

The boy cowers. She reaches for his throat; it's a mistake. He reacts primordially, knocking her arm away, rolling and elbowing her in the chest as he struggles painfully to his knees. He reaches into an open drawer overhead. There's a glint of a blade. Grace arches away from the box cutter as it swipes within an inch of her chin, so close it cleaves away a wedge of her hair. The severed strands rain to the floor. The loss inspires rage, more so than a nick or the drawing of blood. Grace blocks the man's forearm, grabs his wrist and bites into his flesh like a hungry dog. He screams and releases the box cutter. Grace drives a tight fist into his nose, flattening it. Chops him below the chin, disrupting his airflow, then slaps him twice, side to side. His broken nose gushes blood; his eyes roll. She slaps him again.

"Who else did you tell?" she demands, stretching to reach her purse.

"Hong Kong. I swear. Only Hong Kong." No name. Oddly, it's what convinces her he's telling the truth.

"Doors, front and back. Any other way out?"

When he hesitates, she raises her bloodied fist a second time.

"Below," he says. "Romans."

Through the gray glass of the display cases, and out through the equally gray windows to the street, she sees the agent approach the shop. His patience tested, he wants a closer look. She knows such training. When he sees the empty shop, he will call it in and kick the door open. She has, at most, a few seconds' head start.

"Stairs?"

The shopkeeper's eyes direct her to a beaded doorway.

She's fumbling with her phone as, descending too quickly, her feet slip out from under her. She hits the cellar floor bruised and hurting. Using the phone as a flashlight, she takes in low stone arches and a cobblestone floor connecting them. Stone walls form small bins and narrow stalls, which are now filled with crusted furniture and rusting paint cans. The projected light casts a sterile cone out into the dust kicked up by her rapid movements. She hurries through an ancient arch, then backs out because it dead-ends in clutter.

Has he trapped her?

She shines the light to the left of the stairs; hears the crash of the front door coming open. Another arch. Beyond it, another dead end.

Voices from above. The rattle of plastic beads. Grace quiets the light and pockets the phone in her shouldered purse. *Think!*

The lights go on. Two lights. Compact fluorescent bulbs, a faint yellow as they warm to their brighter setting. Grace ducks through an arch, moving away from the stairs, facing a low wall of mortared brick and rock added centuries after the Romans. To her, it marks the start of another building. She has an image now of an alley overhead, a cluster of four structures sharing an interlocking cellar, the livestock sequestered beneath the living space as a source of heat.

It follows that there would have been a ramp to street level. Whether that exit still exists is anybody's guess, but much of the furniture appears to be too large for the stairwells and, as she comes across a crumbling single-horse buggy, its leather cracked and mouse-eaten, her hopes rise. She crosses beneath one building to the next. Here, the low stone archways are of a wider design. The distant light, now a pale luminescence, fails to reach around corners.

Her stalker has gone silent, expertly navigating the treachery of the cellar's contents. He could be two feet behind her; the knowledge puts her head on a swivel and sends her heart into her throat. Sweat catches her ribs and rolls sticky beneath her breasts. Increased distance equals increased darkness. The air smells of rodents and rust.

She ignites her phone, as much for the light of its screen as to check its signal. No bars. Making it dark again, she slips it away and uses the fading mental image to avoid twin stacks of sagging cardboard boxes, turns sideways to negotiate the narrow aisle between. Burned as a gray blue into the complexity of her optic nerve is the graphic of wooden handles collected into a whole. Gardening tools: spades, forks, a hoe, metal rakes.

Behind her, the bump of a leg against a cardboard box. Mingled with her panic is disbelief—how could he be so close? How has he caught up to her so quickly? She stumbles with the surprise.

From a pinprick in the dark pours blue light as her pursuer switches on a penlight. The light—only the light—lunges. Grace defends with a block. A flash of sparks. A jolt of electricity. He's got a Taser. She chops the man's arm and stumbles back, tripping over her own feet but catching herself before fully falling. Throws a basket at him as the device whines, recharging.

Her hand wraps around wood. She lifts the spade from her waist with both hands and stabs for the light. She connects. He belches. The light aims skyward, illuminating cobwebs and gobs of cement frozen between seams. Returning her blow, the man knocks the spade from her hands with such force that it flies into the darkness and crashes. The high-voiced squeal of rats and the scampering of scratching nails on the stone send chills through her. Something hits her ankle and she hops and screams.

The whining of the device stops. The man lunges. Grace crashes, grabbing whatever is nearby and raising it between herself and her attacker. She feels the object drive into him, hears his raw cry.

The device clatters to the cobbles. The penlight rotates through the air like a spinning baton. In the strobe light, she catches the flashing image of the man; he's clutching a pitchfork, its blade embedded in his left thigh.

As the light hits the stone, it goes dark. Grace has the presence of mind to retrieve her purse as she leaps past the staggering man. She collides with a stack. Another. Dust and cobwebs consume her. She spits and coughs and claws at nothing, running, falling forward, fighting against the sticky spider webs most of all. She hates spiders.

She's struck in the back. Stabbed by a tine of the pitchfork, aimed at only the sounds she's making in the dark. Her side clenches into a painful knot. She's on the stone floor and crawling. Hears him dragging his leg as he comes up from behind her.

Somewhere ahead, the air glows a shade other than black. She's drawn to that change. But he's on foot and she's on hands and knees and the accountant can work out the equation: he's closing on her.

Grace reaches out blindly with both hands, searching. Backs

herself into a narrow, angled space between the rough wood of the crates and lowers her head like she's carrying out afternoon prayers.

The sound of his panting and the dragging of his leg draw closer. He has lost the sound of her, the sense of her, and he's professional enough to turn that into caution. She smells him now—sour, slightly metallic from the bloody wound. Perhaps he smells her, too, for he stops.

There is no sound. It is a vacuum of space, without light, without so much as a hum or crackle. They are locked in a three-thousand-year-old vault playing a child's game of who can hold his or her breath the longest.

Grace's lungs burn. Her diaphragm convulses in sharp attacks, begging for air.

She feels it too late—a single bead of sweat runs down her jaw from her hairline to her chin. It settles, grows fat and falls as loudly as a cymbal crash.

49

"xcuse me, sir?" Besim pleads with Knox, desperate to correct his impression of Knox's request.

"Just so," Knox says. He's not going to argue strategy with a limousine driver.

"Please allow me to—"

"No." Knox leaves it at that. "The Holiday Inn. Hurry, please."

It's true they won't be watching the hospital for Victoria, but Knox is a marked man. With each assault, his enemy has escalated its effort to abduct him. With Mashe Okle's "Get Out of Jail Free" business card hot in his pocket, Knox doubts they will be any less forgiving.

He pulls up his pant legs and scratches loose the scabs from the bruised welts on his shins, crying out regardless of his effort not to. Besim checks the mirror. Knox has to pull the scab from his right leg to get the wound open. Blood trickles down both shins.

Just right.

The car slows and pulls to the curb. Knox looks for the hotel.

Too soon, he thinks.

"Please, the address once more?" Besim is turned, looking back between the front seats.

"The Holiday Inn," Knox says, unreservedly impatient and demanding. "It's right there north of the hospital."

Only as the driver's left arm swings around does Knox rehash a laundry list of do's and don'ts. Do thorough background checks on even the most inconsequential contacts. Don't ever become complacent in the field.

A bright flashlight beam stings Knox's eyes as a red laser dot finds his chest. The Taser hides well in Besim's gloved hand. Knox feels the impact—two needles shot at ninety-five miles an hour, capable of piercing two inches of fabric.

But not a passport.

The windbreaker's myriad pockets save him. It's the sheriff with the Bible in his pocket; zipped into his jacket's internal chest pocket, a space meant for his phone, is his passport. It has taken the hit from the Taser's darts. Knox rolls against the stubborn door. Locked by Besim, it doesn't open. Knox reaches for the knob as Besim ejects the Taser's dart cartridge, converting the device into a stun gun. The man's fluidity and speed tell Knox all he needs to know: this man is not a career limo driver.

The door comes open. Knox falls to the curb. Besim dives between the seats, lunging and leading with the Taser. He makes contact, but Knox feels nothing. The Taser has not had time to recharge.

Knox is up and on his feet. His right pant leg is hoisted, his shin bleeding badly. Pedestrians coming toward him jump out of his way, which is not what he wants; he could use the cover of a crowd.

Besim proves himself agile and fast as he claws his way across the backseat and out the open door. Knox's legs are no match for such a man; he is certain to lose this race.

His gift is forethought, the ability to see around corners. The small Taser will be used to buy the owner thirty seconds to flee the scene— or search the victim. Besim is on the team that's pursuing Mashe Okle's dead drop in a humane manner, not the team aiming to put a bullet in the back of their subject's skull. It's all the information Knox needs.

He prepares himself for defeat, an anathema.

The three flags hanging off the building at a forty-five-degree angle signal the finish line. He will accept defeat only once he's there.

He's suddenly looking down the wrong end of the telescope— thirty meters becomes three hundred as an ill-advised glance back confirms Besim is up and shoving pedestrians aside like they're Styrofoam. Knox has ten meters on the man and twenty to go. Eight and eighteen. Six and fifteen. The math doesn't hold up; he won't make it.

A dozen thoughts crowd his brain, none acceptable—holler for help; turn and fight; use a human shield to take the next attempt with the stun gun. Knox works the slalom to avoid giving the man an easy shot, but he stretches out the distance to the flags by doing so. He uses a mother and stroller effectively and is able to move for a few meters in a straight line. But he feels Besim closing, hears him yelling at pedestrians to get out of his way and shouting, "Police!" in a bid to promote himself as an authority.

The stun gun may be the least of it, Knox realizes.

Unable to get up any head of steam because of his injured shins, Knox is bracing himself for the inevitable when the gods of chance give him a gift. Traffic is at its standard-issue Istanbul standstill; a private car has seized upon an open space at the curb and is being loaded far from the three flags at the hotel entrance. The hotel bell-man wears a narrow-waisted black collarless jacket with silver frog button loops and tuxedo pants with a satin stripe down the side. His narrow head hides itself in an oversized purple fez with a gold tassel that has lost most of its sheen, like the unkempt tail of a nag long since put to pasture. The placement of the car shortens Knox's destination by ten meters or more. He eyes the man's jacket again as he crashes into him, screaming that he needs a hospital. Clings to the bellman, panting, sweaty, his blood-covered leg echoing the alarm.

"Nightingale Hospital! Please! At once!"

Besim stops and is immediately shoulder-bumped by a pedestrian who didn't anticipate the obstacle. The collision half spins him, leaving him scowling over his left shoulder at Knox as the two meet eyes. He radiates a predator's determination, tries but fails to contain his seething frustration.

Knox allowed himself to trust the man. Chastises himself for that oversight. Wonders if there's any way to catalogue the damage done by his planning sessions with both Grace and Victoria in the backseat. What pieces of the plan, if any, are out there? How much does Besim know?

Damage assessment is critical, but there's no time. The bellman has called over a pair of his fellow bag handlers; because of the availability of the luggage cart, the three install Knox on its platform like a trio of doting aunts. A group of Turks forms around the injured Westerner, and one rough-faced man has the audacity to stab Knox's shin painfully with a probing finger. The bellman slaps out, pushes away the curious offender.

His head swimming, Knox has a memory of his brother, Tommy, pulling him along an uncooperative sidewalk in their Radio Flyer wagon. It's a painfully vivid and present image, so overwhelming that for a moment he's transported back to Hamtramck beneath the clattering leaves of seasonal maples, shedding their leaves for fall in a sound eerily reminiscent of the plane trees that rattle overhead. The sound stitches with that of a siren blaring, and Knox realizes he's lost more than a few seconds.

"Police!" Knox hears a new voice enter the mix. Besim is coming in for another pass.

Knox grabs the sleeve of the bellhop that rescued him—Furkan, his name badge reads—and pulls him down. "No badge! Not police. He is who hurt me!"

Furkan's head snaps up in Besim's direction; the bellhop comes around the moving luggage rack with alacrity and gets up in Besim's grille, demanding to see his identification—

An instant later, Furkan sinks bonelessly to the sidewalk, a limp pool of flesh and fabric. The man's collapse is so immediate and frightening that his fellow workers attack Besim as a unified tag team, driving him back into a parked car in a resoundingly aggressive move that pins and punishes Besim while simultaneously searching him. The Taser that dropped Furkan clacks to the concrete, followed by Besim's cell phone, which breaks into pieces. A black leather wallet falls. It is snatched up and opened.

Besim steals it back in a flash and makes the two men pay for their insolence, the first with a sprained knee, the second, a stunned solar plexus. Besim bends for the phone, but Knox is off the cart. He kicks the phone beneath the parked car. Besim levels him, shoving Knox onto his back; Knox's head strikes the concrete. Besim empties Knox's pockets like a pickpocket, transferring the contents to his own. Throws open the Scottevest and flattens the nylon mesh lining to inspect the contents. Is given pause by the closeness of the approaching siren. Leaving Knox's passport and money clip on the sidewalk, Besim keeps the rest as he slips away, blends into the growing crowd and disappears.

Knox rolls to Furkan, who is coming awake. Knox stretches for the cell phone, pockets it as the wounded bellmen cuss in English, still trying to help Knox. Any one of them might be a candidate for the ambulance as it pulls up, but it's Knox who's tended to, his shins dressed with bandages before he's loaded into the back of the step van.

Furkan was down for less than a minute. He's groggy but on his feet and trying to help the paramedics, one of whom is a woman wearing a white lab coat and low black heels.

"Thank you!" Knox calls out to Furkan. The young man rubs his forehead; he'll be nursing a powerful headache. He manages a slight nod.

The ambulance's rear doors close with a bang.

WHEELED INTO EMERGENCY on an ambulance gurney, Knox slips undetected past a man who could easily be an agent waiting outside. Knox averts his face—currently obscured by an oxygen mask— while celebrating his decision to complicate his means of arrival. It looks like it's paid off.

In the distance, he spots a group of male nurses smoking cigarettes, their backs pressed up against the building's façade. Any of the staff could belong to the same team as the man watching the emergency room doors. Knox is battling a small army.

Installed in an examination area sectioned off by a drape, Knox goes to work, painfully stripping down to his bare torso and pulling on the hospital gown left for him. He checks his phone—nothing from Victoria. Considers switching out SIM chips, but fears his original chip can be traced. Can't afford the delay of being put into the medical system.

He peers out and spots a line of wheelchairs on the far side of a chaotic, crowded nurse's station. Bundles the heavy windbreaker and his shirt into a football beneath his left arm. His chest wound chooses this moment to be a violent offender; he stifles his own complaint, burying the pain. Whenever possible, hide out in the open. Knox approaches the nurse's station and stands, waiting for attention.

When no one pays him any, he takes a business card from an acrylic stand and moves on, down the hall toward the restroom, passing the line of wheelchairs. Uses the facilities. Takes a seat in one of the chairs and, placing the bundle on his lap, wheels his way past the nurse's station and along the corridor. When the elevator doors open on the eleventh floor a few minutes later, there's an unexplained empty wheelchair in the elevator car, looking lost and forlorn.

True to her word, a text arrives from Victoria. She's in position to call Akram. Knox, head down, wears the patient frock, carries the windbreaker bundle under his arm. He limps slowly down the hall—doesn't have to fake it—ears pricked for the strains of "Brown Sugar," Akram Okle's ringtone for Victoria's phone.

The next people to grab him will find his pockets empty. He will be tortured, possibly to death, for the location of the business card Mashe Okle passed him. A card he no longer has. Referring such people to other agents will only infuriate them and intensify the level of questioning. His presence here, then, has little to do with benevolence: it's a matter of self-preservation. Survival of the fittest. Knox has an angle to play, a way to avoid a fatwa and turn the agents back onto Mashe.

But he must get face time with Mashe, and he must make sure any agents wanting him see that he does. Without personal contact, his plan goes bust.

Victoria, fueled by greed, walked into the snare. Her association with Knox and her history with Akram may put her at risk, something Knox wants to avoid. He's counting on Akram's incoming calls being monitored and traced. She is on their radar—electronically tracked. He believes she has led agents back to the hospital. They have observed her entering. Knox's exchange of texts with her has confirmed his presence here and has hopefully focused attention on the cardiac ward; with any luck, they are monitoring the cardiac ward using the hospital security cameras. Possibly there's a doctor or nurse working with them.

Despite the wall stickers advising all persons in the hospital to turn off cell phones, Knox hears the opening riff of "Brown Sugar" from down the hall. He's still too far away to pinpoint the exact room—but he's moving closer. He pushes his agonized legs faster, finally raising his chin and daring to show his face to the security cameras.

Knox stops abruptly.

From the end of the hall, David Dulwich looks back at him.

50

J ohn!" Grace calls out, just loudly enough to be heard. The cardiac ward's corridor stretches out before her. David Dulwich steps closer to John, which explains why John doesn't turn his head.

She has to assume he can hear her. "It is GPS. The device was modified to contain GPS!"

Now he does look her way, shoots her an expression of shock, disbelief and victimization. John thinks she has betrayed him.

"GPS," she says again.

From the moment she saw the man observing from outside the electronics shop, she knew: it was virtually impossible he'd followed her; beyond any possibility of coincidence that he might be surveilling a random electronics repair shop. No, he had followed the device she'd stolen. Thus, the only possible explanation: the device contained a GPS chip.

She now believes Dulwich's claim that his client did not intend to kill Mashe Okle, but only follow him. Whether such surveillance would result in his death was beyond her ability to determine, but she could make assumptions, as John was now doing. She stands less than a meter from both men.

"The Israelis," Knox says to Dulwich. No one is within earshot, but he wouldn't care if they were. His anger shows as a tightening of muscle and sinew, as though his body is preparing to take a blow. Both men know where this is headed.

Dulwich does not look thrilled about it.

"You are so far out of your element." Dulwich is more mindful of volume than Knox. "You did what you came to do. Now, go home." He reluctantly takes the last few steps and plants himself within striking distance. Lowers his voice further. Grace can barely hear him.

"You two . . ." Dulwich looks past Knox at Grace. "You should have left well enough alone."

"You can't leave something alone unless you know about it in the first place."

"The op is a thirty," he says, indicating that it's over; they're done. "It's a fat paycheck. Don't jeopardize it."

"I'm going in there," Knox says, glancing at the room's door. "I won't be part of his death."

Dulwich shakes his head. "I told you up front: no killing. It's NTK, Knox. Leave it!"

"You made like he was a monster!" Knox spits unintentionally.

"You like things neat. Like your booze."

Knox shakes his head. "The GPS tracks him to a bunker the Israelis have been unable to find."

"N . . . T . . . K."

"They add it to the sortie when the time comes to start taking out Iran's nukes. Those bunker busters the U.S. has been so hesitant to provide. No stone unturned. No bunker left operating."

"You have to learn when to turn it off."

"I'm missing that switch. This model didn't come with one."

Dulwich collects himself. "Come on, John."

Grace adjusts her position, believing she's going to have separate them.

Knox produces his phone. "What say we give Primer a call and sort this out?"

"He'll deny it all."

"Impressive. You didn't so much as flinch."

"We're making a scene. Let's take this down to the cafeteria or outside."

"A scene? You ain't seen nothing yet." Knox moves to push past the man, but Dulwich is faster on two good legs. They stand chest to chest.

"Boys." Grace indeed closes the distance. She stands behind Knox, a gesture he takes as both symbolic and significant. She can be his legs.

"Tell him we don't need a scene," Dulwich says.

"You lied to us," Grace says. "Omission. Commission. No matter. You lied."

"You are both disobeying the directive. You are also misunderstanding what's going on. It's Need To Know."

"I need to know"—Knox emphasizes the words mockingly— "why you lied. I suspect Primer will be interested as well, denial or not."

He focuses on his phone's screen. Dulwich reaches for it, but Knox has several inches more arm span. He holds it at bay. He and Dulwich are practically kissing.

"You have no fucking idea how wrong you have this."

"Enlighten me."

Grace steps forward to pry them apart. Her intervention catches the attention of an orderly down the hall. She spots the man a mile away, thanks to his oversized shoes. He had to change out of his leather-soled shoes to look the part, she guesses, and he couldn't find any his own size in the staff lockers he broke into. In her mind's eye, Grace can see the man panicking and settling for a pair several sizes too large. But he looks like a carnival clown; it might have been smarter to risk wearing his own shoes. He's moving to help her.

"David, your six o'clock," she hisses. The men stop wrestling.

51

Dulwich grabs Knox by the back of the head and presses his lips to his ears. "Thorium," he manages to say before Knox bats his arm away, bruising him. Knox intentionally flares his eyes.

"Can I hel—"

Working from Knox's signal, Dulwich rotates and hits the orderly in the jaw. Grace moves like they've rehearsed for it, catching the man as he sags, unconscious, while driving her fist into his chest and stunning his diaphragm. Dulwich drags the man from behind, Grace catching the door and toeing it open.

Knox watches it all as his thumb directs the phone away from his search for Brian Primer's direct line to its search engine.

thorium

Google.

Dulwich makes excuses to someone who's complaining from within the room. He says the man fainted. He and Grace drag the man into the bathroom, where a soft thud confirms the man won't be interfering further.

a cheap, plentiful source of energy

Knox has it worked out before Dulwich returns. He recalls Rutherford Risk telling him his ID had come up as "on leave." Dulwich is rogue, as Knox suspected, but maybe not the villain he thought.

"We caused the heart problems. Our phones. Forced him here, where your client and his guys put his mother—"

"I know only the client. No part of any government agen—"

"Save it for the congressional hearing. They replace the failed pacemaker with one containing a GPS chip. The Israelis track him back to his bunker lab in the Iranian desert—"

"And we ensure that no one mistakenly bombs it," Dulwich says, staring Knox down defiantly. "You two got it backward, pal. Had it backward from the start. It was never in the plan to harm this guy. His thorium research would be spared. We save him from the firestorm. And, mark my words, the firestorm is coming. Neither he nor anyone else was going to tell us which bunker not to bomb."

"No way Primer sanctioned this," Knox says. A combination of anger and resentment floods him, makes him want to throw a punch. Dulwich put him in the path of an unforeseen dead drop that has put Knox and Tommy at permanent risk. "Unintended consequences," it's called in the business. Knox never wanted to be on the wrong end of it, but he is now, and there's no sense complaining. Not even Dulwich can change an unintended consequence.

"We must move," Grace, ever the practical one, announces. "Now."

Knox bumps Dulwich back a step. He and Grace walk side by

side as he shoves him a second and third time, closing the distance to the exam room housing Mashe Okle.

To his credit, Dulwich doesn't fight back. The man's nervous eyes reveal his search for a solution. If Knox exposes the pacemaker's true purpose, the Israelis lose their op. But more important to Knox right now is distancing himself from any dead drop. If he's believed to be the courier, he'll be followed, hunted and squeezed dry. The Mossad won't rest until they get what they want.

Grace tugs on his sleeve, points out two men at the end of the corridor. They're not hospital employees.

If Dulwich abandons him now, Knox is in the kind of trouble you don't get out of. The magician's trick is sleight of hand.

Knox fishes the business card he stole from the nurse's station out of his pocket. Angles slightly to the right, turning Dulwich with him as he does. He wants both the security camera and these two men to get a good look at what he's doing as he carefully hands Dulwich the card, doing an intentionally poor surreptitious pass.

Knowing no better, Dulwich accepts the card.

Seeing the exchange, Grace covers her teeth—her automatic response to an unwanted smile. Another op, another time, she might have warned Dulwich.

Knox backs up a step. Under no circumstances does he want the business card passed back to him. He amuses himself by thinking: *It's radioactive.*

"Good luck with that," he says.

Dulwich studies the card thoroughly, flipping it over twice. He couldn't play act it any better if Knox had coached him. Then comes the moment Knox hoped for.

Dulwich pockets the card.

Grace tugs Knox away. "Come on, John. We were wrong."

As they walk past Dulwich, the man nods and grins, appreciating her humility.

The door to the exam room in question clicks open. Knox ducks his chin. Grace has the wherewithal to snuggle into him and bury her face in his pajama top as they walk; she partially screens Knox.

Akram Okle comes out of the exam room, passing within feet of Knox and Grace. He doesn't look up.

Knox risks a final glance over his shoulder.

The two agents have converged on Dulwich.

52

―――――

"Thorium," Grace says.

"Sounds like a vitamin supplement," Knox says.

"Poor man's uranium," Grace says, speaking in professorial mode. "Abundantly available. Same energy benefits, but without the degree of waste and nearly impossible to weaponize."

"McEnergy."

"Something like that."

"He should have told us," Knox repeats. Before Grace has a chance to defend Dulwich, Knox cuts her off. "Don't start!"

They step through a door into a fire escape. Grabbing her arm, Knox turns her. "They're looking for two of us."

Grace is already pulling off the scrubs. Knox holds her inside shirt down so it won't ride up and expose her as she strips off the top. Her look softens as she tosses the scrub top into the corner.

"When they see it's a hospital card, they will come for you."

"Yes," he acknowledges. "I'll head up, you go down."

She objects. "Absurd. I will go up. My legs function properly. You leave as quickly as possible."

He nods reluctantly. "We rendezvous at the Holiday Inn across the street. North a few bloc—"

"I know it."

"There's a booth by the café's exterior door. Wait there thirty minutes, no more. If I don't show, I'll see you at your place in Hong Kong."

"I am not leaving Istanbul without—"

"Yes, you are. It's protocol." He hits her where she lives—the front-row student.

"The client is connected to the Israelis. Shabak? Mossad? Does it matter?"

"It's an unsanctioned op," he reminds her. "We both know that. If we appeal to Primer to intervene with the Israelis, the roof'll come down on Sarge."

"You care."

"I care."

"Who shot at us?"

"Not here." Knox has a theory that the Israelis are a house divided, but she won't believe him; Dulwich won't believe him. He checks the door, checks the staircase. The Israelis seem to be the least of their worries; in a few short hours, Mashe Okle's heart troubles will bring down the wrath of the Iranians. They won't care about evidence: they will want words with Knox. "Thirty minutes. Then you abort."

Knox takes off down the stairs with difficulty. Mulls the fact that she switched their assignments. She likes to play so hard-nosed, but Knox is not easily fooled. He waits to make sure he hears Grace ascending.

At the next landing, he quietly opens the door and steps into the hall. It's a patient floor. He walks slowly, peering through partially open doors. The third room is a double: one bed untouched, the other has its bedding turned back and unkempt; it's unoccupied. Knox steps inside, eases the door nearly shut.

"Hello?" He's worried the patient could be in the bathroom.

No reply.

He moves quickly to the bedside phone. Reaches the hospital operator and asks to be connected to a patient. "Family name, Melemet."

Waits, hoping he has guessed correctly—would she, too, now use Okle?

A click, a woman's quavering voice answers in Turkish.

"Victoria Momani," Knox says.

The old woman replies in Arabic.

Victoria answers in Arabic as well. "Yes?"

"This is important. Drop your cell phone in the toilet. Leave the room with it, but dump it as soon as possible. You understand?"

"I understand." Her voice is shaky.

"Not English! Think! Switch taxis no fewer than three times, walking fully around the block each time. Head to the train station. Take the first train east toward Jordan. Wait somewhere down the line and join the overnight to Jordan. Do not wait here for the Jordanian train. You understand?"

She answers in Arabic.

"Calm yourself. Be polite and sweet. Don't tell her you're leaving— say you need to find a vending machine. Something like that. Do not use the hospital's front entrance. There are plenty of others. Wear your head scarf. You understand?"

"Thank you for calling," she says, her voice now relaxed.

A woman's inquiry in Turkish. Knox pivots. Gently hangs up the phone.

The woman coming out of the bathroom is in her early forties.

She's clutching an IV stand and, though facing him, holds her hospital gown closed from behind.

Knox still wears the gown himself, over his pants. He speaks Turkish. "Lost." He points to his head. "Not remember what floor is my room. So sorry." He moves past her. She rotates to keep the back of her gown hidden. Eyes him as the intruder he is. He suspects she may call it in. He thanks her. Hurries.

Stands briefly in the corridor, busier now than minutes before. Weighs the risk of the slowness and pain of the stairs versus the speed and ease of the elevators, knowing full well there are surveillance cameras in the elevator cars.

53

"Getting into trouble is not so difficult," Grace's army intelligence instructor once said in a lecture. "It is getting out of trouble that requires effort."

Grace has climbed three flights of stairs. Is tempted by the thought of an elevator, but knows better. Wishes she had not abandoned the scrubs so quickly, for now she elects to cross the eleventh floor to an opposing set of stairs. She is as much a target as Knox, and they both know it. Any of the interested parties would welcome the chance to dangle her as bait, reel him in.

She wonders if John has a plan. Doubts it. She has gone along with him because he has a knack for thinking on the fly. Given thirty minutes, she could come up with an exit strategy better than his. But she knows she wouldn't have thought to pass a business card to David, to scent the hounds in his direction. A stroke of genius, so typically John Knox, and one that may have bought them enough time to find their way out of Istanbul.

Grace finds the memory of the bloodied taxi and Ali's unmoving corpse unshakable. Distracting. The same instructor warned her about losing one's focus. One can stumble into trouble, but then one must plot a course to find the way out. She feels she is stumbling as she lowers her chin perhaps too far and holds back her stride to avoid running. Still, she senses the deliberateness of her movements, the telegraphing of her intentions. Poisoned by doubt, she begins to crumble, pieces of her confident façade falling to the tile floor. She wants to reach out and hold on, but it would be like trying to catch snowflakes.

Patience! Constant dripping wears away even a stone, her maternal grandmother would remind her.

Mashe Okle's advice to barter his business card with the authorities calls into question what authorities he had in mind. Is he aware of all the players? *The problem with spycraft is facing a faceless enemy,* she thinks. Grace doesn't appreciate being distracted by such regurgitation. Takes it as a bad sign and curses her culture for instilling in her such a strong belief in bad signs. But the point is taken: she and Knox are hindered by having so little idea who, or how many, are pursuing them. It could be three or four; it could be a dozen or more. They might have shown their faces more than once; this might be the first time she and John have seen them.

Yet the opposite is just the opposite—she wears a bull's-eye, front and back. The only upside: she finds it impossible to fear a faceless enemy. Her situation fuels paranoia, suspicion and distrust, but she's not afraid.

Three corridors, a lot of weaving through the chaos of medical practice, and Grace arrives at a set of stairs on the north side of Nightingale. Orthopedics. She hesitates, hoping for someone using the stairs. It pays off. She follows behind two nurses. They leave her at the landing on nine. Her feet pick up the pace of her descent automatically. She pulls on the reins. Anxiety produces boogeymen, jumping out at her unexpectedly. They don't come; it doesn't happen. Her thoughts settle: of course it doesn't happen. They're waiting for her at the bottom in order to limit her options. Either just before she leaves the building, or on the other side of the exit door.

On the second floor, she leaves the stairwell, rejoining a hospital ward. Pediatrics. She feels the cameras burning against her shoulders like the sun after too long on the beach. *Think!*

Only three entities could be monitoring the hospital security cameras: the Israelis, the West or the Turks.

The Israelis will want to protect her and John, will want to see their pacemaker op through to its rightful completion. Western agents will want the contents of the business card, and will go to great lengths to obtain it. The Istanbul police, if present, will want answers about the murder of an innocent taxi driver. The accountant sees the cameras as two-thirds against her, so abandons any consideration of appealing directly to them.

Considering it more dangerous outside than in, yet feeling eyes upon her and unable to leave, Grace begins to feel dizzy. As she was once taught, she free-associates, something that does not come easily nor endure for very long.

Hospital. Health. Patients. Doctors. Healing. Chaos. Order. Patience. Panic. Operations. Prescriptions. Tests. Privacy. Tears. Crying. Diagnosis. Terminal. Cancer. Viral. Bacteria. Flu. Insurance.

She has it: a way out.

54

The heel of his shoe is used to eliminate the fisheye lens in the upper corner of the elevator car. Knox slams his thumb against the buttons, lights up three consecutive floors below him. After an empty stop, he's joined by several nurses and an orderly tending to a young girl in a wheelchair. They all look at him when the elevator makes the next stop and Knox doesn't depart. They disembark at lobby level. Knox rides to the first of three marked basement levels.

He moves quickly for the nearest exit. It's all timing now. They can't cover every exit, every street.

He's comfortable with his chances. His shins feel surprisingly better; he's found the right balance of meds. He's through the exit and into a dark, underground parking garage before he can blink. Ducking, Knox works his way through the parked cars and light trucks, hoping to avoid closed-circuit cameras, though he doubts their existence due to the gloom.

At the exit, he stops to shed the pajama gown, pulls on his shirt, dons the windbreaker and hurries up a concrete ramp to join the crowd on a busy sidewalk. He's all sparks and electricity, his motor red-lining. It's a high that blows away the pain meds, sending him into a giddy mental frenzy that results from this life-threatening game of hide-and-seek.

Two intersections north, he circles the block fully and uses a variety of methods to surreptitiously check for ground surveillance. It's a fool's errand—a small mobile team can easily follow him without detection. But he knows the drill, and he stays with it before mixing with the crowds at the Şişli Mosque plaza where he and Grace stood only days earlier. It feels much longer ago, and Knox wonders for a moment at the outcome had they never pursued the switched FedEx package.

He pictures Mashe Okle's forty-five-minute procedure. The man walks out of the hospital with a GPS in his chest and leads the Israeli Air Force to the location of his thorium research bunker, none the wiser about the protection he'll be rendering. The Israelis will be able to track him for ten years, kill him at a moment's notice.

Knox enters the Holiday Inn minutes later. Heads toward the booth by the alternate exit.

No Grace.

55

It takes Grace time she doesn't have to find the hospital's staff lounge. It's down a fluorescent corridor thirty feet beneath street level on S2, flanked on either side by men's and women's locker rooms where no security cameras cover the toilets and showers. Here she finds an abundance of hospital gowns, rubber gloves, masks, hats and shoe covers. She dons a green jumpsuit, waits for two cleaners to leave, and follows closely behind. By the time she's left all this behind and is on the street again, she's confident she has avoided detection.

She finds Knox in the restaurant booth drinking black coffee. Either the pain or the meds or both have spread fatigue onto his face. He tries to smile for her.

The bench seat is plastic, the lighting environmentally friendly, the buffet picked over. Grace shifts back and forth, unable to get comfortable.

"Making it a few blocks up the street is very different from getting through Customs."

Knox flinches in agreement but doesn't speak.

"Perhaps Besim—"

"He's working for the Israelis." He explains the end of his ride in terse, muttered sentences.

"It's not possible," she says. "I booked Besim, not Dulwich. My arrangements, not his. Dulwich wanted it this way."

Knox grimaces and shrugs. Indifferent. "Fucking Sarge."

"My phone!" she says, still stuck on how an employee of the Israelis had ended up her driver. "The Red Room. When they switched the phone. My new model allowed full surveillance no matter the SIM chips I used. When I called to book my driver . . . they rerouted the call."

"Let's save the CSI for later," he says. Again, she misses the reference.

"He got the business card?"

Another smirk.

"He didn't get the business card." A statement she mulls over. "But if Besim works with the Israelis, then why did he tip me off to the man watching my apartment? A man we assume also to be Israeli."

"We make too many assumptions."

"Your theory doesn't explain anything," she complains.

"They wanted to sell you—us—on Besim's loyalty."

It hits her in the center of her chest. She wants to contradict him. Prove she knew what she was doing as a solo field op. Can't. "I believed."

"They underestimated you. If Besim hadn't given you that guy, we'd never have picked up on the FedEx. It backfired on them because you're way better at your job than they are at theirs."

He's trying to console her. It works. She has a great deal to learn yet, she thinks.

The waiter arrives. Grace orders coffee. Knox waves him away.

"Thorium," Knox says.

"Need To Know," says Grace. "The Iranians have always claimed peaceful use. Looks like they could claim that, however much they lied. A thorium reactor will not save the world, but it could nearly eliminate contamination. This would be a true game changer, John. Licensing such technology—the revenues would be staggering. Perhaps make up for shrinking oil reserves." She lowers her voice additional decibels. "For the Israelis to bomb such research would be a public relations nightmare for decades to come."

"So some benevolent billionaire—the Israeli equivalent of Richard Branson—with ties to the government, or at least a faction of the government, hires Primer, or Dulwich—who knows?—to find a way to exclude the thorium reactor from any future attack."

"We didn't need to know," she says. "What did you mean by 'faction'?"

Knox ignores the question, instead informing her there's been a shift change at the hotel. "When your luck turns, it's hell turning it back. More like a supertanker."

"If I had any idea what you were talking about, it would help." Between the medications and the beating he's taken, it's a miracle he's conscious.

He sips from her coffee. "Shift change. The bellmen, too, I imagine." He drinks more and sets down the mug.

There's an American woman complaining to her husband at the salad bar. Looks like it might be her first time at one. The husband has little tolerance; he moves toward the cherry tomatoes, putting the cough screen between them.

"Another inconvenience," Knox says, then adds, "'If it wasn't for bad luck I wouldn't have no luck at all.' I prefer the Cream cover, in case you were wondering."

A waiter delivers a lamb shank. Knox has half of it gone before Grace can wave the waiter back and order the salad bar. His mouth full of food, Knox shakes his head vigorously at her choice. Orders fish for her. The man writes down the order as he walks away.

Grace knows this particular John Knox personality. He has not shown it in a while, but he can be a confounding, frustrating and sarcastic man—and then there's the John Knox that goes beyond even that.

This is the man she now faces.

"What I meant by faction was hawks and doves. Think about it: what are we doing here, Grace? You and me? Why us?"

"You explained this yourself: if it carried any Israeli fingerprints, Mashe Okle would have run back to Iran."

"I was wrong."

"You are definitely high."

"Extremely."

"Okay. Wrong, how?"

"All these guys we've been fighting, even the ones trying to kill us: they're the same, but different. Two sides of the same coin. Hawks and doves. The hawks, the ones in charge, want every reactor, everything and anything to do with enrichment bombed back into the Stone Age. But there's a catch—they would love to get their hands on any shopping list being couriered by top nuclear scientists in the hopes it gives them all the more evidence to start bombing tomorrow instead of being made to wait. That desire includes taking out possible couriers in hopes of recovering the list.

"The doves," he continues, "seek the higher ground, but lack the political capital to convince others, so they hire—my guess—David Dulwich, not Rutherford Risk, because they know him. Someone who knows of him, or knows him personally. Let's call him the client." Knox meets eyes with her. His are so glassy they look ready to run, so bloodshot it's amazing he can keep them open. "The client finances the op. No connection back to the doves. Not ever. Two different sets of players on two opposite sides of the ball, and all on the same team. And us, you and me, in the middle."

He returns to eating ravenously.

"Explain your reference to bad luck, please." She has grown weary.

"The Chinese put way too much faith in luck," Knox notes through a mouthful of food. "You should learn to care less about luck."

She waits him out.

"An errand," he says. "We need to run an errand."

He wants to tease her into anger, or worse, begging. But he forgets how well she knows him.

"Can I do it for you? I would be happy to."

He stops chewing. She wishes she had her phone's camera at the ready.

"We should do it together. I don't want to get separated."

Grace relaxes. Hoping it doesn't show. Knox has finished the lamb by the time her fish arrives. It's the head and all—looks straight out of the Bosphorus. She doesn't think she wants to deal with it until Knox fillets it for her. She tries a bite, and then consumes the remainder too quickly. Looks up to see him smiling. He has food in his teeth. He's traded the coffee for a beer. This is the dangerous John Knox.

"He should have told us," Knox says.

She's the one with the mouthful. She tries to answer with her eyes.

"The Need To Know makes sense." He's talking to himself. "Here's what I think: I think our friends to the south of here were divided on this issue. I would bet their faction in Istanbul is completely off the books—resources back home, but not on the clock. I think some higher thinker saw a way to contract a third party—us—to do their bidding. No official involvement if it goes south, because official involvement could expose the bigger . . . fish." He looks at her plate. "The fact that these bombs are indeed about to fall. The higher thinker doesn't want to throw the baby out with the bathwater—the thorium project. This guy knows Dulwich somehow. Everyone knows Sarge. Appeals to his sense of patriotism, of higher good. Deep down, Sarge is a pussycat. Plus, he waves some serious change in his face. Sarge takes the bait. Uses the Red Room to sell it to both of us and to switch our phones. We buy into Rutherford's involvement. And here we are."

"If we had done as he—"

"Don't go there." He sips the beer. Then gulps. "We went where we went."

"It's my fault."

"Nonsense."

"I put us on that plaza." She has to raise the question if he won't. "Now that we know?"

"Sarge has his work cut out for him. First, he'll have to explain why there's no microdot on the hospital business card I gave him. Then he'll have to talk them into letting us walk. We'll likely be watched until whatever it is they have planned happens. After that, they can let us be."

"You talk as if we'll be allowed to board a plane and leave."

"A train," he says, correcting her. "But yeah, I get it. That's where the errand comes in." He signals for the check.

His overconfidence makes her uneasy, despite that she finds his courage under fire seductive and alluring. Her defenses lowered, she feels prepared to cross an unthinkable line. If they get out of here, she's going to ask Dulwich for reassignment.

The bill paid, Knox moves surprisingly well on his injured legs as he leads her into the busy hotel lobby. "In case . . . in the event we're separated," he says, "Besim didn't get the business card. As I was going down, I slipped it into the right coat pocket of a bellman named Furkan."

She lowers her voice to a whisper. "What might be Iran's nuclear shopping list? In a bellman's jacket pocket? What if he finds it? Discards it?"

Knox shrugs. "I'm more concerned that he may have worn his jacket home. But I doubt it. It'll be on a rack in the basement."

"The errand."

"Yes."

"Furkan."

"Pinned to the jacket. A name tag."

"Our free pass."

"Nothing is ever lost, only misplaced," he says. "We'll find— fuck, fuck. And double fuck."

She follows his line of sight.

"The receptionist?"

Knox has already swung his head in the direction of the street. A cab pulls to the curb. The driver climbs out at the same time as three others, all Caucasian—including the driver.

"She may have made me. An American hotel! The nerve!"

Grace pulls him away from the front doors. "Quickly!"

He tugs back. "This way."

"We cannot stay." They walk briskly, a pace just short of jogging.

"We won't get another shot at the card. Our only plan, Mashe's only plan is for us to use that card, to play that card." She wants to argue, but he calls her. "You got anything?"

They're engaged in a tug-of-war; she toward the hallway of boutique shops that likely leads to another outside exit; he to the right of the elevators and a green exit sign that depicts a little man running. It strikes her as absurdly symbolic. Stairs.

Finally, she gives in, allows him to drag her along. Her capitulation is based on one thing: she has no plan whatsoever. His plan, regardless how reckless, is better than none. Ahead of her, Knox lumbers down the stairs, stiff-legged but surprisingly fast. She's angry that she has to work to keep up with him, furious that she's gone along at all.

The bang of the door upstairs promises a fight. Knox is not going to turn himself in.

"Two to one," she says.

"Yep." As they exit the stairwell into a musty hallway that smells of cigarettes, Knox says, "Nothing permanent."

He's studying a highway of wrapped pipes overhead. Ethernet, telephone, power and bell wire. Tube lighting. Green skin.

"Twelve o'clock," she says.

Two men wait at the long end of the dim hallway. Knox and Grace move slowly toward them. The idea is for these two to block egress—shield the only apparent choice of exit besides the door she and Knox have just come through.

That implies others coming from behind.

Knox is in bobble head mode. She feeds off his intensity. He appears to be assaying the building's structural components. "Ha!" he says, steering her through the first door to their left. It looks like a backstage dressing room in a seedy rock club.

"Block it," he says calmly.

She drags a file cabinet across the cluttered floor, knocking a coffeemaker to the ground. Wedges a chair beneath the doorknob. All combined, it might buy them a few seconds.

Behind her, Knox is rifling through a hanging rack of black sport jackets. She joins him, starting from the far end.

"Name tag: Furkan," he reminds her.

"Right pocket," she says, letting him know she pays attention to what he says.

He bounces awkwardly to her side and slaps the far wall. He's back in the line of jackets before she manages to speak. His slap has called the dumbwaiter.

"A lift?"

"For laundry carts. But it'll do."

The first charge at the door rings out. She was wrong: ten seconds, at best.

"You knew." She fails to contain her astonishment. "About the lift . . ."

"Old building. Low-gauge, high-voltage power line." He points up to a thick black cable overhead. He followed it into this room.

They are nearing each other at the center of the rack when Knox stops abruptly.

"Go," he says, eerily unemotional.

She moves to the specialized lift. Hauls out the empty laundry cart; it pirouettes on its wheels.

Knox searches the black jackets.

The door blows open behind a determined kick. A man enters. Caucasian. Perhaps not ex-military, but conditioned. Trained. If there was a chance for talking this out, it has passed. The look in his eye is all attack.

Knox spins and pulls down the manually operated door. Something flutters across her vision as Grace is trapped in darkness. A clunk; the groan of electricity. The lift ascends.

It takes her a moment to register the image seared onto her blindness—the flashes of white lingering in her vision like the pop of a camera's flash.

A business card. The business card.

56

Knox unbraids the top of a metal hanger in three quick rotations. He straightens it with two sharp bends and is already swinging the wire whip as he steps around the rolling rack of employee uniforms. It extends three feet from his hands, catching the unsuspecting man across the face, first from Knox's right and then again on the return blow from the left. It raises welts on the man's right cheek, draws blood on the left. By the time his opponent reacts, all the man can do is offer up his hands for a lashing. The whip nearly takes his pinky off. Backs him up a staggering step.

Forehand, backhand. Knox, the matador, marching forward relentlessly. The man cowering now, bent at the waist, bloodied hands clasped over his head, charges Knox like a bull. Hits Knox in the belly hard, reversing their fortunes. Knox drops the whip, gets his hands on the man's shoulders, but it's too late. Two hundred lean pounds drive Knox back and off his weak legs.

The two men wrestle on the concrete floor. Roll into the clothes rack. Knox pulls it over onto them, drowning them in polyester. He breaks loose and crab-walks away, understanding he's no match for this man's coordinated power. A good pair of legs are vital for defending against a man of his opponent's strength.

By the time Knox scrambles out from beneath the pile of black jackets, he's facing two men. One standing; he has a stitched-up ear. One kneeling and not looking good.

All three are winded. Briefly, no one moves—Knox is still inverted on hands and feet like he's in a camp contest. The message is simple: outnumbered, Knox has lost.

Knox speaks first. "You speak English," he tells them. "We're all following orders. I don't have what you want. I passed it off at the hospital. Check on that."

The one who's standing produces a Taser from a side pocket.

"Oh, come on," Knox says.

The man fires.

As he regains consciousness, Knox registers that his hands have been plastic-tied behind his back. His legs are weak but moving, his head pounding, his heart racing.

"Motherfucker," Knox groans behind the electronic hangover.

They're in the hotel basement corridor.

"I like the jacket," the man who didn't suffer the face lashing says. "Could use one of those myself." So they've searched him.

"I passed it off," Knox complains, repeating himself, directing attention back to the card.

"You'll be fine."

Knox doesn't say, "Oh, sure." He doesn't say, "Tell that to my head." He feels something foreign in that moment: hopelessness. Doesn't know how people can live with such a feeling. His head swims but begins to level out, and he's already looking for options, has already left the black hole of despair behind.

The man Knox whipped grips Knox's arm like a tourniquet. Knox won't give him the pleasure of knowing how much it hurts.

"Don't shoot the messenger," Knox says in a steady voice.

"No one's shooting anyone."

The wounded man trips Knox across the shins, hits hard against the bloodstains.

Knox chokes out, "Your boss should make a call. I can give you a number."

"Don't trouble yourself." The wounded one swats the back of Knox's head. It hurts worse than a cop's nightstick. "Shut up, do not lie, and you are to be released. This is over."

Spooks—Israeli spooks?—get away with murder, Knox thinks, knowing he'll never be released because the business card he handed Dulwich contains nothing more than hospital contact information.

"We're all on the same side here," Knox says, not believing a word of it.

"Then there's nothing to worry about."

Knox is searching for Grace as he's led into the lobby. It's a bad sign that these two don't care about being seen by hotel employees.

They reach the outside. It's raining again. The Istanbul traffic is bumper to bumper. Pedestrians slosh along the sidewalk, colorful umbrellas held high overhead. It's the parade of a dozen cultures. A place for lovers, enemies, allies. Spooks. He feels himself spiraling down the drain; blames the meds for his lack of inspiration. He's out of ideas—a first. Hopes this isn't his last glimpse of Istanbul. Wouldn't mind staying a while longer.

"*Hatichat harah!*" the talkative agent says, speaking Hebrew. He wins a flash of scorn from his nearest colleague.

Knox considers himself something of a linguist in that he knows how to swear in a multitude of languages. The agent is not happy with tires of the Audi Quattro 7, parked at an angle to the curb. Two flats.

"What the—?" The agent shouts obscenities at the nearest bellman.

"Taxi!" the other agent says, his English decent. "Now!"

The bellman, no more than a kid, gestures nervously to the street. "Much rain, sir, as you see. One moment, if you please! Right away! Right away!" He runs out into the maelstrom, rain bouncing off his red fez. Blows a whistle, looking left and right.

"You need car? Private car!" A man's heavily accented voice calls out from Knox's left. The driver stands beneath an open umbrella. He moves toward his quarry, extending the shelter provided by the plastic.

"Private car. Very reasonable, very cheap. Where you go, please?"

The whistle for the taxi continues to blow. A crowd of wet Turks gathers around the foreigners, looking curiously at their man in custody. They shout questions in Turkish and English. Wet cigarettes dangle from their lips. Trial by jury on the streets of Istanbul.

Staring bitterly at the incapacitated Audi, the lead agent answers, "Istinye. How much?"

The driver rattles off a price.

The agent launches into negotiations.

"We take it!" the other agent says, moving himself under the extended umbrella while leaving Knox in the rain.

It's not just raining. It's apocalyptic. It's an Old Testament deluge. The wet is a wake-up call. Knox's brain is a computer spinning beach balls; he's processing data from twenty seconds earlier.

"This way, if you please." The driver.

In his dazed and beleaguered state, Knox allows himself to believe he knows the voice. Or is he confusing it with one of the agents?

Someone pushes his head down. He's soaking wet as he lands in the backseat of the private car and is shoved to the center, his bound wrists behind him. The agents climb in on either side. One wet. One dry.

The doors power-lock. Knox leans forward, staring down at his knees, which are practically higher than his shoulders.

"You're going to pay for this," says the agent whose whipped face limits his ability to speak.

No doubt, Knox is thinking. He grunts, looks up and happens to catch the driver's eyes in the rearview mirror.

The eyes. The voice.

Besim.

57

It isn't the first time Grace has faced a difficult decision, so why does she hesitate now? What hold over her does Knox possess? Dulwich hires her because of her pragmatism, her cultural tendency to follow orders to the letter and leave her imagination at the door. She supposes he balances her against Knox for this reason, sees this as the logic behind their recent pairings.

Has she allowed herself to be seduced, corrupted? After all the sacrifices for her career, is she willing to risk a setback? For what? For whom? A testosterone-charged renegade? A maverick, that by his own admission is only in it for the money? A mercenary?

The problem is, she has had the occasional glimpse of the overprotective brother, the defender of women—the sensitivities Knox doesn't want exposed. Dulwich exploits these vulnerabilities for his own benefit. As the op supervisor, he's no doubt willing to sacrifice the troops to win the battle. Turning the opposing loyalties in her head, Grace finds herself uneasy and undecided, two qualities she would never associate with her usual logical assurance.

Cancer or cure, John Knox is under her skin.

In the hotel's lobby bathroom, she uses a safety pin she'd snagged previously to narrow the waistband of her pants to attach Mashe Okle's business card behind the interior garment tag. Her pants slip lower but hold above her hips; it's not a look she would normally tolerate, as the hems of the pant legs drag behind her flats. But if she's searched, the card will be difficult to find. A cursory look at the contents of her handbag and pockets will yield nothing.

The accountant in her ticks off the successes of the op: she and Knox got to Okle and sent him to the hospital, ensuring the implantation of a customized pacemaker in place of the defective model. They did so without the involvement of any government agency. A highly sought-after shopping list of what is likely parts for nuclear reactor maintenance, a list perhaps intended for the Russians, Chinese or North Koreans, is currently pinned by her hip bone. Any such agents could be in the hunt.

Might kill for it.

She leaves the hotel using a side exit; she conceals herself among a group of conventioneers wearing blue lanyards and plastic-shrouded white badges. She hesitates beneath a metal canopy that holds back the steady drum of gray rain. Smothered by conflicting emotion and reason, she battles the two sides of her conscience.

Then she pulls her phone to her ear.

"Xin, I am sorry to wake you. If you inform Dulwich of what I am about to request, I will make what is left of your life a living hell." She knows what it's like in Digital Services, knows the degree to which the myth of field ops pervades the culture. She counts on her bluster to rattle the man, hopes he doesn't identify her words as a hollow bluff.

"You threaten me?"

"I have three phone numbers. I need a 'last-known position' for each of them."

"iPhones?" Xin is already coming awake.

"The numbers won't be registered."

"Understood."

"How quickly?" Grace asks. With a laptop and secure Internet connection, she could do the work herself. She's being polite and they both know it. Xin can accomplish this as fast as he's willing.

"Five minutes," he says, perhaps sensing the trap she's laid.

She rattles off the numbers of Knox's SIM chips. They are committed to memory, not carried in her phone's contact list.

Xin repeats them, double-checking.

"Nothing personal," she says.

The line goes dead.

58

Accustomed to following a navigation system, neither of the men bookending Knox seems to notice that the car has missed the exit for Barbaros Boulevard, the most direct route north to the Istinye district. Instead, they travel the O-1 southeast, and Besim takes a long exit ramp toward Bahçeşehir University. The men look nondescript, Knox thinks as he surreptitiously studies them; the two could be of any European nationality. Judging by the accent of the few words spoken in the hotel's laundry room and the swearing, he's convinced they are Israeli or are on contract to the Israelis. If Israeli, they apparently don't know about Besim. Boxes within boxes.

In point of fact, they could work for any government, any agency, any security company or corporation or individual wanting nuclear secrets.

The man to Knox's left gets twitchy, perhaps sensing the detour. Besim has made the mistake of not averting the rearview mirror, which carries in its upper corner the dull green compass heading: SW. How long until it's noticed?

Knox wrestles his body forward in an attempt to divert attention.

His activity serves its purpose, though it gains him a blow to his sore ribs. Pain is an expected part of the process, but he's worn down by the accumulation of wounds. He resists physical limitations, is able to overcome most of them; it's another part of what makes him valuable to men like Dulwich. The fact that he's succumbing to the toll now makes him question his longevity in this line of work, the thoughts coming in a series of panicked flashes. He hopes to hell Dulwich has not picked up on it, is worried it might make him dispensable.

Thinks of Tommy and the risk he's taking and questions whether or not he's fooling himself by thinking he accepts the work for Tommy's sake.

"Hey!" The agent has it now.

"Traffic bad. Golf tournament, Sahasi," Besim says calmly. "This way better."

Knox wonders how many languages the man speaks; how many dialects; how easily this clipped attempt at English comes to him. It's convincing enough to ease the agent back in his seat.

The car turns right, north, back toward Barbaros Boulevard, but yips to a stop at the entrance to a forested park on the left. Besim auto-unlocks the doors without being asked to do so, and they come open simultaneously. In a flurry of box cutters, swinging arms and fierce shouting, Besim reaches back to contribute the sting of a Taser. Seat belts are cut with razors. Both men are dragged out. It's over in ten seconds or less.

Fucking Israelis.

The two men are replaced by two others, and the car races off, leaving Knox's captors behind, one on his hands and knees, the other unconscious, facedown. The plastic binding Knox's wrists is cut free. He exercises his sore shoulders.

Besim has the car moving fast. South, toward old Istanbul. South, toward the train terminal on the European side and, beyond, the airport.

No one speaks. Knox observes the protocol. Knows better than to mess with Mossad.

After fifteen minutes it's apparent that they are indeed headed for the airport.

So many questions tug at Knox. He understands that he's unlikely to ever get a single straight answer. There is no question—none—that Besim is with these two. The mood in the car is relaxed, other than at stops or when the car slows, which sets the men's heads pivoting like radar dishes.

But then why did Besim attack him to get the shopping list? The only answer Knox can come up with is that Besim is doubled, working for both sides of Israeli security—the side that hired Dulwich and the side that doesn't want to spare a thorium reactor from the fires of hell about to descend upon Iran. So which are these two?

He has to take the risk.

"Just to be clear," Knox says, "I don't have what you think I do. What those guys back there thought I did. I was told it could buy me a pass in a situation like this, but I'm sorry to say I don't have it."

The man on Knox's left eye-signals Besim and the car pulls off the main road and onto a side street. This agent gets out of the car and makes a phone call. A moment later, the agent climbs back into the car, searches Knox's Scottevest, and locates Knox's iPhone. Five seconds later, the phone purrs and Knox answers.

"What's this?" It's Dulwich.

"I don't have it."

"I got that much."

"She has it."

Silence. Then, "Fuck."

"I'll never get through Immigration anyway."

"You think too much."

"So hire Schwarzenegger."

"Not the time for it, pal."

"We stopped being pals a while ago." Knox wonders if he'll ever get a call from Dulwich again and if, by association, he's ruined Grace's dreams of fieldwork. He wonders if Dulwich will pay him for this op if he makes it out. Wonders what the hell to do for Tommy. *Fuck.*

"You think? I was the one responsible for dumping those two back there. Don't be so quick to pass judgment. I'm risking some serious capital here."

"I'm feeling bad for you." Knox notes the use of "back there." Dulwich is close by.

"Where is she?" Dulwich asks.

"Someplace safe, I hope. I thought you and your friends here had teams on both of us?"

A yellow taxi approaches from up the street. Besim backs up expertly, running the rear tires up onto the sidewalk and cutting the wheel sharply. He's about to peel out when the man on Knox's right shouts too loudly for the confines of the car, *"Atzor!" Stop!* Hebrew.

Knox ends the call and returns the phone to the jacket.

He's found Grace.

59

Grace holds the business card in her left hand, a butane cigarette lighter in her right. She steadily brings the two closer.
The two agents are out of the car and pushing their palms
at her in a rush of bodies and limbs.

"No . . . no . . . no!" they say, nearly in unison.

The taxi driver seizes the moment and backs up the Hyundai,
leaving an unsuspecting Grace standing alone. The taxi continues
backing up at an alarming rate all the way to the intersection. Then
it's gone.

"The card for him," Grace says, "or I burn it."

Besim climbs out from behind the wheel, and Knox watches
Grace's emotions get the better of her. Betrayal burnishes her face
angry red.

"Release him!" Grace hollers, the flame now precariously close
to the lower corner of the card.

"We do not wish to possess the card, ma'am," Besim says, "but it
must not be burned." He checks with the man originally on Knox's
left, who nods. "It is truly the only chance for the two of you. We

have promised to do everything in our power to get you out alive. The loss of this card will be our failure. Your failure."

"Get him out of the car, now!" Grace is having none of it.

Besim checks with the agent for a second time. They speak in Hebrew. The three move away from the vehicle. Their hands remain in plain sight.

Grace is unable to keep the confusion from her face.

"The card!" she says again.

Knox comes out of the backseat, grinning appreciatively. He moves around the open door to the front, where he assesses the agents and Besim.

"Grace! Get in," he says, indicating the passenger door. "And don't for a moment take that flame away from the card."

Besim and the others back away slowly.

"In!" Knox says, pulling his own door shut.

Grace climbs in. The flame steadies. Knox glances out his window at the men.

"What the hell?" she says.

Knox shifts into gear. Halfway down the block, he tells her to extinguish the lighter. She doesn't seem to hear him. He repeats himself and she quiets the flame.

"That took balls," he says.

"Always so vulgar."

Knox waits until the car is on Kennedy Avenue, airport bound. He explains his theory that Besim vandalized the SUV and paid off the bellmen to keep their mouths shut, reiterates the likelihood of two Israeli payrolls; one set, Dulwich's, surprising and replacing his hotel captors. His phone buzzes repeatedly, as does Grace's. Neither answers.

"The card?" she says.

Knox answers. "In order for things to remain status quo, they need the dead drop to go as planned. If it fails, it will call for internal review by whatever party of whatever government is supposed to get it, and maybe someone figures out what's really going on."

"Tracking Dr. Okle."

"Sarge spit-balled it for us. Did he lie? Of course. But maybe less than we think. More like he omitted facts."

"You would defend him?"

"Bloodlines. He and I share history." Again, he wonders if he's sabotaged Grace. Feels shitty about it.

"The airport."

"Yeah."

She speculates, "The Israelis had a plane for you." Her voice quavers. "I interrupted . . ."

"Grace . . . we don't know anything. Not a damned thing. These guys are all spooks. Sarge should have known better. Out of our league."

"Railway," she suggests.

"By now, the Israelis dumped out of the car will have called it in. The hawks are not going to roll over for anyone. They'll make the charge of cultural theft against me, play anything they can so I don't get out. The train is too slow. Gives them too long to get their shit together." He can't take the time to switch out SIM cards. "The Turks will have to weigh the claim, put out a Be On Lookout for me. The Israelis supporting the thorium research know you and I have a shot at getting through Immigration or they wouldn't have been aiming for the airport in the first place."

"Or they paid a bribe."

"Or that."

Knox follows the airport signage. They can see it now to their left, and beyond it, the Bosphorus. On the opposite shore starts the Asian half of the city.

"May be a strait, but it certainly looks like a river," she says. "What is it with us and rivers?"

She watches him smile. With more planning, more knowledge, they might have left by the Bosphorus. Always water. Bloodlines.

"We go through security in separate lines."

"Of course."

"If I'm detained . . ."

"I will notify David." It's the best they can hope for. She would gladly make a sacrifice to take this off of him. Has no idea where that thought comes from. Sacrilege. Her career path is entirely singular.

She speaks abruptly. "Everything I do or have done, it is to prove my father wrong."

Knox glances over at her curiously.

"Deepest apology," she says, sounding entirely too Chinese. She hangs her head.

"Well, that's awkward," Knox says.

She starts to laugh, but it borders on tears and she bottles it up as she has learned to do so well in the time they've spent working together.

"My shit's always been about protecting Tommy," he says, adding, "at least that's what I tell myself."

"We never know if we will see the other again," she says wistfully.

"True story."

Her heart races. She's unsure why. "I have feelings for you, John Knox."

The car enters the Departures ramp.

"Yeah," he says.

She waits. The car slows toward the curb. "That is all? 'Yeah'?"

Knox parks. "Yeah." His smile conceals a deeper message; concern for her? Attraction? Whether he means it as such, that smile floods her with warmth.

Knox says, "Check your phone. Find us the first flight out of the country."

60

F ollow me, please." The immigration officer is soft and in his mid-forties, probably nearing the end of his career. The uniform stretches tight across his belly. His pant legs bunch at his ankles as he steps out of his booth to block Knox's exit. The irregular beeping of the magnetometers in the distance is reminiscent of hospital sounds.

All of Knox's worlds are spinning into one, like water down a drain. And he's running down with them. His being detained could be the result of his passport being tagged, but he doubts it. More likely it's the result of face recognition software or vigilant eyes behind one-way glass on the other side of a CCTV camera's video monitor.

Cause and effect matter to him. He can only hope it's the passport.

When two more security men arrive to escort him, that hope is dashed. With his guards the product of steroids and workout videos, Knox knows the depth of the trouble he's in. Out of the corner of his eye he sees Grace, from the back, as she hesitates a fraction of a second before joining a screening line. He wills her to stay out of this.

The walk is longer than he expects. With a guard on either side, he feels like a death-row inmate, a dead man walking. With airports better manned, better guarded than prisons, there's nowhere to go. The thought of Turkish prison stirs his imagination. He's not going down without a fight. The only question is when to start it.

The key is knowing at what point to play his card: too early and it may be ignored; too late, and its significance may be missed. He curses himself for allowing Dulwich to move him into the world of spooks. No one ever accused Knox of being subtle, and this is a game of shades, not colors.

He's treated respectfully. Placed in a chair at a desk alone. The room is undoubtedly locked. Both guards remain on the other side of the door. A ceiling-corner camera stares at him unflinchingly.

The uniformed supervisor who enters five minutes later carries the fatigued eyes of an overworked bureaucrat. His mustache is neatly trimmed above poor teeth. The man's attention is on the paperwork in front of him. He makes no real effort to connect with Knox.

"Name."

"John Knox."

"Nationality?"

"What's this about?" Knox knows the questions to ask in order to appear Joe Normal.

"Nationality?"

"USA. American." The redundancy causes the supervisor to issue a look of complaint: he doesn't want his time wasted. "What have I done? I've done nothing wrong!"

"Last country visited?" The man flips through the passport.

"Jordan. Last week. Amman."

Another disapproving look.

But Knox is not about to act the professional. He won't be lured into it. "I have a plane to catch!"

The man continues working the passport. Knox doesn't like that camera staring at him. Passing Mashe's business card could be construed as an attempted bribe. He has little idea of how Turkish law works. Or doesn't work. Perhaps he's supposed to offer money. He should have studied up in all his free time.

"Purpose of your trip? Business or pleasure?"

The man has set the bear trap; he now invites Knox to put his foot inside. If his being detained has to do with the sale of the Harmodius, a lie could entrap him. If, however, this guy is fishing, the claim of business invites more questions, more chances to answer incorrectly. Knox's position is to lessen the depth of the interest in him.

"It depends if you consider a woman business or pleasure," Knox replies. He wins a slight twist of the man's mustache, like a cat flicking its tail against the cold. "There was the business of a lover of hers in Amman, you see. But the pleasure was all mine once we got to Istanbul." Knox hopes his timing is good. "Victoria Momani, if you need her name. She's returning by train to Amman. Left this afternoon."

Detail, especially unsolicited detail, has a way of authenticating a statement. It can't be forced, can only be used when the opportunity is presented. Knox prides himself on timing, whether in lovemaking or Immigration interrogations.

The man excuses himself and leaves the room. Returns several long minutes later.

This isn't the guy to approach, Knox decides. He's made no attempt at eye contact, has offered not the slightest of signals. He's following up on Knox's statements, moving information from point A to point B. Stalling, Knox hopes.

Knox checks his watch. "My plane . . ."

"This is an airport," the man replies. "Plenty of planes." His teeth look like old patio bricks.

"We stayed at the Alzer Hotel," Knox says. "Separate rooms in case her lover checked up on her." He adds, "My room did not get a lot of use."

The man is clearly titillated. Knox can keep him occupied if need be, but he's supplying information the man already has. He allows himself the fantasy of wondering whether his detention could possibly be random. Such thoughts are dangerous; they allow him to lower his guard. He warns himself to remain alert. Shades, not colors.

The hand-off comes abruptly. A square-jawed man in a worn brown suit and no tie takes the place of Knox's interrogator. Musical chairs. This guy could shave every hour and it wouldn't make any difference. He has the black, infinite stare of a character from a zombie film. He meets eyes with Knox and holds the gaze for a long time.

So this is the guy, and this is the place, and they are both extremely aware of the camera, given that the guy looks over his shoulder, right into it, to make sure it doesn't escape Knox.

Knox's vitals shift into overdrive. The man represents two doors. Monty Hall. Maybe, just maybe, the Israelis or Dulwich could get him out of Turkish prison, but it's a hell of a gamble. Maybe, just maybe, this is the moment that Mashe Okle was referencing when he passed Knox his business card. The Turks have learned to get along with most of their neighbors and the West. The only question for Knox is if he's reading this man correctly.

The man runs Knox through the same questions. Knox responds with the same content, worded differently so as not to sound rehearsed. There are so many traps laid for him that it feels more like a minefield. Is Dulwich going to show up and extract him? Is he on his own?

The fucking camera doesn't so much as blink.

The repetition of the questions grows tedious. Knox expertly extracts the card from his pocket under the pretense of fidgeting. This bastard shows no emotion; he's the Mount Rushmore of Turkish interrogators. Knox wants one more sign, something to convince him. But it's not going to happen. This guy is going to run out of questions and leave the room.

Knox slaps his hands down on the table. "I have a plane to catch!" He shifts his eyes to take in his left hand; nothing more than a twitch and impossible for the camera to see, given the angle.

Knox rises from his chair. "You people—"

"Sit down!" The man places his hands atop Knox's. With his left, he grabs Knox's wrist. His right hand waits for Knox to move, and covers the card fluidly.

Knox sits back down and apologizes. "I . . . I'm sorry. It's just . . . I'm . . . I have the plane to catch. I have a ticket, you see? I miss that flight—"

"You will not miss your flight."

Knox never sees the man pocket the card. He could run the tables in Vegas.

"I have a schedule to keep," Knox says, pitching his voice to sound disappointed.

"Allow me to conclude some paperwork," the man says. "Always the paperwork."

He leaves, replaced by the first man.

Five minutes later, Knox is beginning to worry. Ten minutes in, he's beginning to sweat. The passing of the card wasn't enough. Someone is inspecting it. His plane began boarding five minutes ago. Knox has no idea if the card contains anything or not, has no idea how information would be coded on it. Magnetic? Something in the ink? The supposed microdot? How is it he's allowed his fate to rest in the hands of a man he's met for all of five minutes?

He's released unceremoniously. He wants to shout out that he saved the world the equivalent of cold fusion. Decades of research would have gone up in smoke.

Instead, he's shown to a door and sent back out, bypassing the security lines. The door clunks shut behind him, and for a moment Knox stands, taking in the sounds of the Istanbul international airport. Indians. Africans. Europeans. The crowd swirls around him.

He phones Dulwich from the concourse. Is not worried about revealing his location. Typical of this op, Dulwich doesn't answer. Voice mail.

Knox speaks carefully, using no names. "No one will ever see the objet d'art again. We both know that. Once again lost to history. Your client traded it to preserve what he wanted to preserve. That's his business. But this is our business: there's the matter of the cash, some of which, I suppose, is going to me and my friend. That leaves a bunch left over. There's a family of a recently deceased cabbie— first name, Ali—that deserves the rest. You hear me? Do your homework. Every dime. I'm going to follow up on this."

He ends the call. Steps into the melee, battling his way to beneath a sign indicating his concourse, his sore legs straining to pause. Something tugs at him, urges him to look back at that nondescript door he just passed through, but he won't give in. Aware of the preponderance of CCTV cameras, he doesn't have to act like a disgusted man in a hurry to make his gate; he is.

They couldn't arrange seats next to each other, but maybe someone will move to allow it.

Knowing Grace, she's already arranged it herself.

EPILOGUE

Morning prayers haunt the streets of Amman, echoing, reverberating. A pale but warm sunlight penetrates the small apartment's neat interior, its walls occupied by contemporary art from a dozen artists.

The smell of coffee blows along with a drape out onto a suicide balcony, only deep enough to hold a chair, turned to allow the occupant to stretch her long legs out of the three-quarter-length terry-cloth bathrobe. She's taken up smoking again, a horrid habit she'd thought herself free of. But one is never truly free of one's past.

Victoria sips the coffee, pulls on the cigarette and watches her exhale pinned onto the sky like the vapor trail from a jet. Her laptop is pinched on her waist. She has reread the e-mail six times. Make it seven. Akram's appeal for unification reads a little too much like a business letter, but rather than trouble or offend her, she warms to it; he tries hard to express himself even though he fails. Connects with her, in spite of himself. The possibility of reconciliation excites her.

This, despite the fact she has found it difficult to stop thinking about the romp with John Knox, the tenderness of a Westerner's touch; so different from the men of Amman she has known. She thinks about Knox in other ways too: anger, over the lack of payment he promised; intrigue, over the idea of using him to move the occasional art piece she is offered. She shuts the laptop, trying to silence Akram's voice in her head. Sips more coffee and feels it slide down her long throat. Thinks of Knox again.

She believes she could do business with him. Believes in possibility, like a future with Akram.

The sounding of her apartment's talk box summons her. She uncoils and crosses back into the apartment, careful not to stub her toes on the lip of the sliding glass doors. Pushes the Talk button and is greeted by an express deliveryman with whom she's so familiar she recognizes his voice.

"Mailbox or door?" he asks.

"Bring it up, please," she says, expecting a contract for a show she's arranging for the gallery.

She pulls the robe shut tightly, checks her face in the mirror by the door. Signs for the delivery and locks the door. The air bill's return address is Australia, unfamiliar to her.

She opens the express envelope to find another manila envelope inside that's lined with a metal foil. Not aluminum, something heavier. *Something,* she thinks, *to trick the X-ray machines.* She tips the envelope, loosing its contents onto the maple dining table.

The first thing to spill out is a greeting card with an image of the American president, Barack Obama, by Shepard Fairey. She grins. Shakes the envelope to dislodge the rest of its contents.

Stock certificates. Apple. IBM. Microsoft. Each certificate is marked as a thousand shares. On the back of each is a transfer record listing her name over a signature line she can't read because it's written in Hebrew. There's a *pile* of them.

She licks her finger, pauses, then begins to pull back the corners, allowing her to count. Her finger moves faster and faster. Her grin grows wider.

And she begins to laugh.

ŞİŞLİ PASAJI

FLORENCE NIGHTINGALE HOSPITAL

Feriköy Mezarlığı

Beşiktaş-Kağıthane Tüneli

İstanbul Çevre Yolu

BEYOĞLU

GALATASARAY HAMAM

Kemeraltı Cd

GALATA TOWER

TOPHANE

Vatan Cd

ALZER HOTEL

İtfaiye Cd

AQUEDUCT MEETING

Galata Kpr

FATİH

VALENS AQUEDUCT

TOPKAPI

Atatürk Blv

MUSEUM OF TURKISH AND ISLAMIC ARTS

ATATÜRK AIRPORT

GRAND BAZAAR

BLUE MOSQUE

Kennedy Cd

ISTANBUL